M000102506

The New Badlands:

THIEVES EMPORIUM

Max Hernandez

5/1/15

This book is a work of speculative fiction. All names used are fictitious and bear no relation to any corporation, product, or individual in the real world. In particular, the name 'Apple' does not refer to Apple Computer Corporation, 'Microsoft' does not refer to Microsoft Corporation, and 'Windows' does not refer to any of the operating systems produced by Microsoft. Also, the character Arnold Parker is not one of the Koch brothers and Van de Groot is not George Soros.

Trade Paperback Edition: ISBN 978-0-9887030-0-1

Ebook Edition: ISBN 978-0-9887030-1-8

New Badlands Publishing
Santiago
Dominican Republic
NBP@seabird.us

Dedication

To freedom-lovers everywhere.

Warning

Sexually Explicit Material

The first three pages of Chapter 10 contain graphic depictions of sexual, physical, and emotional abuse. If such material offends you, please skip these pages.

Dear Reader:
Please, I need your help.

I wrote this book because I believe the ideas and issues it discusses are important. If you agree with me, please help me spread the word. In particular, encourage others to read Thieves Emporium by giving it a good review on Amazon or Goodreads, by mentioning it in blogs, and by telling your friends about it.

Your comments are also appreciated. Good, bad, suggestions for future books. It doesn't matter, I appreciate them all. Please send them to me at MaxHernandez@protonmail.ch.

Thank you.

Max Hernandez

Contents

Introduction

For most of mankind's existence, there was a frontier. Those who didn't fit in always had one option: Cross it. Leave. Walk away and live outside ordered society. That gave the rest of us a way to deal with the misfits and the outlaws: Banishment. Throw them out, or just let them go.

For our ancestors, living in small tribes, the border was always close. Crossing it meant leaving for unsettled lands. Those who did were the first explorers, the first to settle in Europe or Asia or Oceania or the Americas. For them, land was plentiful. They picked the best places, the fields of milk and honey.

As mankind grew, those fertile lands were all occupied by regulated societies. Crossing the border came to mean either moving to another country or going to lands that were too rough, hard, or dangerous for any settled country to want.

And still the world became more crowded. Even the harshest places were claimed by some government. Crossing the border came to mean going from England to France, China to Japan, or the U.S. to Canada. No longer did it mean leaving structured society to trade security for opportunity, regulation for risk.

Finally, about a hundred years ago, regulated societies won. All lands, no matter how rocky or dry or cold, became patrolled, regulated, and governed. The wild men, the misfits, the outlaws, and the eccentrics lost their final refuge.

Now, that has changed. Once again, there is a place for misfits. Wild and brutal, beyond the reach of any government, it's the last hope for those who have no other option.

Once again, there is a badlands.

Chapter 1

Recruited

THE NEAR FUTURE

She got to the shelter too late for dinner but still managed to find an empty corner. It got little heat, being near the outside of the building, but the safety provided by two walls was worth the chill. Besides, the late autumn cold kept the other mission guests away, and she appreciated her privacy.

Half-leaning against the two walls, she sat with her bare legs clamped to her chest, her torso cocked sideways to favor her left side. A mission blanket draped over her slight frame, covering bare shoulders and a garish low-cut blouse. A padded bra produced the only curve in her too-thin figure. Earlier in the day, heavy makeup had completely covered her face, but now freckles showed, like small flecks of brown soot, under her weary eyes. Not that they detracted from her appearance. On the contrary, when she smiled, they produced a country-girl beauty that was both disarming and stunning.

Leaning against her shins were two small girls, twins, like identical pearls, also with freckles. They huddled together under another blanket, their matching pajamas providing additional protection against the chill. Softly, knowing it was not a good time to annoy their mother, they played some secret game that required occasional spasms of suppressed giggles.

Pain shot through her left side whenever she moved her back, but she didn't think there was any serious damage. The Bastard was quite good at that, just the right amount of force to change behavior, never enough to damage the merchandise. And, God forbid, never where a john could see it.

Tomorrow morning she would have to be out of here. Back to the Bastard? Unless she could think of an alternative, she would have to make do. Her world offered few choices.

Of course, she could stay here. If she wasn't worried about the twins, that is. Social Services visited every morning, looking for mistreated children. Her girls may not be well fed by the state's standards, but they were hers, the only joys she had left after her husband had vanished. She would never give them up.

As she fretted the alternatives, hoping to find something she had overlooked, she noticed a figure walking toward her from the main room.

The stranger was an older woman of average height, dressed in warm, dark, and dull. Short pepper hair framed her wide face. She wore no makeup or jewelry except for a large silver cross. In her hands was a tray, held with great care as she picked her way through the dim clutter. Stopping at the foot of the young mother's mat, she raised it and asked "Hungry?"

Dinner in bed wasn't standard fare here. Although the young mother hadn't eaten since early morning, she didn't welcome the offer. Being singled out made her nervous. All her life, she'd kept her head down, avoided notoriety. Social evasion had become an ingrained instinct.

But the intrusion was here, like it or not. An unavoidable risk.

"You with the government?" she asked. The last thing she needed was a FEMA ride.

"No," came the answer, delivered with a slight smile.

The young mother weighed it in silence, trying to judge its veracity.

"I just work nights," came a further explanation.

More silence.

"I saw you come in late, just thought you might be hungry," added the visitor as she set the tray on the floor. Apparently she wasn't going to be deterred by silence.

Then the seated woman noticed the smell. Split pea soup, hot and full of herbs. Three large bowls, thick, covered with cheese and flavored with sausage. With rolls on the side. Even in the dim light, she could see steam rising. Her girls smelled it too and looked to her for permission.

With a wave of her hand, she gave it. But, hungry as she was, she was too wary to reach for a bowl. Instead, she kept her full attention on her patron.

"You give room service to everyone?" she asked.

"Only to the ones I think I can help," answered the Cross.

"Why?"

"God tells me to," came the answer.

Oh oh, here comes the sermon.

"Well, thank you, but we're Buddhists."

"Then give back the soup. There's meat in it."

That made the younger woman pick up her bowl. She couldn't ignore the smell any longer, anyway. Her girls were already half finished. Made with a generous helping of oil, the soup would have been good and hearty even if she weren't so hungry. After the first spoonful, she ate with a most unladylike haste.

"You staying the week?" asked her patron. That was the mission's time limit.

The young mother shook her head, unwilling to talk with her mouth full.

"You leaving tomorrow?"

She answered with a nod, not wanting the conversation but needing to be polite.

A shadow flitted across the visitor's face, barely noticeable in the dim light. But the young mother caught it.

After a moment, the woman with the cross asked "Want some Advil?"

That stopped the young mother's spoon just as it touched her open mouth. The mission didn't offer pain medications as part of its standard service, either. Why the special treatment?

The Cross held out a bottle. An Advil bottle.

Was it really Advil? If not, what was it? If it was, why offer it to her?

"I saw the way you carried yourself when you came in," came an answer to the unspoken question.

For most of her life, the young mother had hidden in the shadows. Like a mouse on the jungle floor, she survived by not being seen, by not taking chances. When in doubt, hide. Or run. But take no risks. Say nothing that might attract attention, might offend. Do whatever you have to, please whoever you have to, but do it quietly. And don't stand out.

That attitude had kept her safe and alive. But it had also brought her here: Cold, broke, alone but for her girls, and in pain.

Perhaps it was time for a change.

"Thank you," she said and reached for the bottle. It looked genuine. So did the pills inside. She took four with a spoon of soup.

Meanwhile, the Cross watched in silence, waiting to take back the tray. She seemed to be struggling with some inner decision. Whatever it was, she must have come to a conclusion because she said "Years ago, when I was much younger, I did hard things to keep food on the table." A pause, then "How'd you hurt your side?"

The two sentences were not uttered together by accident. The younger woman glanced quickly at her girls. The Cross must have gotten the message: They didn't know what their mother did to keep food on their table. And she didn't want them to learn now.

"You don't have to take the beatings."

The statement came from out of nowhere. Sudden, but perhaps not unexpected. Vague enough to protect the children, but specific enough for both to understand the underlying meaning.

"I have to work."

"You still could."

"How?" asked the young mother.

"Get your customers anonymously. Get paid the same way. And keep it all. No one beats you because no one knows your name or where you live."

The girls finished their meal and started playing again, quietly. But the young mother just looked back in silence.

"Tomorrow, you can go back for more beatings. Let him rob you again. Or you can take this chance. One shot. Now or never. How about it?"

The moment of truth. Fear and greed were at war for her soul. Dare the mouse come out of the shadows?

"Go on," the young mother prompted.

Without a word, the Cross stooped down to pick up the tray. As she did so, she slipped the young mother a business card. On the front, in a tight, neat hand, was written:

Bring pen and paper

On the back, in the same hand, was:

27.100.199.3:1723

Mai Lee Chang

"Go to any library branch," said the visitor. "Sign up for the Internet. If they ask for a library card, tell them you don't have one. Say you're homeless. You won't need one if they believe you. Don't give your name, your address, or identify yourself in any way. If they push, leave and try another branch. And don't bring the girls.

"When you get on-line, open a browser and type the numbers and punctuation into the address bar. You'll know you did it right if you get an error page from China National Steel.

"Ignore everything except the line that asks who you are trying to reach. Type in the name exactly as on the card. Exactly. Check it. When you're sure it's right, hit the Enter key. When Mrs. Chang comes online, listen to what she says."

"And if I don't like it?"

"Walk away. Go back to your regular beatings. If you don't leave your name, no one will know you were even there. But, whatever you decide, don't come back here again. Don't try to contact me. For your own good, burn this card as soon as you make a decision and forget where you got it."

Finished, the Cross stood up with the tray. The young mother just looked at the card, trapped in her own thoughts, while the Cross watched her in silence. Finally, the older woman spoke.

"What else can you offer your girls? There are no safe bets in this world, not any more. If you don't make a change, it'll only get worse for them. Do this while they still have a chance."

The young mother looked up from the card and their eyes met for an instant. Then the Cross turned and carried the empty tray back to the warmth of the main room, leaving her alone in the chill to consider the life of a mouse in a world filled with elephants.

The next morning, while the streets were still dark, the young mother and her girls walked out of the mission and disappeared into the dirty Cleveland rain.

* * *

The young mother sat in front of the public terminal looking at a Google search page. So far, she had broken no laws. But she knew that would change if she typed in the address from the business card. She could not explain away that overt act if she were caught. Somehow, she knew it would break some unknown law. Just like almost everything else in her life, or in anyone else's nowadays, for that matter.

What would happen when she hit the Enter key? Alarms? Police? Would they catch her when she left the library, take her twins away from her forever?

Those visions scared her into inaction for weeks, until the Bastard started showing an unusual interest in her girls. She could take the beatings, the theft, the degradation, and the filth; she could take it all if it kept them with her. But not what his interest might become.

So now she sat on the edge, worried that it was too late to take this chance. She looked around once more. No one paid any attention to her. Time for the mouse to crawl out of the shadows. So she typed:

27.100.199.3:1723

She checked it. There were no mistakes. After a deep breath and a very non-Buddhist prayer, she hit the Enter key.

Magic electrons did their work.

No alarm bells sounded. Police did not rush into the building.

Instead, the browser changed. A page announced, in several languages, that China National Steel Company had encountered a VPN error. She could either seek help through the main site at www.ChinaNationalSteel.com or contact the relevant individual directly by typing his/her name in the blank provided.

She typed:

Mai Lee Chang

After checking it, she hit the Enter key.

Still no police. The library stayed cold and silent.

Only the browser changed. A chat page appeared along with the promise that Mrs. Chang was on her way.

Seconds later the chat window said:

> Chang: This is Mai Lee Chang. How may I help you?

She hadn't anticipated that question. How could Mrs. Chang help her? What did she really want here, and what did she dare say? She didn't even know who she was talking to. Was there really a Mrs. Chang at the other end? And, if so, maybe she was just some coolie working for China National Steel deep in the hills of Hunan.

So she typed the first thing that came to her mind.

> Guest: Hello

Brilliant.

> Chang: Hello to you, too. You have reached China National Steel. How may I help you?
>
> Guest: I'm looking for work
>
> Chang: I don't normally help with opportunities at China National Steel. Perhaps I may direct you to the Employment Department?

Right. That didn't seem like a good move.

> Guest: No, I wasn't looking for that sort of job.
>
> Chang: What sort of work were you looking for?

How to explain this?

> Guest: I was hoping to meet some men.
>
> Chang: For employment?

She hesitated, then took the plunge.

> Guest: Yes
>
> Chang: Where did you get our address?
>
> Guest: A woman gave it to me
>
> Chang: Can you be more specific? What did she tell you?
>
> Guest: She said I wouldn't get beaten any more and could keep everything I earned if I contacted you

Chang: What did she look like?

Guest: Middle aged. Gray hair, heavy.

Chang: Did she wear any jewelry?

Guest: No

Then she remembered.

Guest: Except for a cross.

Chang: A small one?

Guest: No. Large and silver.

Chang: Where are you now?

Sitting at a computer, where do you think? OK, that probably wasn't the answer Mrs. Chang wanted.

Guest: In the United States

Chang: Which city?

Guest: Cleveland. Ohio.

Chang: Are you at home?

Guest: No.

Chang: Where then?

Guest: The library

Chang: On a public computer? Or do you have one of your own?

Guest: No. I use the one at the library

There was a pause. Somewhere on the other side of cyberspace, Mrs. Chang made a decision.

Chang: Do you have something to write with?

Guest: Yes

Chang: Please wait a moment.

Thirty seconds passed. More time for Cleveland's finest to set up out front...

Chang: On March 12 at exactly 5:12 pm go to Cleveland Boxing Club on 2157 Superior Avenue. Leave your cell phone at home. Ask for Vlad. Tell him you wish to pick up a letter. Can you make this meeting?

The date was over a week away. Well, it wasn't like her calendar was all that tight.

Guest: Yes

Chang: The cell phone part is important. Leave it at home. Got that?

Guest: Yes

Chang: Good. Have you copied the address?

Guest: Yes

Chang: Then thank you for contacting China National Steel Corporation.

The page changed, back to the China National Steel Corporation error page. Trying not to show fear, she logged out. Sliding out of the chair, she slipped out of the room, out of the library, and down the steps into the trudging crowd. Seconds later, she was just another dirty coat walking through the slush.

She had made her first trip to the New Badlands and returned safely. That was reason enough to be pleased. Hostile border crossings are always dangerous.

* * *

Several thousand miles away, in one of the lesser cities of Nigeria, the owner of the GOBI DESERT[*] crossing house stood up to stretch. A thin, dried-up old Hausan, his black frame glistened in the light cast from a battered monitor. Time had been kind to his body, doing little more than wrinkling his skin and bleaching his hair. And thinning it a little. Especially on top. Still, he had no cause for complaint. His body did not hurt and his mind was clear. More forgetful, and a good deal fussier, but still sharp.

Years ago, he started this crossing house to support a young family. His new family. But in that area, time had not been so good. So now he had only this business. And his indentureds, his fallen angels.

He hadn't set out to recruit prostitutes. It just worked out that way. They made good badlanders. Careful, discreet, hard-working. And loyal. They appreciated the new chance he gave them.

* See the appendix for a list of crossing houses mentioned in this book.

And, at the age when at least one of his organs no longer worked at all, they made good friends, too.

So he smiled as he sweated in the humid darkness. Another recruit was a cause for joy. Like a new grandchild. Pink Jade had fallen on hard times. She needed this. Another producer. Tonight he would celebrate her success.

He knew this one came through Jade because 'Mai Lee Chang' was one of the contact names that woman used and the description matched. So did the location, since Jade worked the northern Ohio area.

He knew the recruit really was at a Cleveland library branch because he ran a trace* during their chat. Finally, he knew this newbie was tough enough to take chances since she came across on a public computer, probably because she was too poor to own one of her own.

So he would send her a full contact package now, even though it was a bit early. The alternative was to keep her on public computers with the greater risk that she might get caught. If that happened, he would have to shut down the China National Steel doorbell and might even lose Jade to another crossing house.

Someone from Kumar would pick up the package tomorrow.

* * *

The young mother got off the bus less than a block from the Cleveland Boxing Club with only twenty minutes until her meeting. She planned to have more time to get to know the neighborhood, but the buses were running late because of some lake-effect snow. Now, still with a little time on her hands, she walked past the club entrance.

The small single-story building looked like it had once been a retail establishment, perhaps a cleaners or a pawnshop. She didn't dare linger. Even during rush-hour, few pedestrians walked through this part of town and she didn't want to attract notice. In some sense, though, this worked in her favor as it made it easier to spot anyone else loitering in the area. She saw no one as she moved down the block.

At 5:12 exactly, (by her watch, not her cell phone) she walked up to the open door, stopped at the entrance, and looked in. A counter faced her less than ten feet away, as it might have done for a dry cleaners, except that a wall behind the counter hid the rest of the building from her eyes. It looked

* See the appendix for a detailed glossary.

like patrons checked in at the counter before going through a door to the back area. Behind it sat a frail old man with surprisingly unscarred features and very thin gray hair. No one else was visible. Wet slapping sounds of someone receiving a beating came from behind the wall.

Trying to look like she was a potential customer, she proceeded to the counter.

"Yeah?" the old man said without looking up from his paper.

"Are you Vlad?"

"No Vlad here. What you want?" he asked, finally taking the trouble to lift his eyes from the funnies.

"I was told Vlad worked here."

"Yeah, and I was told boxing was for sissies. We was both misinformed. What you want?"

This is not going well.

"May I speak with the manager?"

"Honey, I own this place. Have for twenty-six years. I never hired a Vlad. I don't know a Vlad. So, unless you want lessons, you better leave."

Having run out of questions, and not really interested in learning to box, she did just that.

As she waited in the light snow for the next bus, she considered her options. They were few: go back to China National Steel and admit the meeting had gone wrong, or forget the entire thing. Either idea made her stomach cramp.

She still fretted the matter thirty-five minutes later as she hung from a bus strap, wedged between slabs of wet coats. As she swayed with the traffic, something tugged at her sleeve. Looking down, she saw the face of a small child looking back from under an over-sized knit cap.

"Can I have some candy?" the remarkably dirty urchin asked.

"I don't have any."

"Yeah you do. Can I have some?" insisted the child.

"No, honey, I'm sorry, I really don't."

"You do, too. I can smell it. In your coat pocket. Please? Give me some?"

When she reached into her pocket to prove the child wrong, her hand brushed an envelope. It hadn't been there when she started this trip. Before she could say anything, her small beggar moved near the door and started panhandling a stooped fat woman. At the next stop, the urchin slipped out and was gone.

The rest of the way home, the young mother reflected on the fact that pickpockets can give as well as take. What she didn't think about, but perhaps should have, was that they can also plant tracking bugs on a person's clothing. This was not a simple game she was playing.

Back home, she didn't dare take out the envelope until the front door was bolted and chained against the Bastard. Locking herself in the bathroom so the girls wouldn't see, she finally pulled it out for a look.

It was plain, brown, and small, about the size a bank would pass out to hold money in. On the outside was a gummed label with a logo that read:

**Kumar's
Discreet Delivery
Service**

***When it absolutely has to get there unseen.
Now making deliveries anywhere in North America.***

There were no other markings. No names. No addresses. Nothing.

Tearing off the end, she shook the contents into the sink: A thumb drive, a letter, and money. Lots of money. Slipping it and the drive back into her coat pocket, she sat down on the toilet to read the letter:

Dear Dancing Fawn:

May I call you that? I hope so, as my records will show this as your badlands name. After all, I have to call you something, and I do not know (and do not want to know) your real one.

So, Ms Fawn, life is full of tests. As you have probably gathered, this is another one of them. You now hold in your hand enough ready cash to feed yourself for months. You are undoubtedly tempted to abscond with it, but are resisting because you fear my associates will hunt you down to get it back. So, let me first assure you that that won't happen. After all, unless you try to contact me again, I won't have any way of finding you. I don't know your name, your address, your phone number, or anything about you except that you live in Cleveland. So, there is really nothing to stop you from just taking the money and disappearing into the night. The bills are not counterfeit, they are not marked. If you take them, you will get away with it as long as you are discreet. Should you decide to take that course of action, all I ask is that you destroy the other contents of this envelope and forget this entire experience. If you do that and, of course, tell no one about it, the money will be yours free and clear.

However, you may wish instead to use these funds to continue to develop our working relationship. That choice is your next test. Should you decide on this latter option, please follow the directions in the attached instruction sheet.

Whatever you decide, life is getting hard for us all. I wish you the best of luck in getting through it.

Mai Lee Chang

Stapled to the letter were two pages of instructions.

There wasn't enough money to get her away from the Bastard for good. So, while the decision might have been a struggle for others, there was really no choice for her. She read the instructions.

* * *

Again, Dancing Fawn found herself sitting in an inconspicuous corner of a branch of the Cleveland Public Library. This was not the one she used before; the instructions warned her to never go back there again. Otherwise, it looked and felt exactly the same except for one fact: She now sat in front of her own laptop.

Two days ago, she purchased a netbook from Walmart. As instructed, she made the purchase with cash, declined all warranty offers, and did not give her name. Taking the computer home, she disposed of the packing in such a way that the Bastard wouldn't know about the purchase. Then, with the front door bolted, locked in the bathroom, she made the machine her own.

Following the instructions, she first set it up to boot from a USB port. Then she inserted the flash drive that came with her cash delivery and rebooted the machine. Unknown to her, the laptop proceeded to completely wipe all data from its own hard disk. Then it started installing a new operating system, one not designed for normal use. Twenty minutes later, the screen told her to remove the flash drive, hide it, go to the library, and log on to the Internet. Following those instructions had brought her here.

She started her computer, logged on to the Internet using the library's Wi-Fi, and then waited while her laptop further arranged its little mind. Finally, after another ten minutes and much hard disk activity, the screen showed the China National Steel error page, along with a new banner at the top that said:

This computer maintained by
HOT WHEELS FOR THE BADLANDS
You're SAFE TO ROLL!

As before, she asked to speak to Mai Lee Chang. Again, the chat page showed up, though this time it looked quite different and was titled GOBI DESERT Crossing House, not China National Steel. After a short wait, Mrs. Chang came online.

> Chang: Welcome, Dancing Fawn. Congratulations on your decision and on your new wheels! How do you like them?
>
> Fawn: Thank you, but I don't own a car.
>
> Chang: That answer begs so many replies I hardly know where to begin. But first, we must keep the civs out. Can you tell me how you got my name?

That question was worrisome. The real Mrs. Chang knew very well how they came to meet, so why ask? Perhaps this was not Mrs. Chang? To delay a little, Fawn typed:

> Fawn: What's a civ?
>
> Chang: A supporter of the Civilized Governments Of The World. Now, please, I need an answer to my question. Where did you get

my name?

Simply because no other response came to mind, she decided on cautious honesty.

Fawn: Someone gave me a card.

Chang: Do you have it with you?

Fortunately, she hadn't destroyed it yet.

Fawn: Yes

Chang: What is written on it?

Fawn: Bring pen and paper

Chang: And anything else?

Fawn: A number

Chang: What is it?

After a pause,

Fawn: 27.100.199.3:1723

Chang: Thank you, you have put my mind at ease. So we don't have to go through that again, please choose two passwords that are different enough from each other that you won't ever get them confused. One will be green, the other red. Type them into the fields on your screen and hit Enter when you're done.

Fawn did as she was told.

Chang: Good. They were accepted. In the future, you can still get me by typing my name (which is also a password) in the doorbell field. However, if you want to go directly to the badlands, just type in one of those passwords instead.

Fawn: Badlands*?

Chang: Here. Where I am.

Fawn: Why two passwords?

Chang: Use one if everything is OK, the other if it is not.

Fawn: I don't understand.

Chang: Use the red password to warn your friends if you get

* See the appendix for a detailed glossary.

caught.

Fawn: Caught?

Chang: Arrested.

The penny dropped. Understanding something intellectually, in one's mind, is much different from really knowing it. Like the difference between looking over the edge of a cliff and falling off it. Somehow, she guessed she was breaking the law. But she never really knew it. Not until now. For the first time, her stomach got the word. Fear started there, a child of cramps and nausea, and scampered down her limbs like cold mice.

Chang: Child? Are you there?

Fawn: This is dangerous, isn't it?

Chang: Yes, it is. Do you want out?

And spend the rest of my life with the Bastard? Or other men just like him?

Fawn: No.

Chang: Are you sure?

Fawn: Yes.

Chang: OK. What is the difference between these two passwords?

Fawn: Right. Green is OK, red is bad.

Chang: Good. Now, next, here are three more doorbell addresses you can use to access the Internet: 187.12.77.90 and 26.22.106.53 and 222.98.2.2. Please write them down and store them in a safe place. If anything happens to the one you just used, you can contact me through one of the others. Lose them all and you will be locked out of the badlands, so memorize them if you can. Let me know when you have them copied.

After a pause,

Fawn: OK, I got them.

Chang: Good, now to the thoughts your earlier comment brought up. First, safe travel in the badlands, like anyplace else, requires the right vehicle. In this case, that is a properly programmed computer. So, one set up for this use is referred to as a 'set of wheels'. I was merely commenting on the fact that you now have your own computer suitable for this sort of thing.

Fawn: OK, thanks. Yes, it's a very nice laptop.

Chang: My second thought concerns security. Do you think there is any reason I need to know if you own a car?

Fawn: No, I guess not

Chang: I agree. If you want to stay out of prison, never give information about your real-world identity to anyone unless it is absolutely needed by the party asking for it. NEVER. Understand?

The word 'prison' jumped off the screen. Mice scampered down her arms again.

Fawn: Yes, sorry.

Chang: No need to apologize. Just, please, be careful.

Fawn: OK

Chang: Which brings up the final thought, one that covers a broader area of badlands manners and ethos. Operating here is not easy. No one would take such pains to stay hidden unless at least one government thought they were doing something illegal. In other words, everyone here has something to hide. Do you understand?

Fawn: Yes

Chang: In such an environment, asking unnecessary questions is a big yellow flag. Anyone who does so may be collecting information to sell to the highest bidder. If you want to get along here, want to establish the trust needed to change your indentureship, then don't ask for information you don't need to know. Doing so will make others mistrust you and, eventually, you will find no one will have anything to do with you. OK?

Fawn: Yes.

Chang: Good. Now, if you felt a pang of worry when you thought I was fishing, you can congratulate yourself. That was the right reaction. If my question didn't bother you, you need to worry more. This is a dangerous place. Paranoia is a survival skill. Understand?

Fawn: Yes. OK.

Then, after a pause,

Fawn: What did you mean by 'indentureship'?

Chang: I mean, at least for the foreseeable future, GOBI DESERT owns you. Before you panic, let me explain. We spent considerable time and money getting you safely through our door. We will spend more getting you a job, mailbox, and holding your hand until you get settled. We are a business. We must get that money back if we are to stay solvent. We do it by charging a commission on all transactions you make in the badlands.

Fawn: I didn't agree to that.

Chang: There was no safe way to explain it until now, so we took the chance that you would agree when the time came. Now is that time. Obviously, we think you will accept, or we wouldn't have put this effort into our relationship in the first place.

Fawn: What if I don't?

Chang: Consider this another test. If you want, just take the computer and leave. The operating system will erase itself if you don't connect to us regularly, so we have little to lose. But you will not get to see what is behind the prize door.

Fawn: Why can't I just go to another business like yours?

Chang: You can. There are hundreds of other crossing houses you could ask. Do you know how to contact any of them?

After a long pause,

Fawn: No

After a further pause,

Fawn: How long will my indenture last?

Chang: That is up to you. The badlands works on reputation. Right now, you have none. We back you in exchange for a cut. When you build up your own rep, when enough badlanders trust you not to turn them in, you will get offers from other crossing houses. When that happens, we ask only that you give us a chance to make a counter-offer. We like to keep our indentures.

Fawn: If I agree, then break my indenture, will I go to jail?

Chang: Heavens, child, there is no government in the badlands! No law, no courts, no jail. The guns are all on the other side of the border. The length of your indenture is determined only by you and the opinion of the rest of badlands society, nothing else. If you accept an offer from another crossing house, no one will come after you any more than Burger King would come after you because you choose to buy your next meal at McDonald's. You are really free to walk away at any time.

Fawn: The woman who sent me said no one would take anything I earned.

Chang: That depends on your definitions. If you sell your house and the realtor takes a cut, is he taking money away from your sale? If an employment agency finds you a job and charges your employer a commission, is he taking money from your pay? If you think the answer is yes, then, yes, Jade lied to you. We are middlemen and take a cut of everything you earn or spend.

Chang: However, we also provide a service, one essential to the transaction. If we didn't provide it, you could not make or spend anything in the badlands because no one would trust you enough to do business with you and you wouldn't know how to go about doing it anyway. So, if it makes you feel better to think that Jade lied, go ahead, but we think of it as just an honest oversimplification made necessary by a lack of time. Now that we have had the time, I hope I have set the story straight.

Fawn: Was that the name of the woman who sent me to you? Jade?

Chang: Her badlands name is Pink Jade. No one knows her real one unless she has told them. She has not confided in us.

Fawn: So. What next?

Chang: If you're still in, we need to get you a mailbox and a job. Are you in?

What was the alternative? Stay with the Bastard?

Fawn: Yes

Chang: You sure?

Fawn: Yes

Chang: Good! You can, of course, choose any email service you want, but we have used CHIANG MAI BOXES for many years and recommend them. If you want, I will tunnel you through when we are finished.

Fawn: Tunnel me through?

Chang: Remember I said that collecting unnecessary information is a no-no in the badlands? It goes both ways. Any businessman who conspicuously avoids collecting unnecessary information is more likely to get customers. One of the ways we do that is by passing all your communications through an encrypted data link called a VPN tunnel. Only you and the business you talk to can understand what goes through it. We cannot eavesdrop. Our customers like that, so we get more business. Understand?

Fawn: Yes

Chang: Good. Now, about a job. What would you like to do?

Fawn: Meet men.

Chang: Be an escort?

Fawn: Well, yes. Like that.

Chang: There are a number of services we can send you to, but first I must be presumptuous and ask a question. Do you really want to continue this type of work?

Fawn: It's all I know

Chang: That is not a good basis for making a decision. Would you like to see what other opportunities there may be for you?

Fawn: I don't know anything about computers.

Chang: There may still be other opportunities. Would you like to hear about them?

Fawn: Yes. What else could I do?

Chang: You could smuggle meds.

Fawn: You mean drugs? Like heroin?

Chang: No, I mean medications. Like beta-blockers for high blood pressure. Not controlled drugs.

Fawn: Like aspirin?

Chang: Yes, just more expensive

Fawn: Why would anyone pay to smuggle aspirin?

Chang: Most prescription drugs sold in America are made in China. American drug companies import the raw pharmaceuticals, repackage them, and sell the pills only by prescription. Not only do they keep 95% of each sale, but doctors and pharmacists get rich because no one can buy the pills without paying a doctor's fee and a pharmacist's mark-up. Smugglers sell these meds at a quarter of what the legal channels charge and still make a very nice profit.

Fawn: If I got caught, would I lose my girls?

Chang: Girls?

Fawn: I have a family.

Chang: If you got caught selling sex, would you lose them? There are no safe choices anymore. Which risks do you want to take?

For the mouse in her, that was a very scary question. But the Bastard left her no choice. Like it or not, she would have to commit to something.

Chapter 2

Seven Years Ago

Seven years before Dancing Fawn made her first crossing, two men sat in a large well-appointed Federal Government office. One, the older, leaned over his heavy desk with the air of patient expectation. The other, the younger of the two, sat at a table in the middle of the room. In front of him were two clear plastic envelopes. Each contained a single $100 bill. One was crisp, new, and uncirculated. The other showed slight wear. The younger man wore a jeweler's loupe and was slowly examining the two bills.

After a full minute of going back and forth between them, Secret Service Agent Joshua Weidemeyer* put down both bills and, with a twitch of his eyebrow, dropped the loupe into his open palm.

"OK, how did we screw this one up?" he asked.

"We didn't," said the older man who was, as of a day ago, the younger one's new boss.

"Except for wear, these bills are identical," said Weidemeyer. "Including the serial numbers. That's not supposed to happen. So, how did we screw up?"

The old man sat in silence, waiting to see how quickly the younger one picked up on the problem. It didn't take long.

"That's not possible. They're both perfect bills."

The older man smiled and shook his head.

"Which one?" asked Weidemeyer.

"The worn one."

Again, picking up his jewelers loupe, Weidemeyer began a close inspection of the worn bill. It was a work of love, for he loved money. Not the value of it, or the accumulation of it, or even its numerical representation in a balance sheet. No, Joshua loved the physical item, be it paper or coin. He loved the art, the embodied history, and the way it had transformed mankind.

His second exam lasted a full two minutes. Finally, with a sigh, he set down

---

* See the appendix for full list of characters.

the loupe and said "You can't prove it by me."

"Nor by anyone else."

"Then how do you know it's not ours?"

"Production irregularities."

"That's all?"

The older man nodded. Weidemeyer muttered a mild vulgarity under his breath.

No two mechanical systems can ever be the same. They vary by machining tolerances when they are made, then by wear differences as they are used and repaired. This is as true for printing presses as for car engines. The Bureau Of Engraving And Printing, which runs the presses that print all the United States currency, know this. They use it to their advantage by taking and filing samples of their press's outputs on an hourly basis. When those samples go out of tolerance, the press is stopped, brought back to spec, and then restarted. The result is that all US $100 bills look the same, even though every one is microscopically different from the others. It would take a precision optical instrument to see the variations, but they are measurable.

This worn bill, like all others, was a little different from the ideal. By going back through the sample files, the Treasury should be able to determine exactly when this one was printed even if its serial number and date were wrong. All they had to do was match the production irregularities to one of the historical samples.

But, for this worn bill, no match. Not to any run. Ever. Someone else printed this bill. In other words, it was counterfeit. But good. So good that no normal method of detection, nothing used by any bank or merchant, could pick up the fraud.

"Paper, too? Watermark and all?" asked Weidemeyer.

"There are differences, but you'd need a lab to find them," the older man said.

"How'd we get this one?"

"Postal inspector. Random drug search. He found a hundred of them. We found the match to that uncirculated bill when the DEA ran a check on the serial numbers."

"Are they all this good?"

The old man nodded.

"All from the same run?"

"No. All from the same press, but the wear patterns show they were printed at different times."

Damn. Not only was someone producing quality counterfeit, but they'd been doing it for long enough to build up an inventory somewhere.

"All worn?"

Again a nod.

"Real wear?"

"No, simulated. But so good no one would notice the difference."

This time out loud: "Crap". Random serial numbers, perfect originals, and worn. The Secret Service's worst nightmare. These bills would be almost impossible to find.

"Did you get the guy they were going to?"

Finally, a smile and a nod.

"He talking?"

"Like the proverbial bird."

"Where are they coming from?"

"He doesn't know."

"How does he know when to pick them up?"

"The Internet."

Now it was Weidemeyer's turn to smile. Ten years ago, they had a ring that tried to organize distribution through the same outlet. Wi-Fi didn't exist then, of course, so all the Secret Service had to do was trace back through the phone company connections. Some of the perps got away, those that were smart enough to use portable computers and connect through a public phone booth. But not many. It was easy.

"So all we have to do is work back through the server address logs."

"If it were that simple, you wouldn't be working for me now."

"Why not?"

"The trace goes to a Mitsubishi computer in Tokyo."

"And from there?"

"Nowhere. Dead end."

"So there's someone at Mitsubishi."

Weidemeyer's boss shook his head. "Tokyo's finest have been over the logs. No one gets the messages. They don't even get through the firewall."

"I don't understand."

"The Tokyo computer never accepts them."

"Meaning?"

"They're messages addressed to nowhere. Dead letters. They just go in the trash."

"No one gets them?"

"I didn't say that."

"Who then?"

"I've set up a meeting so you can hear the answer."

* * *

Larry, Moe, and Curly.

That was all Weidemeyer could think of as he sat with the three network engineers. The vision was unprofessional, but he couldn't get it out of his mind. The resemblance was too striking.

When they had first been introduced, the three engineers had fought a silent combat to decide who would be his teacher. Moe lost. Now he struggled with his burden.

"The counterfeiter you caught gave us a static IP address for a known VPN server-"

Weidemeyer held up his hand. "What's a 'static IP address'?" he asked.

Moe looked at the others, but got no help, so began again.

"Every server-"

"Server?" interrupted Weidemeyer.

"A 'server' is a computer that performs a service without any human assistance. That's why they call it a 'server'. Get it?"

Ignoring the jab, Weidemeyer asked "And a 'static IP address'?"

"An Internet address that doesn't change. Like 123.123.123.123."

"I thought they looked like 'www.google.com'."

Again, Moe looked at his two associates. Neither volunteered, so he continued.

"No, no. That's just a name. A stupid marketing trick. To make it easy for people to remember. If you type 'www.google.com' into your browser, it looks up the real address and uses that to contact Google."

Weidemeyer nodded and waited for more.

"Anyway, the doorbell address your prisoner gave-"

"Doorbell address?"

"The Internet address they use to initiate communications. Like a doorbell button. That's why they call it a 'doorbell address'. Get it?"

Again, Weidemeyer turned the other cheek. "Go on," he said.

"Anyway, it belongs to a VPN server, oper-"

"VPN?"

Again, Moe looked at his two associates. This time, he must have won, because Curly spoke up.

"A VPN server is a server that sets up encrypted communications with other VPN servers. Never mind why it's called 'VPN', it just is."

"OK."

"This doorbell address belongs to a Mitsubishi VPN server in Tokyo. It encodes all communications between their home office and other Mitsubishi and vendor VPN servers anywhere in the world. There must be thousands of them."

"OK, I'm still with you."

That got smiles. Except from Curly, who seemed to be in pain. But he continued anyway.

"Now this master VPN server knows who is authorized to use it, sort of like having a company phone directory in its memory. So, as long as you're in its book, when you ask for a private connection, it sets one up. See?"

"Yes."

"So, if one of your bad guys wants to buy more counterfeit, he just sends a message to the doorbell address."

"And we can't understand what they say to each other because the connection he uses is encrypted, right?" asked Weidemeyer. He was beginning to understand.

"No," Curly said, frustration obvious in his voice.

"No?"

"I mean yes, we couldn't understand anything they said if they got connected, because it would all be encrypted. That's what VPN servers do. But no, because your prisoner is not authorized to establish a link. So they don't get connected."

"Authorized?"

"He's not in the phone book!"

"So?"

"So the server ignores his message!"

Silence descended on the room. After a tense pause, during which Curly calmed down a bit, he asked "See how it works?"

"No. I don't see how having a message ignored will get a connection."

Curly sighed audibly. Looking back at his compadres, he gave each a long pleading stare. For some reason, Larry took pity on him and spoke up.

"OK, think of it this way. Suppose you send an old girlfriend a letter. But she sees it's from you, so she throws it in the trash."

Weidemeyer nodded.

"But lots of people in the post office see your letter before she gets it, right?"

Weidemeyer nodded again.

"What if one of them copies the return address from the outside of the envelope? Then he'd know where it came from, right?"

"Yes."

"So, if he gave that address to someone else, and that person wrote you back, without using a real return address, you wouldn't know who answered your letter, would you?

"No."

"That's why we have a problem. We can't find out who got your perp's message. It wasn't Mitsubishi. Their computer ignored it. The return address on the message your counterfeiter gets back won't be the doorbell server's, either, because that computer didn't reply back to him directly."

"Doorbell server?"

"The one that copied the return address of the message that was sent to Mitsubishi. The doorbell message. That's why they call-"

"I know, that's why they call it a doorbell server. But we can find that other one, right?"

"Which one?"

"The one that finally replied to the doorbell message. That message's got a return address on it, too, right?"

Larry nodded.

"Then we just trace that address back?"

"Not if he uses a proxy server," he said.

"Proxy server?"

"A server that's like a mail forwarder. Substitutes its address for the original in an Internet message before forwarding it on. Try a trace-back, all you get is the address of the proxy."

"Can't we trace through that - what did you call it?"

"Proxy server."

"Right. Can't we trace back through that 'proxy server' to the original source of the message?"

Moe said "Yes."

Curly said "No."

Larry said "Maybe."

"I need a straight answer here."

A long three-way discussion occurred between the technical staff, followed by silence. They just looked back at him, perhaps hoping he was satisfied enough to go away.

"Well?"

Larry must have decided it was still his turn. "We have to give you a firm 'sometimes' on that," he said.

The other two just nodded.

And with that, the meeting came to a close.

* * *

If there were an official King Of The Civs, the current incumbent would be Arnold Wilson Parker. He didn't have many official titles and, according to the IRS, owned little property, but kingship is not about property or titles. It's about control. And Arnold Wilson Parker had that. In spades.

He, and several associates who were, for various reasons, obliged to follow his suggestions, constituted the controlling trustees of a number of very large private foundations. Collectively these financial entities owned enough assets to buy ten percent of all the shares listed in the Dow Jones Industrial Average. That kind of money bought influence.

From his estate high in the mountains of Colorado, he spent most of his time seeing that the investments and donations made by these foundations supported policies that he felt were important, policies that might collectively be referred to as the Globalist Agenda.

Late the night before, in spite of his hectic schedule, Maxwell Stein, Governor of the Chicago Federal Reserve Bank, had flown to Parker's estate by private jet. The trip was necessary because Stein's re-appointment to his first full term was just around the corner.

Now Stein sat alone with Parker in a large study. Bright summer sun streamed in through the open French doors. Aspens sparkled just beyond the veranda, framed by a stunning view across Parker's valley that ended at the gray guardians of the Rockies.

"Confidence is still quite good," said Stein with an obvious sense of relief.

"Meaning?"

"I don't see any risk of inflation in the near future."

"Unemployment? Can you fix it?"

"I doubt it. That's structural."

The conversation lapsed into silence while Parker considered how to ask the most difficult question while Stein, knowing the question was coming, thought about how he would answer it.

Stein broke the silence. "You better plan on more federal busywork because the private sector is not going to recover anytime soon," he said, leaving a broad hint. He hoped it would be sufficient, would allow him to skirt the issue without actually breaking the law.

And that last comment did almost clinch it. But there was quite a bit of money at stake, so Parker was not going to be satisfied with hints. He needed to be sure.

"Next FOMC?" he probed. The Federal Open Market Committee was the body that set short-term interest rates. As one of the Federal Reserve governors, Stein was a participating member. Thanks to Parker's influence, he was a first among equals.

“Where will it go?”

That was the question that Parker was never allowed to ask or Stein ever to answer. If they were sitting anywhere but Parker's den, surrounded by thousands of acres of his Colorado estate, he would not have dared to speak it, as the words drifting in the air, even unanswered, broke dozens of laws. Here, just between the two of them, it was worth the risk.

But Stein had already decided to take the plunge. Without a trace of uneasiness, he answered. "Not much choice as I see it. Unless we want the next depression to start tomorrow, we had better increase the money supply tonight."

"Another QE?"

"We won't call it that, but the result will be the same. We'll-"

"Thanks," Parker said, holding up his hand. He didn't need any more. Knowing which way the money supply would go would be enough.

Tomorrow, Parker would make a few encrypted phone calls to some associates in several of his foundations. They, in turn, would speak with some bankers with whom they had invested considerable funds. And those august individuals, when the time came, would know how to vote when the next election for the governor of the Chicago Fed was held.

The managers of those foundations would also know how to make investments that would return a very handsome profit when a looser Fed policy drove interest rates down further. It's easier to play roulette if you know where the ball is going to stop before they spin the wheel.

Five hours later, Maxwell Stein was back in the air, secure in the knowledge that he would have no problem getting reappointed.

* * *

The counterfeiting business, like any other, has fundamental economic constraints. At one end, operators must produce a product. That, in turn requires very specialized equipment and supplies, all of which cost money. The better the product is to be, the more it will cost to produce. In the case of the bills sitting in front of Weidemeyer, someone had invested enough to dent the budget of a small country.

Assuming the objective is to make money, there is only one way to do it: Profitable sales. And lots of them.

So the second fundamental problem facing anyone trying to run a counterfeiting business is how to run a sales force in the face of violent competition. Until now, distribution had been as daunting a task as making undetectable bills. Hitler printed large amounts of almost-perfect British banknotes, but was unable to do anything with them because wartime security stopped him from setting up a distribution network in the UK.

The problem is more than just the actual distribution of the product, though, since small stacks of bills can be sent by mail rather easily. Someone has to recruit and communicate with the individuals who want to pass these bills, as well as collect something of value back from them to pay for the sales. Until now, this problem had been insurmountable.

Joshua Weidemeyer saw how the Internet changed that. If the Secret Service didn't catch all the rot, stamp out everyone who was involved anywhere in this ring, they risked having the survivors start over with improved ideas. They had to make an example for the underworld by eliminating the entire counterfeiting ring in some very public manner.

Now, once again, he sat in the large office alone with his new boss. For the past hour, they had been working on ideas for how to solve this new problem.

"So we know where they are?" asked the older man.

Weidemeyer nodded slightly, though without a smile to confirm the gesture.

"How'd you find them?"

"We asked Mitsubishi to forward all invalid VPN requests to us. Each one had a return IP address. NSA logged all traffic in or out of those addresses. In about one percent of the cases, a VPN connection was received from a foreign server shortly after Mitsubishi got the bogus request. The encryption stopped us from monitoring what was said, but we could still trace the link back to where it came from."

"And?" prompted the older man.

"The ones that mattered all came from foreign proxy servers."

"Can't we force the owners of those computers to tell where the original messages came from?"

"Sure. If the servers were located in civilized countries, it'd be easy. But they're in Cuba, Iran, Somalia, and North Korea. We could file diplomatic requests forever and never get a trace back from any of them."

"So that's a dead end?" asked the older man.

"No, fortunately not. We asked the CIA to help and they were able to break into two of the servers. Both showed that the connections came from the same IP address in Coro, Venezuela."

"And?"

"Our friends at the agency have contacts inside the Venezuela telephone system. They gave us a physical address to match the Internet one. Unfortunately, it only gets us as close as their last local switch. To get closer than that, we'll have to manually trace the wiring."

"How big's the area of uncertainty?"

"Ten blocks."

"Not good enough."

"No, its not. We also have the physical address they give when they applied for the service, but I doubt it's very accurate."

"Can we manually trace the wiring?"

"Not without the perps knowing. That would scare them off before we could spring the trap."

Both men thought in silence for several seconds. Weidemeyer's boss spoke first.

"They must buy a fair amount of special paper and ink. I wonder who delivers it to them."

One week later, they had a year's worth of connection logs for the Coro IP address courtesy of the CIA. Most went to public access points in the United States, but two with large volumes of traffic did not. One was to an export company in Manila, the other to an IP address in Toledo, Ohio.

For a small discreet fee, a nice man in the DHL office in the Philippines supplied a list of all the ship-to addresses that received packages from the Manila company. One was in the ten square blocks in Coro.

"How many distributors you think there are?" asked Weidemeyer's boss.

"Guys passing the stuff?"

His boss nodded.

"The logs show hundreds of independent contacts."

"A big operation."

"One of the advantages of modern technology."

"So, what's the plan?" the older man asked.

"Since we think their distribution control runs through the Internet, we're going to set up a fake web page to look like the one in Venezuela. Switch all traffic to it after we shut down the real one. That should keep the field perps stupid for a while."

“Only if they don't get warned when we shut down the real one.”

“Right,” agreed Weidemeyer.

“We bring all the counterfeiters back here and keep them under wraps?” asked his boss.

The younger man shook his head. “Operations says they can't keep it quiet with that many prisoners.”

“What then?”

“We'll just have to make sure no one can talk.”

"And after that? We can't keep a fake server going forever."

"Bring the Coro computers back here. NSA should be able to break into at least one of them in a week or two. With luck, they'll have good physical addresses for most of the passers in their files."

"Not all?"

"That's too much to hope for. We think the smarter ones use anonymous mail drops."

"How do you plan on catching them?"

"Wait until they go online for their next shipment. When they log on, we'll have their return IP. A quick trace, a raid, and we're done."

"OK. What about the Toledo site?"

"Extra postal inspectors are hammering all incoming packages. We find one with bogus, we got an address."

"And then?"

"We move."

* * *

Joshua Weidemeyer lived a neat, simple life defined by disposable furniture. Other than his coin collection, he considered little in his small apartment to be of value. All else was expedient.

This evening he sat alone in a folding chair under a single overhead light, leaning forward to examine a small bit of worn silver. Spread out on the card table in front of him, arranged precisely by date, was an assortment of Roman coins similar to the one he held in his hand.

His hard face showed no expression as he inspected his prize. An observer unfamiliar with his character might have considered it cruel, but that analysis would be wrong. He displayed intensity of concentration, not emotional indifference to the fate of others. Joshua Weidemeyer was not unfeeling, just disciplined and focused. This truth could be seen in his eyes, now locked on the lump of metal he held, intense and unwavering.

The rest of his demeanor was unremarkable. His frame was short and wiry, his head crowned with a ring of short-cropped dark hair circling a large bald spot. On his nose sat heavy glasses more appropriate to an accountant than a member of one of the world's best-known police agencies. Perhaps, if he had been a little vain, he would have gotten contacts, but glasses were more practical.

The object of his scrutiny was one of an eclectic mix of coins that were all once used for money in ancient Rome. To Weidemeyer, his collection was a physical record of a civilization's climb to greatness and then its fall back to an ignoble end. Written in it was his confirmation that stable money was one of mankind's greatest inventions. Like language, he believed civilization could never have come into existence without it.

The earliest examples in his collection were little more than lumps of silver, but the quality improved as the dates advanced. The best, those from the late Republic and early Empire periods, would qualify as good art anywhere. Then, gradually, along with the rest of Roman society, they slipped. From fine jewelry, they became silver-washed slugs of bronze which, like aged whores under thick makeup, were covered with a layer of illusion to hide the reality of their baser natures.

Which caused the death of the other, he had often wondered, *the civilization or its money?*

* * *

Pug Ringgold sat hunched in the back of a dark panel van with six other men, trying to make his large frame fit the limited space. There were no windows for him to look out of, but even if there had been, he would have seen little. Dawn in the Venezuelan city of Coro was still three hours away and there were few streetlights in this section of the city to push back the night. Only the skyglow from wealthier neighborhoods far away provided any illumination.

In front of Pug, in the quiet of the unlit van, glowed a laptop. Its screen showed the inside of a warehouse as seen from a pallet containing hidden cameras and microphones. Everything within view of the pallet showed on the screen. Like an invisible god, Pug could see without being seen.

For the past twelve hours, he had watched a print shop in action. Six men worked to feed a press with paper and ink. Four more ran the machine, while nine women removed the large colored sheets that it produced and cut them into individual United States hundred dollar bills. He saw no children, though he had expected some. In Venezuela, at least, counterfeiting was a family operation.

A printing operation of this sophistication was not easy to set up. First and foremost, it required a good press. The one visible on Pug's laptop was over thirty feet long and weighed ten tons. Bolted to the floor to stop it from walking during operation, it had required heavy equipment just to get it inside. Now it provided a significant barrier to Pug's vision, blocking his view of half the building interior.

An hour ago, the printing had stopped. The day's work was finished. Slowly, like an animal stretching before sleep, the operation had gone quiet. The press was cleaned, the produce of the day's efforts was packed, and then the counterfeiters settled down for the night. Now they lay on any level surface that would serve, sleeping the sleep due working men and women after a hard day's labor. The lights were dim, the room was quiet. A single worker kept watch, a lone woman seated on an elevated platform, cooled by the room's only fan. She rocked quietly, an automatic weapon across her lap, keeping a protective eye over her comrades. Outside, on the loading dock, two men also kept guard. They sat in the shadows, watching the only approach to the warehouse, squeezed as it was into a crowded industrial neighborhood.

The pallet that transmitted these pictures had arrived late that afternoon. It was accepted as a normal shipment from Manila, more paper and ink to feed the presses. In fact, it contained only a small amount of paper, distributed to hide its real contents from any cursory examination. Beneath this camouflaging layer were cameras, microphones, and transmitters. And explosives. Mostly explosives, for this package was more than the gatherer of information. It was also to be the dispenser of death.

The long vigil, held quietly until the opposition was asleep, was not a new experience for Pug. A career military man, he had gone from high school directly into the infantry, then the Rangers, Special Forces, and now the CIA. During that time, he had, on many occasions, experienced the dull tension of the stalk, the boredom of the quiet wait. He was used to it, ready for the moment when he would uncoil like a compressed spring to become the messenger of death that his country had trained him to be.

The night before, small cameras were hidden across the street from the warehouse parking area. They allowed him to watch the dock, to pinpoint the location of the two guards who occupied it. From their positions, he knew which sections of the street could be seen and which were hidden. It was time to take advantage of this information. He gave the signal.

Seven men slipped quietly out of the van and walked down the dark street. All wore body armor hidden under worn clothes that were the livery of working men everywhere. If seen in the dim light, they would pass for laborers on their way to early morning jobs. They were (with the exception of Pug) all local men, members of a gang that had contracted with the CIA to do this particular job. Each carried, hidden under his clothing, an AK-47 carbine. All were well trained in the use of that weapon. In the lead, speaking fluent Spanish, walked Pug. He would make sure these mad dogs got to the blind spot nearest the dock, quietly and without being seen. After that, it would be up to them.

When they reached their assault position, Pug spoke softly into the darkness. From down the street, an engine started. Headlights appeared, attached to a small pick-up. It moved slowly, as befitted an old vehicle whose driver made his living collecting scrap. Its bed was filled with samples of that class of metal: Coils of used cable, bed springs, and old cabinets. Hidden under this refuse, lying on their stomachs under the bed's false bottom, were two local specialists. Each lay in front of a small irregular hole cut through the left side of the vehicle. Each held a sniping carbine loaded with .45 ammunition to keep bullet velocities below the speed of sound. That, along with large silencers, sound-proofing inside the truck bed, and the special dampeners in their weapon's actions, would assure that little noise would be produced when they fired.

The disadvantages of subsonic bullets are two. First, they transmit little energy to the target. This was the reason for choosing the larger round rather than the more conventional 9 mm. Even at low velocities, a 45 would tear a large hole in its target. Each carbine would also discharge a three-round burst when fired to maximize target impact.

The second disadvantage was range. Slow bullets do not fly straight but instead arc as gravity pulls them downward. To compensate, a shooter must elevate his aiming point higher than he might otherwise need to for faster rounds such as those used by Pug's assault team.

The accuracy problem was made more difficult because subsonic .45 slugs, even ones that had tungsten cores and Teflon coatings as these did, couldn't reliably penetrate body armor. Since the guards might be wearing some, torso hits wouldn't guarantee a kill. Only a head shot would do, making the target much smaller.

Fortunately, both men had been well trained by Pug for just this task. They would be firing from the nearest street, less than seventy-five feet across the parking lot to the dock. As long as both they and their targets were stationary, they were unlikely to miss.

The truck came to a stop as it pulled in front of the gate-less entrance to the parking lot. Pug watched it intently, waiting for the snipers to fire. Nothing happened. The dim silence remained unbroken. Then his earphone cracked to life, issuing a single Spanish word, repeated three times so he could not miss it, confirming that both guards were down. Pug hadn't even noticed the shots.

With a quick wave, he sent in the contractors. They ran hunched over, as quickly and quietly as they could, across the exposed space of the dirt parking area towards the protection of the loading dock wall. Most, but not all, reached its shelter before a small door opened in the back of the dock. A large Hispanic in body armor stepped out, weapon at the ready, a wary look on his face. Perhaps he heard one of the guards fall, or perhaps the sound of an overshot striking the common wall. Whatever the reason, he was now a serious threat to the assault. As nearly as Pug knew, there were twenty-two armed counterfeiters in that building, far more than his meager force could tackle without the advantage of surprise.

The snipers on the bed of the pickup also saw the door open. Pug had trained them well, for they acted quickly. Both fired as the interloper stepped out of the dim warehouse light into the darkness of the dock. Pug never heard these shots, either, but the big Hispanic felt them. Spinning back into the building, he yelled at the top of his lungs. Whether it was because the snipers had not had time to aim properly or because the man was moving, they had failed to make an instant kill. The element of surprise was about to be lost.

Pug held a radio detonator in his right hand. Acting instinctively, he flicked up the safety cover and pushed down the button underneath it. This time, he didn't miss the result.

Even when contained by cinder block walls, the sound of twelve Claymore mines detonating was unmistakable. The blast sent thousands of small steel balls across the shop in every horizontal direction, shredding anything that stood (or in this case, lay) in its path. The dock protected his contractors, even the two that had not yet reached the shelter of its lip, because they had dropped to the ground when the big Hispanic opened the door. But the small pickup truck across the parking lot was not so lucky. Pellets from at least one of the mines punched through a closed overhead loading door and stuck the vehicle, injuring the driver and one sniper. Only the distance and the door slowed the pellets enough to prevent fatalities.

Before the last of the debris came to a stop, his contractors vaulted over the dock lip and ran into the warehouse. They took advantage of the confusion caused by the blast and the grogginess of the counterfeiters to kill before anyone could shoot back. It helped that his contractors wore body armor. It also helped that the Tungsten-core ammunition their carbines used cut through their opposition's body armor like a shotgun blast through a dirty t-shirt.

Pug waited until the shooting died down, no more than thirty seconds, before he moved in. He walked into the warehouse just as the second van, the one with the clean-up gear, backed up to the dock. As he moved through the building, marking equipment for destruction, one of his contractors ambled ahead of him and placed two shots in the head of each counterfeiter. Only the woman by the fan had put up any resistance. Stunned by the Claymore's blast, she died before she was able to hit anyone.

Walking through the chaos left by the blast, Pug directed the final disposition of the facility. Behind him, thermite charges were strapped to the printing press. Each would produce a flow of molten iron when it went off, fusing delicate parts together and irrevocably defacing all the plates. Satchel charges went under each pile of printing paper and all inventories of finished counterfeit. Their explosives wouldn't destroy the paper or scrip, but would scatter it around the warehouse like loose confetti so it could be consumed by the fire while it still drifted in the air.

Two web servers were located in a closet near the back of the warehouse. Both had been damaged by gunfire, but one hard drive was intact. Both drives, along with samples of the counterfeit bills, would go back to Washington in the next diplomatic pouch. Within a week, the supercomputers at NSA would brute-force the password and the counterfeiter's site would be up again, only this time under new management.

Ten minutes later, as he supervised the installation of the last of the incendiary charges, one of his contractors yelled for him from a side room. Going to the door, he walked in to see three small children, eyes wide with fear, huddled together in a corner. They had been found hiding behind a pallet of printing paper, missed during the initial attack.

"What do you want me to do about it?" asked Pug in almost-perfect Spanish, the frustration clear in his voice through a slight accent. Then, after waiting a long heartbeat for the point to sink in, he turned and left. Seconds later, as he walked towards the dock to set the final charges, he heard shots from the room. As agreed, there would be no witnesses.

Minutes later, before the local police were even sure something had happened, the raiders were gone. The warehouse grew as silent as the tomb it had become. Then the thermite ignited, followed by satchel charge explosions. Two seconds later, the incendiaries created a wall of flame that filled the building. It burned for hours, leaving little behind except traces of cocaine left by the raiders. These drugs would give the Venezuelan government a cover story, a way to save face. Officially, they could claim a local drug gang made the attack to settle a dispute. The alternative was a diplomatic confrontation they knew they could not win.

But the mangled printing press put the lie to that explanation for anyone who had eyes to see. For them, the message was clear: The U. S. dollar's status as the world's reserve currency existed because the American Government did whatever was necessary to prevent its debasement. Mass counterfeiting by any power would be considered an act of war and would be dealt with accordingly.

* * *

"Father, I'm confused," said twelve-year old Arnold Wilson Parker II, known to his acquaintances and family as Junior.

"Not uncommon. At your age. Not at all," answered his father, expecting to begin a discussion of the world's most confusing subject.

"Yes, sir," answered young Parker. He was home from Exeter and his father could see all the signs of budding puberty. Well, a father had to be ready for these sorts of questions.

"Can I help?" he prompted.

"Yes, sir." After a short hesitation, the boy blurted out "It's about money."

"Good stuff. Money. Good," said Parker with some relief. On that subject, at least, he was quite ready to talk. On the other, well, he was still not all that sure of himself.

"Yes, sir. What is it?"

"Money?" asked the father, surprised by the esoteric nature of the question. His son, after all, was little more than a child.

"Yes sir. Some of my friends say it's dollars, others say gold. Which is it?"

"This is what you boys talk about?"

"In Social Studies, sir."

Well, at least boys were still boys, thought Arnold. Aloud, he said "Profound question, son. Tough, too. Profound and tough. What does your teacher say?"

"He won't give us an answer."

"Shows good sense."

"I don't understand."

"Never mind. It's simple, really. Simple. Money is what people think it is."

"Sir?"

"Not easy to understand. Like all great truths. Even when you state it. Ambiguous. Subtle. But still true."

The boy looked very confused so Arnold paused, letting the words sink in while he decided where to start.

"Know the definition of money, son?"

"No, sir. Sorry, sir. We haven't gotten to that yet."

"Teacher needs to get on the ball."

"Yes sir."

"Money is anything used regularly for three-party transactions."

The boy looked back in uncomprehending silence.

"Suppose you give me a sack of wheat. For a week's work. I take it, I eat it. What we did was trade. Barter. Just a trade. No money changed hands. None. See that?"

"Yes sir. Wheat isn't money."

"No. Didn't say that. When it's only traded between two people, it isn't money. But suppose, instead of eating it, I give it to my landlord to pay my rent. It's still wheat, right?"

"Yes sir"

"But not a trade. A three-party transaction. My landlord is really getting the wheat from my employer. I'm just the go-between. Passing it along, so to speak. Then wheat is money. See the difference?"

"No sir. Sorry."

"Enough of the 'sorry', boy. Don't be sorry. Never be sorry. Never. Do what you have to. But never be sorry. Never."

"Yes, sir. Sor-. I mean, yes sir."

"Think about the second example. Doesn't matter what my employer gives me. Only matters that I know how much of it my landlord will take for rent. See that?"

"Yes sir."

"Can be anything. Shells. Pretty stones. Tobacco. Gold. Colored paper. Anything. Doesn't matter. As long as everyone accepts it, it's money. See that?"

"Yes sir. I think so, sir," the boy said with a smile. "So which is it? Gold or dollars?"

"Right now, today, if you try to buy groceries with a lump of gold, will the cashier take it?"

After a thoughtful moment, the young man answered "I don't think so."

"No, he won't. Not officially, anyway. Might pocket your gold and pay for your groceries himself. But the store won't take it. Right?"

"Yes sir."

"Do you see why?"

"No sir."

"They don't keep their accounts in it and can't pay their bills with it. Can't pass it through. No three-party exchange."

The boy just looked back in silence.

"Try a three-party transaction with gold, you get turned down. Right?"

He got a nod in response.

"So, is gold money? I mean right now. Today."

"No sir."

"Right. Because right now, today, it won't be accepted for a three-party transaction. What will be?"

"Dollars?"

"Right.

"So gold's not money?" asked the child.

"Not today, it's not." answered the older man. Then, after a pause to let his son think about the point, he asked "Want a trick question?"

With a smile, the boy nodded. Father always made trick questions easy.

"Will dollars be money tomorrow?"

The smile vanished. Father hadn't come through this time. The young Parker was at a loss for the right answer. There was a pause while he considered trying to guess, but decided against it. With Father, guessing was rarely a good idea.

"I don't know," the boy admitted.

"Good. Right answer. No one can predict tomorrow. When it comes, how will you find the answer?"

"Buy something?"

"Right. And, tomorrow, if you do the same thing, but they won't take dollars, only gold, will dollars still be money?"

Junior took a second to be sure of his answer, then said "No."

"Right. What would be?"

"Gold."

"Smart boy. Money is what people say it is. And sometimes, people change their minds. So money is not always the same thing. Today, the answer to your question is dollars. But, tomorrow, it might be gold."

Junior became pensive, trying to digest a difficult concept. He had just been told that a rock of his existence, one of the framing members of his world, was not solid. That was a scary idea for a twelve-year old to accept.

"Father," he finally asked, "That can't really happen, can it? Gold can't really become money someday, can it?"

"Yes, son. Afraid it can. But don't worry. It won't. Not as long as I have anything to do with it, it won't."

* * *

Eddy sat alone in his battered Civic by the edge of a warm New Jersey parking lot. Balanced on the dash next to him, a homemade Yagi Wi-Fi antenna connected him to the Internet through a small cafe on the other side of a busy highway. Around him, a crowded parking lot provided cover. His laptop sat open on his lap, powered by the same inverter that ran his antenna amplifier.

He was in his car rather than the cafe because what he was doing was illegal. The extra separation gave him a better chance of escaping if anything went wrong. As most members of his family could have told him from personal experience, always have a good get-away plan when dealing with the law.

Two years ago, Eddy quit college because he ran out of money. The loans ended when he was still six months short of graduating. With thousands of dollars of debts, he learned that 90 percent of a computer science degree only got you food stamps. Alone, depressed, and almost on the street, one of his uncles gave him an IP address and told him to visit the site.

Now he was working on his graduate degree, free and clear.

Thank you FUNNY MONEY.

Now he was logged on to order another shipment of bogus bills. Everyone else must be doing the same thing, though, because the site was taking forever to complete his order.

While he waited, he rested his eyes on the cafe across the street. Without warning, two sedans sped up to it and stopped in the fire zone. Six clean-cut men in business suits jumped out and ran through the front door, guns drawn.

Eddy knew what a raid looked like, though he had never seen one. Until now, that is. Jerking the remote antenna off the dash, he shoved the laptop to the floor, slid over into the driver's seat, and backed quickly out of the parking space. Seconds later he was exiting the far end of the Stop & Shop lot.

Meanwhile, Agents from the two cars moved quickly through the cafe, targeting everyone with a computer. A third sedan blocked the rear exit, ready to catch anyone who tried to leave by that route.

All those without computers, including any employees, were identified, logged, searched, and sent home. But possession of a laptop got the owner a free ride to the new Federal Building. Three customers, along with their laptops, made the trip. The cafe's computers and router also went, as did the manager. The building was searched, then closed for the rest of the week. Finally, the suits left.

And Eddy, now sitting comfortably in front of his TV, decided it was time to do something else for a living. But what?

* * *

"Father, can silver be money, too?" asked Junior Parker.

They were sitting at the informal dining room table, the one that overlooked the veranda and the Rockies. At one end sat the boy's mother, thin and straight, leaning over her soup at just the proper angle. At the other sat his father, Arnold Wilson Parker. And, as usual, Junior was in the middle.

The question caught both parents by surprise. Arnold was pleased by it, his wife much less so. The interest his son had shown in money earlier in the week was something Arnold hoped to encourage, so this question was a blessing. If the boy was ever to grow into the job his father planned for him, that interest had to be encouraged.

Turning to his son, he said "Of course, Junior. Anything can-"

"Not at the table" interrupted his wife, not shrilly, but with the razor in her voice. Arnold turned to see her looking back at him, the displeasure on her face masked by the tight smile she used for appearances. He knew that face all too well.

When they decided to marry, he had not known of her proclivity for the proper. She had been a young woman then, attractive in many ways, in particular because of her family connections. Those contacts still held, as did her looks. And her determination to raise her son to fit in with the right people. Learning correct manners, including the social skills, was high on her list.

Most of the time, he simply acquiesced to her demands. The proper schools, the proper friends, the proper sports. Usually, he accepted her control of the boy's upbringing. But this was different. Curiosity was hard to cultivate in a young man. For whatever reason, his son had shown some interest in economics. That had to be encouraged, not squashed. Ignoring his wife, he turned back to Junior.

"Yes, of course it can-" he began.

"Junior, honey," his wife interrupted again, "didn't you just get a new computer game?"

The boy knew what was coming. Nodding silently, he waited.

"Why don't you and James go play with it?" James, their servant of many years, knew the drill. Stepping forward, he assumed the role of babysitter for the storm that was to come. Quietly, the boy slipped away from the table and, under James' reassuring hand, left the room.

When both were out of earshot, she turned back to her husband. Arnold was prepared for her assault. Eyes flashing, she hissed "I will not have my son raised in the gutter."

"Money is not filth," he responded, the familiar retort slipping out easily.

"It's base and ugly-"

"It runs the world."

"You will not encourage my son to wallow in it."

"How'd we get all this?" he asked, gesturing around in a wide sweeping motion.

"A vulgar necessity. Talk about it in the toilet, if you have to, but not at the dinner table!"

Stupid cow, Parker thought. But she wasn't, not really. Stupid women don't graduate from Vassar, no matter how rich they are. In his less angry moments, he saw that her limitations lay, not in intellect, but in depth.

His wife was just another soccer mom. Richer than most, but still as limited as the rest of that class. Her life's objective was ease and comfort for her son and herself. To her, money was for buying another chateau on the Riviera. But nothing more. She made it vulgar because she used it only for base purposes.

Of course, she supported the correct boutique charities. Social standing required it. But the idea of using money for a greater good, of using it to force noble goals on a society that would otherwise not undertake them, that had never occurred to her.

No, she was not stupid. Just shallow.

Well, his son mattered to him, too. He couldn't allow the boy to be subsumed by the vapid and simple. This was one battle he would not give up on.

"Strike when the iron's hot. Have to. When there's interest. Can't wait," he tried again.

"No," she shot back. "There is a time and place for everything. You must learn that."

"He must understand money. Must."

"Why? So he can be a good accountant? I will not have my son be a damned bookkeeper."

Well, at least we agree on something, thought Arnold.

"It's not about keeping track of it."

"What then?"

"Making it and using it."

"So? You run the presses. Just print more. See? Is that so hard?"

Yes it is. If you want people to keep accepting what you print, that is. But how to explain it to a cow? How could he show her that they were all at the mercy of the public? If everyone stopped using the dollars he printed, just stopped, it was all over. That money controlled the people who held the guns. If those men and women couldn't spend their pay, she would be dead. Our whole society would be. The dollar brought order. Without it, humanity would sink into a new dark age. *And most of us would die.*

He had to work for the only alternative. A unified world, with no more nuclear war. Hell, no more war anywhere. Peace. For the first time in humanity's history, peace everywhere. And it was so close. Just within his grasp.

His son had to learn how to control people with money. Not just for his own sake, but for the future of the world. Had to.

But how do you tell all that to a cow, even a smart one?

Chapter 3

Four Years Ago

"I want a lawyer."

The speaker wore an orange prison suit and a three-day beard. He sat hunched over, arms folded, fighting the chill of a room that was intentionally kept too cold. Since his arrest, he had slept on the bare steel bed frame on which he now sat, without a mattress, blanket, or pillow. Overhead, recessed behind a grill in the ceiling, the light never went out. Since his cell had no windows, a stainless steel toilet and sink were his only comforts.

Joshua Weidemeyer sat on the other side of the bars in a folding metal chair. He smiled at the request, then took an envelope out of his jacket pocket and handed it through the bars to the prisoner, who opened it to read:

Warden
DHS Detention Center
Madison, WI

RE: Thaddeus Svensen Olsen, 332-46-9986

The referenced prisoner has been determined to have engaged in terrorist activity against the United States Of America. You are therefore instructed, under Presidential Directive 2412, to detain this individual until such time as the status of the charges against him are resolved.

This individual is to be held in solitary confinement. He is not to be allowed communications with any unauthorized persons, nor is he to be permitted legal counsel. You are not to acknowledge his presence at your facility.

Please contact my office if you have any questions regarding this matter.

```
Matthew Hood
Deputy Secretary
Department of Homeland Security
```

Sven Olsen finished the letter and started to set it on the bed frame.

"I need it back" said Weidemeyer.

Without hesitation, Sven handed the folded paper back through the bars. Then, after a moment of silence, he asked "What have you told my family?"

"They got letters, just like yours."

"You haven't let them go yet? They haven't done anything. Are they here?"

"Yes, though in better accommodations than you have. And, yes, we don't think they've done anything, but we need proof before we can release them."

"What about my farm? Cows need tending."

"A nice young couple is taking care of them. Your neighbors think they're your cousins from Michigan, helping while your family sits by your hospital bed. You've had a bad stroke, you know."

"What do you want from me?"

"Passwords."

"And if I don't give them to you?"

"Until we're sure who's passing these bad bills, no one leaves here. No one. I'm sure your family would like to get back to the farm."

Sven sat in silence for a moment, head in hands, tired and cold. Then, with a short shake of his head, he gave up the passwords.

"Thank you. If your computers show your family is innocent, they'll be released."

"What about me?"

"The Constitution provides for death for counterfeiters. Article 1, Section 8." The lie came easily to his lips.

"You gonna kill me?"

"We should. But, no, we're not. You could disappear for a very long time, though. Do you understand why the Constitution has such a strong penalty for counterfeiters?"

"No."

"Other than traitors, it's the only class of criminals for whom death is prescribed."

The big farmer just stared back at him in silence.

"Do you understand why?"

"I don't care."

Sudden anger surged through Weidemeyer, almost overwhelming in its intensity. Then it retreated, as quickly as it came, suppressed by a cold iron will. As far as he was concerned, civilization would cease to exist without sound money. Its preservation was his duty, his sacred trust. Science, technology, art, government, industry. You name it, without stable money, it would all die. Humanity would go back to grubbing in the dirt with sticks. And this animal, this walking piece of dog excrement, after doing his best to destroy it, was completely indifferent to the damage he caused.

He took a second more to vanquish the last of the anger, then tried to speak. But "You should be shot," was all that came out.

"OK, so I'm a shit. What do you want?"

Finally, back in full control of himself, Weidemeyer said "Tell me who runs the badlands."

"How should I know?"

"Right now, you shouldn't. We want you to find out."

"And how can I do that?"

"We'll walk you through it, from the comfort of your own little cell."

"And if I say no?"

"Your family gets used to this place."

Sven Olsen looked hard at his visitor. Weidemeyer stared right back, unblinking. After briefly considering his limited options, Sven said "OK"

"Good. I'll get you a mattress and blanket for tonight."

With that, Joshua Weidemeyer stood, picked up his chair, and left.

* * *

Arnold Wilson Parker sat by the mountain stream with his teenage son, enjoying a fine summer day. Next to them, still unused, lay two fishing poles.

"Father, do you remember explaining money to me?"

"Sure, Junior." His son preferred not to be called Junior any more, but the habit was hard to break. Arnold would have to keep working on it. Still, the boy took his occasional lapse with good grace.

"Why are there different kinds?" Junior (make that 'Will') asked. He was a sophomore at Exeter and cutting his teeth on his first economics class.

"Of money?" his father answered.

The boy nodded.

"You mean different currencies?"

"No. That 'M' stuff," came the answer.

"Ah. Velocity. Taught you about that yet?"

"No sir."

"Inflation. What causes it? They tell you that?"

"Too much money chasing too few goods?"

"True. They say what 'chasing' meant?"

"No sir. Not really."

"OK. Cabbages. Suppose you sell cabbages." As he had hoped, that got a smile from his son. "Lots of money around. But everyone saves it. Don't buy cabbages with it. How do you sell yours? When no one spends money, I mean."

"Advertise more?"

"Talking economics, son. Not marketing."

"Lower the price?"

"Right. See that? Lots of money, but cabbage prices still go down. Is that inflation? When prices drop?"

"No sir."

"Right. What's it called?"

"Deflation."

"Good. Now imagine everyone gets extra money. Doubles what they have. But they save it all. Don't buy more cabbages. Would the price change?"

"If they don't spend more?"

"Right."

"No. I guess not."

"Price stay the same?"

"Yes, sir."

"Good. Money doubled but prices didn't change. See that?"

The boy nodded.

"Why?"

"If no one spends anything, it doesn't make prices go up."

"Right. Willingness to spend is called 'velocity'. For inflation to happen, there has to be both. Money and velocity*.""So why are there different kinds of money?"

"Different velocities. Cash in someone's pocket gets spent faster than in a six-month CD. So their velocities are different. Money supply's a mix, not just a single number. M0, M1, M2*are all attempts to describe that mix."

"And the Fed controls them all?"

"Probably not. Not easily, anyway. Interest rates let them do it for short-term money. But not bonds. Control's a lot harder there."

"But they do control it?"

* See the appendix for a detailed glossary.

"With difficulty. Great difficulty."

"How?"

"Deception."

"Sir?"

"They lie, Will." *Good, got his name right.* "If they want people to spend money faster, make everyone think inflation's just around the corner. Want it socked away? Make everyone think deflation's about to hit. It's a game. A confidence game."

"Like a con game?"

"Sort of. Make people confident their money will be worth more tomorrow and they'll save it. Convince them it'll be worth less and they'll spend it. Control confidence and you control velocity."

"And the Fed lies to do this?"

"Misleads. Misleads is a better word."

"They don't lie?"

"Sometimes. When they have to. But deception is better. Honest deception."

"They trick people?"

"It's the only way, son. The only way."

* * *

Four years before the young woman would become known as Dancing Fawn, she let herself into her dark apartment. It was past midnight, so she moved like a mouse to avoid disturbing her husband. But she need not have bothered. He was already awake, dressed to go, sitting on their mattress with his back against the wall. In his lap, leaning against his chest, slept the two girls, one small head on each shoulder.

After she closed the front door, she watched them in the darkness. He knew she was there, of course, but didn't look up. Instead, his face moved back and forth, first to one fuzzy head, then to the other, breathing in their scent. He loved their sleep smell, the warm that filled his nostrils when he nuzzled their small ears.

Not wanting to disturb them by turning on the light, she slowly picked her way through the darkness for a fresh towel. Going to the bathroom, she stopped by the door to look at them once more. This time, he looked back, lifting his eyes but not his face, which still touched the twins.

How could he leave them like this? she wondered as she closed the bathroom door.

Quickly, trying to keep her world under control, she stripped off her McDonald's uniform and turned on the shower. If she didn't wash the fryer smell out of her hair right away, it would follow her, like a miasma in a bad dream, for the rest of the night.

The hot water felt good, a pleasant distraction. She needed that right now, needed anything that helped her fight back the tears. She had promised not to cry.

Coming out of the bathroom, wrapped in a towel, her light hair fell loose and wet against her neck. He had moved, now sitting at the far end of the sofa where the fabric was still good, his bare feet supported by a corner of the mattress. The twins slept next to him in a plastic laundry basket wedged against the wall.

Stepping over the mattress, she sat down next to him, leaning against his side without looking into his face. The towel printed a damp spot on his shirt while her wet hair soaked his collar.

They sat like that, silently, for several minutes. And she did all right. Until he kissed her forehead. Then, softly, she began to cry.

"Hey, what's this?" he asked.

"Please. Please don't do this."

"Do we have a choice?"

"I can't care for them without you."

"We have a sitter, remember?"

"It's not that," she answered without elaboration. Try as she might, she couldn't explain. It was not any specific thing. It was everything. The overwhelming everything. Leaving her to deal with it all. By herself. Alone. They had been over it many times, there was no longer any need to enunciate the words. They had agreed he would leave this night after she came home, but now it seemed so wrong.

"What about your girls?" she asked.

The ultimate weapon. They need you. Don't leave your girls. Not 'our girls', but 'your girls'. What he once viewed as a burden, forcing them to marry, was now the great joy of his life. Yes, they were his girls.

"They have to eat."

The telling argument. He had not worked for over a year. Construction in Cleveland had stopped. Try as he might, he found nothing else to take its place. Unemployment ran out long ago. What she earned wasn't enough.

Then this job came up. The Prometheus project, out west someplace. Contract work, expenses included. Also twelve-hour days, bad food, and nights spent bunking in small plastic trailers. But the pay was good. It would arrive automatically in her account. And every three months, a flight back home to see his girls. And his wife.

Time passed slowly, as for the condemned awaiting execution. Small talk helped, but still his departure trod heavily on her thoughts.

"We need to go," he said, finally, breaking their last quiet moment. His flight was less than three hours away. With one car, she would have to drive him to the airport.

Reluctantly, like a child getting ready for a doctor's visit, she got up to dress.

* * *

"Congratulations, Joshua. How'd you find him?" Weidemeyer's boss asked.

"He sent a doorbell request from his home. Didn't try to hide it with a proxy. NSA was watching the Mitsubishi server, traced it back and put a watch on all his traffic. We knew he was passing when he got a VPN from outside the country."

"You have something hard on him?"

"Had the post office watch his mail. Got a pack of bad bills."

"Anyone outside know you got him?"

"Don't think so. Grabbed the whole family on an empty stretch of road. We had a jammer going, so they couldn't have gotten any calls out."

"Rest of the family still in custody?"

Weidemeyer shook his head. "Couldn't keep them without causing questions from their neighbors."

"Think they'll tip anyone off?"

"They know Sven doesn't get out unless we catch more bad guys, so I think they'll cooperate. Besides, their 'cousins' are staying there to keep an eye on things."

"Think you can turn him?"

"Easy. He's no hero, just in it for what he can get."

"Like the rest."

Weidemeyer nodded.

"You been leaning on him hard?"

Weidemeyer gave a snort of disgust as he shook his head. "A few cold nights on bare bed springs. Badlanders aren't hard-core. No higher virtues. Nothing matters beyond their own petty existence."

"How long before he decides to help us?"

"Already has. He just doesn't know it yet."

After a pause to reflect on the matter, the older man asked "Why do you think he did it? Solid citizen, lived on the same farm all his life. Family business, four generations. Why'd he risk it all?"

"Wasn't risking much, he was about to lose it all to foreclosure."

"Why not a loan?"

"He tried, but couldn't get anyone to approve one. They didn't turn him down, just kept asking for more information. No answer means no money, so he had to act."

"How was he paying for the bogus?"

"Used some of each delivery to buy coins in Madison, Milwaukee, and Chicago. Sent them back by mail."

"Any luck finding out who received them?"

"We're still working on that."

* * *

Arnold Wilson Parker sat with his back to the French doors of his upstairs study. Light from a gloriously clear winter sky streamed past his shoulder, fell on the bare wooden floor, and filled the room with a golden glow. Facing him, across a coffee table on a worn leather sofa, sat Maxwell Stein, the recently re-elected Governor of the Chicago Federal Reserve Bank. Together, they were discussing the primary question all central bankers forever grapple with: How to milk the most out of your country's currency. The objective was to create as much spendable money as possible without causing noticeable inflation.

"The key" expounded Stein, "isn't how much you create, but whether you maintain confidence while you're doing it."

To those not in the know, it would appear that central bankers have many tools to accomplish this task, but, in fact, they have few. One, of course, is lying. Make a credible promise that you are going to keep a tight money supply and the public to expect their dollars will purchase more tomorrow. Velocity will drop. Then you can do the opposite as long as (and this is a key) the public doesn't notice you are doing it.

The second tool of central banking, then, is the ability to hide new money creation. This can be done in several ways. For instance, you can loan money to another country in the form of a 'currency swap'. The other country will have some of your currency and you some of theirs. Both of you can spend it, putting more money into circulation, but hiding what happened because those funds only show on the books as international loan guarantees. The complexity of the financial world makes it easy to hide money printing, even in large amounts, if you just exercise a little restraint.

The problem now facing Parker and Stein was not the stealth creation of money, which Stein had gotten very good at, but the suppression of the inflation that had begun to rise in spite of all measures taken to maintain public confidence. The specific solution now under discussion was one of the favorite deceptions of central bankers.

"So you think it's inevitable?" asked Arnold, speaking of a loss of confidence in the dollar.

Stein nodded. "At the rate we're going, the slide will start sooner rather than later. When that happens, you won't have many arrows left to shoot."

"Back to the gold standard then?"

"We'll have to hide behind it sooner or later. Better start planning for it now."

There was no arguing with the assumption inherent in the first part of Stein's analysis. Politicians had to buy off the voters to stay in office. That cost money. Lots of it. Right now, tax increases weren't politically feasible and bonds were dead. The only way to come up with the money was to 'print' it.

"Isn't there something else we can do? To maintain confidence, I mean?"

"Financial manipulation has its limits. Eventually, it will fail. We better be ready with the gold standard dodge," said Stein.

"OK. I see that. What should we do? To get ready, I mean."

"The Fed has to own more metal."

"You don't have enough already?"

"Not enough to be believable. If we announce a new 'gold standard', we have to own enough physical metal to make it credible."

"How do we get it?" asked Arnold.

At first glance, this didn't seem to be a very difficult question. On paper, at least, the United States held very large stores of gold in Fort Knox, West Point, and New York. In fact, at the moment, the country was the OPEC of gold possession. Unfortunately, possession is not the same as ownership. All three stockpiles had either been pledged, sold, or already belonged to some other country or financial institution. The metal still on U.S. soil was only there for safe-keeping. On deposit, so to speak. The Fed owned almost none of it.

So, one option was to simply appropriate it all. Steal it, if a more honest word may be used. Tear up the agreements with private bankers and foreign governments. It was an act worth considering, but the risks were too great to undertake just now. Private bankers constituted a large percentage of Stein's political backing. Any act that alienated them was not a good idea.

As for foreign governments, they were the same people that Parker would need when it came time to organize a unified world government. To steal their national gold supply now would not only sink his dream of the ultimate Globalist objective, it would be construed as an act of war by many of those countries. He did not want to risk an open conflict with a united Europe, as absurd as that idea might seem at the moment.

In extremis, expropriation might be the only option, but it would be a very bad one. Much better for all concerned if the Fed established physical ownership by some more subtle means.

How to increase the Fed's gold holdings?

"We'll have to do it the hard way, I'm afraid," said Stein with a sigh. "We'll have to buy it."

Thank goodness we own the presses, thought Parker.

* * *

Under Weidemeyer's direction, Sven sent another gold package through the mails. After requesting instructions through the badlands, he got an address for a vacant house in Las Vegas. One of the growing army of bank repossessions, this one had stood empty for almost six months, maintained by a service company hired by the bank.

Before the package was delivered, the local Secret Service agent set up remote cameras to watch the mailbox and the surrounding property. This would be the only close surveillance for several reasons, including economics. To have personnel on site full-time would require three shifts of two agents each, meaning (if time allocated for travel and overtime is to be avoided) that ten officers would be required to perform a single 7-day/week stake-out.

The second problem was secrecy. This house, like most of the 200 serviced by this maintenance company, was on a small residential street, meaning a street with few curbside parked cars. A surveillance vehicle would inevitably arouse suspicion even if it were a delivery van with the observer hidden in the back.

In this instance, however, the Secret Service decided to spend the money. Two teams were stationed at the site, one at each end of the street hidden around the corner so as to minimize suspicion. Both were vans equipped to monitor the mailbox continuously.

About twenty four hours after the package was delivered, a lawn crew showed up. They proceeded to clean up any trash, collect old newspapers, mow the lawn, and check the mailbox. The latter was necessary because, somehow, the post office did not have a hold-mail notice for this location. As a result, the box was full of junk mail and circulars. Several of the crew gathered around as the box was emptied, all taking delight in looking at the junk mail. From the vantage of the surveillance van, it was impossible to tell which laborer actually took the package.

Now the agent in charge had to make a decision. He could order an immediate intercept, block both ends of the street, and arrest all the perpetrators. But on what charges? Part of their contract with the bank required them to empty the mailbox once a week. It specified that mail other than advertising be marked 'Return To Sender' and re-deposited into the postal system. If they were picked up now, the crew boss would say that was what he intended to do with the package, he just hadn't had time to do it yet. In other words, all would get away.

The alternative was to follow the lawn truck back to its shop. That, however, presented its own set of problems. At the shop, the crew would disperse, each in his own vehicle, as it did after every work day. All would have to be followed, stopped, and searched to determine who had the package. If any of them were found with it, he would say he was given it to drop off at the Post Office the next morning on his way to work.

If one of the crew managed to slip away with the package, what could the authorities say? All had been handling the mail, all could say they saw the package but didn't take it. The Secret Service had no evidence to the contrary, so no arrests could be made.

Regardless of which action the Secret Service took, the results would likely be the same. The package would be consolidated with many others in a larger box that would be smuggled past outgoing Customs through the Las Vegas International Airport. And the address would never again be used as a re-mailer drop.

So the agent in charge chose a third alternative. He waited until the crew finished and left the scene. Together, returning to their shop, they were concentrated in a single vehicle. It was stopped at a sterile location, one where everyone was arrested without any opportunity to hide the package in surrounding shrubbery or buildings. Then the van and all its occupants were taken to a central facility where they were all placed in individual isolation.

For three days, three laborers and a supervisor were held incommunicado and sweated. The crew van, along with all the yard equipment, was inspected in excruciating detail. Hundreds of man-hours were expended in the attempt to find some further leads. In the end, the only accomplishment was the disruption of the yard service company's business week. True, this would hurt the badlanders that used this organization as a front, but they would more than make up for that expense through their re-mailing of future shipments.

* * *

Mr. Wu had a problem. Twice, after years of careful work, he had set up a counterfeiting ring inside the United States using the new Internet. And twice, that ring had been wiped out. Had his investors been solely interested in a financial return, he would be looking for other employment. Fortunately, that was not the case. So he had access to funds to make another attempt if he could come up with a good explanation for why this new effort wouldn't also become a smoking hole. Getting that explanation had stumped him until now. However, he had high hopes this meeting would change that.

Sitting across from him was a brash young American who claimed to have a solution to his problem. That young man, known as Eddy, had been shooting off his mouth for the past year. Usually, such indiscretion was bad, but not this time. Eddy had been mouthing off to his family, telling them why the last counterfeiting operation Mr. Wu set up had failed and outlining to them, in painfully technical detail, how it could be made to succeed. And, because he asked them to, they had discreetly spread the word.

It eventually reached Mr. Wu. So, two weeks ago, he made it worth Eddy's while to fly halfway around the world for a little talk. Now Eddy, Mr. Wu, three Chinese technical experts, Mr. Wu's most trusted adviser, and a translator sat together in a posh penthouse overlooking the city of Shanghai.

"Yes sir, you see, Mr. Wu," said Eddy, "the guys I worked with were caught because the Feds traced their communications. Found their servers. Kept tracing until they knew where everyone hooked on. Waited until most were online, then BAM."

Mr. Wu's people had come to pretty much the same conclusion, though without the hand gestures.

The translator said "Thank you for your analysis, Mr. Eddy. Mr. Wu finds it quite insightful. However, the issue that concerns him now is how to prevent it from happening again."

"Easy. Make the communications untraceable."

"And you have a suggestion for how to do that?"

"You bet! Ever hear of trojans?"

There was some chatter as the translator, who was familiar with colloquial American English, discussed with the other participants the possible meanings of that question. After rejecting the thought that a male birth control device was under discussion, they picked the only other likely possibility.

"You mean the occupants of the ancient city of Troy?"

"Naa. I'm talking about the software programs those guys invented." Then, seeing that the joke didn't translate, he held up his hands, palms out, and tried to salvage what he could. "Sorry. Hoboken humor. Just kidding. You had to have been there."

Confused, but undaunted, the translator asked again: "Please. What is a trojan?"

"Right. A trojan is a program that's running hidden on some guy's computer. He doesn't know it's there because it was slipped in and camouflaged to look like something that belongs there. This particular trojan turns a computer into an Internet relay."

The translator turned to the others and spoke. Eddy took advantage of the pause to watch their responses. Under his flip demeanor, he was an astute observer of human nature. Here, in this opulent room, furnished with examples of all that was great from three thousand years of Chinese history, he watched their expressions for a sign of support or rejection. He particularly watched Mr. Wu.

That man listened without expression. He was a sphinx, somber concentration personified. Dressed, as were all of them, in expensive Western suits, he projected an air of superiority over his subordinates. In the discussions, he seemed more intent on listening than talking. Only at the end, when all had said their piece, did he speak. He asked a few questions, listened carefully to the answers, then gave instructions to the translator.

"Isn't that what a proxy server does?" the latter asked.

"Right. Same thing, actually."

"Then Mr. Wu wants to know how such a program would be better than a proxy server."

"Proxy servers keep logs. It's the law. But trojans don't care about the law. So no records for snoopy Feds."

The translator spoke to his colleagues. When he finished, Eddy continued.

"Now suppose four or five of these zombie computers connect in a chain. When one end gets a message, it's passed along until it gets to the other end. At one end is your customer, at the other is you. If the Feds catch your customer and try to trace communications back to you, all they get is the first zombie."

Some chatter went back and forth between the technical experts and the translator.

"What is a zombie?" asked the translator.

"A computer that's been infected with a trojan."

The translator turned again to his associates. More discussions, then the translator turned back to Eddy.

"Mr. Wu wants to know what is to prevent the authorities from putting a trace on the output of the first 'zombie' - is that the right use of this word?"

"Right. Yes, good on you, boyo. Yes."

"Thank you. I think. Mr. Wu wants to know what prevents the authorities from just running a trace back up the 'zombie' chain?"

"Good question. Good question. Tell Mr. Wu that's a very good question. The answer is that nothing stops them. Not, that is, if the second zombie is in the same country as the first. If it's not, though, the Feds have to go through a diplomatic dance to get someone in the country where its located to continue the trace for them."

"Won't they get permission?"

"Eventually, maybe, if we wait. But we don't. Every few seconds, we send a message to all the zombies to break up the chain. At the same time, we tell four new zombies to start another one. Now the feds have to start over. Hell, we could make a new chain after every transmission if we wanted to."

"Wouldn't the government just go to the owner of the first relay computer and arrest him?"

"Not if the owner shows he didn't know the trojan was there. It could have been slipped in by a hacking program or email virus. As long as the owner shows he ran software scans, had some anti-virus programs installed, he'll be covered. Even if he put the trojan on himself. Besides, do we care if some teenage girl gets arrested because she didn't keep her computer clean?"

Chinese chatter resumed, ran on for a bit like a quick shower on a tin roof, then subsided. The translator turned back to Eddy and asked "If they wait long enough, won't they eventually get the addresses of all your infected computers? Then all they have to do is put a trace on all of them and wait until one connects with our server."

"Good question, boyo. You got some smart guys there, you know? I'm impressed. But, no, if you have thousands of zombies and you keep adding new ones to the pool faster than the old ones are cleaned and you choose your chain of computers at random, they'll never trace more than a few deep before they have to start over with a whole new set."

This triggered another chatter session. After several minutes, the translator said "Mr. Wu wants to know if any of this has ever been done before."

"Hell's bells. Yes. Of course. All the time. Usually, trojans are put on some guy's computer to record all his keystrokes to steal credit card numbers, bank accounts, passwords, stuff like that. Linking them together in botnets is done to flood company servers, crowd out customers. For blackmail."

More chatter, then "What is a botnet?"

"It's what I'm talking about. A network of zombies. Hey, this stuff isn't new, I'm just suggesting a new use for all of it. The names have been around for a long time."

More Mandarin discussions occurred, after which the translator asked that the meeting adjourn for the day so Mr. Wu could digest the issues presented.

The next morning, Mr. Wu proved why he had risen to his present position. Long ago, he learned not to join any enterprise unless the person running it had a deep personal commitment to its success. This young man did. He also knew the American market, had the necessary underworld connections, and, most important, was not Chinese. The latter was critical because, should this effort fail, the U. S. government must never suspect any connection with the Peoples Republic of China.

"Mr. Eddy," the translator asked, "Mr. Wu wants to know if you would build, manage, and rent such a botnet to one of his organizations in exchange for a large cash advance fee."

Suddenly, the expression 'skin in the game' came home to Eddy. Mr. Wu was clearly not a man to accept failure from a business associate. Eddy had a mental vision of his erect male organ sitting under the knife of a paper cutter as it sliced downwards. If he lost Mr. Wu's money, that would be the best fate that might befall him. This man was not to be trifled with.

Still, the genes in Eddy's blood didn't come from a family of milksops.

"Hell, yes. Tell Mr. Wu I said 'Hell Yes'."

The world's first botnet* house was about to be born.

---

* At the time of this writing, www.shadowserver.org is actively tracking over 2,600 botnets directing over 60,000 zombies. Estimates of the total number of botnet zombies run as high as 24 million computers.

Chapter 4

Two Years Ago

Two years before Dancing Fawn made her first crossing, Arnold Wilson Parker sat on the veranda of his estate overlooking the Rockies. Next to him sat Edgar Kohrob, CEO of ENGCO, a conglomerate of the largest engineering, design, and construction companies in the United States. For the past five years, they had conspired, planned, and worked to bring into existence the world's first thorium nuclear power plant. If it was successful, over twenty more would follow and the United States would finally be on the way to solving its energy needs.

"OK, where are we? Now, I mean?" asked Parker.

But Kohrob didn't answer. He waited instead, in discreet silence, as Parker's butler, James, having approached unseen by his host, delivered their lunch. Both men knew that the large veranda, like the rest of the estate, was swept daily for bugs. They also knew, being both born to wealth, that a servant's mouth can never be trusted. Instinctively, they suspend all conversation whenever any help was present. So they sat in silence until this particular security risk finished his duties and went back into the house.

"Sorry," said Parker after the door closed. "Where were we?"

"The Project status. It's moving well," said Kohrob. "We expect warm-up next week."

"And seed injection? How soon?" asked Parker.

Thorium is only slightly radioactive and produces no heat. To generate power, it must be converted into a type of uranium called U233. When U233 atoms explode, they produce heat and also radiation that changes some of the thorium into replacement U233. A new reactor is started by adding a small amount of radioactive U233 to the fuel. Until that is done, the fuel is no more dangerous than a bucker of molten sand.

"Two weeks. If they let us."

And that, thought Parker, *is the big question. Will they let us?*

"What are you doing about it?" Parker asked, referring to the group of self-appointed watchdogs that had found construction anomalies in the containment vessel. They were threatening to go public, meaning to Van de Groot, with the evidence if ENGCO didn't fix the dome before start-up.

"We've calmed them down for now, but if we seed the core without a fix, they'll blow the whistle on us."

"And you're sure there's no way to repair it?" asked Parker.

"Not without a major rebuild."

And not without years of delay and bankruptcy for ENGCO and most of its partners, all of whom were patrons of Parker. His leadership could not stand the loss. Damn Van de Groot. The bitch would get him good if that happened.

Parker had been over this time and again with independent experts, people who did not have an axe to grind. Their opinion had always been the same. Because a thorium reactor did not produce radioactive steam, it did not need a containment vessel. A small bunker, maybe, but nothing bigger.

But the issue still worried him. Could a man ever trust his advisors? What if they were wrong? He was in this fight to save the environment, not flush it down a radioactive toilet. There would be no American Chernobyl on his watch.

Then why even risk it? When Parker looked at the big picture, the answer was painfully obvious. Without massive amounts of cheap energy, the nation couldn't even build, much less deploy, an effective military. During a time of growing shortages, those armored divisions and carriers stabilized the world. Civilization depended on them to keep the peace. Chaos, famine, and nuclear war was, now more than ever, just under the surface. If American power ever withdrew, the great collapse would begin.

Windmills and solar panels could never provide the tanks and ships. No matter how many covered the country, there just wasn't enough space. Without oil, nuclear power was the only option. This project, or one like it, had to go through. For humanity's sake.

"OK. Again. Why don't we need one? A containment vessel, that is," he asked.

"To begin with, no water."

"Explain."

"All nuclear power plants now in operation cool their reactors with pressurized water. So it gets radioactive. If there's a leak, it turns into radioactive steam. The dome stops that steam from getting out."

"Thorium reactors don't make steam?"

"Not radioactive steam. It doesn't use water to cool the core."

"Why the dome? If it's not needed, I mean. Why is it there?"

"Ask your friend Van de Groot. Her people pushed that through."

Parker didn't have to ask. *Damn that woman's ambition. Damn her megalomania.* She lusted after power, wanted to run everything. *As if she had some special vision, some divine knowledge of what was best for mankind.*

And she knew the only way to the top was to embarrass Parker on a major project, something like Prometheus. Van de Groot had done all she could to make it fail for her own political motives, not for any scientific or technical ones. She pushed through a statutory requirement that all power reactors, regardless of type, must have a containment dome.

Out loud, Parker asked "Fix the design? On future reactors?"

"This isn't a design problem. Someone just cut a corner building the thing. And, yes, I can promise you it will not happen on any of the rest of the series."

And I know who did the cutting, thought Parker. *You greedy shit, putting all of us at risk for a few dollars*. Still, you couldn't always choose the human resources you had to work with. For some men, money was more important than honor. He had learned to accept that long ago.

"OK. The troublemakers. You got names?"

Kohrob handed him a sheet with thirty-seven names.

"None of these people critical? I mean, can you finish without them?"

Kohrob nodded.

Two hours later, while Edgar Kohrob was on a private jet back to California, Arnold Wilson Parker put in motion the final solution to the Prometheus whistle blower problem.

* * *

It wasn't a very small group, but, given the nature of bureaucracies, it was probably as small as Matthew Hood could manage. Speaking was Hood himself, Deputy Secretary of Homeland Security. This was his baby. The Committee To Insure The Safety Of Cyberspace. CISC. They should have thought of a catchier acronym. Unofficially, Weidemeyer had already heard it called the Badlands Sterilization Committee, or BS Com for short.

Hood was droning on about the importance of this committee to the safety of the country. Whatever skills he had as a bureaucratic infighter, he was a poor speaker. His voice was high-pitched, with little intonation. Overweight, with an unpleasant complexion, he did not make an imposing figure. But his eyes compensated for these faults. They darted around the room, riveting first one, then the next attendee in a piercing stare. They were quick, intense eyes, the eyes of a man determined to dominate those around him.

Weidemeyer was here representing the Secret Service. In theory, it would look good on his resume. In reality, he felt like someone was trying to get him out of the way. If it weren't for the fact that he still kept full control of his badlands agents, he would have worried that this was an upward demotion. Still, if that were the case, then some powerful people in other sections of the government had also been demoted. From DHS, there were representatives from TSA and Customs. Also present were key people from the FBI, DEA, NSA, CIA, DOD, the BATF, and FEMA.

Thank God they left out the IRS.

"This thing started out as just a little counterfeiting," Hood said. "Drugs, a little piracy, some fraud. That was about all. Just a bunch of petty criminals trying to get by."

He paused to again sweep the room with his gaze, singling out two of his listeners for a special stare. Neither the CIA nor DEA representatives seemed comfortable with the extra attention.

"It's gone way beyond that now. They're getting organized. Linking up. This has all the makings of a major crime organization. A new syndicate, developing right under our noses. A new threat.

"That's why you're all here today. This committee has been formed to coordinate our attack. No longer will it be a lonely effort by Customs or FBI or DEA to stop smuggling or bribery or corruption. Beginning today, we will act together. Today we turn the tables on these vermin. Today begins a new chapter in man's struggle against evil.

"These people aren't supermen. They each have an Achilles' heel. They're like roaches, hiding from the light. All we have to do is turn it on, expose them wherever they hide.

"How? The answer is so simple it's hard to believe. Just get a traceable address. That's it. Anything that links back to their registered Internet address. We can find them from that. Names, physical addresses, family. We can hunt them down. All we need is a traceable IP.

"So, as we end this meeting, I want to ask all of you to think about that. Think about how we can get those addresses. Bring me ideas.

"Until next time, ladies and gentlemen, keep that one thought in mind."

And with that, the first meeting of the BS Committee came to a close.

For the next week, the sessions continued. Each BS Com (sorry, CISC) member outlined what resources his organization could bring to the table and a history of his organizations efforts to date. When it was his turn, Weidemeyer went over his six agents, the difficulty of detecting the new counterfeit currency, and how they caught the half-a-dozen badlanders that they now ran as counter-spies.

Today the NSA representative got to strut his stuff. After four sleep-inducing hours of charts, data, and self-aggrandizement, the man finally finished. The room opened for questions. No one raised a hand.

Weidemeyer didn't want to prove his ignorance to the rest of the group by opening his mouth, but the lack of questions from anyone else gave him no choice. If he wanted his questions answered, he would have to ask them himself.

"You mentioned that you had access to the 'National Security Upgrade' resource," he asked. "Can you explain what that is?"

The room suddenly became very quiet.

"If you give us an IP, in most cases we can give you the technical information about the computer that is using it."

"Like?"

"Serial number of the microprocessor, MAC addresses of all Internet interface cards, the Product Key, and registration information for the operating system. In addition, if you wish, we can activate a keystroke logger on the machine and give you a listing of the results. Audio and video, too. We can record those if the computer has a camera and microphone."

It took a moment for that to sink in.

"Can you go over that again?" asked Weidemeyer, startled by the length of the list.

"If you give us the Internet address of almost any computer, we can get almost any information you want about it and the people using it as long as it's running Windows or an Apple operating system."

Weidemeyer was impressed. "Any computer? Even a foreign one?"

"Yes, in most cases, unless it's behind an unusually sophisticated firewall."

"How do you do that? "

The NSA rep looked to Matthew Hood for guidance. When none came, he turned back and said "We have national technical means that I may not discuss. The important thing for you is what we can do, not how we do it. I hope I have satisfied your questions in that regard."

In other words, drop this subject! Perhaps he had just proven that, while there may be no such thing as a stupid question, the same can't be said for the person asking it.

Twenty minutes later, the meeting adjourned for the day. As Weidemeyer walked away from it, trying to get as far as possible from anything that reminded him of the day, FBI representative Daniel Shelton slid next to him and asked if he had time for a drink. Since he had, not only time, but a burning need for some friendly company, he accepted.

Now they sat in a dark corner of Shelton's favorite bar, one whose only claim to fame seemed to be the size of the waitresses' nipples. The music was loud, the lights low, and their backs were against adjacent walls. Shelton sipped a whiskey and soda, while Weidemeyer nursed a tonic with a twist.

Leaning together so their heads were close enough to talk over the music, Shelton asked "Was that your turd in the punch bowl this afternoon?"

"What happened?" asked Weidemeyer. "I just asked a simple question."

"You asked about a subject that was classified above your pay grade."

"How was I to know? And why such a big deal anyway?"

"Because the answer was above the pay grade of everyone else in the room and because they knew the answer anyway. You were asking about a secret that is practically public knowledge and could easily become a public disaster."

"It was painful."

"Yeah. For us, too. Look, if you forget where you heard this, I can give you a few details so it won't happen again."

"Done. Give."

"Know what source code is?"

"No."

"Basically, there are only two kinds of programs: Those that can be read by a computer and those that can be read by a human being. One's called an 'executable', the other 'source code'. Source code looks strange, but it makes some sense. At least to a weirdo who's spent most of his life learning it. Sort of like French. But a computer couldn't make heads or tails out of it. Programs are all written in source code so the guys who write them can understand what they wrote.

"Since computers can't understand that format, it's converted to another one called an 'executable'. Unfortunately, the change is a one-way operation. If you want the source code and all you have is the executable, you're fucked. Going backwards can be done, but it's a bitch."

"So?"

"So most software companies take advantage of this. They never supply source code to their customers, only executables. That way, no one can steal their ideas or write software that uses their code without their cooperation. It makes their programs more difficult to copy and almost impossible to modify."

"The point being?"

"The point being that no one outside of Microsoft or Apple knows what their operating systems really do when they run on a computer. Their customers sure don't.

"About a year ago, the DHS leaned on both companies. If they wanted to keep working in the US, they had to add a special feature to their operating systems. Hush-hush, no legal reason they had to, but a promise that no one would hear about it if they did. So they added it.

"On-line updates went out six months ago. Since then, if NSA sends the right Internet message to a computer running either a Microsoft or an Apple operating system, this little bit of code hears it, sucks up all the local ID information, encrypts it, and spits it back to the NSA."

"Is there a punch line here?"

"Hey, you were doing pretty good at busting badlanders for a while there, then everything dried up, right? How come?" asked Shelton.

"The perps started using proxy servers and VPNs."

"So you couldn't trace back their connections anymore, right?"

Weidemeyer nodded his head.

"Well, this changes all that. Now, this little bit of snitch code will get the NSA message, even though that message got routed through Vladivostok, and still spit back the data. The stuff may go back through Russia before the NSA gets it, but they'll still get it, it'll just take a few seconds longer to get there."

"All we need now to catch a badlander is the doorbell message?" asked Weidemeyer.

"Yep. Don't need his real IP, just a link that eventually gets the message back to him."

"Crap."

"Yep. You been fighting this for two years the old way and you've turned, what, five badlanders?"

"Six" interjected Weidemeyer. *Why make it worse than it was?*

"OK. Six. Using these snitch messages, we caught that many last month."

At this rate, Weidemeyer thought, *the badlands would be a memory in a year.*

* * *

Although the lone woman seemed to be sitting in a dark corner of Marty's Pub, the appearance was deceiving. She was not there. She was in the badlands, at the MEET THE BEST chat room, fully engaged in a flirt with David Bowie, who got his badlands name because he was lucky enough to indenture with the ROCKY ROAD Crossing House.

She, on the other hand, had originally indentured with DARK CITIES and so must forever bear the badlands name of Nairobi Bombay. She had no choice in the matter, DARK CITIES always chose cities for their names. They considered it good publicity. Still, if she had a choice, she might have preferred something more Nordic, as she was tall, lean, athletic, and a natural blond. Unfortunately, nature had also given her a plain face and the bones of a gorilla. One can no more choose one's genes than one's badlands name, so she had long since resigned herself to make the best of both.

The flirt was fun, but all things must come to an end. She had a meeting with her editor that required her physical presence. So, over Bowie's strenuous protests, but with a flutter of her virtual eyelashes, she signed off, packed her things, paid the bill, and headed out to the street.

She had gone a hundred feet down the sidewalk when the first black Humvee squealed around the corner. Two more followed, lights out but moving fast. They sped past her, jerking to stop in front of the entrance she had just left. A dozen helmeted blackjacks jumped out and sprinted into the club.

It wasn't until two more vehicles pulled to a stop in the intersection ahead of her that she came out of her shock. Her first impulse was to run but, turning quickly back away from the club, she saw that the intersection at the other end of the block had also been closed.

To her left was an alley. She ducked into it. Even if they weren't after her, she knew they would welcome an excuse to have a long conversation, one that she didn't want to be part of. She also realized that her computer was that excuse. She began looking for a way to ditch it.

The alley was a dead-end. Before FEMA solved the homeless problem, it would have been an open sewer, stinking of fresh excrement and swarming with flies. But now the rain had washed most of that filth away, leaving only mildewed bedding and decaying cardboard.

Running quickly down it, picking her way past piles of trash, she leaned over a broken shopping cart to try one of the two doors that provided possible escape. It was a blank slab of rusted steel, bolted closed from the inside. She didn't need to check the other one since it didn't even have a handle. There was a window next to it, but that was covered with burglar bars.

She looked back towards the front of the alley and saw the last of the pedestrians pass by. Soon police sweep teams would be moving down the street. She had to do something now and catch up with the end of that crowd if she were to avoid suspicion.

Quickly, stooping down behind an overturned garbage can, she pulled out her laptop. After a quick wipe against her coat to remove fingerprints, she slammed it hard against the alley wall. The first time it only cracked, but the second strike shattered the plastic case. Two more swings and the computer lay in pieces about her feet. Picking through the debris, she found the hard drive and wrenched it loose from its connector. After slipping it into her pocket, she kicked the remaining larger pieces under a pile of sodden clothing. Then, with more than a little fear, she stepped back out onto the sidewalk and moved down the street.

It was occupied only a short distance ahead of her. Catching up with the end of the crowd, she followed the last of the other pedestrians as slowly as she dared, hoping for some inspiration. Then she saw it. Picking her spot, she stepped off the curb as if to cross the street diagonally. As she did so, directly over a storm drain, she slipped the hard drive out of her pocket and let go. It bounced through the grating and splash in the runoff below.

At the end of the block, she went through a pat-down and wand scan, as well as an inspection of the contents of her purse and pockets. Nothing incriminating was found. With no more than an hour wasted in line, she was again on her way. Hopefully, her editor wouldn't be too angry about her having missed the meeting.

She considered herself lucky to have gotten out of the pub before the raid began, but she didn't know the half of it. She had bought her laptop on Ebay using a money order purchased with cash, and hadn't taken the time to re-register it. So all the information sent by the Windows snitch program that was running on her laptop implicated the original owner, not her. That poor woman would spend an anxious few hours proving that she no longer owned the computer and didn't know where it was. But DHS would not be making calls on Nairobi that night.

Her problem now was how to avoid having this happen again.

* * *

The ambulance arrived quickly, at least by camp standards. This was especially surprising because no one had actually called for it. No dispatcher had sent the vehicle, no record of this visit existed in the system.

The patient lay on the concrete floor of the latrine, not sure which end he should put over the pot, as both were spewing filth. The symptoms implied food poisoning, something that wasn't at all uncommon in the camp. And, of course, it could be nothing more than that, though, to anyone who has suffered from the condition, that is quite enough. But food poisoning didn't warrant an ambulance visit. His friends could carry him to the infirmary, just like they would if he had broken his leg.

To understand the reason an ambulance arrived, you have to appreciate the conditions in this camp. It was crowded, packed with dirty, poorly-nourished men. Sanitation was poor at best, awful the rest of the time. While food poisoning is a self-limiting phenomenon, one that might, at worst, carry away one poor soul, gastric flu had the potential to run through the population like a squall line across a wheat field, laying flat forever the weak caught in its path. Those that thought about it considered the fear of this disease to be the cause for the prompt response to a man puking his guts out.

But nothing is as it seems in a FEMA camp, especially this one. Located in the remotest part of northern Wyoming, it was set up to serve as an overflow for camps located near each major city. When the population of one of them got too large, this was where the overflow went.

The camp authorities worried constantly about disease, using all their meager resources to maximize public health, but those resources were stretched very thin. Gastric flu might take the old, weak, and infirm, but most would survive it unaided. The same could not be said for cholera. That disease has been a scourge of mankind from the dawn of the written word. If left untreated, it can literally make a person shit and vomit himself to death in hours. The only treatment for strains resistant to antibiotics is intravenous replacement of lost fluids, something that the camp infirmary could do for no more than 500 patients. The rest of the 30,000 population would simply have to take their chances with a disease whose untreated mortality rate for healthy men was over 50%. And the men in this camp were anything but healthy. Those in the know realized that the real fear, the real reason the ambulance came, was not the risk of flu, but of cholera.

Whatever the reason for their prompt visit, the two attendants picked up the sick man, dumped him onto the gurney, and wheeled it to the ambulance, leaving the hut wardens to clean up the filth their patient had left behind. After the gurney was secured inside the vehicle, one attendant got in to drive while the other climbed in back. With little fanfare or hurry, just as they had arrived, they drove slowly off towards the Detention compound gate.

For this illness had occurred, not in a FEMA Shelter camp proper, but the smaller attached Detention camp. To get to the infirmary, the vehicle would have to pass through the guarded gates of that smaller camp into the larger one, and then make its way through several miles of packed huts, plowing through muddy roads that had never seen a load of gravel.

In the back, the patient leaned over the edge of his gurney and vomited into a bucket on the floor. As he did so, the attendant sitting next to him swung an improvised sap in a quick whipping motion, striking the retching man on the back of his head with an almost-silent thump.

A manufactured sap consists of a short flat spring with a pad of lead shot attached to one end. The entire assembly is encased in several layers of leather, sewn flat so as to look like an amputated beaver tail. It's held by the narrow part of the tail, the portion, if you will, that would have been attached to the animal, and swung so the spring flexes through the arc. If timed correctly, its unflexing near the end of the swing and the rotation of the wrist combine at the instant of impact to drive the flat of the weighted end against its target with devastating speed. A determined blow to the head could easily cause a concussion, skull fracture, or death from bleeding in the brain.

The beauty of this weapon is that a blow by the flat, though causing considerable internal damage, will leave no mark on the surface. The softness of the leather, backed by the loose shot that conforms to the surface of the head, will spread the blow over a large area, thus avoiding trauma to the skin or, in this instance, scalp.

The ambulance attendant did not, however, have a manufactured sap. He did not want one because, if it were found on his person, he would be questioned uncomfortably about it. Instead, he had nested several heavy athletic socks, one inside the other, to make a single strong padded sheath. The toe of this sheath was filled with two pounds of pennies. True, he did not have the advantage a spring would have provided when he delivered the blow, but he was very good at his job and made up for that detail with skill. The net result was the same. The patient slumped into an instant coma, possibly mortal, without a mark showing on his head or scalp. An MRI could reveal the injury, but this man would never get one.

The attendant pushed the limp body back onto the gurney, then emptied the coins into a drawer and threw the nested socks into the trash. Rolling the patient onto his back, the attendant tied a gauze mask over the man's nose and mouth.

With the threat of flu, not to mention drug-resistant TB, spreading through the camp, the use of gauze masks was common and encouraged by the authorities for those who showed symptoms of an upper-respiratory infection. Should someone see a mask on this patient, they would not consider it unusual. And, given the threat of contagion that such a mask implied, they would not make an effort to examine it. That was fine with the attendant as, unlike other masks, this one had an airtight plastic film sandwiched between the gauze sheets. The patient now wearing it could easily breathe out, as the mask moved away from his face with the force of an exhaled breath, but he could not recover that breath, as, when he tried to breathe in, the mask would settle over his mouth and nose, blocking them.

As the patient's subconscious mind fought its struggle for breath against the mask, the attendant frisked him, removing everything from his pockets, including his identification. Then he pulled out an opaque black body bag and slid it under his charge, beginning at his feet. After he had secured the hood around his head, the attendant reached into the bag and clipped a new ID badge to the man's pocket, one that displayed the correct picture but a different name.

Fifteen minutes later, after an unhurried drive through the camp, the ambulance pulled up to an unused side door of the infirmary. The attendant removed the mask from the now-cooling body. After placing an envelope on the corpse' chest, he zipped the bag closed. The driver came around to help him pull the gurney out of the ambulance and held the door as he pushed it into the building. As soon as he cleared the entrance, the attendant turned to the right, towards the camp's small morgue, rather than left towards the emergency room. After all, why bother the doctors? The patient was obviously dead. For anyone who doubted that, the envelope on his chest contained a completed death certificate to prove it.

This body would go to Cody tomorrow, to a small crematorium there, along with the other six that had accumulated in the morgue this day. By tomorrow night, all that would remain of this patient would be a FEMA database record under the name on his false ID. It would show he had arrived at the camp about two weeks ago, ill at the time, and died today from a heart attack.

Should his friends ever ask about the man taken from the Detention latrine, the same FEMA database would show that someone using his name had recovered and had managed to contact a relative by phone. That good soul had come and picked him up, taking him back to a fresh new life on the outside, something that everyone in the camps hoped to personally experience.

Chapter 5

A New Life

THE NEAR FUTURE

Fawn slipped out of her old apartment without a word to the Bastard. One minute she was there, watching TV with the girls, and then they were all gone. They took only pictures, papers, and the clothes on their backs. She didn't even take her phone.

The money she saved from her new badlands business let her do it. She delivered black-market meds for a wholesaler located outside the country. He received orders from the general public through an offshore web site, paid with a credit card. No prescriptions required, very cheap prices. As often as she could accept a delivery, he would smuggle a shipment of prepackaged meds to her. Her job was to slip them into the U. S. mails without being detected. Payment was in gold, deposited automatically to a badlands account in her name.

She started her business while she still lived with the Bastard. On the sly, when he wasn't there, she would take the bus to the international airport and pick up a package using a driver's license she had made herself from an ID IN A BOX kit. Then, dumping the contents into her backpack, she would start walking, a meander that went from one blue corner mailbox to the next, leaving a few packages in each one. Those packages looked like they had been sent by domestic mail-order drug retailers, complete with company logos, advertising, return addresses, and postage. If they had all shown up at a single mailbox, some postal inspector would have become suspicious. This way, no one noticed.

Now she had her own apartment, furnished with a mattress, pillows, three folding chairs, and a cinder block table. It wasn't much, but she didn't have to have sex with anyone to keep it, and her girls were safe.

In the closet was a locked trunk, big enough to hold several hundred meds. Her supplier had told her that she could have as many as she could deliver. All she had to do to grow her business was figure out how to move them without walking herself to death.

* * *

"Fucking hell," cursed FBI Special Agent Daniel Shelton, expressing the feelings they all had concerning their lack of 'recruiting' success. "We had them dead. What happened?"

"Somehow, they figured it out," answered Weidemeyer.

"'Somehow?' Fuk-Ing-Hell. It was open secret. Everyone knows we bug their computers. That's not the point. How are they turning the damn things off? That's the point."

The BS Committee was in session. They had just gone over the latest capture figures. Until three months ago, they were exploding. Then they tapered off, eventually dropping like a rock. Last month they hadn't turned a single badlander.

"Obviously, either they've found a way to clean the snitch code-"

"No, it's too well embedded in the OS" said NSA

"- or they're using an operating system made by someone other than Microsoft or Apple."

"Meaning who?"

"Linux?" suggested NSA.

"OK, so let's get snitch code installed there, too," suggested BATF.

"Not that simple, sorry. First, there're multiple manufacturers of those systems. We would have to cut a secret deal with at least a dozen vendors, many outside the country. Second, they all distribute open-source code, so, even if we did get them to slip in a snitch program, their customers would find it, remove it, and then warn the rest of the badlands about it."

"What's 'open-source' mean?" from the DEA rep.

"It means the vendor distributes his source code so all his customers can see what they're getting. We can't slip anything in because, unlike an executable, people can and do read source code. Someone would find it."

"So where to from here?"

"The badlands isn't never-never land," Matthew Hood said. "It touches reality every time anyone connects to it. Its inhabitants live here, in this physical world, not in 'information space'. They walk, they eat, they breathe. So we look for them like we look for any other criminal, because that's all they are, just another set of criminals."

"It's back to street-cop basics. Get your snitches to work harder to turn in other badlanders. We don't need much. A name, IP, physical address, picture. Even a voice print. Anything is a start. We can work from almost anything."

"We can also stage more searches. Roadblocks. Checkpoints at major transportation hubs. You get the idea. We catch them with evidence on their person, we got them."

"What counts as evidence?"

"Anything you can think of."

"Like running Linux on their computer?"

"Yeah, that would be a good start."

* * *

The bullhorn jerked Fawn back into the humid, sweaty present.

"This is a TSA Security Inspection. Please place your hands on the seat in front of you. If there is no seat, place them on the handrail overhead or in your lap. Do not place them in your pockets or open any of your carry-ons"

Moving quickly down the transit bus aisle, weaving through the few passengers that were standing, were four TSA agents in blue uniforms, black bulletproof vests, and garish yellow "TSA" logos. They carried nightsticks, though otherwise they seemed unarmed. As they walked, their eyes darted quickly to either side, looking for any passenger careless enough to disobey the bullhorn's instructions.

Standing next to the driver at the head of the bus was the agent with the horn. Next to him stood another, recording the position and movements of the passengers.

From behind Fawn came a yelp.

"Please do not move your hands from sight. Keep them on the seat ahead of you, on your lap, or on one of the overhead rails. This is for your own safety," announced the bullhorn.

She had not noticed the bus come to a stop. Her eyes had been closed, mind drifting in the peace that comes after a good workout, when Mr. Bullhorn had rushed up the steps. But now her stomach lurched, her vision narrowed, and her mind was frozen by fear. She was more than just alert. She was terrified.

Last week, she had picked up a large box at an air freight carrier's cargo desk. She had taken it home and transferred over a thousand small envelopes and boxes to the two locked trunks hidden in her closet.

Three times since then, she had put on her 'rich yuppie' bicycling outfit (including streamlined helmet, large dark glasses, and gloves), hopped on her new mountain bike, and pedaled away into the dawn. On her back was a pack with water and about two hundred med mailers. By bicycle and bus, she would travel along an erratic route, wandering from mailbox to mailbox. Each one got a few packages, none more than four. She never lingered long, just scooted by and shoved them in. Between boxes, she would stop, pull out a few more, check them, and have them ready in her jacket pocket when the next ugly blue box came up.

This morning, she had done it for a fourth time. Now, as the sun was setting, she was on her way back home. All but one of the meds were safely in the post. Her pack was empty. In her pocket, though, was one small bulging envelope that she hadn't mailed. It had carried a stamp rather than a meter mark and that had fallen off so she hadn't mailed it, planning instead to re-stamp it after she got home and drop it off tomorrow.

This surprise TSA inspection made that a bad idea. In a mailbox, that package would seem normal, but, in her pocket, it would raise questions because neither address on it carried her name. If she were caught with it, they would search her apartment and find the others. Then she would get a cell and they would get her girls.

Slowly, the bus emptied. Row by row, the blue-clad agents ushered the passengers out, a seat-full at a time, up and off the bus. As they left, other agents with mirrors and wands would go over the seats just vacated. Even if she could get the package out of her pocket without being seen, slipping the pills under the seat wouldn't do her any good. The searchers would find them and know which seat she had come from.

Come on, brain, get in gear!

She thought briefly of making a run for it as soon as she got to the bus door, but the TSAs outside were armed and seemed to be expecting just that sort of bolt. If they caught her after a try, they'd be sure she was guilty of something and search until they found it.

Perhaps she could just brazen it out with some sort of story. Had she picked them up for her grandmother? Nice try, but she didn't even know who they were addressed to and didn't dare take the package out now to look. Besides, she had no explanation for the absence of a stamp.

Outside, those passengers that had left the bus were wanded and frisked. At a portable table near the entrance, two bored agents hand-searched bags and packages. When cleared, everyone went to a separate waiting area to stand in resigned annoyance. Some just gave up and walked away.

From across the street, the smell of stale burnt wood and sewage distracted her. Still no ideas. Perhaps a run for it was the only way.

Her turn came. She stood up with her seat-mates and began the shuffle down the aisle, an agent standing on either side to keep an eye on their movements. As she reached Mr. Bullhorn, a shout came from behind her. Turning, she saw one of the agents by her old seat holding up two small plastic bags of white powder. The agents on either side, as well as at the entrance to the bus, became more alert. Running for it was now out of the question.

"Keep moving, keep moving." Mr. Bullhorn advised.

There were four in her group, she was third in the line. When they got outside, she watched as the two ahead of her got an unusually careful search. Her mind now empty of any ideas, she took slow deep breaths to try to calm herself.

It was her turn. She held her arms out, spreading her feet slightly as the wand ran over her body. Satisfied, the female TSA agent put down the instrument and began the pat-down. Her grandmother was the best she could think of, she had better make it sound good.

Then confusion. Shouts. Slammed from behind, she spun and flew forward. Her foot tripped on the broken sidewalk. As she turned, she saw a flash of running legs, then a man sliding off-balance against an inspection table. Recovering her feet, she turned to see him struggling with three TSA agents.

And no one looked at her.

Seeing her chance, she picked up her pack and slipped towards the cleared passengers.

"Not that way," barked an agent.

She stopped.

He took her pack and led her to the still-standing inspection table. He began going through it with great care, even feeling the seams for any unusual stiffness. She stood in silence, watching him.

Of course, he found nothing, because there was nothing to find. The unmailed package sat in her coat pocket, missed in the confusion.

A blue Humvee pulled up, the doors opened. Two TSA agents pushed the runner, hands cuffed behind his back, through the open door. One agent followed him. The doors closed and the vehicle departed.

"OK, over there," her agent said, pointing to where her two seat-mates were standing as he handed her back her pack.

The transit bus filled in the growing dusk. Sweating and sullen, the passengers lined up to re-board under a single streetlight. She realized that, when they were all inside, the bus would leave without her.

"I have a bike on the bus, I have to get it off."

Another Humvee pulled up. The back doors opened and her seat-mates, now bound, were ushered in and told to slide across. The agent gestured for her. They were going to take her in anyway, even though they didn't find anything, just because of her seat-mate.

"I have to get my bike off the bus."

"Just get in the truck"

"I can't leave it on the bus, it'll be stolen at the next stop."

The bus was almost loaded.

"Please, I can't afford to buy another one."

The agent sighed, looked annoyed, and then realized there might be contraband in the bike.

"That one in front?" he asked.

It was the only one in the rack.

"Yes."

He yelled to the agent who was supervising the last of the bus loading. She watched as her bike was pulled from the bus and wheeled to where she stood.

"Is this yours?" the agent asked.

"Yes."

He looked at it, not sure what to do next. For a moment, she actually thought he might try to wand the metal frame, but he settled for an intimate pat-down. Finished, his blue vinyl gloves were now black. His annoyance at that brought her a smile that she barely suppressed.

Meanwhile, the bus drove away without her.

It was obvious that there was no room in the Humvee for the bicycle, her, the other two passengers, and two TSA agents, so her fastidious agent made an executive decision.

"OK, you sit there" he said, pointing towards a curb that was wet and green from a water pipe leak somewhere nearby. She remained standing, hoping it wouldn't be interpreted as an act of confrontation.

The Humvee left. Now the only passenger, she watched as the tables were folded and loaded into a blue van. Her agent had a quick conference with a man in a suit, then came back to her.

"ID?"

She stood, fished in her backpack, and handed him her real one, not sure if he had access to an on-line driver's license database, or how capable he was of spotting her fake.

Clip board in hand, he copied her name and number.

The blue van left.

"OK, you can go," he said as he handed back her license.

Her mind still locked up, she watched as he got into the last vehicle, a blue TSA sedan. It wasn't until the car had pulled around the corner, leaving her standing alone in the night, that she realized she didn't even know where she was. Worse still, she had no lights on her bike. Now very tired, she decided to wait for the next bus, since she couldn't afford a cab.

One other thought popped into her mind as she stood alone under that single streetlight: She better find another way to make her deliveries. Public transportation was no longer a good idea.

* * *

Mrs. Chang suggested that it was time for Fawn to make some badlander friends, so Fawn now sat at her kitchen table, music on, red wine in hand, and wandered through the MEET THE BEST chat room. She noticed that one of the patrons was named David Bowie and, never having met a rock star before, struck up a conversation.

> Fawn: So, are you really David Bowie?
>
> Bowie: Yes, that's right. By some fluke of chance, I was also given that badlands name.
>
> Fawn: How about a song?
>
> Bowie: Sorry, love, but I'm not very good on the keyboard.
>
> Fawn: Where's your next gig?
>
> Bowie: Uh Uh. You got the last question. It's my turn.
>
> Fawn: OK
>
> System: Nairobi Bombay, female, DARK CITIES, has entered the room
>
> Bowie: What are you wearing right now?

Somehow, 'dirty t-shirt and panties, no bra' didn't seem like a good answer. Or, perhaps it was, but she wasn't going to give it.

> Fawn: A long tight evening dress. Black, long sleeves, high neck, with diamond earrings.
>
> Bowie: God, I bet you even have your hair up, too?
>
> Fawn: Of course.
>
> Bowie: Well, love, this is a good time to let it down. I promise I won't try a grope. Honest.
>
> Nairobi: Hells Bells, he's at it again. God save the women of the world.
>
> Bowie: Christ, just like you were me sister. And me about to ease her into a private, too

Nairobi: Hello, since he has no manners, allow me to introduce myself.

Bowie: Nairobi Bombay, cub reporter. This is Dancing Fawn, someone who has some manners.

Fawn: You write newspaper articles?

Bowie: Aw, criminy, I guess this lot's done for.

Nairobi: Bye bye Bowie, catch you later, OK?

Bowie: Right, love, when I can get you alone. Later, Fawn, don't pick up any bad habits.

System: David Bowie, male, ROCKY ROAD, has left the room

Fawn: He's a hoot. You known him long?

Nairobi: Years. At least it seems like it. He's fun and spices up the place, at least I'll give him credit for that.

Fawn: You think he's really David Bowie?

Nairobi: You're new here, right? No, I think he's a twelve-year-old boy hiding in a closet.

Fawn: I suppose that's no worse than the kitchen table.

Nairobi: You sitting at your kitchen table right now?

Fawn: Oh, was that one of the things I wasn't supposed to tell anyone?

Nairobi: No, but, please, which OS are you running?

Fawn: Excuse me?

Nairobi: Your wheels. Whose software are you running on it?

Fawn: I don't' really know. GOBI DESERT set it up for me.

Nairobi: Good. OK. You're covered. They use a good wheel house.

Fawn: Explain?

Nairobi: Two years ago I was almost caught in a raid. I managed to get away, but had to chuck my wheels. Not knowing why it happened, I decided to change everything: login site, computer manufacturer, OS, VPN, proxy, doorbell address, everything but my crossing house.

Fawn: And that fixed it?

Nairobi: Well, I haven't been in a raid since.

Fawn: Did you figure out how the civs found you?

Nairobi: Probably. Several other badlanders had the same experience about that time. The only common thread was that we all used either a Microsoft or Apple OS. No one who used an open-source OS ever got caught in a raid.

Fawn: Open-source?

Nairobi: Apple and Microsoft both compile their source code and then supply only executables to their customers. Other vendors supply the source code instead. In fact, they make a point of advertising it, calling their software 'Open-Source' because anyone can get get the source code and look at it.

Fawn: So why did that make a difference?

Nairobi: Because you can have an independent cracker check what's in the code and then have a buddy compile it into an executable. That guarantees that there isn't anything hidden in your OS that you don't want there.

Fawn: And you think there is in the Microsoft and Apple systems?

Nairobi: No one knows for sure, their executables are too hard to pick apart. But no one running an open-source OS has been caught in a raid, so everyone thinks they installed some sort of tracker in their code to rat-out anyone who entered the badlands.

Fawn: So how do you know I'm safe?

Nairobi: The reputable crossing houses only install checked open-source code on their wheels. If you're using an OS you got through GOBI DESERT, you're safe.

Fawn: Good, thank you.

Nairobi: That doesn't mean you can feel comfortable, though. Are you connecting to the Internet through your home Wi-Fi?

Fawn: Yes.

Nairobi: The badlands is a belt and suspenders kind of place. Just to be safe, in the future, you should only make a crossing from someplace away from home. I suggest a pub with lots of exits and good beer.

Fawn: Should I disconnect now?

Nairobi: No. If they've traced you, it's already too late to do anything. But next time, hit the pub. And wear something that will blend in. Slinky and black probably won't do. Even if it is your normal kitchen outfit.

Fawn: You caught that?

Nairobi: I snoop a lot.

Fawn: You're really a reporter?

Nairobi: When I have something to write about.

Fawn: How do you get your ideas?

Nairobi: I hang out here. Any suggestions?

Fawn: No

Nairobi: Yeah, I seem to be hitting a dry hole everywhere. Well, next stop is the snitch market. It's expensive, but usually fruitful.

Fawn: Snitch market?

Nairobi: Emporium.

Fawn: What?

Nairobi: Thieves Emporium. Damn, you don't know?

Fawn: I'm new here.

Nairobi: Come on, girl. We got shopping to do!

* * *

The Thieves Emporium was not a place for the faint of heart. It was the dark underside of the free market, where merchants from all over the world came to sell every form of exotic good. If it was prohibited, illegal, or immoral, it was for sale here.

Women love shopping. They have since one first dropped from a tree to pick up a shiny stone. Fawn and Nairobi were no different. Any market, especially one as free-wheeling as this, excited a deep thrill in both of them. The implicit danger and forbidden nature of the wares only made the experience more enticing.

Fawn sat enthralled, alone in her dark kitchen, transfixed by the display on her wheels. Before her, a home page shimmered and dazzled like something out of the Arabian Nights. The index of services included:

Botnet Rentals
Custom Cracks
Custom Wheels
Discreet Delivery
Escorts
Escrow
Extraction
Forgers
Investigations
Investments
Persuasion
Termination
Waste Disposal

Or, if she just wanted to buy something, there was:

Counterfeit Currencies
Cracker Products
Documents
Goods w/o titles
IDs
Kiddie Porn
Meds
Narcotics
Snitches
Snuff films
Weapons
Wheels

And for everyone who wanted to sell, someone was also advertising to buy. There were even Help Wanted ads if she ever decided to give up her business.

What did she want? Jewelry made from prohibited stones? Blood diamonds? How about exotic woods? Or genuine ivory? Or perhaps clothing made from some protected species? How about a polar bear coat?

Something with a missing title? Here was a diamond necklace at 1/10 the retail price. Or a Maserati with updated VINs and papers.

Perhaps she preferred intoxicants? Everything from plain marijuana leaves to refined cocaine, from magic mushrooms to processed and certified heroin. Taxes were getting so bad that even cigarettes were now for sale in bulk. Or, if she wanted to grow her own, there seemed to be a complete seed bank and nursery at her disposal.

How about a fast poison instead? Want something quick-acting? Tasteless? Undetectable in an autopsy? Hey, and for the old folks, some are even painless.

And, of course, there was her specialty: Meds. This is where the old folks came to buy on the cheap, everything from blood pressure to check-out pills. It was all here, reasonably priced and quick.

Any form of intellectual property also seemed to be available: Music, books, videos, software, everything you might buy on Pirate Bay. And guaranteed safe delivery. Want to build a nuclear bomb? A better IED? The plans are here.

And, if all else failed, there were 'Persuasion' or 'Termination' services.

Persuasion. Termination. Euphemisms for torture, maiming, and killing. Long ago, Fawn had developed a live-and-let-live attitude towards victimless crimes. Even the open sale of stolen goods didn't bother her. But offers of violence hit her hard. They were wrong. Just evil and wrong.

A text message arrived on her screen:

> Nairobi: Well, what do you think?

She thought how dangerous her life had become, and how little she could do about it.

> Nairobi: It bothers you?
>
> Fawn: Yes.
>
> Nairobi: The first time I came here, it was hard for me, too.
>
> Fawn: But you're still here.
>
> Nairobi: Good with the bad.

When no reply came back again, Nairobi asked

> Nairobi: What bothers you the most?
>
> Fawn: The violence. The killing.
>
> Nairobi: And that doesn't go on in the real world?

Fawn: It's just so open here.

Nairobi: Does that make a difference? If a killer gets hired here or in some real-world bar, does it matter? Someone still dies.

Nairobi waited for that to sink in, then asked

Nairobi: You still live your life, don't you? In the real world?

Fawn: Yes.

Nairobi: Do the same here. You can't control what other people do, so don't accept the burden of their actions. Just forget about it, like you do in the real world, and go on with your life.

Fawn: Doesn't it scare you?

Nairobi: Everything scares me. Here and the real world. Be careful everywhere, but don't dwell on it.

After another pause to give Fawn a little space, Nairobi asked

Nairobi: Questions?

Fawn: Is there anything that's not for sale here?

Nairobi: If it's not illegal, you won't find it here. The overhead is too high. If Ebay has it, buy it there. But if some civ wants to throw you in jail for buying it, it's here.

Fawn: Ebay's the same thing, only for legal stuff?

Nairobi: No. This place is unique on earth. It's a meeting place for double-blind transactions. In all history, there has never been anything like it.

Fawn: Never?

Nairobi: Buy something on Ebay, the site operator knows who you are. Buy through the mails, you have to send someone a check or take delivery somewhere. Both leave trails. Even if you trade drugs on the street corner, someone still sees your face. Until now, there has never been a market where both the buyer and seller are anonymous.

Fawn: That's what you mean by double-blind?

Nairobi: Right. Anonymous in both directions. The badlands is a shifting web of double-blind links with this place at the center and crossing houses around the edges.

There was more silence on the chat line. After a short pause, Nairobi asked:

> Nairobi: Well? What do you think?
>
> Fawn: Let's shop!
>
> Nairobi: Want a diamond necklace to go with the black evening dress you wear in your kitchen?
>
> Fawn: OK, cut it out. You ever buy any of this stuff?
>
> Nairobi: No. If I get caught, I want as clean a record as possible. So I just come here for business.
>
> Fawn: Where?
>
> Nairobi: Where all the good dirt is buried. The Snitch Market.

Half an hour later, Fawn was still sitting at her kitchen table, her third glass of red wine almost gone. In front of her was her laptop, logged into the Thieves Emporium Snitch Market. Along the top of the screen was a chat bar, below it two browser windows took up the rest of the display.

The chat bar said:

> Fawn: Look, I know where Elvis is buried!
>
> Nairobi: No you don't. See, I have his phone number and address.

One window read:

> ELVIS PRESLEY. Elvis Presley did <u>not</u> die in 1977 as claimed, but was killed by the CIA on 1/1/2000. I have <u>proof</u>, as well as all the details, including where he is really buried! An autopsy will confirm my proof and make you famous and rich. For more details, please contact me NOW! Wild Bromeliad

The other said:

> ELVIS PRESLEY. Yes, he is alive! You can actually talk with him! See him for yourself. For details, contact me. My rates are very reasonable. Red Fly
>
> Fawn: You rely on these people for serious leads?
>
> Nairobi: Yeah, I know. But I have no choice.
>
> Fawn: Can't you just hang out in bars, or, you know, whatever?
>
> Nairobi: The times, they are a-changing. No one wants to speak up any more unless they're sure they won't be caught.

Fawn: Hasn't that always been the case?

Nairobi: No. It used to be that, if you got caught, you might get fired, maybe sued, but that was all. You could always get another job and you could defend yourself in open court by just proving that what you said was true. Truth was always a perfect defense.

Fawn: So that's changed?

Nairobi: Now everyone is beholden to the government. Get caught snitching and they cut off your rent subsidy or your food stamps or your social security. And that doesn't even count what the IRS can do. And none of it requires legal justification on their part. If you don't like it, you have to sue them to get your benefits back. But good luck, they're the government.

Fawn: This place is different?

Nairobi: Just like anywhere in the badlands, whistle-blowing here is a double-blind activity. You pay them, they give you the dirt. If it can't be traced back, the government can't find out who they are even if you wanted to tell. They know that. This is the only place where a source is guaranteed anonymity.

Fawn: So how do you decide if one of these guys is for real?

Nairobi: Good question. I doubt that Red Fly has a very good approval rating. He might be a solid and trustworthy guy, but he probably hasn't sold enough snitch to build a rep. So I don't actually go to these guys. If I was considering contacting Elvis, I would go to a reputable snitch house with the lead. They would act as an escrow service.

Fawn: Like a middle-man?

Nairobi: Right. They'd find out what I wanted and then look at what Red Fly had to offer. If it looked like he really had something I wanted, the snitch house would arrange a negotiation for a fee and put their rep on the line to back up what I bought.

Fawn: So if I want to find out where Elvis is buried, who should I contact?

Nairobi: Screw Elvis. I'm getting hints that something stinks in FEMA's homeless camps. So, I offer to buy snitch about anything going on there. Leads get sent to me c/o the EVERYTHING REVEALED Snitch House. If they get anything interesting, they let me know. Then we negotiate.

Fawn: Anything good so far?

Nairobi: What paper did you say you write for?

Fawn: Sorry. First rule, right? Never ask too much.

Nairobi: It's just that I do have something, I'm just not sure what. If I publish, you'll get the first copy.

On a whim, Fawn ran a search of her own.

Five minutes later, alone in her dark kitchen, she stared at her laptop. The search turned up a lead, one she never thought she would ever see. Reaching out from the screen, hitting her between the eyes like a thrown martini, was an offer to sell snitch on her missing husband.

Chapter 6

Husband Hunting

Nairobi began her investigation by getting copies of every FEMA death certificate issued over the past five years. 27,836 of them. All, fortunately, in electronic format. Each came from a homeless camp and was electronically signed by a physician, a real person with a real phone number. Using an alias she set up for the purpose, she started making phone calls.

Dr. Hiram Goodman was not the first physician she was able to contact, but he was the first one willing to give her a telephone interview.

"I'm doing a story on the FEMA homeless camps-" she began.

"Shelter Camps," he interrupted.

"Excuse me?"

"They're called Shelter Camps. Promise me you'll use that term in your story? Not any other, just that one?"

"Yes. Sorry."

"What do you want to know?"

"Are you a doctor at one of the Shelter Camps?"

"Yes."

"Heart Mountain?"

"Beaumont."

"Not Heart Mountain?" She had certificates from that camp that bore his signature.

"Only as a fill-in. My full time position is in Beaumont, Texas."

"Do you sign death certificates?"

"Not in Beaumont. I'm just a staff physician there."

"And Heart Mountain?"

"I'm the designated Medical Examiner when I'm there."

"I don't understand."

"Only the Medical Examiner can sign a death certificate. There's one at each FEMA camp. At Beaumont, it's someone else, another member of the staff. When I get duty in Wyoming, though, I'm the only physician on site. By default, I have to be the M. E."

"So you sign certificates there?"

"Yes."

"Why do you work at two camps?"

"Perhaps I could be more direct with my answers if I had some idea what you are looking for."

"Sorry. I've got copies of all the FEMA death certificates for the past five years."

"And?"

"Camp death rates are higher than for the general population."

"Have you ever been to a Shelter Camp?", the annoyance clear in his voice.

"No."

"You should visit one. They're filled with people who have no other option. Families. Children. Houston and New Orleans, we take the desperate from both cities. They have no place else to go. Most lived on the streets for months before they came to us. Weak immune systems. Poor nutrition. Parasites, skin lesions, infections of every sort. Diabetes. TB. Dysentery. Some so overweight they can hardly walk. We manage to keep most of them alive. Do miracles with what little we get. You should praise us for keeping the death rate as low as it is."

"Yes. I see that."

"Without these camps, our cities would overflow with homeless. Hunger. And crime. Hungry people do bad things to eat. And sanitation? How would you like a vagrant defecating on your front porch? They have to go somewhere. You have to tell the country why we need these camps. You will, won't you?

"Yes" answered Nairobi, well aware of the reason for their existence. When the homeless overwhelmed private charitable institutions to become a national emergency, FEMA was mobilized to house them. The camps were supposed to be a stop-gap measure, to be eliminated when the economy improved. But when the crisis became permanent, they did also.

"It's not like these people can turn anywhere else," continued Goodman. "They don't have addresses. No address, no EBT card. Many don't have IDs. Some are illegal. How are they going to survive? And families? How could they feed their children if we didn't have the camps?

"Good point."

"Every camp is on the edge. Right on the edge. It would be a holocaust. Measles. Mumps. Chicken Pox. These kids didn't get vaccinations. Flu. Anything. The crowding, the poor sanitation. One spark and thousands will die in an epidemic. That's what you have to tell people.

"I'm doing my best. We all are. But without more money, FEMA is just delaying the inevitable. Please, write about that. I don't want this on my conscience. Please."

"OK. I will. I promise." She paused for a minute to try to clear the images out of her mind. Then she started again.

"Can you tell me about Heart Mountain?"

"What do you want to know?"

"The death rate is three times higher than any other camp. Why?"

"They're not a primary camp. They're overflow."

"Meaning?"

"When someone new is sent to Beaumont, the camp Administrator has a problem. We're full. Can't take any more. So he sends a current guest to Heart Mountain to make room."

"The new person doesn't go to Heart Mountain?"

"No."

"Because?"

"No Administrator wants trouble in his camp. They're big places. Beaumont is rated for 125,000. Packed tight. Limited medical facilities, minuscule police force. The best way to avoid violence and disease is to ship off the bad apples. The sick and the mean. The bottom of the barrel gets transferred to Heart Mountain. Not just from Beaumont, but from every camp.

"But it's worse than that. FEMA allocates resources according to rated camp capacity. Heart Mountain's is 30,000. But its population is half again over that. There's no provision for too many people in an overflow camp. But they keep coming. And Heart still only gets resources for thirty thousand."

The frustration and anger came through clearly in his voice. She paused a minute to let him calm down, then asked "You work at Heart Mountain?"

"When I have to."

"How often is that?"

"Two, three times a year. Maybe ten days total."

"Who's the regular doctor?"

"There isn't one. No one will take the job. So we rotate through, every FEMA physician. We're all temporary."

"You all sign certificates?"

"Yes."

"Why are there so many more deaths at that camp?"

"Haven't you been listening? Heart Mountain gets the dregs. The scum, the infected, the hot potatoes that everyone else wants to get rid of. To deal with them, Heart Mountain gets almost nothing in the way of resources. No Shelter Camp gets much, but Heart gets even less. Poorer food. Worse medical facilities. Fewer marshals. The place is a cesspit under the backside of hell. You really want answers? Go there. Walk through the filth. Smell the stink yourself. I'll get you a pass. Well?"

Nairobi couldn't answer at first, then stumbled for an excuse. He cut her off.

"Give me a call if you change your mind. Until then, I have work to do. Good day."

And, with that, the phone line went dead. She considered calling him back to take him up on his offer, but her stomach wouldn't let her.

* * *

Fawn had sent a message to Caper Oleander asking for details on his snitch ad about her husband. His reply suggested a meeting at the WAREZ Chat house. So now, although she was hunched alone in a dark corner of a local pub, the two of them were also sequestered in a private chat room in the badlands.

Oleander: Yes, I know where he is now.

Fawn: What can you tell me?

Oleander: A fair amount. Once you pay for it.

Fawn: When did you last see him?

Oleander: Listen, he was a good guy, I would really like to help you, but I need the money.

Fawn: How much?

He told her. She hoped it was just an opening offer, not a bottom line.

Oleander: What's he to you?

If I tell him the truth, he'll know my real-world name.

Fawn: One of his friends is looking for him.

Oleander: Well, tell this friend that I have the goods when he has the money.

Fawn: He'll want proof.

Oleander: I have it, part of the package.

Fawn: What kind of proof?

Oleander: A complete FEMA file. Logs. Pictures. The works. Encrypted with FEMA codes. And the passwords.

Fawn: When did you last see him?

Oleander: I never said I saw him, only that I know where he is and can prove it.

Fawn: You said a FEMA file. Was he in one of the homeless camps?

Oleander: Yes

Fawn: Which one?

Oleander: Did I mention that I need money?

Fawn: You still haven't given me any evidence that you really have a file.

Oleander: He went into the camp thirty-seven months ago.

She did a quick calculation. *A little over three years. Yes, that was when the checks stopped.*

Fawn: I don't have that much money. Will you come down any?

Oleander: Maybe if I know the money is really there. But you're a newbie. Your rep doesn't give me much confidence that you can deliver.

Fawn: I can get it if you can come up with a reasonable price.

Oleander: Hey, listen, I really want to help you, but I got a family to feed, you know?

Fawn: OK, I got that part. Thank you. I'll get back to you.

Oleander: Listen, if you're really interested, I got other bidders, so you need to act soon, you know?

Fawn: Who else is bidding?

Oleander: They want it quiet. They're bidding to get all these files off the market and they don't want their names spread around.

Fawn: There are other files?

Oleander: Yeah, lots of them, but this is the only one on your guy.

Fawn: The others from FEMA camps too?

Oleander: Yes.

Fawn: They all for sale if I can find a buyer?

Oleander: Sure.

Fawn: Who are the other files on?

Oleander: I'll send you the list.

Fawn: Will you throw this one in for free if I get you a buyer for the rest?

Oleander: Yeah, maybe.

Then maybe, Fawn thought, *there might be a way.*

* * *

All Fawn could think about was how to get enough money to buy her husband's file. One obvious way was to borrow it.

Chang: That's an awful lot of money, child. Are you in some kind of trouble?

Fawn: No. I just thought maybe you might make me another loan.

Chang: I was willing to make the last one because it made good business sense. If I can get some details, I might be able to help.

Fawn: No, I would rather not.

Chang: Child, I wish I could help. But your income won't support any more debt.

The text stream stopped as Fawn thought about what the rejection meant. Somehow, Mrs. Chang must have understood how important it was to her, because she typed:

Chang: There might be another way. You could always leverage what you make by taking your real-world payment in counterfeit.

Fawn: Dollars? You mean pass counterfeit dollars?

Chang: Yes.

Fawn: Isn't that dangerous?

Chang: Of course. That's why we decided to have you go with meds in the first place. But, if you really need the money, this is probably the safest way to get it. You are already running a distribution route, you could just pay your expenses in bogus scrip.

Fawn: How likely am I to get caught?

Chang: Not very, but if you do, the penalties will be much stiffer than for med smuggling. The fake bills are very good, so good that I doubt that even the banks can detect them. If they can't, none of the merchants you deal with will, either. If you spread your spending around, it's unlikely that anyone will ever connect you with the bad bills.

If I ever want to find out what happened to my husband, I have to make a lot more money than I'm making right now. What other alternative do I have?

Fawn: OK, I'm in. Where do we go from here?

Chang: Order another kit ID. Use a different name and address from the one you used for your meds. Open a mailbox with that ID at the other end of your delivery route. Plan on picking up a package only about once a month. I suggest ID IN A BOX, just like last time, and FUNNY MONEY for the bills.

Fawn: Thanks.

Chang: One other thing.

Fawn: Yes?

Chang: Please, child, keep your head down. It's getting very dangerous out there.

* * *

"You've got a serious problem. Serious," said Arnold Wilson Parker.

Across from him, on the large leather sofa that was the centerpiece of Parker's well-furnished study, sat Edgar Kohrob, CEO of ENGCO. His face had the look of concern that only an emergency trip from half-way across the country could induce.

"You stopped paying on the files, Edgar. That was a bad idea," began Parker.

"He won't do anything," came the dismissive reply.

"He put them on the market."

"No. He wouldn't dare."

"He did."

"Shit." Kohrob had obviously underestimated the blackmailer. "How do you know?"

"Never mind how. He even has a buyer sniffing around."

Kohrob's face showed the struggle as his mind tried to reject the news.

"Start the payments again, Edgar. Now," demanded Parker.

"Why me?"

So no one else will get blamed if it blows up, you greedy ass, thought Parker. Instead, he said "Because it's your mess."

"It wasn't my mistake. I didn't lose those files. FEMA did. Make them pay for it."

"No, Edgar. FEMA was cleaning up for you. You cut the corners. You pay the tab."

"I had to stop, Arnold. ENGCO has auditors. They were getting too close."

"Find a way, Edgar. Hide it deep. Where no one will ever look. I have faith in you. Find a way."

The plea got no reply.

"Edgar, you're at risk here."

Both men knew Parker wasn't just talking about an audit. Not many people could threaten the chairman of ENGCO and make it stick. The change in Kohrob's face showed that Parker was one of that select group.

"You need to do this. Absolutely need to. For your own good, Edgar."

"All right," came the grudging answer.

"Now, Edgar. Time is running out. We have to get him paid right now. Before he actually sells some of the damned things. Do you understand me? This is urgent. Very urgent."

"Yes, yes."

"Now."

Kohrob nodded.

"When, Edgar?"

"By tomorrow night."

"Don't mess this up, Edgar."

* * *

Fawn sat alone at a small table in the play area, her back to a corner. Scraps from two Happy Meals fought for space with her wheels. In her field of view, but no longer the main object of her attention, her twins did their best to wear out the play-set.

Concentrating on her wheels, she typed.

> Fawn: What's encrypted chat?
>
> Nairobi: It's what we're doing. Just the two of us.
>
> Fawn: I know that. Why not just a chat?
>
> Nairobi: A private chat, which is the alternate, can be monitored by the chat house. An encrypted chat tunnels communications so they can only be monitored by the participants of the chat.
>
> Fawn: You don't trust this chat house?
>
> Nairobi: Badlands rule #666: Never trust anyone you don't have to.
>
> Fawn: Right. OK. What did you think of the list?
>
> Nairobi: Why do you think this chat's encrypted? Where'd you get it?
>
> Fawn: And which paper did you say you worked for?
>
> Nairobi: OK, I deserved that. Share?
>
> Fawn: Everything?
>
> Nairobi: Yes.
>
> Fawn: Partners?
>
> Nairobi: That's a bit much.
>
> Fawn: Please?

After pause, the answer came back:

> Nairobi: OK. Now give.
>
> Fawn: I got it from a snitch. Caper Oleander.
>
> Nairobi: Where'd he get it?
>
> Fawn: No, your turn.

Nairobi: I've managed to pick up the names of six protesters that have disappeared after being seen in FEMA camps.

Fawn: Any on this list?

Nairobi: All of them.

Fawn: Where'd you get their names?

Nairobi: Your turn.

Fawn: I was looking for someone for a friend. Oleander was selling files on him.

Nairobi: Was he selling files on all the names on this list?

Fawn: Yes.

Nairobi: How did you get the list?

Fawn: I just asked for it.

Nairobi: Damn. I need a new snitch house. How much does he want for the files?

Fawn told her.

Nairobi: Damn again.

Fawn: It's a lot of money?

Nairobi: It would set Donald Trump back.

Fawn: Any chance we could find a buyer?

Nairobi: What did he tell you about the names on the list?

Fawn: That they all disappeared from a FEMA camp.

Nairobi: One camp? He said 'a' camp?

Fawn: Yes.

Nairobi: Is your friend's friend on this list?

Fawn: Sorry, that's on a Need-It-Now basis only.

Nairobi: You mean Need-To-Know. Need-It-Now means something else.

Fawn: Right. I knew that. Just a typo. What's next, partner?

Nairobi: Partner? Was your friend's friend on this list? Partner?

Fawn: OK. Yes.

Nairobi: Thank you.

Fawn: What's next?

Nairobi: We get a good snitch house to talk for us.

* * *

Fawn and Nairobi set up an encrypted chat with Nobu Bara, owner of the KISS'N TELL Snitch House.

Bara: Bad news. Caper Oleander says the information is no longer available.

Nairobi: He took it off the market?

Bara: Well, actually, he claimed it was never there, said he knew nothing about it.

Fawn: I got the list from him.

Bara: I know, I know. We keep a running record of everything offered for snitch. A history, actually. We have his listings.

Fawn: All of them?

Bara: Yes. Files on everyone on your list were offered for sale.

Nairobi: And he just pulled them? All 2,192 listings?

Bara: Yes.

Nairobi: And he claims he never offered them?

Bara: At first, yes. When I showed him our records, he changed his tune. Admitted they were listed, but no more.

Fawn: Did you tell him we wanted to make an offer?

Bara: No good. Perhaps he doesn't believe you have the money.

Nairobi: What if we escrow the funds with you?

Bara: That might change his mind. But it's a considerable amount of money. Your reps aren't that fat. Where will you get it?

Nairobi: Thank you, Mr. Bara. We will be in touch.

* * *

"OK, Sandra. What do you want?" asked Luke Abbas.

His ex-wife just smiled back. She rarely missed an opportunity to squeeze him. Why should this be any different? He and his son had been planning these outings for over three months. The Subway Series. The Yankees vs. the Mets. And he had box tickets for the two of them, purchased through his company. Now, when they were about to go to the third game, she said Samuel had to do homework.

So now he stood on his old doorstep, double-parked while she put the squeeze on him. Just like old times. Fortunately, she hadn't noticed that his car was a rental, one that he got using a false driver's license.

"Please. I'll get a ticket. What do you want?"

She liked to draw these things out, savor the authority she had over him thanks to the court's one-sided custody decision. A long pause emphasized her position, then she said "The washer and dryer are worn out." Shamelessly, she spit the words out. The child support and alimony weren't adequate for her and her boy toy. She wanted more. She always had.

"All right. Now can he come?"

"Soon as I see the cash."

"Please, Sandra, we'll be late for the game."

Actually, that wasn't true. He had planned the day's schedule with an ample allowance for delays. There was too much riding on some hard deadlines for him to have done otherwise.

"Your bank has a branch just down the street."

"How much?"

"A thousand should do it."

Without a word, he turned and walked quickly back to the car. Half an hour later, he handed her the money. She counted it, then called inside to their son.

"Samuel, honey, I've changed my mind. Hurry up, your father's waiting."

The boy came out of the door at a run. He must have been waiting just inside, ready for a sprint to the car as soon as the word came that he could go. Luke quickly followed. Seconds later, they turned the corner at the end of the street.

Later, after they had merged into the expressway traffic, Luke looked at his young son and said, in mock seriousness, "I have bad news."

This was a game they often played, had been for the past year. Samuel would know the news was never bad. When his father used this tone, things always got better, never worse. But how could they get better than this? Box seats for the third game, with the Mets ahead 2-0. If the Mets won, it would decide the series. It couldn't get better than this.

But it did.

"You know how we've always talked about going deep sea fishing?"

"Yeah."

"Well, I just won two plane tickets to Cozumel."

"Where's that?"

"Mexico."

"Mexico? Where banditos live?" Samuel was very big on Westerns.

"The same."

"They go deep-sea fishing there?"

"Yep. Best in the world."

Cowboys and deep-sea fishing. What could be better? His father was so lucky.

"Want to go?"

That got an even bigger smile and an eyeball-jarring nod.

"When?" Samuel asked.

"Well, that's the bad news. The flight's this afternoon."

"But we're going to the game."

"Yep. That's the bad news. We can't do both.

"Can't you change the tickets?"

"Nope. Non-refundable."

"Wow. Which we gonna do?"

"That's up to you. I promised you the game. I won't renege if you still want to go."

"Do I have to decide now?"

"Yep. Afraid so."

Samuel scrunched up his face in thought. And Luke's heart skipped a beat. This would be much tougher if the boy made the wrong choice. Perhaps he could help it along a bit.

"The Mexico trip is for two weeks. You'd have to miss school for two weeks."

That decided it. A grin as wide as the Hudson flashed across the boy's face. "Mexico!" he yelled.

Forty five minutes later they stood in front of Aero Mexico's first class counter. While still in the car, he had explained another game to his son. They were going to pretend to be banditos on the lam. Fake names and everything, just for fun. Samuel understood. He would play along.

Luke handed the clerk two badlands passports. Samuel's had his correct first name and the last name of Sandra's boy toy. His said he was that boy toy. With luck the name choice would cause some embarrassment, especially since he didn't think the punk's papers were quite in order.

Both passports looked genuine. Any errors were too small to be detected by anyone unless that person was both suspicious and well trained in fraudulent ID detection. Neither passport had a database record to support it, but since the ticket agent did not have access to the Department Of State Passport Database, that would not be an issue. Luke stated, correctly, that Samuel was his son. The common last name on the two passports confirmed his claim, thus giving him the right to take the child out of the country. On the scale sat their luggage, just barely under the allowed weight limit.

Had the agent taken the time to grill Samuel, the boy would probably have slipped up and revealed his real name. There was, however, a line of other first class passengers who wanted to board the aircraft. Delaying them with excessive questions was not in the ticket agent's best interest. So, within minutes of presenting his documents and luggage, Luke and Samuel had their boarding passes and were moving through security.

One hour later, just before boarding the aircraft, Luke called his ex to tell her that his car wouldn't start. They would be delayed getting back from the game as they would have to wait for a tow truck.

Seven hours later, they missed their connection to Cancun. Instead, using another pair of badlands passports issued under different names, Luke and Samuel flew out of Mexico City for South America.

* * *

Buying cheap is easier to do if the owner has an incentive to sell. If you want to buy a dry cleaning business, have a buddy rough up the owner's wife. The principle is obvious. And it works for gold as well as dry cleaners.

To say Arnold Wilson Parker had considerable influence with the IRS would be an understatement. Oh, he paid all his taxes. In fact, he even paid a little more than he had to. After all, he had 'bribed' the legislators who passed the tax laws to give him all the loop holes he needed to keep his tax payments small, so why not pay a little more than that? It was good PR.

No, the area in which he most appreciated his influence was in the field of other people's taxes. Not any one person. That would be too easily noticed. No, he influenced policy. The way the IRS dealt with everyone, so no claim of favoritism could ever be made against him or his minions in the IRS.

Today, he changed the tax policy on gold. It was already punitive, of course. At the moment, anyone making a profit from the sale of gold would have to pay the highest tax rate and forgo any capital gains protection. Those rules had been instituted to discourage the ownership of that metal. But they didn't seem enough any more.

So, beginning today, all owners of gold would have to declare their metal holdings every year beginning with this year's filings. If they didn't make any profits on sales this year or the next, they wouldn't have to pay any taxes, but any failure to declare those holdings would result in total confiscation if they ever came to the attention of the IRS.

And, beginning today, gold could not be taken out of the country without an IRS letter stating that all taxes had been paid on any 'unrealized' profits made on the metal. Any attempt to do so without a letter would result in confiscation of the metal, just as it already did if an attempt to take out more than $3,000 worth is made without informing the Census Bureau (of all people) ahead of time that it was going to be 'exported'.

Also, beginning this year, the tax rate on profits from the sale of gold would be raised from the current 28% to 50%. Of course, capital gains exemptions would still not be allowed.

Finally, today the IRS would announce that a 'hoarding' tax would be placed on all gold owned by U. S. citizens and residents beginning in two years. Any gold held after that date would be taxed at a rate of 10% per year on the market value of the metal.

Hey. You. Mr. Dry Cleaner. I only roughed up your wife this time. But two years from now, I'm going to really hurt her. You sure you don't want to sell?

Chapter 7

The Riot

"So why do they call you 'Butterfly Killer'?" asked FBI Special Agent Daniel Shelton.

They were sitting at their favorite booth in Shelton's favorite bar, though Joshua Weidemeyer had to admit that the nipples were growing on him. But, now, this question. It was not one Weidemeyer appreciated. And, though Shelton couldn't see it in the dim light, the question brought a look of annoyance to the other man's face.

"Because of Weidemeyer's Admiral."

"What?"

"A butterfly. Discovered by my great-great grandfather. You can see them stuck on pins all over the world. So, I got the name 'Butterfly Killer'." *And thought I had shaken it.*

"Your great-great grandfather was a butterfly collector?"

Weidemeyer nodded.

"He collected butterflies, you collect old coins. I guess it runs in the family, right?"

That got a weak smile along with another nod.

"Hey, at least you're related to someone famous. Should I start calling you 'Butterfly Killer'?"

The look FBI Special Agent Shelton got back was very clear and very negative.

"OK. OK, forget I mentioned it. I will, I promise."

"I've been trying to shake the name since high school. I thought I had succeeded."

"You came pretty close. As far as I can tell, almost no one remembers it. And you have my word, I've forgotten it already. Honest."

"Thank you," said Weidemeyer, now with a genuine smile.

"There is something I've been meaning to ask you, though. Why don't you just catch your counterfeiters through their bank accounts?"

"Because" Weidemeyer said, "they don't use banks to transfer their money."

"How, then?"

"Through the mails, for one thing. Get their scrip through a re-mailer. Same when they send gold back."

"Wait. Don't they send back cash?" asked the FBI man.

"If you had access to undetectable counterfeit currency, would you accept banknotes as payment for anything?"

"Yeah, OK. So why don't you just have all the mails inspected?"

"All inspections go through manual scanners. That takes manpower. We don't have the people to check more than one piece in every thousand."

"You catching them when they pass it?"

"How? Merchants can't recognize the bogus before the passer leaves. The stuff's too good. It even gets by us unless the serial numbers haven't been issued yet."

"Fucking hell. They're that good?" asked Shelton.

Weidemeyer nodded.

"You've given the banks the issued serial numbers?"

"No."

"What? Why not? They could be looking, too."

"One bank employee on the take and the counterfeiters would have it, too."

"Then no more duplicate numbers?"

"Right. And no more detections. Period."

"How many passers your people caught?" pushed Shelton.

"I told you. None."

"None?"

"Yeah, none!" replied Weidemeyer with growing annoyance. "The only guys we've ever caught were nabbed through postal inspections, something that almost never happens with the current inspection rates."

"Hell, we can't even tell which merchants send bogus to the banks. About all we know is which banks send them to us. Without knowing who the merchant is, we can't even get a description."

Shelton lapsed into silence to give his friend a chance to calm down. After a short period, he asked "How you going to deal with this?"

That was a question for which Weidemeyer had no good answer. "We had planned a new currency issue," he began. "In fact, it should have been out by now, but the RFIDs don't work."

"Tag the money?"

"Put an RFID in each bill and a reader in every post office. Any money, either real or perfect counterfeit, will trip the detector."

"Great. Why didn't you do it?"

"First, getting a tag into the paper. Anything you put in a bill has to be soft and flexible or it causes a wear point. Destroys the bill. We found a way around that, though.

"But we can't solve the interference problem. Stack bills together, the RFID antennas sit on top of each other. That causes interference, so none of them work. We can find a single bill just fine, but a stack slips through."

"Any idea when you'll have a fix?"

With a sigh, Weidemeyer shook his head.

* * *

Summer had come. Glorious summer. No snow, no ice, no slush. Just sun. Mostly, anyway. And, more important for Fawn's morale, school was out. Her munchkins were free.

In winter, every week was a trial for them all. For four days, while she made her deliveries, she had to leave them with a widowed neighbor. All three had to do without cuddles or laughter or play. It was more depressing than the cold gray winter rain. But it was also the only way she could be at her weekend flea markets and they could still be in school, so they all put up with it.

Every Tuesday morning, she would climb into her cold van before the sun came up. Then she would depart for Buffalo or Detroit or Cincinnati or Indianapolis, stopping along the way to buy gold coins with counterfeit scrip, show her antiques, pick up her meds, and distribute them. She never went to the same cities twice in a row, never used credit or debit cards, and always obeyed the traffic laws.

But it was now summer! No more Monday night goodbyes, no more sneaking out early Tuesday morning to avoid a scene.

Now both her beauties lay under the covers on the high platform bed that turned her unmarked white cargo van into a camper. They were quiet, sensing their mother's tension, but not knowing why. They did, however, know the drill. When she told them to, they would lie flat under the covers, still as real fawns, not a move or sound until they were released from the exercise. They were good girls.

A few blocks from the cargo forwarder, she pulled into a strip mall and stopped. Going up front as if to check a rattle under the car, she slipped a clear plastic cover over her license plate The cover bore just enough stains and crazing to make it impossible to read the number. She did the same thing on the rear.

Now, as she turned into the industrial complex, she yelled back "OK, girls, time to hide."

There was a flurry of giggles and a little shoving. Blankets flew and flapped in the air, then came silence. She looked in the rear view mirror and saw nothing but an unmade bed. They were very good girls.

Fawn parked as far as she could from the freight office without causing suspicion. Busying herself with gathering her documents, she took the chance to scan the parking lot and surrounding docks. Nothing stirred in the early morning light.

If they were to catch her, this was the most likely place they'd do it. The message she got saying her package was here had included one of the safe words they had agreed on. It was supposed to prove that the sender wasn't sending the message from a DHS hotel. That was the theory, anyway.

This was one of those times when theory might not match reality, though, so she worried. Getting out, she stood near the door and scanned the area again, stopping to tie her shoe to give her the excuse to linger.

Nothing looked out of place. But then, if they were waiting to arrest her when she picked up the package, they wouldn't show themselves yet.

There was no use delaying it any longer. With a deep breath, she walked slowly back to the rear of the van. Opening the doors, she took out a hand truck.

One more scan. Still nothing usual. So, cart in tow, she began the long walk to the shipping dock. Dragging it up the steps and through the door, she made her way to the counter.

"Yes?"

"Got anything for Fastway Delivery?" she asked in as normal a voice as she could muster.

"I'll check," he answered and turned his attention to the computer in front him. As he typed, she waited, watching him for any sign of suspicion. She knew she should make small talk, say something to make him more comfortable, but no words would come to her. Only the fear that she dare not let him see.

So she just stood there, outfitted in dark green work pants and jacket, a cap over her light brown hair. No makeup, clean hair pulled back in a French braid. All business, freckles showing like buff stars scattered over a tan sky. She knew she should take advantage of her looks, smile at him a little. But she couldn't do that, either.

"Yeah. We should. You got ID?"

She handed him her kit license, then stood there, frozen, while he examined it. He seemed to take longer than normal, then handed it back and turned to the boxes behind him.

This was the hard part. If something had gone wrong, this was where she would find out. Had they caught the shipment going through customs? She had no idea what arrangements had been made to slip it through, but, like everything else, they were subject to failure. Were agents closing in on her van right now?

Or perhaps he had seen the small defects in her ID and had signaled the front office to call the police. Were squad cars pushing fast this way, lights flashing but sirens off to avoid warning her? Was he just stalling for time or was he really searching for her shipment? Because she was a badlander, every day really was the last one she might have with her girls.

"Four boxes. Check 'em and sign here. You wanna pull up to the dock?"

"No, thanks, they're not heavy." she said as she signed the name she had used on her kit ID. Then, stacking them on her hand-truck, she struggled with the door until he came around to hold it.

"Thank you," she said, more relieved than she showed. If he was willing to hold the door, the police weren't on the way and Customs wasn't waiting outside. She whispered a small prayer: *Thank you Lord, for one more day with my girls.*

She put the boxes and the hand truck in the back under the platform bed. After opening them to confirm their contents, she slammed the back doors and drove out of the parking lot, doing everything she could to avoid attracting attention.

"Come OUT come OUT wherever you are!" she shouted as the van turned back on the main street. Wild squeals were the only reply, along with bouncing she could feel through her seat.

"Hey, hey, hey, simmer down OK?

"Did we do good?"

"Are you kidding? Sherlock Holmes couldn't have found you!"

"Can we go to the museum next?" The Chicago Children's Museum had been the official objective of this trip.

"Next stop! I promise!"

And so, with a chant of "GO GO GO GO..." blasting out of the back, they were off.

* * *

They left the museum about 2:30, after lunch and what Fawn (though not the girls) considered a very long day. Walking back to the car, west along Illinois Street, they passed empty store windows covered with For Sale and For Rent signs. She didn't notice anything unusual until they came out from under Michigan Avenue, when it dawned on her. The sidewalks were almost empty. Fear of the camps kept panhandlers and loiters away, of course, but even normal traffic was light.

A block later, she noticed an unnatural murmur, almost a rhythmic throbbing, in the background. Faint and hidden, noticeable only because the rest of the city noise had gone quiet, it got louder as she walked.

At Wabash, she noticed the people. They filled the intersection with State. Her car was parked down State.

Her girls, noticing the crowd, lost the last of the bounce in their steps. Falling back, they lagged behind, only keeping up because holding their mother's hand required it.

"Momma, what are all those people doing?" asked the braver of the two.

That was a good question. The intersection was packed with them, all clad in black. That should have generated a mean traffic jam, but Illinois was almost empty of cars. Then she noticed police were directing cars away from the crowd. She had seen this at every intersection for the past few blocks, but it had not registered until now.

"I'm not sure, honey" she replied, beginning to become a little concerned herself. "Stay close to Mommie, OK?" She need not have worried.

Their car was parked in the Hertz garage, two blocks south down State. With the entrance off of that street, she continued towards the intersection.

The closer she got to the crowd, the more she noticed the police. Looking back, she saw several squad cars parked along the last block, with more ahead. Uniformed officers stood near them, clustered in small groups, as if waiting for something. Beyond them, a solid wall of black cloaks and clown masks extended in either direction through the intersection.

The protesters stood, facing south, chanting and gesturing. Many carried signs. Since the sounds echoed off the surrounding buildings, she couldn't understand what was being said, but they seemed to feel strongly about the subject.

"Honeys, stay close and hold tight. It's important," she commanded, more than a little concerned. But turning back and walking around the long way seemed unnecessary. After all, either way, they would still have to get on State to get to the garage entrance, and it was only another block down that street if they kept going. So, she continued to the corner.

There she found, to her relief, that most of the crowd stood in the street, with parked cars forming a barrier that protected the sidewalk. Encouraged by the emptiness, she turned left and walked south. They passed a bakery and the Marriott. Reaching Hubbard, she noticed a wall of police blocking that street. All wore black armor and helmets with plexiglas face masks. Gripping her girls tighter, she hurried past their dark faces, walking along the no-mans land that existed between their line and the shouting black clowns filling the middle of the street.

"Momma, how much farther?"

The child's classic plea.

"One more block, honey. Please hold tight to momma, OK?" she answered, picking up their pace. Moving at just short of a run, she pulled them behind her like a fishing boat might drag two nets. In response, two sets of small arms grabbed hers as if for dear life.

For some reason, turning left off of State onto Hubbard didn't occur to her. The wall of police looked solid and impenetrable, but it would have parted had she asked. They were human and she was a woman with two small children. She could have escaped the reverberating chants of the protesters if she had just asked.

Instead, because she had made up her mind earlier and was now too scared to reconsider, she forged on, taking the shortest route to her car. The Hertz sign was only half a block away. Crossing the intersection, she weaved around the scattering of protesters that now spilled onto the sidewalk.

As she approached the alley that separated a windowless building on her left from the Hertz garage, the mood of the crowd changed. It seemed to come in a wave, like a wall of rain racing under a squall line. Somehow, she knew it would happen, but had convinced herself that she would be safely in her car before then. Now, she realized she had been wrong. The sound around her changed from chanting to yells, roaring in from ahead like a tsunami. Grabbing her girls, she ran for the Hertz entrance.

Then the crowd turned. Before she could reach the garage, it became a black flood, surging against her. Blackjacks vomited from the alley in front of her, slamming into the howling mob to merge into a single writhing black monster of flashing plexiglas and flailing nightsticks. She lost sight of everything but black cloth, overwhelmed by the wave of running cloaks and clown masks. They slammed her face into the concrete wall, rolling her along it as they ran past.

She tried to wriggle free, make herself and her girls flat enough for the packed screaming mob to get by, but they carried her along with them. Worse, they ripped at her girls. One stumbled, almost pulling her down, but Fawn wouldn't let go. Both screamed, open mouths and wide eyes, but she couldn't hear them over the howl of thousands of black cloaks running in terror and pain. They slammed her against the wall again, and dragged her along it. But worst of all, worse than anything, she felt her girls slipping from her hands. First one, then the other, wrenched from her grip by the black torrent. Another hard slam pinned her against the wall, and she felt the breath leave her body. Unable to turn, her legs buckled and her face slid down the rough concrete surface.

But she didn't hit the sidewalk. Instead, she floated, dragged against the rough wall without falling. Somehow, she was being supported, held up as if by a flooded river as it swirls around rocks, supporting her in its rush to fling her downstream.

But her girls were gone. She could see nothing of them, only black cloaks and clown masks.

And then the wall disappeared. She fell away from the blackness, into an open space, striking the base of a heavy glass door. Pushing herself up onto all fours, she spun around to dive again into the maelstrom for her girls.

Then she saw them. Each was held aloft by a battered black clown, safely above the crowd. And she realized that she had also been held up, supported by a third black laughing mask until she reached the safety of this entry-way.

They fell together into a small space, a shallow building alcove. It was barely big enough for them all. She and the girls collapsed against the glass door, cracking it in the process. Clinging to her, their tears came in yelling sobs of terror while the crowd ran past. Their three dark knights fell over them, pushing to get whatever shelter they could from the howling black banshee that ripped by.

After the flood of clowns came the jackboots. Not as many, slowed by their armor, and without shields, but with sticks swinging. As they passed, also on the run, she saw one of them swing at her clowns, hitting one as he tried to get out of the way. It was not a hard blow, poorly aimed and made weak by the stumbling speed of the jackboot, but it still connected. The clown mask jerked back with a spurt of red. As the last of the riot police streamed by, the injured clown slid to the ground in front of her, supported as much as possible by his companions.

An then, as suddenly as it had arrived, the wave of noise receded down the street. A quiet borne of exhaustion and shock descended around her. Only the sobs of her girls, coming in great gasping breaths, reached her ears.

"Honeys, are you all right?" she demanded as she turned each precious head over slowly, fearing the worst but seeing little blood.

She got two nods, two of the most precious gestures ever made by God. Both were bruised and scraped, but that was all.

"Where you parked?" came a demand from above.

What?

She looked up and saw her three clowns. They had removed their masks and cloaks, turning themselves, as if by a magic looking glass, into tall, gangling teenagers.

But that wasn't true. An hour ago, it might have been. But not now. They had stood against the banshee, risked their lives to stop her girls from becoming sacks of pounded meat. However young they looked, they were men.

"Come on. Where are you parked?" repeated the tall one, pulling her arm for emphasis.

"The Hertz garage," she answered, too dazed to think beyond that statement.

"Let's go," he said. And, half lifting her to her feet, trusting her to motivate her girls, he pulled them out into the quiet chaos of the empty street. The other two moved after him, one helping the other along. She had no choice but to follow.

They moved quickly over a sidewalk covered with the debris of battle. Only a few stragglers were visible, men and women trying to find shelter now that the storm had passed. Around her, the remains of a bad day covered everything with the smell of blood, fear, vomit, and tear gas.

As she reached the alley they had almost crossed only minutes ago, she looked down it. This time, there were no police, only cruisers with flashing lights blocking the other end. More of the same were parked across State Street on the other side of the river. But no one left either set of vehicles to come after them.

Under the Hertz sign, the garage office was open but deserted. The glass on the window had been broken by something that left blood behind, but, otherwise, all was intact. To avoid the glass, they took the ramp next to the office, eventually reaching her van. It was undamaged. The riot had not come into the building.

She took her daughters to the ladies room. Washing off the dirt, she straightened their clothes, combed their hair, and dried their tears. Again, she checked, but no blood. Both were quiet with shock, eyes big and skin pale, but otherwise truly unhurt. *Thank you, dear God.*

When she got her brood back to the van, she saw the three defrocked clowns sitting next to it on a curb. The injured one was no longer bleeding, but was covered with dried blood and leaned against the tall one for support. All looked battered, much the worse for the day.

The two uninjured ones sat more erect when they saw her approach. Then the tall one stood up.

"We need a ride," he said. It wasn't phrased as a request, but she knew it was. It just didn't come out that way. Perhaps he was too young to know how to ask properly. But the way he said it, just spitting it out, told her as much as the words could. He was scared. They all were. This was very important to them.

But also to her. She knew what the request really meant. This morning, she might not have, but the past hour had taught her much. Now, she knew her answer would be as significant as was her first badlands visit. Until now, she could be excused for anything that had happened, but giving these three a ride could not be explained away. It would be an unacceptable risk for her girls.

"Please," he added, as if suddenly realizing that he needed to rephrase his statement, but not knowing how.

Inside her van were several thousand illegal meds, packaged and ready for mailing. A false compartment in the bottom of her bed hid the gold she purchased earlier this trip. Next to it were bogus bills, hundreds of them. If she were searched because these three were found in her van, the authorities would find everything. She would face years in prison and never see her girls again. Whatever dangers they faced if she refused them a ride, it was nothing compared to what she risked if she gave them one.

Only one answer was possible. Only one would keep her girls safe. For their sakes, she must never take unnecessary chances, never stand out. She had no choice. These men would just have to understand that. Just like she understood about the brutal crushing chaos of that street, knew about those hands that held her girls above it all until they reached the alcove. Her sweetest darling girls.

Her mind told her mouth to say "No".

But it said "OK".

* * *

She was ready before she made her first turn out of the garage, so she had nothing to do but deal with the butterflies when she saw the roadblock ahead, across the Dearborn Street intersection.

Behind her, on the floor under the platform bed, lay the three young men. They were lying in various awkward poses, wrapped around packages and antiques in contortions that wouldn't look like human shapes from above the tarp that covered them. On top of it lay other treasures, enough to obscure the forms underneath but not enough to block the view down the length of the vehicle.

Next to her sat her two girls. Calmed and coached, they were good girls, and they were ready. They would need to be.

Less than a minute later, a Chicago police officer was standing next to her window.

"Hello, ma'am. May I see your driver's license and registration please?"

"Of course, officer," she said, handing him her genuine documents.

He handed them to another officer who took them away while he scrutinized her for any sign of worry. On the passenger side, another officer stood several feet away from the door and examined her girls. They looked back and, to their credit, smiled.

"What were you doing in the riot area, ma'am?"

"Hiding."

"Hiding, ma'am?"

"Yes, we were hiding in the Hertz parking garage in this van, waiting until we could get out safely."

"May I see the parking ticket?"

She was ready, having expected that question, and handed it to him. He examined it briefly, noted the date and time, then handed it back.

"Why were you in the area?"

"We came to visit the Children's Museum."

"Why didn't you park closer?"

"Officer, have you ever tried to find parking downtown after rush hour? This was the best we could do." Which was easy to say because it was true.

The other officer brought her documents back and, with a nod, handed them to her interrogator. He handed the registration back to her, but kept looking at the license. *Thank God it was the real one.*

"Do you have something to show you were at the museum? Tickets or anything?"

That stumped her. She had stubs at one time, but the day had not been normal. What had she done with them? Checking her pockets and purse, she got lucky and handed them over.

"Were you at the protest?" he asked as he examined the stubs.

"No, Officer. I have two small children. Would I risk their lives in something like that?"

The point seemed to tell.

"Thank you, ma'am." he said as he handed back her license and the stubs. "I would like to look in the back, please."

Now came the time for prayer. She sent the Lord a long silent running plea as she got out and walked around to the back of the van. As she opened the rear doors, she took the chance to catch his eye and gave him the warmest smile she could muster. As he bent over to examine her antiques, she tried to distract him by asking "What were they protesting?"

"Don't know, ma'am. I just work here," he said as he flipped the bedclothes.

Nothing, so he squatted down to look through the space under the bed, seeing all the way through the clutter to the front seat backs.

"What is all this stuff?" he asked as he straightened up.

"Antiques, officer. I buy and sell antiques." After a moments pause, she added "Can I interest you in a nice set of cuff links?"

Finally, that brought a smile.

"No, ma'am, thank you," he said as he closed the rear doors.

Two minutes later, as she was driving across Dearborn Street, with the first whiff of new smoke in her nostrils, she realized that she had sold her last set of 'antique" cuff links earlier that week. What would she have done if he had taken her up on her offer?

* * *

The men stayed under the tarp for some time, coming out only after they had crossed the Chicago River. The tall one sat on the floor, rocking in silence with the motion of the vehicle while the injured one half-lay next to him. Behind her, the stout one leaned forward between the seats to monitor their progress.

As they approached Desplaines, he said "Right here."

She hadn't promised taxi service, so she pulled to the curb instead. But, when she turned to tell them to get out, she saw meds scattered all over the floor. An open box had been knocked over in the ruckus. The tall protester was holding one of the packages, examining it with some interest.

"Please put those under the tarp," she asked.

He looked up, met her eyes, and then, without a word, swept them back into their open box.

And she changed her mind about the taxi service.

Five minutes and three turns later, the stout one asked her to pull over. They all got out and spoke briefly. Then stout one hobbled away down an alley, half-carrying the wounded one as he went. She watched them slide out of sight in the shadow.

"Thank you for your help."

Startled by a voice from behind her, she turned around to see her tall passenger standing next to the window. He must have walked around the back of the van while she was distracted by his companions because she hadn't noticed him until he spoke. Looking up at his face, she was struck again by his youth. Had she ever been that young?

"I'm sorry. I didn't mean to startle you." Her surprise must have shown.

"Thank you for saving my girls." she answered, expecting that that would end the conversation and he would leave. But it didn't. Instead, he stood there for a moment, as if in thought. Then, reaching some decision, he looked into her eyes and said "Join us."

It came out of the blue, as unexpected as a meteor.

"Excuse me?"

"Join us. If you don't fight now, while there's still a chance, what future will your girls have? You owe it to them."

"March in a clown suit?"

"There other things you could do. We need your help."

She looked back at him, too shocked to know what to say.

His next request hit her between the eyes. "Please, text me next time you cross" he blurted out and, with an awkward motion of his hand, offered her a note. In the fading light, she was able to read the words 'Angelo Pisa, RENAISSANCE Crossing'.

She looked back up at him, thinking there was more that she should say, but not sure what. It didn't matter, though, because he was already walking away down the alley.

Chapter 8

Why We Fight

"Any luck?" asked FEMA head Cassandra Carter in her deep, resonant voice.

"You want to get lost, you can't find a better place than the badlands," answered Mathew Hood with a shake of his head.

One of the ironies of life at the highest levels of American government is that privacy is hard to guarantee. Carter and Hood sat in a rented golf cart on this sunny morning specifically because of that problem. This meeting could have been held in either's spacious office, but neither could be sure some other organization, some group not directly under their control, would not have bugged the place as part of a criminal investigation. They were both, for good reasons, worried about such an investigation.

They didn't even have access to the obvious techniques of their opposition in the badlands. If they tried to use a government computer to cross the border, their VPN connection would not get through the firewall that protected bureaucratic Washington's cyberspace. Officially, it was there to prevent crackers from breaking into government databases. Not so officially, it also prevented corruption of the minions who worked behind its protection. If a Federal employee couldn't contact anyone anonymously using a VPN, he couldn't arrange transfer of and payment for any data he might steal.

So, like it or not, they were forced to use the old techniques. Sitting in a stationary golf cart, they looked like an Amazon and a troll dressed for the cover of Golf Digest. They picked the rental cart at random so they knew it was clean. It sat in the open at a randomly-chosen location. And boom box speakers broadcast their favorite musical noise out to the rest of the world. If anyone did manage to get into position to use a directional mike, all he would hear would be a compilation of Twisted Sister's greatest hits.

"I don't understand why you haven't been able to follow the payments," complained Carter.

"We've been over that," answered Hood. "Kohrob sends the gold to a re-mailer in Mexico. Pick that guy up, he'd say someone with a false ID picked up the package. Staking out the place wouldn't work, either, even if we could, since he's just reshipping the metal to another address."

"Can't the Mexican authorities help?"

"Supposed to. But all we get are roadblocks."

"So this guy keeps getting paid every month?" asked the tall woman.

"What's the alternative? We tried to stop, remember? He put the files up for sale, just like he said he would."

"We could eliminate all the physical evidence and claim the files were fabricated."

"OK. Good idea. How do we suddenly kill a thousand people without anyone noticing?"

"Move them back into the general population?"

"Cassi, most of them have relatives, right? Relatives that will come and get them after they make their legally-mandated weekly phone call. Then we have a thousand witnesses loose and eager to talk."

Carter was silent.

"No. We follow the plan."

"I could speed up the ambulance visits."

"No," answered the ugly man. "Someone would notice. Just keep the targets away from the Shelter population, and nature will take its course soon enough.

"I can't keep the lid on forever."

"If we have to, we'll stage something. But for now, just keep doing what you're doing. Who knows, maybe we can find this guy, what's his name?"

"Caper Oleander," said Carter.

"God, where do they get these names? Yeah, anyway, maybe we can get rid of him and solve everything."

The two lapsed back to silent thought, if it could be called that behind two speakers playing Twisted Sister. Neither liked the solution any more than the music, but it would work, and it was the best they could come up with.

As if to signal that the meeting was officially over, Hood reached back and turned off the boom box. It was time for a little golf.

* * *

Fawn sat in a quiet corner of a dark pub nursing a bottle of Dos Equis. With her back to the wall, she could scan the entire room as well as see her wheels' display that sat in front of her.

On the screen, in the world of the badlands, she and Angelo were 'sitting' alone together in an encrypted chat at MEET THE BEST.

Fawn: How's your friend?

Angelo: Stitches and a concussion, but he'll recover. We've got hard heads.

Fawn: Who's 'we'?

Angelo: Troublemakers. According to the governments of the world, anyway. That's why we have hard heads.

Fawn: Why?

Angelo: Lots of practice stopping nightsticks.

Fawn: Do you have any idea what I owe you?

Angelo: No, other way around. We owe you our lives.

Fawn: That's a bit extreme.

Angelo: Eight protesters disappeared after that riot. If you hadn't sneaked us out, it would have been eleven.

Fawn: Why you?

Angelo: Those eight were most of the coordinating committee. We were the rest.

Fawn: How do you know the police did it?

Angelo: Booking records show they were arrested and released. Station videos show each walked away from the station. No one saw any of them after that. Who do you think it was?

Fawn: Anyone could have picked them up off the street.

Angelo: Each was released alone about two in the morning. None of them called for a ride or an escort or even to say they were getting out. All were released from substations in bad parts of town, not from the main jail. What do you think?

Fawn: A setup?

Angelo: See why we owe you?

Fawn: Do you have children?

Angelo: Not that I know of.

Fawn: Sorry. I shouldn't have asked that.

Angelo: It's OK. You already know what I look like.

Fawn: Yeah. I guess so. If you had kids, you'd know why I owe you.

In her real-world pub, she took another pull on her beer.

Angelo: So, not that I don't appreciate it, but why this meeting? Ready to join us?

Fawn: Not tonight. Tell me about the protest. What were you trying to do?

Angelo: Shut down the Federal Reserve. You stumbled on fifty thousand of us making a public point on the subject.

Fawn: The guys that print our money? Aren't you people usually after the CIA or the cheating rich?

Angelo: We still are. Their paymaster seems like the best place to start. The Fed bankrolls them.

Fawn: So, if you're successful, won't they just start using Euros or Yen or something?

Angelo: No, sorry, I wasn't clear. I should have said the Fed creates the financial backing for both the CIA and the 'cheating rich', as you put it. Without that support, they would both die. The pieces of paper are actually printed by the Treasury Department. They don't matter anyway, they're just tokens. It's the creation of what underlies the printing that we're trying to stop.

Fawn: OK, I'll bite. If they don't print the money, how do they create it?

Angelo: Loans that are never repaid. They loan the banks money to pay each other's debts, so the owners and managers of those banks get rich spending the loans. It also buys most government debt so it indirectly finances their darker activities. Including the CIA.

Fawn: Won't those loans have to be repaid? They're not gifts, they're loans, right?

Angelo: Someday. If a dollar is still a dollar.

Fawn: I don't understand.

Angelo: You ever pass counterfeit?

Fawn: Excuse me?

Angelo: Sorry. I was going to make the point that counterfeiting is considered wrong because it dilutes the money supply. Pass a bogus dollar and all the real ones in circulation buy less.

Fawn: Why?

Angelo: There's a rough balance between all the money in existence and the amount of goods and services for sale. Increase the money by passing counterfeit and you make all dollars worth less.

Fawn: You're saying counterfeiting is wrong because it's stealing from people who hold dollars?

Angelo: More than that, it's stealing from anyone who is owed dollars in the future.

Fawn: Getting deep here.

Angelo: If I loan you ten dollars and then the money supply doubles, you only have to work half as hard to repay me. And, when I get it, it will only buy half of what it used to.

Fawn: Inflation?

Angelo: That's what it's called.

Fawn: OK. So what? Why take it out on the Fed?

Angelo: They're the biggest counterfeiter in the world. Last year they increased the number of dollars in circulation by $1,000 for every adult in this country.* And it all went in their pockets, not ours.

Fawn: I've had too many beers to go further down this road.

Angelo: Pretty and likes a drink. I could work with that.

Fawn: Down, Clown face. Why did it turn riot?

Angelo: It shouldn't have. We assembled at Lincoln Park, then

* M1, the paper bills we exchange with each other and money in our checking accounts, increased by $245 billion in 2012. www.federalreserve.gov/releases/h6/current/

planned to march down LaSalle to the Fed. But the police blocked LaSalle. So we took State. They reformed and blocked us where it crossed the river.

Fawn: So you sidestepped again?

Angelo: Couldn't. They closed the side streets back for five blocks so our only option was to back up. That's not something a large crowd can do easily.

Fawn: But you could do it?

Angelo: We were trying when they charged us. Boom, instant riot.

Fawn: You make it sound like they wanted it.

Angelo: What do you think? You were there. Did you see any violence before the tear gas?

Fawn: Why would they do it? What would be the point?

Angelo: They wanted arrests. You can't lock up a peaceful protester, but you can if he becomes a rioter. Or make him vanish.

The word hit home. *Vanish,* she thought. *Just like my husband.*

* * *

Chang: Where did you get this idea?

Fawn: Someone in chat suggested it.

Chang: In open chat?

Fawn: Yes.

Chang: Thank goodness you came to me before you tried it.

Fawn: Why? It sounds great.

Chang: Not even close. First, smart phone operating systems are all proprietary executables. That means you can't know what's in them.

Fawn: So?

Chang: So they could put snitch code in the OS. You would never know if they did.

Fawn: Why would they?

Chang: To comply with a government mandate. If DHS wants them to, it's the only way they can stay in business.

Fawn: So someone could be listening when I cross?

Chang: Not could. Would. And not just someone. DHS. No cell phone manufacturer is going to turn down a DHS subpoena.

Fawn: How would they know to pick on me? There are millions of phones out there. They can't listen to all of them.

Chang: No, but they could be recording all of them. And they will be listening to the ones that make overseas VPN connections. So if you use a phone as your wheels, they will be listening to you.

Fawn: OK, but so what? It can't help them. If I use a false ID to get the phone, they can't trace me, can they?

Chang: DHS can tease an amazing amount of information from a set of seemingly unrelated facts. If they have snitch code in your phone, they will know everything you say. Not only you, but all your friends will be recorded. That is a pretty good block of data. They will find something in it. The only way you can protect them and yourself is to not let DHS get those facts.

Fawn: OK. I see that now. Thank you.

Chang: No, child, it is worse than that. If you cross with your phone, they will know who you are even if they don't have snitch code running on it.

Fawn: How? They have to know it's my phone first, don't they?

Chang: They know. You had to registered it with an ID or traceable land-line when you bought it. That's civ law now.

Fawn: What if I use a false ID? I'd be OK then, right?

Chang: Do you know that all cell phones have GPS trackers embedded in them?

Fawn: Just for emergencies.

Chang: Child. Do you really believe that?

Fawn: It's not true?

Chang: It is true. But not the whole truth.

Fawn: Meaning?

Chang: Meaning the tracker also tells DHS where your phone is at all times, not just when you dial 911.

Fawn: Great if I lose it, I guess.

Chang: Fawn. This is serious.

Fawn: Can't I just turn the tracker off?

Chang: No.

Fawn: But there's a menu option to turn it off.

Chang: That is just for commercial use. Turning it off that way will only stop people who want to sell you something from learning where you are. It doesn't turn off the tracker.

Fawn: I thought it did.

Chang: Then you were wrong, child. Even turning it off won't help. Your phone sends your location as long as it is connected to the system. Unless you pull the battery or go out of range, your phone company will always know where you are.

Fawn: But that's not the DHS, is it? Doesn't the DHS still have to get a court order or something?

Chang: There is a secret anti-terrorist court that issues blocks of pre-approved search orders to the DHS ahead of time. All they have to do is fill in your name.

Fawn: Are you sure?

Chang: The fact that you can't turn the tracker off proves that it is there for DHS use.

Fawn: So a false registration won't help?

Chang: No. Regardless of whose name your phone is in, it will still tell DHS where you spend the night. In the morning, they can still pay you a visit.

Fawn: But it seems so nice, not having to lug a laptop around.

Chang: Sorry, child, until they make open-source operating systems for smart phones, it won't be safe to use them for wheels.

Fawn: What a shame. It would have made life so much easier.

Chang: Get lazy and you get caught. Your sloth is worth more to them than a thousand policemen.

She let that sink in for a moment, then she said:

Chang: Child, did you check the rep of the guy that was pushing this idea?

Fawn: It was just open chat.

Chang: Meaning 'No'?

Fawn: No, I didn't check him.

Chang: Child, what am I going to do with you? Always check out everyone you deal with. Always. Got that?

Fawn: Yes.

Chang: OK. Let's do it together. What was his name?

There was a pause in the text stream as Fawn looked at her logs. When she found the name, she passed it over. More time passed while Mrs. Chang made a check.

Chang: Heavens, child. Look at his rep. Look at it now. Go ahead. I'll wait.

Fawn called it up. There was a long pause while Mrs. Chang gave her time to read and think.

Chang: Are you looking at it?

Fawn: Yes.

Chang: What do you see?

Fawn. Just normal stuff.

Chang: Do you see that three badlanders have flagged him as a possible DHS snitch?

Fawn: Yes.

Chang: Is that what you call 'normal stuff'?

Fawn: No. Sorry. I understand.

Chang: Good. Then you must do something for me.

Fawn: OK.

Chang: The ideas this man is pushing are more than just negligent. They are intentionally deceptive. You owe it to your fellow badlanders to tell them so.

Fawn: I do?

Chang: Just because we do not have a government does not mean we are not moral people. Do you understand that?

Fawn: No.

Chang: No society can exist without morals, ours included.

Fawn: People here commit murder!

Chang: No one gets killed in the badlands, so our moral code does not include murder.

Fawn: What then?

Chang: Dishonesty, for one thing. Deceit hurts everyone here. That's why reps are so important.

Fawn: Is that why you want me to file on this guy?

Chang: Yes. If you don't warn other badlanders, DHS will get more of us.

Fawn: Like that red-green password thing?

Chang: Yes. Just the same. Protecting each other is very much in our moral code.

There was a pause in the text string as Fawn thought.

Chang: Will you file?

Fawn: How?

Chang: Put a note in his rep file.

Fawn: But that's so much work.

Chang: Someday, Fawn, someone may save your life for no other reason than they think it is the right thing to do. Consider this payback in advance. That's what moral codes are all about. Write the note.

Fawn didn't answer.

Chang: Fawn, this is not all about you. Will you do it?

Fawn: OK

Chang: Do I have your word?

Fawn: Yes. I promise.

Chang: Good. And, child, be more careful in the future. Please.

DHS really is trying to get you. This is not paranoia. It is real. Unless you want to spend the rest of your life sleeping with the lights on, you have got to be more careful.

* * *

A week later, Fawn found herself in another private chat.

Angelo: Where did you get this list?

Fawn: A snitch. Any of your friends on it?

Angelo: All of them.

Fawn: Which is?

Angelo: Twelve. Who's the snitch?

Fawn: Someone offering files for sale on all those names.

Angelo: All the names on this list? He has files on them?

Fawn: That's what he claims.

Angelo: What's in them?

Fawn: FEMA data. He says everyone on the list is in a FEMA camp and he's selling copies of the files.

Angelo: Which camp?

Fawn: He won't say.

Angelo: How much?

She told him.

Angelo: Let me see what I can do.

Not 'Ouch'. Not 'Wow'. Not 'Hey, bimbo, you think I'm rich?'

Fawn: Are you rich?

Angelo: No.

There was a pause in the text string while she waited him out.

Angelo: I know someone who is.

Fawn: Rich enough to buy the entire list?

Angelo: Rich enough to consider it.

Fawn: Who?

Angelo: He doesn't want his name used.

Fawn: Well, tell him I get one of the files. That's my price.

Angelo: Which one?

She sent him her husband's name.

Angelo: Got it. I'll get back to you.

* * *

"So how serious was that thing last week?" asked Arnold Wilson Parker.

Late the night before, in spite of his hectic schedule, Maxwell Stein had flown to Colorado by private jet. Now they sat together, alone in Parker's large study.

"You mean the riot?" asked the Governor of the Chicago Federal Reserve.

Parker nodded.

Stein shrugged. "Cops had it under control. I'm surprised they got so far, but that gave us a chance to hit it hard. Press looks better that way."

"Did it get close to you?"

"Naa, never got across the river. Couldn't even see it from my office." Stein's office was the top floor of the Chicago Federal Reserve building, as befitted the most influential governor of the system. Both men knew that influence was exclusively due to the fact that Parker's Foundations owned a large number of member banks in the system. Their votes put Stein's agenda through.

"Are there more coming?"

"Protests?"

Parker nodded.

"Probably. Police will handle them, just like this one. That's not why we have to stop these people."

"The demonstrators?"

"The badlanders," answered Stein.

"You're worried about the criminal element spreading?"

"No, no. Police take care of that, too. I'm worried about the example they set."

"Meaning?"

"Central banks have convinced the world that debt is the best form of money. That's why we can print as much as we want. No central bank anywhere in the world could survive without the public believing it."

"That debt is money?"

"Right."

"So the badlands demonstrations are hurting that?"

"Yes. No. I mean not the kind that turn into riots. But their very existence is a demonstration that will kill us if we don't get them first."

"Why?"

"Because they use equity for money."

"Instead of debt?"

"Yes. They use ownership of something tangible. Equity. In this case, it happens to be gold."

"So why is that a problem?"

"Because of the example it sets. If they run a successful economy on equity, run it publicly for the entire world to see, it will destroy our ability to control the public through debt. Through their money. Neither of us can afford that. You've got to break the badlands."

Of that Arnold Wilson Parker had no doubt. To do it, though, someone had to get at their organization. Their communications, planning, and leaders. Someone had to find the head of the snake. So far Matthew Hood had not been very successful at the effort.

Chapter 9

Life In The Badlands

The evening gown was wedged between heavy coats like a fashion model in a bread line. Fawn passed it by the first time she saw it, more interested in finding something warm. But the sparkle pulled her back. Silver threads dancing on black silk. Impractical. But she couldn't stop looking at it.

She had never owned such a dress before, never even held one in her hand. Grandeur and impractical beauty. Taking it to the only mirror, she admired its lines as it draped over her torso, almost touching the floor. High-cut, with no cleavage, it covered her chest all the way to her throat. Restraint in the age of garish sexuality.

The fit was good. And so was the price. But it was just too impractical. Perhaps that was why it had been on the rack for so long. And she needed a coat. Reluctantly, she put it back.

So, when the invitation came the next day, she knew exactly what she would wear. She needed that dress. It's one thing to see a good bank statement, quite another to feel it. Right now, she needed to touch some real, physical proof. And that dress, that exotic ebony trophy, would do just fine.

Four days later, she sat alone in one of the more expensive restaurants in town, sheathed in that magnificent statement of her new worth. Small pieces of cut glass dangled from each ear, visible under a short haircut. Only her face looked out of place, bare of any makeup.

But that, too, was a statement. Everything else about her appearance was so different from her old life, she wanted it all to be new. Makeup would ruin that, chaining her mind to what she had been. So her freckles, like her earrings, danced as she spoke to the waiter.

Not that it mattered. Even without makeup, she was the most striking woman in the room. She sat with her back to a dim corner, her open wheels nestled in front of her among the cloth napkins. The screen read:

> System: Nairobi Bombay, female, DARK CITIES, has entered the room
>
> Fawn: This is weird.
>
> Nairobi: What's the matter? Never been to a dinner party before?

Fawn: Not one where I can't eat.

Nairobi: Don't you have a plate of food in front of you? Those were the rules, remember?

Fawn: Yes. Well, no, actually, but it's on order. That counts, doesn't it?

Nairobi: As long as it gets there and you eat it, it counts. Think of this as going out to dinner with friends.

Fawn: But we're not at the same table.

Nairobi: Use your imagination.

System: David Bowie, male, ROCKY ROAD, has entered the room

Bowie: Oh, God, what luck. I got two beauties all to me self.

Nairobi: Hello, Bowie.

Fawn: How you been doing?

Bowie: Good. Thank you, love, for asking. Business has been good.

Nairobi: Can you talk about business?

Bowie: You mean what do I do? Buy low and sell high, like everyone else.

Nairobi: Sell what?

Bowie: Anything that doesn't have a title. And you, Fawn?

Fawn: Meds. I distribute meds, pass a little scrip.

System: Angelo Pisa, male, RENAISSANCE, has entered the room.

Nairobi: You're late, Angelo.

Bowie: Bugger all, competition's here.

Fawn: Welcome, clown-face.

Angelo: Traffic, sorry.

Fawn: Traffic in the badlands?

Angelo: No, getting to the pub. Sorry.

Nairobi: S'OK.

Fawn: Get money for the names?

Angelo: Maybe. Later, OK?

Fawn: OK. Hey, know anything about the riots in Los Angeles?

Angelo: Not a good dinner topic.

Nairobi: Why? I heard they weren't bad.

Bowie: Who told you? The sodding civ press?

Angelo: People are getting too hungry. Food stamps aren't enough any more.

Nairobi: What do you know?

Angelo: We had people there. They count, with names, over 200 dead. We don't know what started it, but the cops fired on the crowd and some of them fired back. I expect cops were hit, but I don't know how many. One of our guys gets the Spot satellite feed real-time, says at least 10 city blocks are still on fire.

Nairobi: Any word on what touched it off?

Angelo: No. Maybe a roadblock, but no one knows for sure.

Fawn: Hey, my food's here. Lets do pictures so I can eat.

Nairobi: Right. Has everyone got their food now?

Angelo: No, wait, I just ordered.

Fawn: Yeah, but you were late. I'm hungry.

Angelo: I couldn't help it, the roadblocks make everyone late.

Fawn: You should have left earlier.

Nairobi: OK, take a picture and then eat. They don't have to all be posted at the same time.

Fawn: Hey, clown face. My girls want to know why you wear masks when you protest.

Angelo: Because the only way to be free anymore is to be anonymous.

Fawn: Meaning?

Angelo: Protest the government, they cut your food stamps. Or sic the IRS on you, cut your Social Security benefits, kick you off Medicare, or get you fired. No one speaks up anymore unless its anonymous.

Fawn: OK, got my picture. Here it is.

A picture of a plate of food posted for all to see. There was a tablecloth, real glasses, and fine cutlery. The light looked like it came from candles.

Nairobi: Damn, girl, your business is doing well.

Bowie: Hey, can I eat with you next time?

Angelo: OK, what's on the plate?

Fawn: Chicken, potatoes, broccoli.

Bowie: You're having wine!

Fawn: Of course.

Bowie: You sure I can't eat with you?

With a smile, Fawn took her first bite. The satisfaction of being here, of being accepted by people who cared about her, gave her a warm glow that surpassed anything the good food could provide.

Nairobi: Hey, partner, did you see the first issue of Badlands Sources?

Fawn: You got it out? Our new newspaper?

Nairobi: Our new blog. BadlandsSources.net. Check it out after dinner. We hit the street with a bombshell.

Fawn: The list?

Nairobi: All 2,192 names.

Bowie: What list?

Nairobi: Fawn got a list of people held by FEMA.

Angelo: This the same list you gave me?

Nairobi: Yes. I just published it.

Fawn: We just published it.

Nairobi: Right, partner. We just published it.

* * *

It took almost three weeks for Nobu Bara to ask for another meeting. When it came, Fawn found herself sitting alone in a dark pub, huddled over a glowing laptop, while simultaneously living in a private chat room that had no physical location.

Nairobi: He said no?

Nobu Bara, owner of KISS'N TELL Snitch House, explained the bad news.

Bara: Yes. Oleander said no. The files aren't for sale.

Angelo: How much more do you think it would take?

Bara: I'm sorry. He didn't say 'not enough'. He said 'no'. Not for sale.

Angelo: I can get the bid raised.

I wish I had rich friends, thought Fawn.

Bara: It won't help. He is simply not interested. Believe me, I'm as disappointed as you are. But he seems firm.

Nairobi: Why? With a good offer on the table?

Bara: Perhaps he has a better one.

Angelo: No. If he did, he'd play us off against each other. Hold an auction.

Nairobi: Blackmail.

Fawn: What?

Nairobi: Someone is paying him to keep the files off the market.

Fawn: Can we find out who?

Nairobi: I'll look around, but I doubt it. Secrets are hard to break in the badlands unless someone wants them broken.

* * *

The Bastard sat at a red light, second car in the right lane, when he spotted his runaway whore. She drove the first car in the oncoming left turn lane. Crossing traffic filled the intersection. He took advantage of the opportunity to examine her face, her hair. If that woman wasn't the bitch, then it was her twin. Shorter hair and no makeup, but otherwise she looked the same. And she hadn't seen him yet. Unlike his restless vision, hers concentrated on the left turn signal.

Ever since she ran on him, he had been consumed with the need for revenge. In the pimp game, you can't let them leave you, can't give them that power. But she did just that, embarrassing him in front of his fellow businessmen, turning him from a threat into a laughing stock. Women loved the threat, that little tingle of fear when he looked at them hard. It filled his stable. By leaving him, by escaping without pain or scars, she didn't just hurt his ego. She made it hard for him to keep the other whores in line.

But now he had found her. Time to set things right.

The cross traffic stopped, the signal changed. She pulled into the intersection and turned left, passing in front of him. As she did so, her profile showed itself to him, outlined in a brief close-up that left no doubt in his mind. Yes, this was his best whore, the one that thought she could escape. He smiled as he considered the ways she would have to pay.

When the last turning car cleared the intersection, the one in front of him pulled out. He followed it, also making a right, and dropped in far behind her but still within sight. Moving quickly, he worked his way through the pack, closing to within three cars of her vehicle. The weather was cloudy, with intermittent rain. That, along with the dirtiness of his windshield, was enough to hide his face from her even at this short distance.

He wanted to close and sideswipe her, force her off the road, then beat her senseless. Once, not long ago, he would have done just that. But age mellows us all. Instead, he followed. Carefully, sometimes in the lane behind her, sometimes to the left or right, skillfully avoiding potholes and missing pieces of pavement. Always, he was ready for a quick lane-change if she chose to make a turn. But she did not turn. She drove straight, like a cow down the slaughterhouse chute.

As he followed her, he realized she must be doing well. She was driving a new van, unescorted, not even working. Her new pimp was too soft. He would never have let her keep that much money. Perhaps the van wasn't hers. Almost certainly, it was not one of his competitors. They had better taste.

A plan formed in his mind. If the van wasn't hers, tracing her through its tag wouldn't work. She was driving very conservatively, though, and the traffic was not heavy, so following her was easy. He would spend the day doing that, find out everything he could about her new life: Where she lived, where she worked, where she shopped. Once he had that information, he would plant a tracker and bug in her van. Patience would pay off. If he was careful, learning everything he could about her new life, he would know all he needed to make her and her little cunts pay for running out on him.

Chapter 10

The Bastard

Two weeks and his patience paid off. Early on, he had copied the VIN from her dashboard. That, the right contacts, and a little financial persuasion got him a door key. Two days later, after darkness came, he slipped a tracker and cell phone bug under her dash.

Now he followed her from a safe distance. His laptop did all the work. He knew where she went and even what she said to her twins when she took them to school. He knew everything there was to know, yet he was more puzzled than ever. He knew she was getting money from somewhere, but she wasn't making it on her back. He couldn't see where it was coming from.

His first thought was drugs. That was an obvious source of income, one that he had often used in the past himself. Yet she didn't seem to associate with any of the right sorts of people. In fact, the unusual thing was that she didn't seem to meet anyone at all. And that was a shame, since he would have liked nothing better than to catch her breaking the law. The law protects those that follow it. But step outside it, and you don't dare call it for help. He smiled again at that thought. If she were dealing, she was free meat. Just thinking about it gave him an erection.

Four days later, when she stopped at a UPS store to pick up a package, it hit him. She was selling drugs, just not the way he was used to. Someone was mailing them to her in bulk and then she was repackaging and distributing them through the mail.

What was she selling? Cocaine? No, she would have too hard a time sealing the packages. The drug dogs would find them. That was also true for any of the obvious other substances like heroin, marijuana, or hash. It had to be something that was already smell-free. Pharmaceuticals. She was selling pills, prescription pills. Painkillers? Yes, probably painkillers, they would pay the best. *Good for her,* he thought, *she would be very well off by now.* When he paid her a visit, he would make his dick and bank account happy at the same time.

Fawn, of course, knew nothing about the new turn of events that was about to transpire in her life. Two days later, she was thinking of an evening with her girls, about their dinner together, as she wheeled her grocery cart up to the side of the van. Unlocking the windowless cargo door, she opened it as she turned towards her cart. From within the darkness of the open vehicle, a hand reached out and grabbed a fistful of blouse, catching as much of her left breast in its grip as possible. The pain would have brought her to her knees, but he never gave her that chance, instead jerking her into the darkness with the force of a catapult. Her shins struck the door-sill, her left hand the edge of the rear door. As she slammed against the far wall, she screamed. But, before sound could get up, he struck a sharp blow across her ear with a pistol.

"Quiet, bitch," he whispered, then struck her again. The second blow wasn't necessary, the first had made his point, and they both knew it. The second was solely for his amusement.

"Hey. bitch. See this?" he asked, pushing the muzzle painfully against her cheek.

She nodded, too scared to do anything more.

"This will kill you and your little cunts if you give me any trouble. I'll hunt them down after you bleed to death through your pussy." To make the point clear, he pushed the muzzle hard into her crotch and cocked the hammer. "Are you going to be a good little whore?"

Again she nodded.

"Good. Now reach out and pull those groceries into the car." Shaking, trying not to vomit, she did as she was told.

He made her drive, kneeling behind her seat in the darkness. In his right hand was his pistol, muzzle driven forcefully into her right armpit. His other arm reached around the seat. His left hand was under her bra, squeezing her breast for support. At the same time, he pinched a thumbnail as deeply as he could into her nipple, making him so hard he had to keep reminding himself not to do any permanent damage to the merchandise.

She was sobbing silently when they pulled into the parking spot he had picked out earlier. After they stopped, he grabbed her hair, jerking her back onto the cargo bed and shoved her facedown against the floor. She tried to struggle again, briefly, until he slapped her ear with his cupped hand. Pain got such good results that he had to constantly remind himself not to overdo it.

Through her whimpering, he tied her face-down on the floor, one wrist to each front seat and her ankles together, pulled tight to the rear door. Reaching under her hips, he undid her belt, pulling her pants and panties down below her bottom. With one hand, he grabbed her hair and jerked her head back as he straddled her thighs.

"Now, bitch, it's time for school. Pay attention, OK?"

With his free hand, he guided himself into her. His first thrust was done quick and sudden, giving her sphincter no time to relax. Her screams only encouraged him, each new thrust buying him more pleasure at the cost of her pain.

When he finished the lesson, he wiped himself clean on the back of her blouse. Then he pulled his pants back on while the results of his instruction pooled inside her, mingled with her blood and feces.

Moving to the front of the van, he turned and faced her, sitting down between the two seats. Looking into her wet face, he let his gaze linger for a moment, meeting her puffy eyes. Then, reaching under the front seat, he pulled out a thin stick, about ten inches long. One end was enclosed in a small wad of duct tape, about the size of a golf ball. Snaking out from the tape next to the stick was two feet of stiff colored string. He held it in front of her so she could see it clearly.

"Know what this is?" he asked.

She shook her head.

"Sure you do. Look good. I made it myself. Tricky, you know."

He held it closer for her inspection, twirling it slowly between his thumb and forefinger.

"The bird shot is the most important part. Powder's important too, of course, but getting the shot right is the key."

He admired his work for another second, then asked "It's kind of pretty, don't you think?"

Then she recognized the string. It was fuse. He wasn't holding a ball of tape on a stick, he was holding a firecracker. Suddenly she knew what he was about to do.

He smiled when he saw the terror wash over her face.

"You've figured it out? Good." Then, without another word, he half-crawled over her back. She felt his hands on her naked bottom as she begged, pleaded with him to forgive her. It did no good. The searing pain still came as he used the stick to shove the taped ball deep into her injured rectum.

She heard the flick of a disposable lighter.

"Now, now. Stop squirming, you're making it hard to light".

The fuse begin to sputter. As he moved back to the front of the van, the first whiff of burning powder reached her nostrils.

Reaching the dash, he turned around and sat so he could look into her face.

"Like I was saying, the key is to get the amount of shot right. Too much, and you die right away. Too little and you live. If you call having to shit in a bag for the rest of your life living, that is."

"I think I've got it just about right, though. The last bitch took three weeks to die."

She felt the first warmth against the back of her thighs. The fuse must be laying against her pants, the heat from the ash soaking through. Closing her eyes, she screamed.

He slapped her, using the sharp sting of it to get her attention.

"Look at me, bitch. Look into my eyes. I want to watch you when it goes off."

Bits of burnt fuse were falling on her bare bottom now. Normally, that would be quite painful, but her terror masked the pain. She felt nothing but the fear, saw nothing but his eyes and the smile on his face.

"No one walks on me and lives, bitch. No one."

The heat advanced into the cleft between her cheeks. Searing heat. But there was nothing she could do. Try as she might, she couldn't expel the deadly suppository. Her rectal muscles were too damaged by his earlier assault.

"Wait for it. Wait for it. This will be so good."

She felt the fuse burn past her sphincter. Mucus and blood now provided some protection against the flame, but she could still feel the heat advancing steadily inside her. She couldn't tell how close it was to the end, but the flame couldn't be more than seconds from the fuse end.

"Here it comes. Here it comes. Yes!"

Nothing happened. Time passed, but nothing happened.

"Aw. It must have been a dud," he said with mock disappointment.

Her sense of relief was overwhelming. It flooded through her like a drug, sweeping all other emotions away. She would live. At least for a while longer, she would live.

"God must love you."

More silence.

"Don't ever test me again," he said, then looked into her eyes in silence, watching them as she quietly cried. Her muted sobs brought back the smile to his lips. In a conciliatory tone, he said "None of that had to happen. If you had just stayed with me, you could be happy right now. You know that, don't you?"

She had been with him long enough to know the expected response. Silently, knowing that any sound might provoke him again, she nodded.

"What's in the box?" he asked, pointing to the delivery she picked up earlier that morning.

She didn't know what to say, so, fearing more pain, she said nothing.

He reached behind the driver's seat and picked up a long thin tube. As soon as she saw it, she started shaking again. Uncontrollably. She knew what a cattle prod looked like.

He saw her reaction. "Ah, you remember this, don't you? Good. Then you know I'm only going to ask once more. It will be in your best interests to make me happy by answering. OK?"

She nodded.

"Good. Now, what's in the box?"

"Pills."

"Ah, good. That spirit of cooperation will get you far. Now, where's the money?"

"What money?"

He put the end of the prod against her lips, his finger on the trigger and said "Aw, don't do that. You were being so good."

Then he shoved harder, jamming it past her lips until it struck her teeth. "I know you have money, you have to in this business. Where do you keep it?"

She had no money, only scrip and gold that hadn't been sent out yet. But he wouldn't know the bills were counterfeit.

"I'll show you."

"No. You will not. You will tell me where it is."

And she did.

He opened the cargo door and stepped into the alley, leaving her tied face down. Pulling a clasp knife from his pocket, he opened it. A polished serrated blade glinted in the dim shadows. Reaching back into the van, he slashed downwards. The line that bound her right wrist parted with the snap of a rubber band.

"I know where you live, cunt," he said as he closed the weapon and slid it back into his pocket. "I'll be in touch."

Then the door slammed closed. In the silence that followed, she lay sobbing on the hard steel floor.

Dusk settled. The van interior dimmed through the colors of the sunset.

Still she did not move. She was pinned, not by her pain, but by her loss. She had seen the way out, had almost escaped to it. But now that dream was gone.

The brutal world of organized meat-space had dragged her back. Once again, she was trapped between clashing governments, corporations, and mafias, to be ground into filth by their struggles. The Bastard was just their representative, their agent. He existed because he did their bidding or because they wouldn't stop him. Either way, it didn't make any difference. What mattered was that he was again her lord and master.

* * *

> Chang: It is all right. It is all right, child. Please, calm down. Losing a shipment of meds is not the end of the world. These things happen.

Fawn: cant

Chang: Of course you can. Take a deep breath.

Fawn: not that cant

Chang: Can't what, child? Is there something more?

Fawn struggled to type the words, to say she wouldn't be crossing any more.

Fawn: y

To put it into writing, to actually see the words, would be the final step in making it real. Tears streamed down her face again. She could just walk away without saying anything, but she owed Mrs. Chang an explanation. Yet her hands wouldn't type it.

Chang: Please, child, tell me about it.

Still, her fingers wouldn't move.

Chang: Child, are you still there?

Fawn: y

Chang: Perhaps if you could tell me how you came to lose the shipment?

Fawn: he took it

Chang: Someone took it?

Fawn: yes

Chang: Who took it?

Fawn: bastard

Chang: How did he get it?

No answer came back.

Chang: Did he attack you?

Fawn: yes

Chang: Where are you now?

Fawn: bar

Chang: Are you crying?

Fawn: little

Chang: Please, child, this is not serious. But attracting attention by crying in a public place is. Please, compose your face. Can you do that?

Fawn: Yes

More time passed before the next message.

Fawn: OK better

Chang: You're not crying any more?

Fawn: No.

Chang: Good. Now tell me exactly what happened. How did this man know you had a meds shipment?

Fawn: He was in my van. Hiding.

Chang: What happened?

Fawn: I opened the door

Another pause in the text stream occurred.

Chang: Fawn?

Chang: Fawn, are you still there?

Chang: Fawn Please Answer

Fawn: Sorry. I'm OK now.

Chang: Did he hurt you?

Fawn: y

Chang: Fawn, please, you have to pull yourself together if I am to help you.

Fawn: OK

Chang: Take a deep breath.

Fawn: OK

Chang: Are you crying again?

Fawn: No

Chang: Good. Now, please, tell me everything that he did.

Fawn: He stole my meds. Scrip. Gold too.

Chang: Is that all he did?

Fawn: n

Chang: Did he hurt you?

Fawn: y

Chang: How badly? Do you need to go to a hospital?

Fawn: No

Chang: Child, did he rape you?

Fawn: y

Chang: Did you call the police?

Fawn: n scared

Chang: Are you in any danger now?

Fawn: n but girls at home.

Chang: Your daughters? Fawn, are you worried about your family?

Fawn: y

Chang: He knows where you live?

Fawn: ys

Chang: If you give me your real name I can get them a bodyguard.

Fawn: No.

Chang: Do you own a gun?

Fawn: No.

Chang: I can ship one to your box overnight. You'll have it tomorrow.

Fawn: no pls no

Chang: It may make a big difference. Please, just as a backup until we get another solution working. Please. OK?

Fawn: No cant touch one NO.

Chang: OK. Do you know the man's real name and address?

Fawn: Yes.

Chang: Will you send it to me?

There was a pause in the text string.

Fawn: cant cross any more

There. She had finally said it.

Chang: What child?

Fawn: I cant come back

In the Nigerian night, a sweating black man suddenly became very cold. One of his fallen angels was slipping back into the darkness.

Chang: Why?

Fawn: he real u not

Chang: That is not true.

No reply came back.

Chang: Please, child. Let me prove you wrong. Please.

Fawn: How?

Chang: Give me his name and address.

She knew that act would be fatal if the Bastard ever found out. Her girls would die. No mouse could ever take the chance. Better to live the rest of her life hiding in a dark hole.

Fawn: He'll kill them.

Chang: Give me his name and I can stop him. Forever.

Fawn: What if you don't?

Chang: If you go back, he will kill them some day anyway.

And she new that was true. It was why she had left in the first place.

Chang: Child, he may kill them either way. But what if he doesn't? What kind of life will they have then? Do you want them to live the rest of their lives as victims?

Fawn: But they could die.

Chang: Yes. Life is dangerous. It always has been, always will be.

Do you want them to live it as mice, waiting to be stepped on, or as tigers, in control of their own destinies?

* * *

The Nigerian male known to Fawn as Mai Lee Chang sat in a private chat with Milk Weed, owner of the LET'S DO IT MY WAY Persuasion House. They had been friends and business associates for many years, though Milk Weed knew the Nigerian by his real badlands name*, not the one he used with Fawn.

Chang: He raped her and robbed her.

Weed: Are you sure?

Chang: Yes. I trust this one. If she said it happened, it happened.

Weed: What do you want to do?

Chang: Whatever we do, it has to be soon and hard. Her life is in danger.

Weed: She give you a name?

Chang: Yes. And an address.

Weed: Pass it over.

There was a brief pause in the text string, then

Weed: I'll have someone get a picture to confirm the ID.

Chang: Will that take long?

Weed: Maybe 24 hours. I can put a guard on her till then.

Chang: No. I suggested that, she said no. Won't give up her real ID.

Weed: Then all you can do is get her to hide.

Chang: She's already gone to ground, used her kit ID and cash for a hotel room.

Weed: That ought to do.

Chang: And if she confirms the pictures?

Weed: We'll have someone fix the problem.

---

* To avoid confusion, the Nigerian owner of GOBI DESERT will be referred to as Mai Lee Chang throughout the rest of this book.

Chang: How?

Weed: You just want a message delivered? Or more?

Chang: Let me talk with her, find out exactly what happened. Let me know as soon as you have the pics.

* * *

Milk Weed got the pictures in less than 12 hours. It took a little longer for Chang to get them confirmed and get details on the attack. Still, in much less than a day, they were back in a private chat.

Weed: How is she?

Chang: He hurt her pretty bad.

Weed: She still safe?

Chang: Well hidden. With her girls. We can't keep them there forever, though.

Weed: She confirm the pics?

Chang: Yes.

Weed: OK. How do you want to handle it?

Chang: I want more than a message.

Weed: The STALINGRAD boys?

Chang: No. They enjoy their work too much, get carried away.

Weed: You don't want him dead then?

Chang: If it were up to me, I would use him for a Juju rite. But she says no. Says vengeance is wrong.

Weed: What then?

Chang: No killing or maiming. But anything short of that would be fine.

Weed: You want him scarred? It's easier with the cops if we don't leave marks.

Chang: OK, no marks. But give him great pain.

Weed: Does he know she's a badlander?

Chang: No, he thinks she is a pusher.

Weed: I assume you want the badlands link to stay hidden?

Chang: Yes.

Weed: We'll play up the pusher angle instead?

Chang: Fine.

Weed: This won't be cheap. Does she have the money?

Chang: If she cannot cover it, I will. She is one of mine.

Weed: OK.

Chang: How long?

Weed: Two days max. She should be able to come out by the end of the week.

* * *

They came up behind the Bastard as he walked to the grocery store, one on either side. The one to his left hit him with a Taser, the other supported him as he slumped.

They did it as he passed a parked delivery van. The side door slid open and his assailants shoved him through it. Seconds later, all were gone in the Cleveland traffic.

Not that anyone cared, but, if someone had been looking for him, they would have noticed that the Bastard disappeared for a week. When he showed up again, he was lying in the filth of a local dump, alive and unmarked, but otherwise seared for life.

Electric shocks, psychosis-inducing drugs, and insulin injections had scarred his soul. Burned into it as if by a branding iron was a message: Fawn works for very powerful drug dealers who don't like having their employees raped. Stay away from her or die.

To say that the Bastard had friends would be to torture the definition of friendship. It would be more accurate to say he had business associates. One of the first things he did after cleaning himself up and regaining control of his bodily functions was to make calls to several of those individuals. One in particular was quite interested in what he had to say.

* * *

Two of them were waiting for Fawn when she came out of the grocery store. One fell into step on each side as she pushed her wobbling cart over the cracked parking lot. Neither made any menacing gestures, but both were big enough for their size alone to cause concern.

"You. Come with us," grunted the one on her left as they closed in on her van.

"Shut up," said the other to the first. Then, turning to Fawn, he said "Forgive my partner. He's not good at following instructions. We have been sent to ask you politely to come to a meeting with our boss. We was told specifically to say 'please'. Would you please be good enough to follow us?"

Fawn had lived on the hard side of Cleveland long enough to know this was not a request. Or, rather, it was, but if she turned it down, the next encounter would not be so pleasant. So, twenty minutes later, she found herself seated in the living room of Leroy Washington. His two assistants, the ones that led her here, stood discreetly but noticeably off to the side of the room.

He greeted her cordially enough, first with a handshake and then with an offer of refreshments. But now, it seemed, it was time to get down to business.

"I represent individuals who control the drug trade in Cleveland. It has come to our attention that you may be attempting to get a bit of this business."

The image of grandma getting B12 injectables from the corner pusher flashed briefly across Fawn's mind. "My efforts don't compete with your principals in any way," she said while trying to keep a straight face. "I assure you there is no business conflict."

"Perhaps not. We certainly hope not. Still, we have it from a reliable source that this is not the case."

She started to answer, but he raised his hand to silence her.

"Please. No debate. We feel it would be better for everyone, you included, if you were to leave town. In particular, it would be better if you were to do so without leaving a forwarding address."

This was not a request.

"Why?"

"We know you have a history with one particular individual, someone who is tangentially part of our organization and over whose actions we have some limited control. We also know, by the way that individual was recently treated, that you have excellent contacts with some very powerful people. My objective is to prevent conflict between our two organizations."

"You want me to get out of town so that Bastard doesn't kill me."

"Yes. You and your daughters, to be more specific. He has made it clear that he fantasizes about some very sexual ways of murdering all three of you. Should he do so, we don't want the splatter to cause a war between our organizations."

"You said you controlled him."

"If you know this man, you know that anyone who thinks they can control him for very long is a fool. We are not fools. He will break his leash if you are around to tempt him. So, we must ask you to leave. Please."

* * *

Fawn: So what can I do?

Chang: Well, first, leave Cleveland. There are too many people there looking for you.

Fawn: You want me and my girls to move?

Chang: Yes. The only question is where. It needs to be someplace large and far away.

Weed: The Orlando Police are badlands-friendly.

Chang: Good point. That's far enough away, big enough to hide in, and with a large population of retired. You should have plenty of business there. What do you think of Orlando? Want to take your girls to Disney World?

Fawn: I've never been further away than Chicago.

Weed: Trust me, your girls will love Disney World.

Chang: What about the Bastard problem? Orlando solves Leroy, but the Bastard will still find her. That kind doesn't quit.

Fawn: Why can't I just get a new identity there? Like a badlands witness protection program.

Weed: That's not as easy as it sounds.

Chang: There are records everywhere. You have to get your new name into all of them. Social Security, driver's license, passport, credit cards. Miss just one and someone starts to ask questions. Miss several and Homeland Security takes you away for an interview.

Weed: A false ID isn't good enough except when you want to get past a very specific obstacle, one where you are sure no one will check a database.

Chang: No one in the badlands has your picture, right?

Fawn: Yes. Right.

Chang: And keeping it that way is important to you?

Fawn: Yes.

Chang: Well, you can't get a good ID from a kit. If you want a passport, you have to get it produced at a lab and they will need your picture.

Weed: Changing your identity is out.

Chang: We don't dare kill him now, either.

Fawn: No. NO NO KILLING.

Chang: OK, Fawn, OK. We promise. We can't do it anyway, now, though. Leroy would take it as an act of war. He would have to hunt you down and retaliate. He may not take as much pleasure in it, but the result will still be the same.

Weed: We'll just have to get someone else to deal with the Bastard, someone that won't put Fawn in the crossfire.

Chang: You have an idea?

Weed: Yes. It might take a little time, though.

Chang: How long?

Weed: A week.

Chang: That is OK. We will get you out of Cleveland tomorrow. That should give us at least that long.

Fawn: I can't pack by then.

Chang: Forget packing. Take your girls and go now. Drive to Orlando. Tomorrow. Promise?

Fawn: OK. But no killing? You promise?

Weed: Promise.

Ten minutes later, Milk Weed started contacting operators of Badlands Kiddie Porn sites. He found one who was willing to make a deal.

* * *

They got his keys, of course, so the first thing he did when he got back to his fortress apartment was change the locks. And his passwords.

Next was an inventory. They'd ripped off the meds he stole from Fawn as well as her money and gold. Other than that, he couldn't see anything missing, but the place still felt dirty, used.

Finally, he went over everything with a bug detector, but found nothing. He hired a business associate to do the same, but still, the place was clean. To be on the safe side, he collected everything that might be even the least bit illegal and moved it all to a remote hiding place.

So he wasn't too worried when there was a knock on his door accompanied by the yell 'Police'. He opened the steel slab a crack, protected by three chains. They flashed a warrant at him, but he knew he was safe, so he complied.

Three hours of searching passed. They left with nothing more than his computer. Fat lot of good that would do them, he hardly knew how to use the damned thing.

* * *

Detective James O'Malley of the Cleveland Police Homicide Department was working a cold case. Two days ago, he received an anonymous tip regarding the murder of a prostitute. Her dying statement implicated her pimp in her torture-killing but, until now, the police could do nothing because the pimp had a perfect alibi.

The email claimed there was evidence on the pimp's hard drive proving he was at the murder scene. It also gave passwords for his login and the encrypted files where the data was allegedly stored. That was enough for O'Malley. It had also been enough for a judge. So yesterday they executed a warrant.

Now O'Malley sat next to the department technician, waiting for a verbal summary of his findings while they looked at the computer screen.

"Well," O'Malley asked "Is it Christmas?"

"Yes and no."

"I need Christmas. Don't make me cut you from my Christmas list."

"Your tip was wrong. Sorry."

"Shit. No Santa for you this year, buddy."

"Ah, but wait. There is good news."

"Yes?" O'Malley's conviction rate was not good. He needed good news.

"We found this." A picture appeared on the monitor. It showed a young boy being sodomized by an older man.

"So he likes fag porn. How does that get me Christmas?"

"Ever hear of a web site called BarebackKiddies.com?"

"No. My wife keeps me too busy."

"It's a hard-core homosexual kiddy porn site. Set up through the badlands. Very high on Vice's hit parade."

"And this guy visits it?"

"No. This guy runs it."

"How do you know he's not just a customer?"

"We found the design files. Only the guy that runs that site could have them."

"Oh, Santa, come to papa!" If he couldn't get a conviction, an assist in a major vice bust would be a great consolation prize.

Then O'Malley thought a minute.

"You said it was run out of the badlands?"

"Right." said the tech, smiling while he waited for that to sink in.

"Then this guy's a badlander?"

"Right again."

"Proof?"

"He had a file in the encrypted section of his drive with his badland passwords. Unencrypted. I guess he thought one password was enough."

"You got his wheels, too?"

"Backed up on his drive."

"Santa shares. Drinks on me tonight." A gift-wrapped badlander for DHS was at least as good as a vice assist any day. Santa had blessed him twice. *Between state and federal laws,* thought O'Malley, *this guy won't see daylight for twenty years.*

And he was right.

The Bastard would shortly learn the price of not maintaining his firewall. Crackers, like pickpockets, can give as well as receive.

Chapter 11

Prometheus Exposed

"They're an existential threat. For all humanity. Not just for this country. For humanity," announced Arnold Wilson Parker.

Matthew Hood sat quietly in Parker's Colorado estate study, absorbing the thoughts of his unofficial boss.

"Humanity. We've all crawled too far out on the resources limb. Too far. Can't allow chaos to cut it off. We must preserve order. At all costs. Must. You do see that, don't you?"

"Oh, yes, of course" Hood agreed, there being little else he could say under the circumstances.

"There is literally nothing, no action, beyond consideration if this government is to stave off the chaos that the badlands is thrusting upon us. Starvation. War. Environmental disaster on a global scale. Billions and billions dead. The end of civilization. Maybe of humanity. That's the only alternative to the path we've chosen. Only one. You see that, don't you?"

"Yes, yes, absolutely."

"It's not just economics. We have to guide the thing in the right direction. Have to. How can we if corruption becomes unstoppable? You understand, don't you? The badlands makes corruption unstoppable. You see that?"

Hood nodded, encouraging his mentor to continue.

"Any petty thug can organize his own gang. Recruit, coordinate, pay for anything without being detected. We don't know what he's planning, we can't stop him. Can't. Right?"

"Quite right," came the nasal reply. "We can't."

There was a period of silence as both men considered the problem. Or perhaps only one considered it, while the other waited for opportunities.

"You must act decisively, Matthew," said Parker as he leaned forward, tapping the table to emphasize the point. "Quickly and decisively. If you hesitate, we're all lost. Lost. You see that, don't you?"

"Well, yes sir. Of course."

"Our only failure so far has been not acting firmly enough. Not committing enough resources. Not using them ruthlessly enough. Don't fall short in the future, Matthew. Don't hesitate.

"No, I won't."

"Your teams. How's the SWAT expansion going?"

Finally, a question Hood had come to address.

"Not as well as I would like. TSA has proven a poor source of recruits. All the qualified personnel seem to be locked in the military."

"What if I made it easier for them to transfer? Cut the red tape. Would that be enough?"

"Well, they'd still need an incentive to move."

"Money? Yes, you mean money. That can be arranged. Tell me what you'll need to offer. I'll get you the funds."

"Thank you."

"What else?"

"Can we make these transfers official?"

"No. Too early. On the books, they still need to be military. OK?"

"Yes. Thank you." *One problem solved. Maybe not as pretty as I wanted, but solved* thought Hood. "What about training?"

"Let me know what you need. I'll push it through. See to it."

"Good."

"But see here. Don't miss this. If you don't triple SWAT by the end of the year, we're in trouble. Understand? Big trouble. You're all we got. It's chaos otherwise. Chaos."

"It will be done."

"What else you need?"

"Well, right now, we share authority for SWAT with the local jurisdictions.

That sometimes limits our ability to act."

"The local guys depend on DHS grants, right?"

"Yes."

"OK, I'll make sure everyone understands that those grants are conditional. Anything else?

"Can't SWAT be put under one command?"

"No. Attract too much attention. We need camouflage. Got to seem to have local control. When the time comes, you'll get uniform command. Not now. Wait. Anything else?"

"The postal inspection thing has collapsed. The terrorists send anything they want anywhere without getting caught. We have to stop that."

"What if I get postal inspection authority moved under DHS? Will TSA be able to handle it?"

"Yes, good. What about private carriers? UPS, FedEx, those people?"

"No, we can't let them become an alternate route, can we? I'll get authorization for your people to inspect any shipment by anyone anywhere in the country. Will that do?"

"Yes." *That was too easy.*

"Anything else?"

"We need a national firewall, something to stop unauthorized international VPN traffic."

"Yes, I thought you would come to that. What do you propose?"

"DHS should be authorized to set one up."

"Can't swing that. Work with NSA. Can you?"

Oh, well, you can't get everything you ask for.

"Sure, of course. We're willing to cooperate with anyone if we can shut these guys down."

"NSA could get one up pretty quickly if they're given the authorization and funds. I'll get started on that at this end. Anything else?"

"No, that should cover it." *More than cover it.*

* * *

Two days ago, Nairobi received a text from someone she didn't know asking for a meeting. Now they sat in chat for the first time.

> Nairobi: What can I help you with?
>
> Oak: I seen your blog. One with the names.
>
> Nairobi: Did you recognize anyone on the list?
>
> Oak: No. Well, yes. That not be why I ask to talk.

The text string stopped. Nairobi waited for details.

> Oak: I have papers. Want them published.
>
> Nairobi: Why don't you ask the New York Times?
>
> Oak: Don't trust them.

Well, thought Nairobi, *at least you have some common sense.*

> Nairobi: Why trust me?
>
> Oak: Because I know you be taking a risk to print those names.
>
> Nairobi: This is the badlands. They can't hurt me here.
>
> Oak: But they can in real world. If they catch you. Or me.
>
> Nairobi: Are you worried about your safety?
>
> Oak: I got copies. Look at them? I don't trust no one else.
>
> Nairobi: OK. Send them over.

Nairobi received pictures of 37 hand-written documents. The originals all seemed to be done in varying shades of reddish-brown ink on frayed cloth. All were stained, dirty, and badly creased. Each was written by a different hand, usually with a different pen or brush. Judging by the overlap shown in the pictures, each consisted of a scroll rather than individual sheets. Cut marks and unraveling of the fabric on which they were written showed along the edges.

She picked one at random and attempted to read it, but, because of the penmanship, the lightness of the ink, cross-outs, and the dirt, finally gave up and instead transcribed it, piecing the bits together until she could read:

I attest that I am Samuel Edward Cohen. I am 23 years old, having been born on (***) in Mobile, AL. My mother (Sara Lane Cohen) can attest to my identity because only she and I know that, at the age of four, I was attacked by a flock of swans at a park in Boston, MA.

I further attest that this document is written by my hand using my own blood and so can be verified by DNA analysis. It is written of my own free will, without any form of coercion. I swear that all the information provided in it is the truth to the best of my knowledge, unaltered or slanted in any way. The whole truth, nothing but the truth, so help me God.

On (***) I was installing rebar for the containment dome at (***). We were short on finished one-inch pieces so I was told to use 1/4 inch spacers until the correct sizes arrived. When I came back two days later to assist with the concrete pour, I observed that these spacers were still wired in place. I pointed this out to my supervisor, thinking they would stop the pour, but was told to mind my own business. The pour continued, encasing this section of the containment dome in concrete.

I later checked the drawings when no one was looking and saw that no changes had been made authorizing the reduction in rebar strength.

The supervising engineer signed off on the work.

The document continued for another two pages, outlining three other instances where corners were cut to finish the containment dome.

Samuel Edward Cohen's name was on the snitch's list of FEMA files that had been for sale.

Nairobi began transcribing other photostats. All recounted details of instances where significant corners were cut in the construction of the Prometheus containment dome.

And all 37 of the men and women who wrote these documents were on the snitch's list.

* * *

In encrypted chat, Nairobi asked:

> Nairobi: Where did you get these testaments?
>
> Oak: Will you write about them?
>
> Nairobi: That depends on how authentic they are. Where did you get them?
>
> Oak: They be given to me.
>
> Nairobi: By whom?
>
> Oak: Don't know.
>
> Nairobi: I need details.
>
> Oak: Why?
>
> Nairobi: These are no good to anyone unless I can prove they're genuine. Where are the people who wrote them? I need to talk to the authors.
>
> Oak: They be dead. Most, anyways. All, I expect. Dead.
>
> Nairobi: You want my help?
>
> Oak: I writ you, didn't I?
>
> Nairobi: Then you have to give me details. No one will believe these without supporting evidence. I have to know.
>
> Oak: Can you call me?
>
> Nairobi: You mean telephone?
>
> Oak: Yes.

Nairobi: Why?

Oak: I don't like to write.

Nairobi: It's dangerous. Phone calls can be traced.

Oak: You got some kind of badlands phone?

Nairobi: You mean audio chat?

Oak: Yeah. I guess so.

Nairobi: You understand there is a security risk?

Oak: Somebody overhear?

Nairobi: More than that. Someone could recognize your voice. The civs maintain a voice print database.

Oak: That be why you all write everything?

Nairobi: Yes.

Oak: I understand. But I still don't write so good.

If she went verbal, he wouldn't be the only one at risk. Her voice would be out there, too. Did she trust him enough to let him hear it? She would be talking to him through his computer so he could easily record everything she said. No, more than that. If he was working for DHS, he would record everything she said and use it to try to locate her through the National Voiceprint Database. The chances of such an effort succeeding were high, so the real question she had to ask herself was how much she trusted him.

As she considered the matter, her eyes ran over the copies he had sent her. Maybe they were fakes. Maybe he was, too. But her gut said it was safe and the story was too damned hot not to take the chance.

Nairobi: Are you someplace where you can talk out loud?

Oak: Yeah. Of course.

Nairobi: You know how to set up an audio chat?

Oak: No.

For the next ten minutes, Nairobi walked him through the procedure. Then they went verbal.

"Can you hear me OK?" she asked.

"Yes, ma'am. Fine," came the reply. The voice was deep and raspy, old and

Cajun with the accent of the Mississippi delta.

"OK. Go ahead."

"What do I say?"

"Everything."

"All of it?"

"Yes. Everything. The more detail you tell me, the more believable you will be."

"Where I start?"

"Try the beginning."

But Nairobi got no response. At least, none that could be considered coherent.

"There's no rush, Oak. Just start wherever you want."

"You recording this?"

"Yes."

More silence was her only reply.

"Oak, I have to convince other people you're telling the truth. The recording will help."

"OK." Then more silence, intermixed with small vocal sounds.

"Anywhere, Oak. Just start talking anywhere."

"Right. Well. Let's see." More silence, then the sound of a breath being drawn in. Finally, she heard "They roust me in Billings. Should I start there?"

"Good, Oak. Start there."

"Well, I be standing by the freeway ramp. My thumb not out. Just my sign. Cardboard. Made it myself. This be what you want to hear?"

"Yes, Oak. Please continue."

"Well. OK. I got this sign, see?"

She waited through the silence for him to continue. Finally, he spoke again.

"It be asking for a ride. Back home. Back to Louisiana. Anyway, this cop pull up and tell me to get in the back. I guess they don't like southern folk. I see a FEMA camp coming, so I run. Stupid. I be tired. Cold and tired. Real tired. Not thinking straight."

He paused again, as if thinking, then continued.

"I get away, though. For a little while, anyway. But, Lordy, they be angry. I don't think they get that mad just cause I run. But they do. More cops than I ever seen before. Chase me down like dogs on a coon. Box me in, knock me down. All over a damned sign. Tell me I be a 'hostile vagrant', cuff me and take me away."

Another pause, but shorter this time.

"Two days later, I get to Heart Mountain. Then, wham-bam-thank-you-ma'am, I be on a bunk in Detention with thirty days sentence. Thirty days. All I done was run. Well, maybe mouth off a little, too, but not much."

"This was the FEMA Camp in Wyoming?" asked Nairobi.

"That be the same. Anyway, I be in Detent when the funny happen. I be in the hut for maybe an hour, lying on my bunk. Alone. They all working, I guess, so I just keep low. Alone. Then the Marshal come in. With two deputies. The Marshal. He come for me. Like I was somebody important or something. They come up to me and he say 'There be a mistake'. He say 'Detent's full'. Say I gotta do my time in Shelter camp. Now I ain't too bright, but I know what empty bunks look like. They look like what's next to me. Both sides. But Shelter's a damn sight better than Detent, so I say 'Yes, sir' and jump fast. Don't look no horse gift in the butt, if you know what I mean."

Then came another pause.

"Am I doing OK?" asked the Cajun.

"Just fine, Oak. Go on."

"Well. When I get to Shelter, they tell me I get to call for release. Never heard anyone doing time get to call for release. But, OK. OK. So I call. My baby niece back home in Cut Off. I get her on the phone. She nice and all. We chat. But her car's busted. She can't come get me."

"They would let you go if your niece came to pick you up?"

"Yeah. That's what 'release' means, don't it? All I got to do is prove I got a place to stay. Have her sign for me and take me home."

"Anyway, when I tell them, they say I get another call! Damn, it's like they really want me gone. But I got no one else to call. Knocked-up Katie is it. Her boyfriend's split. Her car's busted. So, no ride. I stay put. Back to my hut.

"Now, I been places like this before. First rule is kiss-up. Second, too, I guess. If I keep calm, I be good at it. So I do it now. Kiss Kiss Kiss. Before long, I be a trustee. That mean I get to pick my job.

"We all got to work. You sick, you still got to work. Everyone. Big FEMA rule. So we all work. Laundry or kitchen or infirmary or field. All gotta do it. No work, no food. And I be fond of food. Since I be a trustee, I get to switch around, don't get too bored, have fun sometimes when no one be looking. Get to try new things.

"So, two months later, I be working the field behind Detent. I work hard, it make time go by. Also, good kiss-up. I hear a voice, look up, see some thin guy standing next to the last hut. He call me. Ask how I got out of Detent so fast. Say he saw me there. And I hear the accent. He be Cajun, just like me.

"We all been warned. Never talk to no Detent. Never. But I be raised friendly, hard not to answer. He lay down behind the hut, next to the fence corner, so no one see him. So I answer. I don't look up, just keep hoeing, but I answer. And, know what? He be from Cut Off, same as Katie. Same high school. Even said he knew her. Knew her name, anyway.

"I don't got no friends in that camp. Kiss-ups don't got friends. So I start asking for field work, just to hear his accent. Every time I work close to the back, he come out. He lay down low by the fence corner and I keep hoeing. I trustee, no one watch me. So we talk.

"He be sick. Got a bad cough. And hungry. Cold, too. Wyoming be cold even in the summer. I tell him I get him food when he get out, but he say no. He not get out. Been in Detent for four months already. That not right. FEMA say thirty days max. He laugh, say they never let him out. Ask me to tell his family when I get home.

"And he look so thin. I think fever, maybe. My only friend, and he be sick. So I steal food. Sorry, Momma.

"I not always be a good man, but I try. Momma taught me right. She be a good woman. Taught me right from wrong. Besides, he be my only friend. Katie broke, so she not fix her car. I not get no ride. So, sorry momma, I steal. I get kitchen duty. Steal sausages. Slip em in my shorts, next to my real thing. I be hung, so no one notice.

"Next day, I get field. I see him lying on the dirt when I near the fence. I pitch the meats to him, they land by the fence. He see em, just look at me. Go on, I tells him, I got extra. He reaches under the fence. Gets em. Starts to thank me, don't finish. Then he crawl back to the hut. Through a window. But he don't eat them sausage, just hold them, some in each hand, keeping them clear of the dirt, all the way to the window.

"Maybe three day later. I see him again. He reach under the fence, pitch something at me. I look around, no one see it, so I hoe it to my shoe. It small, dark cloth. Knotted. I bend down, like I tie my shoe, slip it in my sock.

"Then, when I stand up, he ask me. He want a sheet. A bed sheet. Not food. He want a bed sheet. They got no sheets in Detent. Lucky to have blankets. No sheets. He want a white one. If it too big to hide, get him pieces. Wide strips. A little each time. He say it very important. More than food. He never ask me for food, but he beg for that sheet.

"And vinegar. Just a little. Maybe a small jar. Pickle juice if that all I can get. He make me promise. Tell me to use what he give me if I have to.

"Why the vinegar?" she asked.

"Don't know. But they writ on them sheets."

"Good. Please, go on."

"When I get alone, I look at what he give me. In the cloth. They be wedding bands. Gold. Six of em. Just bands. And a note. It say use these to buy the sheet if I have to.

"So I get laundry duty. Staff, they got sheets. When they dirty, we wash them. So I drop one behind a machine. Careful, no one see. Later, when I do baggies, I slips the sheet between them. Then I push the laundry cart back myself. It filled with baggies. Also the sheet. I tip over the cart when I pass my bunk, kick sheet under it when it fall out. No one see, so I hide it in the latrine that night when it be dark."

"What are baggies?" she asked.

"Coveralls. Work coveralls. We don't get no shirts. Not even in Shelter. Just coveralls. And shorts. Socks, too, if Red Cross bring 'em."

"OK. You're doing well. Go on."

"So that night, I tear the sheet to strips. Take one, roll it up. Hide the rest.

"Next day, I work the field. My friend come out. When no one see, I pitch him the sheet. Do it again on three more days. A bottle of pepper sauce too. He be a happy coon-ass.

"Not long after, it get too cold to farm. We pick greens, leave, not come back.

"Did you ever see your friend again?"

"Yes ma'am. Come winter. After the fire."

"What fire?"

"A Detent hut burn down. His hut. It be winter, during a big snow. And the hut catch fire. Burn fast. Kill some, not my friend. But he burned. I work infirmary, help when fire start. I seen him brought in. Burns. Not too bad, but he sick. They set him on the floor, beds all full.

"I be real busy. Cleaning sheets. The floor. Everywhere. They all sick. Puke. Shit and piss. Blood and ooze, too. Doctor run out of bandages, I tear up sheets. Everyone screaming. No morphine. All got to stay in camp, roads closed by snow. Too windy for helicopter. Doctor do his best. I help.

"My friend, he not screaming. Too sick, I think. Cough a little. Can't get his breath. Dies in the morning."

"I'm sorry."

"Thank you."

"Go on."

"Right. Anyway. Before he die, I sit by him when I can. We talk. About home. About Cut Off. He be a good man, too. Like Momma. He be in pain. I sit with him, try to help. That be when he give me the roll."

"The roll?"

"Yes ma'am. Like a newspaper rolled tight. Wrapped in waterproof they tore from the walls. Tied tight. He hand it to me, ask me to take it. Hide it. He say it very important. Say it be the reason they there, why they all be dying. He want me to get it out. Tell someone. Say it big. He be my only friend, so I say yes. Take the roll, slip it inside my baggies. Put the end in my shorts. When I get back to my hut, I hide it in the latrine."

"What was in the roll?"

"The sheets I give him. But writ on.

"Come spring, Katie gets a new boyfriend. He got a car, so I gets out. Hide the roll in the field when I work, pick it up after I be out. When I get to Cut Off, I open it and read them all. Then I know why it be important, but don't know who to tell. So I do nothing. Tell the wrong man, they kill me. Katie, too. So I wait. You understand?"

"Yeah, Oak. Sure. You did the right thing."

"Anyway, I seen your list. Ask around, learn it come from you. From the badlands. So I figure you be safe to tell. Especially if I be in the badlands, too. I find a friend, he help me cross. And now I be here."

"That's quite a remarkable story, Oak."

"I got more to say."

"Sorry. Go on."

"I been working oil patch all my life. Onshore. Offshore. Everywhere. That's why I be in Montana. I be working gas fields.

"So I know pure gas don't smell. Right out of the well, it not pure, smell of sulfur. But they clean it, make it pure, on account of the sulfur stink be poison. Then it don't smell. So they add chemical back to it. Stink chemical. Make it smell, but not poison. For leak warning. Sell only stinky gas for your house. Commercial gas all stinky. But pure gas don't smell.

"When my friend's hut heater go out, there be a safety. All heaters got safety. No flame, it shut off gas. Supposed to, any way. But his don't. It be broke. So gas just go into room.

"So air should stink. Be bad, wake everyone. But it not stink. Because it not be commercial gas. It be pure. Why they use pure gas in that hut? That be against FEMA rules.

"I check my hut gas. It stink. I check other huts. Stink be there, too. Stink be everywhere. But not my friend's hut. I know. I check gas bottle for his hut after fire, smell no stink.

"Know what happen if hut fill full up with gas? Everyone die. Sleep to death. Suffocate. No fuss. No mess. Just be an unfortunate accident. And all quietly dead. Whoever break heater, use pure gas, make flame go out, they want that. That why they wait for snow storm. So all windows in hut be closed tight. Want to kill all quietly."

'But that not happen. Someone make a spark when some air still in the room. Air and gas burn. Boom. Now big deal. Everyone notice. Not planned. But still murder. Either way, still murder. This not be accident."

The conversation paused, then Nairobi asked "What happened to the rings?"

"Still got them."

Another pause. Then "You haven't asked me for money."

"Money be good. Katie need it. Me too, truth be told. So, whatever you think be fair, be OK by me. But I give you papers anyway, even if you not pay. This be for my friend. What they do to him, it not be right. Nothing in that camp be right. So you pay me what you can, I be happy. But you get them fucking peckerwoods, you hear?"

* * *

Fawn: Hi, partner. What we got?

Nairobi: ENGCO!

Fawn: Who?

Nairobi: ENGCO. One of the largest engineering companies in the world. Prime contractor for the Prometheus project. We got them.

Fawn: What about FEMA? I thought we were going after FEMA.

Nairobi. That's not working out so well.

Fawn: What about the deaths at Heart Mountain?

Nairobi: FEMA's got explanations for them. All documented. Nothing we can get anyone on. But we got ENGCO.

Fawn: Will that help us get FEMA?

Nairobi: Hey, partner, you don't sound very happy.

Fawn: I want to tell my friend what happened to his friend.

Nairobi: Sorry. Maybe later. We'll keep looking, I promise. But for now, this will keep us going.

Fawn: It's big?

Nairobi: A bombshell. It'll blow ENGCO out of the water. Prometheus, too.

Fawn: And Prometheus is what?

Nairobi: Nothing short of the resurrection of nuclear power. The solution to all our energy problems. The start of a new Golden Age. That's what their press says, anyway.

Fawn: OK, partner. Details, please. I Need-To-Know.

Nairobi: We have thirty-seven testaments from various construction people saying that ENGCO cut corners on the Prometheus project. Big corners. In other words, it's not safe to operate it. And, since ENGCO did it, they're in big trouble.

Fawn: What are these testaments?

Nairobi: Statements written by witnesses in their own blood, no less, on scraps of cloth telling what they saw.

Fawn: OK. Roll the presses.

Nairobi: Not just yet. We need interviews to back them up.

Fawn: OK. Ready for that, too.

Nairobi: I can't locate any of the authors.

Fawn: Why not?

Nairobi: The ones still alive didn't leave good forwarding addresses when they left the camp.

Fawn: Some are dead?

Nairobi: Almost half. At least according to the public FEMA database. A heater blew up in their barracks last winter, put nineteen in the infirmary. Twelve died.

Fawn: And the rest?

Nairobi: Released. FEMA claims they don't have any more of them in their camps.

Fawn: These people were all working on the Prometheus project?

Nairobi: Yes, as nearly as I can tell.

Fawn: Then what were they doing in a FEMA camp?

Nairobi: Good question. Damned good question. Give me a few, I'll check the FEMA records.

Several minutes passed.

Nairobi: FEMA claims they were all laid off from the project and were having a blow-out farewell celebration. It got out of hand, they all got arrested, and, through some mess-up, were sent to Heart Mountain Detention.

Fawn: Sound reasonable?

Nairobi: No. Especially since Heart Mountain is an overflow camp. If they were sent to any FEMA camp, it should have been a primary one. Why did they go directly to overflow?

Fawn: Sounds like we have something on FEMA after all.

Nairobi: We have more than that. Even if FEMA is telling the truth, they should have all been out of Detention in 30 days. None of them were ever moved to the general population. Fourteen were released directly from Detention, four died prior to the fire, and four were transported to other camp hospitals after it.

Fawn: How long did they stay in Detention?

Nairobi: Some were there as long as four months.

Fawn: FEMA give any reasons for that?

Another pause, then:

Nairobi: The records show they tried to escape from Detention and were given new sentences for it.

Fawn: How long were the new sentences?

Another pause for a records check.

Nairobi: The max, thirty days.

Fawn: All of them? They all tried to escape every thirty days. All of them?

Nairobi: Doesn't sound likely, does it?

Fawn. No. What happened to those last four, the ones sent to other hospitals?

There was another pause in the text stream.

Nairobi: No idea. The records don't even say which camp they went to, only that they were transferred out for medical reasons.

Fawn: Hey, this is great, partner! Sounds like we do have something to ask FEMA after all.

Nairobi: Yes, it would appear so.

Fawn: Tell me more about these testaments.

Nairobi: I'll send them to you. They pretty much speak for themselves.

A pause, then

Fawn: Got them.

Time passed as she looked at the scans and transcripts.

The twelfth one was written by her husband.

She had been hoping to find out more about what happened to him, knowing that his name was on the secret camp list, but there were thousands in that camp. To actually find his name, to see his handwriting in blood in front of her, was tough.

She read the text through twice. Then she studied the original, not just to check the transcription, but to see the actual handwriting. It was his. The father of her two girls, the man with the candy smile. The phrasing had a ring of truth, it was exactly the way he would have talked. He'd been trapped in that damned camp. All that time. If she had known, she could have come for him. If she had only known.

She took a few deep breaths, then typed:

Fawn: I found him. My friend's friend. One of these testaments is his. What happened to him?

Nairobi: Who? Which one?

Fawn gave her the name. There was another pause while Nairobi looked him up in the public database.

Nairobi: He's alive. He wasn't in the fire.

Fawn: Where is he?

Nairobi: Well, I can't tell you that, unfortunately. That's my problem right now. I don't have good addresses on anyone who was released. The records just say he was released from

Detention and left right away. Before the fire.

Fawn: Don't you have to have someone pick you up to get out?

Nairobi: Yes. Someone has to sign for you.

Fawn: Well, who picked him up?

Another pause, then

Nairobi: His wife. FEMA says he was picked up by his wife.

Chapter 12

Life In Florida

Fawn: How did you get your badlands name?

Jack: Yeah, pretty cool, eh? I came through a crossing that's a little flexible about names. After I was here awhile, I decided I wanted to start my own cracker service, so I had them change my name.

Fawn: How did you get the entire badlands to go along?

Jack: I didn't. The old name's still out there, I just never use it. All I did was convince my crossing house to change my name to Cracker Jack.

Fawn: How did you transfer your reputation?

Jack: Didn't do that, either. Had to start over in the rep area, but I didn't lose much because I was new, so my old rep was small. But it was worth it. That name is a gold mine. You came to me because of it, right?

Fawn: Well, in part, anyway.

Jack: OK, business. I assume you need a cracker exploit. What can I break into for you?

Fawn: I want to cross from home. No more road trips for my wheels. Too many roadblocks, you know?

Jack: But you don't want to use the Internet you have at home because it's in your name, so you want to set up a long-range antenna and steal someone else's service. Right?

Fawn: Yes.

Jack: I get a lot of that. It's easy, I can do that for you. Let me shoot you a description of what you have to do to get set up. When you're ready, get back to me and we'll do it, OK?

Fawn: OK.

Four days later, a tripod sat in front of Fawn's bedroom window. Clamped to it, pointing towards the apartment building across the street, was a long black cylinder with a small 5x spotting scope attached. The scope was aligned with a directional antenna mounted inside the dark tube. The electronics that connected to that antenna also activated several LEDs inside the scope, ones that she could see when she looked through it. From the back of the antenna tube came a USB cable which was plugged into her wheels.

For the past two hours, Fawn had used this antenna to scan her neighbor's windows. Most didn't show any signal, but some were active. Methodically, she had made notes on the location of each window that gave her a green LED. Twelve Wi-Fi signals were strong enough to use.

She had checked each using one of the open-source programs that Cracker Jack had asked her to download and install. In each case, the signal was locked, meaning it was protected by some form of encryption. It was time for Cracker Jack.

In addition to the high-gain antenna connection via her USB port, her wheels were hard-wired via an Ethernet patch cord to her cable modem. Through that connection, she had established a VPN to a proxy server outside the country. She communicated with Cracker Jack through that server, using its return address. He could never learn her physical location through the link because a trace would show a return address no further back than her proxy server.

She made the crossing and told him she was ready.

On her laptop ran, not a normal chat program, but the second program he asked her to install. She granted him access and a chat window for that program popped up.

> Jack: Hello, are you there?
>
> Fawn: Yes. I think everything is ready.
>
> Jack: OK, from what you sent me, I think we should try the HOME-58EE network first. Can you point your antenna to that router?

She checked the table she had made and saw that the window that provided that network signal was 3 floors down from the roof and 17 windows over from the left edge of the building. Moving the antenna, she counted windows until the one she wanted showed up in the center of her spotting scope. The green signal light came on.

> Fawn: Try that.
>
> Jack: Got it.

The chat went quiet. She waited.

Fawn: Can you talk?

Jack: Sure, I'm just waiting for my program to break in.

Fawn: That's it? All you do is run a program?

Jack: Not all, but, yes, I let a program do the work. My part is deciding which program to use and how to set it up.

Fawn: Can these programs break in anywhere?

Jack: No. Not any more than a safe cracker can break in to any safe.

Fawn: How can you tell if you can break into a particular computer?

Jack: It's like breaking into a residence. To get into any one of a thousand low-end apartments, I'd just start trying doors. Eventually, I'd find one that wasn't locked. That's how most trojans are installed. BOTS R US doesn't care where its computers come from or how good they are, so they send virus programs to every computer they can. When they find one that's not locked, they plant a trojan.

Jack: OK. Just got into HOME-58EE.

Fawn: Wow. So I can get Internet through that router?

Jack: Yep. I know the password. Until someone changes it, you're safe to cross anytime using that network.

Fawn: So that was like one of the thousand apartments?

Jack: No, it was a little more difficult than that. It was more like one of a dozen middle-class houses. Their doors are locked so I have to get out my pick set and go to work on each one. The program I just ran did that. Like an automated set of lock picks. Sometimes it works, sometimes not. This time I got lucky. Lets try another.

Fawn: Which one?

Jack: NETGEAR69.

She pointed the antenna at that window.

Fawn: Got it?

Jack: Yes. Hang on.

A minute passed.

Jack: OK, we're working on it. Now, where were we? Oh, yes. To continue the example, if you asked me to break into a specific rich guy's house, one with good locks and an alarm system, it'd be harder. I'd have to case the place, pretend I was a meter reader or something. And I still might not get in.

Fawn: But you usually can, right?

Jack: No. Sometimes I can't ever get in. If I tried the White House, where they have great locks, alarms, and guards on duty all the time, not only would I not get in, but I would probably get caught. Some computers are just too hard, even for the best. And, while I'm good, I'm not the best.

Some few minutes passed.

Jack: No luck here. Let's try another.

So it continued for most of the afternoon. Cracker Jack was able to break into three systems, getting her anonymous Internet access through any one of three apartments. When he left, she was happy with his services.

But, perhaps she shouldn't have been. While he was in one of those computers, without telling her, he took a look around. Like snooping through the desk of a house he had broken into, his efforts got him the physical address of the person who owned that computer. He didn't know Fawn's address, but he knew where one of her neighbors lived.

* * *

"Hey, did you see the papers? Are you happy?" asked Nairobi. She was in a private encrypted verbal chat with Oak

"That be good. I be one happy Cajun. Thank you."

"Got you some money, too. Put it in the account you gave me. Hope that was all right."

"That be good, thank you. Katie need it."

"I'll try and get you some more, but I need help in return."

"What you need?"

"Physical proof."

"What that mean?"

"I have to prove that the documents you sent me really came from the people who signed them."

"What you want from me?"

"Send me the roll."

There was a long pause.

"Oak? You there?"

"I be here."

"Oak, I need you to send me the originals."

"Why?"

"I need to get them analyzed."

"Analyzed?"

"DNA. Cloth. Dirt. I need to be sure everything matches what you've told me."

"Why? You think I be liar?"

"No. No, Oak, I trust you. But others don't. We're trying to bring down some big people here. We have to have rock-solid proof."

"What you do with the roll if I send it to you?"

"Give it to a lab to analyze."

"Then I send to lab."

She hadn't considered that idea. It had several virtues, including the fact that she wouldn't have to ask him to entrust her with the precious originals.

"OK. Set it up with a badlands courier and have them bill me."

"I never done that before. It be hard?"

"No. If you want, I can set it up with a courier. They'll contact you to arrange pick-up."

"OK" came the answer.

Twenty minutes later Kumar's Discreet Delivery Service had a new order.

* * *

After her stressful move, Fawn's life was settling down. She learned the landmarks in a plastic landscape and memorized where the main roads ran. Her girls got used to their new school and made new friends. Just knowing where the shops were, not getting lost every time you got in the car, was a stress-reliever.

Each Tuesday morning, after seeing her girls to their bus, she left Orlando to run deliveries. Sometimes south, sometimes north. First, as in Cleveland, she would go to the far end of her route and pick up her shipment. Then, for the next four days, she drove and dropped. A mailbox here, another there, no more than three deliveries per box. And, always, in between drops, she visited antique events and shops to keep up her cover.

The girls usually had to be in school, so she traveled by herself. Four days alone. The badlands and central Florida can both be very empty places. Her twins had managed to make new friends, but she had not.

Her last experience with the Bastard still haunted her. Even though she couldn't afford it, she began camping less, sleeping more in hotels. At first, they were the cheapest she could find, but the filth and smell of stale air-freshener drove her away. Fortunately, her business did well, so she started treating herself to nicer places. And always, looking over her shoulder. Never use her real ID, pay only with scrip, and never stay in the same place twice. That wasn't hard. Florida overflowed with hotels.

Some had bars. A few were even good. Anonymous faces, tired and sad. Some handsome, most just human. And real. Faces she could watch as they talked. Eyes that looked back at her. People who laughed. You never heard that in a chat room.

But, just as she missed the physical communication in chat, she missed the honesty here. And not just from the other patrons, either. She never really expected them to speak without illusion, sometimes deceiving themselves more than anyone else. No, she missed being able to speak her own mind, to be as honest with another person as she tried to be with herself. But here in the dim light, she never dared bring down her guard, never dared to talk about herself lest it go too far. She could hardly tell anyone what she did for a living, could she? Young as he was, she missed Angelo's smile. Cleveland was a long way away.

Even when she was home, enjoying the glow from her twins, she felt a hunger. Often she thought about her husband, wondered what had happened to him. Even at home, the nights were long. On the road, when she awoke not knowing which city she was in, they were intolerable.

So she went on a quest. It was a common one for single woman of her age, but made complicated by her badlands connection. She had to find someone who not only fit all the other criteria that women have hidden away in their bridal chests, but he had to come to terms with her illegal activities. He had to, if not join her, then at least accept that she was a badlander.

At first, she visited isolated pubs, ones not associated with the hotels where she stayed. She told herself it was for security. It would be harder for people she met to trace her if she didn't go to bed next door. But, really, she was looking for a different class of patron. Not better, just better looking.

Now she sat in a dim booth across from an attractive man of average build and rugged demeanor. His clothing was tastefully semi-business, as befitted a lawyer out on the town after hours. If anyone had seen them together, they would have been considered a handsome couple.

"The problem is that our government has been taken over by Fascists," he said.

"Fascists? Like Nazis?"

"Yes. Fascists. Fascism is big business controlling the state. That's what we have now."

Not sure what to say in reply, she just nodded and smiled encouragement. She knew well from her previous professional experience that nothing makes a woman look more attractive to a man than a visible interest in his opinions.

"Like big agriculture. They force poison down our throats. Insecticides. Antibiotics. Growth hormones. Frankenfoods. They get away with it because they own the FDA. A government really concerned about the people's health would throw them all in jail."

"Wouldn't that make food more expensive?" she asked.

"More expensive than what? Cancer? Birth defects? People have to be protected from these corporate thugs.

"But what if people don't want that? What if they can't afford it?"

"There are assistance programs. They just need more funding. If we put up the money and make people do the right thing, it'll work out in the end."

Fawn knew all about assistance programs. After her husband disappeared, she went through the list: WIC, AFDC, TANF, TAFDC. And that was just for starters. In her head, she could put a tune to the list and hum it like her ABCs.

Every one had a catch. No address? Living in an apartment with an adult male present? Married? Where is your husband? There was always an excuse, one hoop too many, a Catch 22, or a price too high. If you could live your life their way, and prove it, they might throw you a scrap to chew on. Otherwise, you were on your own. Like she had been all her life.

"What if you don't qualify for those assistance programs?"

"Anyone in real need can qualify. You just have to prove the need. To prevent fraud. Anyone who really needs assistance will accept the minor inconvenience of proving that need."

The road to hell isn't paved with good intentions, thought Fawn, *only minor inconveniences. We're controlled, not by their truncheons, but by our own sloth.*

But he was still talking. "All we have to do is organize. Throw the Fascists out. Get good men and women into power who will do what has to be done. Clamp down in the name of the people. Then we can pull out of this mess."

Left or right. Stalin or Hitler. It doesn't matter, thought Fawn as she silently nodded her head. *The poverty and the prisons will still smell the same.*

* * *

> Chang: Congratulations. You have reached a new milestone. Do you know what it is?
>
> Fawn: No, I'm afraid not.
>
> Chang: You are now officially out of debt.
>
> Fawn: You mean I'm no longer indentured?
>
> Chang: No, you will always be indentured to some crossing house

as long as you are in the badlands. No, I mean you have paid off all the loans we made to you when we decided to take you on. You have been working very hard and saving a great deal.

Fawn: Thank you.

Chang: Are you saving for something in particular?

Fawn: Yes.

Because, if he's still alive somewhere, the money might get him back.

Chang: And for what is none of my business, right?

Fawn: I don't mean to be rude, but I'd rather keep it private.

Chang: One thing we in the badlands understand is privacy. Please forgive me for prying. Still, this change in your financial status brings up a new problem that you must deal with.

Fawn: What?

Chang: You now have savings and must decide what to do with it.

Fawn: Can't I just put it in a bank?

Chang: Yes, of course, but that has a different meaning here than on the other side of the border. Before you make a decision, we should talk about those differences.

Fawn: OK.

Chang: Here, a 'bank' is just a place to store your money, like a safe deposit box. Oh, they will transfer your funds at your request to pay your bills, just like real world banks, but they don't make loans. They don't loan your money out.

Fawn: So?

Chang: So they don't make money from your money. All it brings them are expenses, since they have to store it, keep track of it, and insure it. So they don't pay you to let them keep it, they charge you.

Fawn: You mean they don't pay interest?

Chang: No, just the reverse. They charge you a storage fee.

Fawn: That doesn't seem quite fair.

Chang: It is when you realize how our money system works. A badlands 'bank' is not a physical institution any more than is anything else here. It doesn't hold any money, only accounting books. Your money is actually held by many small depositories, like coin dealers, jewelers, or pawn shops. They are businesses, just like yours, and, like yours, they have to make money to pay their expenses. They do so by charging the banks they work for a storage fee which, if the banks are to stay in business, has to be passed on to you.

Fawn: So, they don't loan out the money I deposit like real-world banks do?

Chang: No.

Fawn: Why?

Chang: Because no one here trusts banks. We have all seen what they do in the real world when they are allowed to make loans with their depositors money, and no one wants that here.

Fawn: What do they do?

Chang: Oh, my, that is more complicated than I had thought to discuss. The short answer is that, if they are allowed to loan out any of their customer's money, they will eventually loan out all of it. Sometimes several times over. No matter what regulations are instituted, this inevitably happens. When one of those loans fails, the bank either defaults, meaning their depositors lose their money, or the government bails them out. Of course, that just transfers the bad loan problem upstream and eventually forces the government to fail. The only way to guarantee that sort of thing won't happen is to never allow banks to loan out money, which is why depositors in the badlands demand that of their banks.

Fawn: So, if I put my money in a bank, it will be safe but I'll have to pay a deposit fee each month?

Chang: That is right. The reason I bring all this up is that there is an alternative.

Fawn: What?

Chang: You could make a loan. Even in the badlands, loans do pay interest.

Fawn: I thought you said banks didn't make loans.

Chang: They don't. But you could, either indirectly through a badlands broker, or directly to some credit-worthy borrower.

Fawn: Isn't that more risky than if I put my money in a bank?

Chang: Of course. If you mean a badlands bank, that is. That is why you get interest, to pay you for taking that risk.

Fawn: How would I find someone to loan my money to?

Chang: If you want to go through a broker, I can suggest several that have good reputations. However, I would like to propose an alternative.

Fawn: Which is?

Chang: The GOBI DESERT Crossing House is a business like any other. As such, we also need working capital. We would welcome the chance to borrow your money and will offer you an interest rate higher than you can get at any broker.

Fawn: How much would that be?

Chang: I suggest a rolling 90-day term at a rate of 0.61% per term.

Fawn: How much is that a year?

Chang: If you didn't take any money out, about 2.5%

Fawn: That doesn't sound like very much.

Chang: On the contrary, it is quite good. I suggest you shop around before you make a decision. There are many good brokers listed in the emporium. Check and see what they will give you.

Fawn: Why does that rate seem so low?

Chang: You are thinking in the wrong monetary units. You are used to loans made in a dollars. That is a unit of exchange who's worth is constantly being debased by inflation and further decreased by taxes that the government charges you on the inflation. Since everyone in the badlands has already had enough experience with government-issued currencies, they are only willing to deal with institutions that quote prices in gold. The loan rate I quoted you will be repaid in that metal, not a shaky government currency.

Fawn: So, if I loan you a thousand grams of gold, at the end of three months, you would pay me back 1,006.1 grams?

Chang: Yes. And, if the dollar price of gold has gone up, you will have more dollars because you made the loan in gold, not dollars. Of course, you won't have to pay taxes on your profit.

Fawn: That still doesn't seem like a big return.

Chang: It's not. Unlike the real world, you won't get rich by making loans in the badlands. Here, because we don't have inflation or other games played by central bankers, you can't get rich by manipulating money. You have to do it by producing goods and services that someone else wants to buy, just as you are doing now with your meds business. Here, the rich do get a little richer, but most of the increasing wealth of our society is accrued by those that work for it. Like you.

Fawn: I can't just save dollars?

Chang: Of course you can, child. But if you want to keep your money, you have to stop using theirs.

There was a pause in the text stream.

Chang: Well?

Fawn: This is a lot to think about.

Chang: I know. Sorry, but you have to start thinking about it now. It is your money. If you do not worry over it, no one else will.

For the first time in her life, Fawn was about to become a capitalist. She was also about to learn that the job wasn't as easy as it sounded

* * *

Thanks to Parker's efforts, new funds and TSA personnel produced a major improvement in mail inspection. Now every post office displayed a notice declaring that all mail was subject to x-ray inspection. Patrons were warned they should write DO NOT X-RAY on any package whose contents might be damaged by the procedure. What the signs didn't say was that such a request would guarantee a hand-inspection of that package.

Like most badlanders, Fawn knew that, so she made no such declaration. The gold coins her package contained wouldn't be damaged by the radiation anyway, so she wasn't deceiving anyone. The only precaution she took prior to mailing her week's earnings was to place an untraceable return address on the package. Not false, as the post office used automatic address scanners to verify all return addresses. A false address would guarantee a manual inspection. The address was real, perhaps belonging to a little old lady who ate dog food for dinner. At least that was what Fawn hoped since she knew there was a chance something would go wrong with her delivery and, should that happen, she liked to imagine her gold going to a worthy recipient.

Her package consisted of eight coins laid in three lines, staggered on top of the other, then wrapped in padding and taped between two strips of steel flat stock. A deposit slip made out in her badlands name was taped to the outside of one of the bars. Over that was padding, then two layers of wrapping. The inner one showed only her badlands name and crossing house, while the outer one contained full addressing and stamps for the benefit of the post office.

The package was light enough that postal regulations would allow it to be mailed on the street and large enough to decrease its chances of being lost. She dropped it in a curbside blue box as she drove her girls to school.

The post office processes millions of pieces of mail every day. Even with the new funds, checking such a large volume of mail was still a numbers game. It's like a fish trap: Stakes channel fish into a net. The net forces them into a trap. That last, like a manual inspection, catches the prey. The more packages you can inspect automatically, the more packages you can afford to screen.

To begin the process, automatic optical scanners check both addresses. Any that are false, on the suspect list, or illegible are sent directly to x-ray inspection. Next, the mail stream goes past a series of sniffers to detect the smell of explosives, flammable liquids, narcotics, and newly-printed money. The latter is detectable because the Treasury Department adds chemical tracers to inks to give bills that 'new money' smell. Unfortunately, these tracers are volatile, meaning they gradually evaporate which is, after all, why they can be smelled. Eventually, after a period of a few months, their smell is too faint for chemical detection. Packages that smell wrong are sent directly to hand-inspection.

Finally, all the packages are run past a metal detector. Those without metal, including those containing older currency and counterfeit (unfortunately not detectable by smell) go back into the system for delivery. Packages that contain metal go directly to x-ray inspection.

These checks all have the virtue of being automatic and so are cheap to perform. However, x-ray inspection requires an operator to interpret the pictures making the use of that station expensive. Any package that an operator thinks might contain gold, explosives, currency, or flammable liquids is sent for manual inspection.

In the case of Fawn's recent mailing, the metal detector flagged it for an x-ray inspection. The new TSA operator couldn't detect the circular shapes of the coins because they were masked effectively by the two metal bars. But he was suspicious that the bars themselves might be gold, so he ordered a manual inspection. Of course, it found Fawn's coins.

Officially, there was no law against sending gold through the domestic mails. But the act screamed 'badlands'. For that reason, Homeland Security was very interested in meeting anyone who shipped or received that metal. The obvious way to do this was to simply watch the delivery destination after the package was delivered, but that had proven both time-consuming and ineffective. Fortunately, there was now an alternative.

Following procedure, both the inner and outer sets of wrappers of Fawns package had been carefully removed to avoid damaging either of them when it was opened. A GPS tracker was padded with lead strips to duplicate the size, weight, and feel of her coins and bars. It was then re-wrapped using the original materials and sent quickly on its way.

When the re-mailer it was addressed to (a UPS store) received the package, they were allowed to replace the outer envelope with a new one, one that was addressed to the next forwarder down the line, and drop it back into the mails. By electronically following it, TSA was able to trace it all along the way, through as many re-mailers as the smugglers used, until it arrived at an international air freight terminal. Only when the tracker indicated that the package was about to be placed on an aircraft did SWAT move in. Four badlanders from two mail-forwarders and a freight company would be spending a long time as guests of the DHS.

Fawn heard about the loss of her gold almost as soon as the consolidated shipment her package was supposed to be in failed to arrive in Moscow. Her gold was gone, of course, but life went on. This sort of thing was part of the cost of doing business in the badlands. If it got too expensive, she could always resort to recasting the coins into something an x-ray operator wouldn't notice, like a machine part or a box of bolts. But that was time consuming and expensive. So, for now, she would just shrug off the loss and go on with her life.

Meanwhile, an elderly lady of limited means got a surprise visit from Homeland Security. After days of interrogation and an extensive search of her property, they found nothing. They had to conclude, correctly, that she had no involvement in the badlands.

As for the gold, Fawn would have been disappointed. Since the old woman convinced DHS that it wasn't hers, they impounded it, waiting for the rightful owner to come forward and claim it. And they still have it. If you want it, just speak up.

* * *

No one eats or sleeps in the badlands. Comfortable furniture doesn't exist. It's never too hot or too cold. Bandwidth is the only physical commodity that's really consumed. The amount of data that can be sent and received by a badlander at any given time is the only metric that determines the quality of his virtual life.

Fawn's previous Internet connections had all been through public access points and so, for either policy reasons or because of heavy usage, had offered little bandwidth. She had been limited to audio at best, text at worst. Video, especially fast video, was impossible. For this reason, she had never been able to participate in one of the badlands greatest social and recreational activities, on-line gaming. It simply required too much bandwidth.

That gaming should be one of the badland's greatest recreations seems odd. Real-world recreation or social activities all require physical sensations such as feeling the effects of alcohol, or physical interactions, such as hitting a golf ball. Virtual games do not require any of those, yet they still provide the rewards of mental challenges in the presence of one's peers.

So, thanks to her new Internet connection, Fawn had her first chance to join her friends in a serious on-line game. She and Bowie were now the sole crew of a sub-space fighter. He wasn't her favorite companion, but in the world of on-line video games, like in war, you don't always get to pick your comrades.

Together, they drifted with the rest of the fleet behind one of the moons of the enemy's home planet. An ambush was in the making.

Bowie: How's the new link working?

Fawn: Fast, thank you.

Time passed.

Bowie: What made you do it?

Fawn: Do what?

Bowie: Get a connection from home.

Fawn: The ID check thing.

Bowie: You were worried they'd catch your kit ID?

Fawn: Not likely. For what McDonald's pays, none of their people check ID's very well. No, it's just the whole thing: bandwidth, roadblocks, fake ID's. On and on. The civs requiring ID's to get online was just the last straw.

More time passed in silence.

Bowie: You see Nairobi's latest series on the Prometheus thing?

Fawn: Hey, mine too. We're partners.

Bowie: Yeah, I know, love. Sorry. Did you read it?

Fawn: Yes. Of course. We're partners!

Bowie: A bombshell.

Fawn: You really think it was good?

Bowie: Criminy, yes. The testaments. DNA, signatures, cloth it was written on, even the brand of the pepper sauce. It all checked out. ENGCO is dropping like a rock.

Fawn: Pepper sauce?

Bowie: The snitch said he gave them a bottle of Texas Pete to stop their blood from clotting so they could write with it. The lab confirmed that's the brand they used. She did great.

Fawn: We did great.

Bowie: Yeah. Sorry, love. You both did great.

More silence.

Bowie: Hey, love, you free tomorrow?

Fawn: Aw, sorry, love. Laundry day.

Bowie: Really?

Fawn: Really. Monday's always laundry day.

Bowie: Why Monday?

Fawn: Only day it's not crowded.

After a brief pause:

Bowie: How about Tuesday?

The spacecraft alarm cut him off, saving her from having to think up another excuse. Their target had appeared. Time for some fun.

* * *

"Weidemeyer" he said into the phone.

"Data has a match. Hood told me to give it to you." No name, FBI Special Agent Daniel Shelton knew his voice would be recognized.

"Tell me more, my good friend."

"Six months ago a badlander hired one of our stoolies to put in a remote antenna. He got a local address. From the ranges, antenna angles, and building geometries, we can work backwards. Our perp's location is one of about three hundred units in three apartments."

"OK, go on."

"Two days ago another snitch filed a report. Seems the same badlander does laundry on Mondays at a public facility. None of the three apartments have laundry rooms and there's only one laundromat in the area."

"So why are you giving this gift to me?"

"According to the file, the biggest thing this perp has admitted to is passing scrip. We figure you could make a counterfeiting charge really hurt, so it should be yours. Besides, I want you to owe me."

"Thanks, I do owe you. Who's the perp?"

"Badlands name is Dancing Fawn."

* * *

"Have you seen the latest quotes?" asked Parker. Maxwell Stein, the Governor of the Chicago Fed, nodded. The grim expression on his face didn't change.

"Suggestions?" asked Parker.

"I warned you this day would come."

"Ideas, Stein. Not lectures."

"We have few options."

For the past week, the dollar slid against everything but the Euro. Collapsed might be a better word. The currencies of China, Taiwan, Korea, and OPEC all exploded upward. If this went on much longer, the U.S. military would run short of almost everything but beans. Fuel, spares, even uniforms and body armor. Production lines for everything that used semiconductors or exotic metals or computers would shut down. Critical components that the military could not do without would become unavailable. All were bought offshore and paid for with dollars. If the slide continued much longer, the U. S. military wouldn't be able to afford any of it.

"Gold Standard?" asked Parker.

Stein nodded again. "We're down to that."

"Does the Fed have enough metal? To back it up? Make it creditable, I mean."

Stein gave a very uncharacteristic shrug, then answered with "Probably not."

For many months now, the organizations controlled by Parker and Stein had been strengthening the central bank's balance sheet by buying gold as quietly as possible. But their stockpile still seemed light. No one could say for sure, of course, what would satisfy the country's trading partners. Controlling a market, like controlling a currency, was also a confidence game. But the only way to be sure the suckers would fall for it was to get more metal.

"You're not helping me here, Maxwell. Ideas? I mean, what can we do?"

"I see only one practical source for more metal." As Stein had made clear often in the past, he favored compensated confiscation. Take the metal from the citizens of the United States. Pay them a little for it, but take it. Call it eminent domain. A lump of gold was no different from land sitting in front of a freeway expansion. No one objects to the government buying out a homeowner if his house stands in the way of progress. Why should gold be any different? As long as the public felt the owner was paid a fair price, they would probably go along.

"How do we do it? Get them to turn it in, I mean. We can't search every house. Send a cop to each one. We can't."

"You don't have to. The IRS has a list of gold owners." Last year, every taxpayer in the United States had been required to declare all gold ownership on his tax return. These records, along with those of sales from all the gold dealers in the country, would supply a pretty complete list of everyone that owned or had owned gold within the past seven years.

"So what are you suggesting?"

"Executive Order. Just like in '33."

"The President's Van de Groot's man."

"So work something out. Van de Groot has as much to lose if this thing goes south as we do."

"What should the order say?"

"Same as '33. The Fed will pay for the gold at the market price on the day before the order is issued. Make it a felony to not turn the stuff in. Have the IRS back it up with a letter to everyone who declared gold ownership on a tax return. Get your pals at the commodity exchange to drive the price down before the announcement so we won't have to pay as much. I could even get the Fed to dump a little physical a week ahead of time to push the price down even more."

"Wouldn't everyone just ship their metal out of the country?"

"If they didn't tell the IRS they had any then, yes, I guess that could be a problem. Have the order make it a felony to export gold, too."

Both lapsed into thought, considering the matter. The moral issue of robbing his fellow citizens didn't bother Parker. After all, the future of American military power was at stake. No, it was the practical problem that bothered him. And, Parker had to admit, Stein seemed to have a solution for that.

Not only would it provide gold to support the dollar, it would also, in one stroke, cripple the badlands. After all, they refused to use anything but gold for money. Deny them the use of that metal and their economy would collapse. Their only other alternative would be some form of fiat currency, but their own counterfeiting efforts had so disgraced that class of money that no badlander now had any faith in it. And, even in the badlands, money was about trust. Without a medium of exchange that they could all agree on, their society would be reduced to barter. That change alone would destroy them as an effective opponent to Globalization.

"Tell me again. How will this help the dollar? I know, but go over it for me again," said Parker.

"The point of a gold standard is to induce trust in a currency by allowing those that use it to redeem it, if they wish, for gold at a promised rate. To get that trust, you have to let someone do some exchanging. In this case, its foreigners. If they become convinced that the redemption offer will stay valid, the dollar should stabilize. Maybe even go up a little."

"Can we afford to do that?"

"Sure, as long as we set the price high enough."

"How high?"

"Twelve thousand an ounce. That should be high enough to allow for the wave of inflation that will hit after we do this. "

"Where do we get enough money to buy at that price?"

"We don't. We force the sale at the price gold was at the day before the Executive Order is issued. If we drive it down hard enough ahead of time, we should be able to get the metal for well under a thousand.

"Still, where do we get the money? To buy, I mean. Even under a thousand? That's still a lot of money."

Stein smiled. "We own the printing press, remember?"

Chapter 13

Caught

We all carry cravings that come from deep within our genes. For men, it is the desire for the hunt, the need to bring fresh meat home to the hearth. For women, it's their children, their nest. For reasons that are beyond any man, one of the primary symbols of nesting, something that every woman feels the need to have at an atavistic level, is her own washing machine.

Fawn was no different. Part of the reason she chose this apartment was the utility room. That was to be the altar on which she could make one of the sacrifices needed for female happiness. There she could install her own washer and dryer.

They arrived yesterday from Sears, packed in neat, efficient boxes. She was ready, having bought the tools weeks ago, one at a time, like Christmas decorations to reassure herself that Santa would really bring her a present.

Now the installation was finished. Her two white servants squatted together in their nook, ready for her first command. The hoses and plugs were hooked up, both water valves were open. It was time.

She checked her first load one last time, then closed the lid and hit the button.

The machine, her machine, thunked. A little thrill surged up her spine. Then came gurgles and splashing. It was happy. Her washer was happy. And she was happy.

Twenty six minutes later, the first load she had ever washed in her very own machine was clean. As she transferred damp clothes to the first dryer she had ever owned, she made herself a promise. Never again would she see the inside of a public laundry.

* * *

One advantage of being higher up the enforcement food chain is that you don't have to do your own leg work. Well, at least some of the time you don't. This was not one of those instances. So Weidemeyer personally spent the day visiting the offices of the three apartments in question, collecting the names of all the residents in each one.

Turning them into pictures was a little more difficult. Florida DMV did most of it, matching all but three of the them. Two didn't drive, while one had a license from Ohio.

A request to the Ohio DMV produced a picture for the out-of-state name. It also turned up an interesting bit of information. Two years ago, a child pornographer claimed he saw gold, cash, and drugs in the subject's van. For some reason, DHS never got a copy of the Cleveland report. Orlando did, but the cops there declined to pursue the matter, so it died.

If this woman shows up tomorrow, thought Weidemeyer, *I'll give her special attention.*

Monday found Weidemeyer and one of the local Secret Service agents sitting outside the laundromat taking pictures of everyone who went in or out. Public laundries are open long hours, so it had been a tiring day, but worth the effort. He got six good matches.

Now, to kill time, he was on line getting the plates for every vehicle owned by any of the suspects. Tonight, he would walk quietly through the parking lots, attaching a GPS tracker to each one. Then it would be a waiting game. With luck, one would take a long trip with lots of stops. Otherwise, he would have to wait until some other probable cause showed up.

* * *

It wasn't summer, but Fawn didn't care. She took her girls out of school anyway, telling the teacher they needed to visit a sick relative in Miami. Once, she might have felt guilty about the lie. Now, all that mattered was the freedom to sing with her girls at the top of their lungs as they drove back north. Three more stops and she would finish her day's quota. Then it would be time for, what, maybe a visit to the beach?

She wasn’t thinking about how well her new washer and dryer worked or how she would never again have to use a laundromat. Of course, she had no idea that staying home had saved her and her girls from arrest.

Almost, anyway. Unfortunately, Weidemeyer had decided to track her vehicle, even though she hadn't shown up at the laundromat, because the Cleveland police report justified the extra surveillance.

So there would be no beach today. Instead, blue lights began flashing behind her.

* * *

"Where are my girls?"

These were not the first words Joshua Weidemeyer usually got when he met a new prisoner for the first time. And they were not even uttered in the belligerent tone he had grown to expect.

The woman who asked the question was dressed in prison orange, huddled small against the cold room. She sat on the edge of the lower bunk, sitting on the same bare steel springs she slept on for the past three nights. Her hair had been cut short. Without makeup, her freckles showed through the dirt on her face. In short, she looked exactly like she felt: Scared and tired.

"They're here, in this building. They're all right. In fact, they're considerably better off than you are right now," answered Weidemeyer.

"Can I see them?"

"Perhaps. But, first I must give you this," he said as he handed her an unsealed envelope through the bars. She took it and, in the always-on bright bluish light of her solitary cell, opened it to read the letter inside.

It was the same document he had been handing prisoners for six years, ever since they had first arrested Sven Olsen. The difference was that, thanks to Presidents Bush and Obama, it was now true. Now he really could keep her forever without telling anyone. Now, for the first time ever in American history, the threat in this document wasn't an illegal bluff.

She put the letter down. There was no longer any need for him to ask for it back.

"Can I see my girls now?"

Weidemeyer begin to sense he was dealing with a one-track mind. That was good. Trains are easier to control if they only run on one track.

"Help us."

"Doing what?"

"Find out who runs the badlands."

"No one runs it."

"We're not children. We don't believe in fairy tales. Will you help us?"

"What if I can't find anyone because there really isn't anyone?"

"As long as you try your best, that will be enough."

"OK. Can I see my girls now?"

Weidemeyer got up, the interview over.

"Yes," he said as he started out. "And I'll see what I can do about getting you a mattress and some linens."

"Thank you," she said in a quiet voice as he turned to go. And as he walked out the door, he thought about the fact that no one else had ever shown any gratitude for any part of this interview.

* * *

Two men sat alone in the large comfortable office. The older asked "How have the interrogations gone so far?"

"Well enough." answered Josh Weidemeyer to his former boss, and now friend, of ten years. "I think we know everything she can tell us about the badlands."

"Has she told you who's running it?"

"No. She truly believes the place just grew like Topsy."

"Like everyone else we catch."

"Whoever's running it is doing a great job of staying under cover."

"Have you put her online yet?"

"No."

"Because?" asked his boss.

"I'm still not sure which password she'll use."

"Keep pounding until you can trust her. We'll just have to wait until then.

"We may not have a choice." said Weidemeyer.

"How so?"

"We've had her for almost two weeks. No med pick-ups. No metal going back. If we keep her much longer, someone's going to notice. That would destroy her rep as quick as if she used a red password."

"We could have one of our people pick up her meds and scrip. Send some metal back from here."

Weidemeyer shook his head. "We've tried that before with other snitches. Eventually, they all get flagged. You know that."

"You have a suggestion?"

"Let her out to run her business."

"Christ, Josh, we can't do that! Badlander connections are too damned good. Let her out and she'll have new papers and be out of the country before the weekend."

"Not if we keep her kids."

That gave his boss pause. In the long tradition of statecraft, the taking and holding of hostages has always been a very successful technique for controlling an adversary. Why not use it now?

"She care that much about them?"

"More. She'd rather die than see them in a foster home." The irony of the statement slipped by them both.

"How you going to stop her from warning her friends while she's out?"

"We'll just have to trust that fear of losing her daughters will control what she says."

"Can we at least put a spy program in her laptop?"

"Not in the software. Her wheel house sweeps her computer every time she crosses. They'd find it and that would destroy her credibility, too.

"What about hardware? Is there room for a logger?"

A keystroke logger is a small hardware device that records, and sometimes transmits, all keyboard entries. And, most important for this situation, the simplest ones can't be detected by software sweeps.

They also need space and must match the interfaces used by the other boards. That's rarely a problem in desktops because those units have plenty of room inside and use standard connectors. But laptops can be difficult.

Sometimes a logger will fit, sometimes not.

"Maybe," answered Weidemeyer. "They're working on it."

"Well, I guess we've nothing to lose. Like you say, she'll go stale soon anyway if we don't act. Do what you think best."

Thank you, Josh thought, *and good luck to me.*

* * *

Weidemeyer handed another letter to her through the bars. She read it, her worst nightmare. The signed, approved court order delivered her girls to foster care and authorized their adoption. All her fears and terrors, all her nightmares brought to fruition by a single piece of paper. She began to cry. Not loudly, not noticeably, but profusely. Without moving, tears welled up and streamed down her cheeks, dripping from her chin to fall on the damning paper.

"Can I see them before they go?" she asked without looking up.

Weidemeyer waited a few heartbeats for the horror of the letter to sink in a little more, then he threw out the carrot.

"They don't have to go."

That got her attention. She looked up at him, desperate for any shred of hope.

"If I ask the court to delay the execution, they'll stay here."

"Why would you?"

"I need your help. We could make a deal."

She'd heard enough deals in her lifetime. The offer of another brought no new hope. She just waited for it to come.

"We fly you back to Orlando. Your girls stay here in boarding school. You work on your business, just like before. Every weekend you come back here, see them between trips."

"And you want the king of the badlands."

He nodded.

"There isn't one."

"Like I said earlier, do your best. Keep us updated. That'll be good enough."

"Will I have to turn in my friends?"

Weidemeyer knew this would be a sticking point. With luck, he would get her to change her mind later, but for now, he already had enough small fish. He wanted the king. But he also didn't want his agreement to be on a recording for some future enemy to use. So, rather than answer, he shook his head no.

She just sat, staring back at him, drained. He saw he could push no more, but he also saw he didn't need to. She just hadn't realized it yet.

Turning to go, he said "I'll tell the matron to send your girls in. You can give me your answer tomorrow."

Chapter 14

Terrorists

Jane Doe's car carried a new spare tire. She didn't realize it, had never checked it. But sometime in the past month, someone changed it without her knowledge. Perhaps when her car was last serviced. Or, since she parked on the street, maybe someone crawled under it one night and made the switch. When and how didn't matter. It was done. That was all that counted. Because of it, Jane Doe's life would shortly be over.

The spare was winched up under the rear. Had she bothered to lay down and look at it, she would have seen nothing unusual, just a dirty doughnut clamped into place with a cable.

Getting a flat is one of life's unlucky events. At least it would have been for most people, but not for her. On the contrary, it would have been a lifesaver. Then, in the process of changing her tire, she would have lowered the spare and found it very heavy, so heavy that she couldn't lift it into place over the wheel hub. She would have had to ask someone to help her and whoever she asked would have had a hard time, even if her assistant were a man, because this tire was filled with something other than air.

Probably, she would have given up and called a tow truck. More good luck for her, because the operator would have known enough about tires to see that there was something very wrong with this one. He would have taken it back to the shop and eventually cut it open to find what was inside.

But she wasn't lucky enough to have had a flat. Instead, she was stopped by another roadblock. They sprang up everywhere. There a day or two, then gone. They stopped traffic, caused long lines, and made everyone angry. At first, they were manned by local police or state troopers, but now it was usually TSA inspectors backed by national guard troops. Their attitude showed they didn't like the duty any more than she liked having to wait for the check.

Finally, after almost twenty minutes in line, she pulled to the head and handed her papers to the agent. As he examined them, a small computer embedded in her spare tire made a decision.

In its cockroach-like mind it had a list of geographic coordinates that were updated via a cell phone connection roughly every half-hour. Except for that call, the cell connection was turned off so it couldn't be traced. Every few seconds, this artificial insect brain checked those coordinates against the ones from a GPS chip mounted next to it on the same circuit board.

Now, for the first and only time in its dumb existence, one of the downloaded coordinates matched its present location. So, without hesitation, it closed a small relay. That sent a current to a detonator which ignited the 20 lbs of ammonium nitrate/oil mixture that filled the spare tire.

Twenty pounds of explosive doesn't sound like much and, perhaps, it's not. But it is enough to end the lives of four drivers (including Jane Doe), six TSA inspectors, and two citizen-soldiers who had the misfortune to be near the vehicle when it exploded.

Someone had finally had enough of surprise roadblocks and had done something about it.

* * *

"Let's start off with an introduction."

Hood was chairing another session of the BS committee. At the long table in front of him sat the ten key bureaucrats in the war on the badlands: Representatives of the Secret Service (Weidemeyer), the FBI (Shelton), the NSA, DOD, and the CIA. Also present were the heads of the Coast Guard, FEMA (Carter), the Border Patrol, and the TSA. All now made a big show of giving him their undivided attention.

"Please join me in giving a warm welcome to our newest member, Pug Ringgold, National SWAT Team Coordinator. He comes to us via the Army Special Forces, DIA, and the CIA. His responsibilities will include all SWAT training, recruiting, and equipment throughout the country. A big hand please," he said as he started the clapping.

Pug stood up, towered over those still seated. The room fell silent, expecting him to speak. But he kept his own counsel. Without breaking the silence or showing a smile, he sat down.

"Questions?" Hood asked.

"Are you responsible for directing local forces, too?"

Hood took the question before Pug could respond. "No. Not in normal circumstances. His shop will only be responsible for finance, training, personnel, and procurement. But in the event of a declared national emergency, he will also be responsible for all operational aspects as well.

That would include local forces, but only after a Presidential Executive Order."

There was a pause for other questions. None came.

"OK, let's do some announcements." Then, after a barely noticeable pause, which Hood used to gain eye contact with his audience, he said "First, we've had another roadblock bombing."

"When?"

"Last night. A little before midnight."

"Where?"

"LA. That's twenty-two so far. Everyone get the point now? This is war. Not just rhetoric. A real people-killing war. Our people."

He paused to let that sink in.

"Over two hundred dead. Almost a hundred were your brothers and sisters. Soldiers like you in the fight to preserve order. We're not fighting petty crime any more. Anyone want to see the pictures? I got pictures. Anyone?"

He paused for effect. Some of his committee gave slight shakes of their heads, the others just looked somber. None spoke. But everyone was really paying attention now.

"All right, then, it's time to act as if this is a war. Time to get with the program. Effective immediately, I'm issuing shoot-to-kill authority to all personnel under my command. Similar directives are going out right now to all other departments. This is no longer a game."

"Exactly when are we authorized to use deadly force?" asked the head of the Border Patrol.

"Anytime you have reason to believe that the suspect has access to the badlands and you have no other way of preventing his escape."

"Anytime? Shoot-to-kill some geeky kid that's running away? In the back?"

"That 'geek', as you call him, is part of a terrorist conspiracy. Catch him if you can, we want to know everything he does. But, if you can't do that, don't let him get away. Pump a full mag into his back if you have to, but no get-aways"

Another pause for questions. None were asked.

"We used to call them badlanders. I say 'used to' because that terminology has now changed. From now on, those people will be called exactly what they are: Terrorists. Period. No more use of the word 'badlanders' to describe these animals. Is that clear?"

It must have been, there was no response to his question.

"Next item. The National Security Firewall is now up. NSA is monitoring access and should be able to give us the IP of anyone who attempts an international VPN connection without proper certificates."

"Is making such an attempt a crime?"

"Yes. If the perp can prove it was just a mistake, fine, but otherwise we Get Him And Sweat Him. For as long as we need to. Questions?"

Silence answered.

"Finally, we now have our own badlands crossing house. It's been named COCHISE Crossing to honor the original occupants of our own badlands. It's available to any of your personnel."

"How do we get to use it?"

"Apply through my office for a set of approved wheels."

"Approved?"

"Yes. Let me stress what most of you already know: All crossings must be monitored. Until now, that meant using some snitch's laptop at one of our facilities. Now that's changed. After you get approval for a plan of investigation, we will authorize you to cross from any physical location as long as you use COCHISE and an approved computer."

"Does this mean we won't have to file weekly reports?"

"No, they'll still be required. It only means that more of you will be able to cross at once. Your conversations will still be logged by your laptop, as will your movements, for use in filling in the details around the statements you make in your reports."

The room fell silent.

"No questions? Good. Now on to..."

* * *

It was dark outside when Fred Delling activated the office alarm. When the warning beeping began, he stepped out the front door, then closed and locked it. Inside, he could see the alarm indicator turn from flashing red to steady green. He had left the cocoon of safety that his small company provided, closed the envelope of security behind him, and was now literally alone out in the cold. Tired, after another long day of trying to save his dream from collapse, he turned to walk to his car.

But, instead of making the trip, he stopped. Standing in the middle of the empty lot, directly under one of the two light posts that still worked, was a dark figure in a trench coat and hat. The coat was not unusual given the cold, wet weather, but the hat was. Men rarely wore hats nowadays.

The face of the watcher was only partly visible under the shadow of the wide brim. It was an average face, neither handsome nor ugly, hard nor soft. Yet it caught his attention. Not the face, actually, but the eyes. They were not the eyes of a stranger. He had seen them before.

"Hello, Delling. How's business?" asked the man. The voice, like the eyes, was familiar. There was no hostility in it, no sign of any threat. The question seemed to be no more than that, just a question.

"Well enough, thank you." Delling answered, more from habit than for any other reason. Then his curiosity got the better of him. "Do I know you?"

"Probably," said the stranger and removed his hat. In the harsh parking lot light, a face appeared, coalescing into existence. It was the face of Luke Abbas, the man responsible for the current financial crisis of Delling's own company. Not long ago, Abbas had stolen his own son and his company's funds. The latter went bankrupt, defaulting on debts it owed to Delling's firm. It all flows downhill.

"I should call the police," Delling said. Luke was, after all, a wanted man.

"Perhaps you should. Perhaps you still will, even after you hear me out. But, please, listen to what I have to say first."

Delling pulled out his cell phone, flipped it open and got ready to dial. "You have one minute."

"And you have money waiting for you in an account in your name. Enough to pay what my company owed you. If you don't want to hear more, go ahead. Call 911."

Delling did nothing. Right now, money was important. More to the point, except for his last erratic act, Luke Abbas had always been a reliable business associate. And, maybe, even a bit of a friend.

Luke walked up to him, slowly, as he might to a dog he didn't want to startle. Raising his right hand, he held out two business cards. Lowering the phone, Delling took them both and examined them in the dim light. One said only 'Lucius Magnus' and 'BARABBAS Crossing House'. The other bore a series of numbers and the name 'Cato The Elder'.

"What are these?"

"Have you ever heard of the badlands?"

"Maybe."

"My name there is Lucius Magnus. If you go to the badlands and contact me, I'll give you the bank account for your money. The other card gives you the details on how to get there, to cross over the border."

"Why do you have a bank account for me?"

"Because I owe you."

"Yes, you do. So what?"

A prowl car pulled into view from up the dark street. Slowly, looking for some of the trouble that had become so common of late, it drove by. As it did so, one of the officers panned a spotlight over the unlit ghost mall across the street. Both men watched it slide past and disappear back into the darkness. Neither made any attempt to attract the attention of the two officers who were its occupants.

"I want to make up for some of the damage I did," Luke began again. "I'm trying to do that now. If you'll let me."

"Why give me my money in the badlands? Why not just send me a check?"

The drizzle started up again. Luke, who wasn't standing under the entryway awning, held up his hat and asked "May I?" After getting a slight nod, he put it back on.

"Because giving you a check here, in the real world, would just be giving it to a government that I despise. As soon as they knew you had funds, they'd steal it. Taxes, fines, fees, inflation. It doesn't matter how, they'd still get it. This money is for you and your people, not them."

"My bills are in the real world. If it's not in a real bank, I go out of business."

"Maybe. Or maybe you just move your company to a different place. Like I did."

"I owe my people too much to ditch them."

"I didn't ditch mine."

"They got letters of recommendation instead of paychecks. What do you call that?"

"I call it a temporary expedient. One since made good."

"How?"

"By hiring them back or finding jobs for them elsewhere."

"Elsewhere?"

"In the badlands. They all feed their families now."

"And you want me to do the same?"

"I want you to do what you think best. Protect your people any way you can."

Delling handed one of the cards back, the one with the numbers.

Taking it, Lucius looked at in the dim light. "You'll need this to get across," he said.

"How do you think I've stayed solvent so long?" answered Delling as he moved towards his car. "There's not a business in this country that isn't either on the government take or working through the badlands. And I don't do government work."

Then he paused, took one last look at Lucius, and said "But I will be in touch, Lucius. I promise. I intend to collect what you owe me."

And, with that, Delling got into his car and drove off into the darkness. And Lucius Magnus realized that more people were already in the badlands than he had ever before suspected.

* * *

"I've been thinking," said Weidemeyer. Under the circumstances, that was a good trick. Thinking, that is, not speaking, although that was also not so easy. The loud bass, in particular, made thought difficult, but Joshua Weidemeyer's powers of concentration were unusually good. Not having alcohol in his system helped.

"Ten years ago, we shut down a ring by hijacking their server," he continued.

"Coro?" asked Daniel Shelton, his regular drinking partner (if tonic with a twist could be called 'drinking').

Weidemeyer nodded.

"I heard of it."

"Why can't we just do that here?"

"How?"

"The badlands is built around their 'Thieves Emporium'. Right?"

Shelton nodded.

"What if we hijack its server? Just find the hardware it runs on and grab it? Then we'd have the whole badlands, right?"

"Nice try. No cigar."

"Why?"

"It doesn't exist."

"The Thieves Emporium?"

Daniel shook his head. "The server. It doesn't exist. The Emporium doesn't run on a server. At least not in the sense that you mean."

"I don't understand."

"Badlanders are a paranoid bunch of fuckers. If you were one of them, would you risk having the core of your world all in one place?"

Weidemeyer just looked back at his friend, waiting for the punch line.

"That's what their Emporium is, right? The heart of their world? The central exchange for the badlands? Right?"

"Yes. I guess so."

"So the fuckers don't have one."

"An Emporium?"

"No. A single market. They don't have one big exchange, like some giant fucking Walmart. Instead, they stitch lots of little piss-ass markets together. That's why they call it an Emporium. It's a matrix of little markets."

Even sober, Weidemeyer was having a hard time grasping that concept. It didn't help that a waitress with a lovely set of nipples chose that particular moment to check up on their table.

"Who connected them together?" asked Weidemeyer after the nipples were out of earshot, which, because of the music, was about the length of an outstretched arm.

"No one. It just happened."

Daniel could see from the look on his friends face that the idea hadn't found a new home.

"Think of a big fucking flea market," he tried again. "Or a trade show. Better yet, an old Arab souk. In a big fucking building. Lots of stalls down every hallway. No one runs more than a couple of them. If you want something, go up to any one of them and ask. If its owner doesn't have what you want, he'll know who does. If he trusts you, he'll point you in the right direction.

"The place works because everyone cooperates with everyone else. No one runs it, no one owns it. But if you want something, and they trust you, eventually you'll find what you're looking for."

"And the badlands is like that?"

"Yep. Just faster. If you wanted to open a shop in the badlands, you'd rent space from a market house. Your new landlord would have a list of doorbell addresses for other markets. When you open for business, he'd forward a copy of your shop to everyone on that list, updated automatically to stay current.

"Every market house maintains its own address list. If another house trusts yours, it sends your house its doorbell address and copies of its shops. As a courtesy, all houses display each other's shops along with their own to anyone that visits."

"If I open a shop, can I get a copy of my landlord's address list?" asked Weidemeyer.

"Nice try. But, no. You get the names only. If you want to contact someone, your market translates the name to a doorbell. Being too loose with other people's doorbells will lose a market operator trust real fast."

"So there's really no one in charge of their markets?"

"The Thieves Emporium? Nope. Sorry. Not as far as I can see, anyway."

The two lapsed back into silence again as Nipples brought them refills. After she left, Weidemeyer asked "How do you know all this?"

"Every crossing house runs it's own market, or at least has a connection to a market house. Has to, or its indentureds wouldn't know how to contact anyone. There aren't any phone books in the badlands."

"So?"

"So when the FBI set up COCHISE, they had to start their own market from scratch."

"I thought COCHISE was a DHS thing."

"It is now. We couldn't get it to go so they took it over. So far, that asshole Hood hasn't done any better than we did."

"It's not working?"

"Oh, it works, it's just not trusted."

"Who cares as long as you can cross through it?"

"Changing doorbells is a pain, no one wants to do it, but it's the only option if DHS snags yours. So everyone is cagey. They only hand out their addresses to markets they trust. But it takes time to get that trust. COCHISE is too new. So, right now, we don't have many other markets listed in ours."

"Meaning?"

"You can cross through COCHISE, you just can't go anywhere afterwards."

"So, if I wanted to look around the badlands, you'd recommend I not use

COCHISE?"

"Just between friends?"

"It stays here."

"Maybe someday. For now, fuck no. Don't bother. Use one of your snitches instead."

* * *

What can you say about a man who falls twelve stories from the balcony of his apartment? Other than noting that he dies, that is. Would you call it suicide? An accident? Or murder?

Would it make a difference if he had a high alcohol level in his blood? What if it happened after midnight? Would it matter if no one was seen going into or out of his apartment? What if the security cameras for his condo complex were not working when he fell? Should the fact that he was under considerable financial pressure be taken into account? Or the fact that the FBI, several state prosecutors, and a Congressional Committee were conducting investigations of his activities as CEO of ENGCO?

This was the conundrum that faced the authorities when Edgar Kohrob's body was found broken across the edge of a swimming pool. It was not an easy question to ponder. Be thankful that you are not the Medical Examiner responsible for ruling on the cause of his death.

When his demise was announced to the public, more than a few individuals did breath easier. Not only could Kohrob's testimony have implicated many working for ENGCO, but it might have spattered as far upstream as FEMA, Homeland Security, and even Parker himself. Most of the relatives of those that he had killed to cover up the problems with the Prometheus project would also be pleased, though many of them would have wished for him to take longer to die.

Regardless of what the authorities decided on the matter, three points concerning his death were worthy of comment. First, before he died, he stopped the blackmail payments to Caper Oleander because the investigations made it too risky to continue them. Second, he made extensive arrangements to hide the fact that past payments had been made. And finally, he died before he could tell Arnold Wilson Parker that he had stopped those payments.

Caper Oleander might be the only person who would not be happy because Kohrob had died.

Chapter 15

On The Street Again

System: Angelo Pisa, male, RENAISSANCE, has entered the room

Fawn: Hey, clown-face. Good to see you.

Angelo: Yeah, good to see your login, too. But you can cut out the clown-face bit. We don't wear funny masks any more.

Fawn: What, you don't need to be anonymous?

Angelo: Oh, we need to hide more than ever. It's just that now, a plastic mask isn't enough protection.

Fawn: Against what?

Angelo: Tear gas. Batons. Water cannons. We still cover our faces, but now it's with dust masks and goggles.

Fawn: Are things getting that bad?

Angelo: I wear cardboard armor under my poncho and a bicycle helmet to protect my head, but I still come home bleeding and bruised.

Fawn: Maybe it's time to stop.

Angelo: What would I tell my kids?

Fawn: You have kids?

Angelo: No, not yet. But I want to. And if I do, I don't want them to be slaves because I didn't fight.

Fawn: And you still want me to join?

Angelo: What will you tell your girls when they grown up? What will you say when they ask why you let it all slip away?

Fawn: Time to change the subject. I need your help.

Angelo: Ready.

Fawn: I have to convince somebody that no one runs the badlands.

Angelo: Why? It's obvious.

> Fawn: I made a bet, now I have to back it up. Any suggestions?
>
> Angelo: It's pretty hard to prove a negative. But, in this case, unnecessary. All she has to do is look around and see for herself.
>
> Fawn: He doesn't have border privileges.
>
> Angelo: Oh oh. Competition?
>
> Fawn: No, no. Just a friend.
>
> Angelo: OK, 'he'. Just get 'him' across and he'll see for himself. Otherwise, I don't see how you can win your bet. I don't know of any way to prove that someone doesn't run the badlands.

* * *

Weidemeyer was standing on the sidewalk outside her apartment when Fawn drove out. As she stopped at the entrance, waiting for traffic, he walked up and handed her an ad for a local coffee shop. Could she give him directions to it? When she answered, honestly, that she didn't know where the place was, he thanked her and, dropping a note into her lap as he retrieved the ad, left. The note had directions to the shop and told her to meet him there in an hour.

Now they sat facing each other across two orders of scrambled eggs.

"So, how you settling in?" he asked.

"I've been settled for over a year. What do you want?"

"Straight to the point, eh? OK. I want to stress how important your cooperation is."

"Got that."

"How you going to do this?"

And that, she thought, *was a good question.* As she considered her answer, her gaze fell on an abandoned motel across the street. Had its owners asked the same question? *How am I going to do the impossible?* They to save their business, she to find someone that didn't exist.

"You want an honest answer?" she asked.

"I wouldn't have asked if I didn't."

To her surprise, she found herself willing to give one. If it existed, that is.

But only to him. Not to his bosses. And certainly not to the entire civ organization, for ever and ever.

"You got your phone with you?" she asked.

He nodded.

"Give it to me," she demanded, holding out her hand.

He stared back, startled by her tone.

"You want honesty?" she demanded.

He nodded again.

"Then give."

After a second of indecision, he reached into his pocket and gave it to her. She pulled hers from her purse and handed both back to him, saying "Lock them in your car."

He didn't respond, even though he knew why she made the demand, because he didn't want to encourage the rebellion he saw in her eyes.

"Now."

Another second of thought, then he took them and left the table. Two minutes later, he returned. "OK. Talk," was all he said as he sat down.

"You been at this badlands thing long?"

He nodded, offering no more than necessary.

"How long?" she pushed.

"Five years. Maybe. Why?"

"How many agents you got looking?"

"Quite a few."

"Couple hundred?"

"Maybe."

"For five years. And you're still looking. So you got nothing."

"Maybe."

"Why do you think I can do better?"

"No one's watching you. You're outside. That might give you an edge."

"You overrate me," she answered, frustration clear in her tone. Looking back out the window, she struggled for an idea. Any idea. But none came.

Across the street, the motel looked back at her in lonely silence. *Am I like your owners?* she asked it. *Committed to fail in an impossible quest? Please, God, please. Help me keep my girls.*

"What else can I do?" he asked, interrupting her thoughts.

Then, perhaps, God answered her.

"Stop relying on someone else," she said.

"Meaning?"

"Go after the King yourself."

"You mean cross on my own?"

She nodded.

"We've got procedures. I'd have to get clearance, use a monitored computer, log all my contacts, file weekly reports. It could be done, but it'd be slow."

She studied his eyes, trying to decide if the moment was right. Finally, she said "Why not use your own computer?"

"You mean get my own 'wheels'?"

She nodded.

"Strictly against the rules."

"Obey them, you go nowhere."

He considered the matter, looking at the collapsed motel as he thought. Was he thinking about its owner, too?

"Suppose I decided to go on my own. How would I do it?"

"Use a crossing house. Like everyone else."

He'd actually thought about it. Often, in fact, because nothing else had worked. At first the unauthorized nature of the act stopped him, but, as time passed without success, that worry faded, overwhelmed by his desperation to try something new. Now, the only thing that held him back was not knowing a way to do it.

"How would I contact one?"

"I could do it for you."

And turn me in afterwards, he thought. *Of course, if she did that, I'd activate the court order. And she knows it. A Mexican standoff.*

"Which crossing house?"

"Mine."

"I'll think about it."

Four days later, he found out that GOBI DESERT had a rep to kill for.

* * *

> Chang: Heavens, child, are you feeling all right? Don't you understand that he's the enemy?
>
> Fawn: Yes, but he's the enemy we know. Flag him, but let him through.
>
> Chang: Why? Why should we risk our reputation?
>
> Fawn: If he worked for the State Department and wanted to cross, you'd take him in a minute, wouldn't you?
>
> Chang: That's different.
>
> Fawn: Why? Because someone from State could get you false passports? How would you know he wasn't snitching every time you gave him an order? You wouldn't, would you? You'd just make a risk-reward decision, hedge your bets by not telling him anything you didn't have to, and go with it, right?
>
> Chang: Yes.
>
> Fawn: Well, how is this any different? He's working for DHS, not State, but he's still in deep enough to be worth a lot to us.
>
> Chang: He hasn't asked to join us, has he?
>
> Fawn: No.
>
> Chang: Then he's not just a potential snitch, he's a self-confessed

one.

Fawn: At least you'll know where he stands. Flag him so everyone he deals with is careful what they say, but let him in.

There are no courts in the badlands. You can't sue to claim damages, so you check reps on everyone you meet. Everyone. You do this by subscribing to a reporting service. They, in turn, use bots to scan all of the badlands, looking for gossip on everyone. Had a bad experience with a snitch house? Post a complaint. Worried someone you know is a civ spy? Post a warning. Happy with your crossing house? Post an attaboy. They all get sucked up, digested, and spit out by half-a-dozen different reporting houses. Subscribe to whichever one you trust the most, but do subscribe. Everyone in the badlands does.

Josh Weidemeyer had no rep because he hadn't dealt with anyone there yet, or at least anyone who had posted a report. But, according to Fawn, he did have one in the real world, and it was very clear: He was a sharp cop. A dedicated civ. And he stood against everything the badlands was. Yet now he wanted to cross. How could any reputable crossing house handle that? Would it be enough to just post a report saying he was a civ spy and leave it at that? Would all your customers drop you if they knew you sponsored a known snitch? Or would they accept it as long as you posted a clear and strong warning? The man that Fawn knew as Mai Lee Chang had to weigh risks and rewards, something that, in this case, he couldn't do without talking to some of his customers.

Chang: OK. I see your point. Let me ask around, but no promises. What is his name?

Fawn: He wants this confidential.

Chang: You have my word it will be. But I have to know more about him or I cannot approve. That is the best I can do. What is his name?

Fawn knew if she asked for Weidemeyer's approval, the entire thing would fall through. She would lose what little hold she had over him and her girls would suffer for the rest of their lives. On the other hand, he hadn't explicitly told her not to give his name.

Fawn: Promise you won't tell anyone why you're asking about him? And you'll erase his real-world name as soon as you decide?

Chang: Are you in a position to bargain?

Fawn: It's important to me. Please, will you promise?

Chang: Yes, child. I will promise.

Fawn: To both requests?

Chang: Yes, child, yes. Now, what is his name?

Fawn: Joshua Weidemeyer.

Chang: Thank you. I will look into it and get back to you as soon as I can.

Fawn: How soon?

Chang: Why are the young always so impatient? I have no idea, it will take as long as it takes. Maybe next week, OK?

Fawn signed off with some hope.

* * *

The Smart Grid had browned out Fawn's air conditioning earlier this morning, but her refrigerator still had power. So she sat alone in her warm kitchen, a glass of chilled wine in her hand, and enjoyed the conversation that was beginning on her wheels.

Nairobi: Raw fish? You're going to make us sit here and watch you eat raw fish?

Bowie: Criminy. You can't actually see me eat it, you know.

Angelo: Hey, I like sushi.

Fawn: Doesn't anyone want to know what I'm eating?

Nairobi: Please, Lord, let it be cooked.

Bowie: OK, pass the pictures so we can eat.

A pleasant twenty minutes passed while all looked at pictures, texted each other, and enjoyed good food.

Fawn: Hey, did anyone have trouble crossing today?

Angelo: Yeah, I think they're getting that National Security Firewall running.

Fawn: What's that?

Angelo: They're trying to stop badlanders from getting across by making it hard to go to a foreign VPN server.

Bowie: They can't do that.

Fawn: Why?

Bowie: They'll shut down international trade. All the Globalists will shit. GM isn't going to talk shop with China unless they know Ford isn't listening.

Angelo: They're issuing certificates that allow the right companies to tunnel through. They only work on Windows or Apple systems, though.

Fawn: That sounds serious.

Angelo: It only affects us at the doorbell. After that, badland systems use port spoofing anyway.

Fawn: Port spoofing?

Angelo: Internet messages have a port number as well as an IP address. The address is the location of the computer, the port is the door through the computer's firewall. Spoofing is sending a message to a port that may not actually be set up to read that kind of message.

Fawn: I've never sent anything to a port.

Nairobi: Sure you have.

Angelo: Your communication software does it automatically.

Nairobi: But you've sent one to a port manually, too.

Fawn: When?

Nairobi: Remember the first time you crossed? The address you used? It was something like 111.111.111.111:1723? With a colon and that number at the end?

Fawn: Now that you mention it, yes, it did have that. What was it for? I've never seen it since.

Nairobi: That was a spoofed port. You were using a web browser to communicate with a doorbell server. The decoy server expected a VPN request. If you had sent a request to port 80, which is what web page requests from all browsers automatically ask for, anyone monitoring the communications would have thought that odd.

Fawn: Meaning they might decide to track it back to me?

Nairobi: Right. So you specified a port by putting a colon after the address. You used 1723 which is the port used for initial requests for VPN service. So your browser sent its web page request to port 1723, not port 80 as it would have by default. To anyone listening on the line, it looked like a normal request for VPN service.

Angelo: The request was ignored because your return address was not on the authorized VPN users list, but it still looked like a valid request to anybody monitoring the link.

Fawn: So what are the certificates for?

Angelo: Under the new rules, if you try to go to port 1723, your communications software has to show a certificate or the request won't be allowed through the national firewall.

Nairobi: If you're Ford trying to establish a real VPN link, that's a big deal. But if you're you, just trying to get a message through to a doorbell server, it doesn't matter much. You could still just address your request to port 80. It would get through because those ports don't require certificates. The doorbell server would still get it. There would be more risk of some civ detecting it as a doorbell request, but that would be all.

Fawn: So you're saying that I don't need certificates, but, just to be safe, I should use them?

Nairobi: Right. At least for the initial contact.

Fawn: Not after that?

Nairobi: No. After that, you're dealing with some botnet zombie. It probably expects all communications to come over port 80. Since that's the most widely used, specifying it makes your message harder for a civ to detect. A firewall that blocks messages to port 1723 won't have any effect on it.

Fawn: So how do I get a certificate? And how do I get it to run on my wheels? You said they only run on Windows or Apple right now, didn't you?

Angelo: Yes, officially that's right. But the Emporium already offers software that will run certificates on open-source machines.

Fawn: So how do I get a certificate?

Nairobi: Officially, you can't, unless you're GM or Siemens or someone like that.

Angelo: But unofficially, they're in the Emporium. Someone bribed someone and bought a bunch. But you probably don't have to worry about any of it anyway.

Fawn: Why not?

Angelo: Do you have someone doing your wheels' maintenance?

Fawn: HOTWHEELS.

Angelo: You're covered. They'll take care of it all.

Bowie: It's kind of sad. They throw this stuff up to block us, and all they do is make it harder for the IBM's and DuPont's of the world to survive.

Nairobi: Yes. Those guys have to spend more money and pass the costs on to us. No wonder things keep getting more expensive.

Fawn took another sip of wine.

Bowie: Hey, Nairobi, you hear about any more IRS murders?

Nairobi: Four. Two agents, one wife and a kid.

Bowie: New?

Nairobi: Since last week.

Bowie: How? I thought they only ran in packs now.

Angelo: During business hours. But they still go home.

Bowie: Someone hit a residence?

Nairobi: Parents were both agents. Someone did them all to make a point.

Angelo: Home addresses are for sale in the Emporium.

Bowie: Shit.

Nairobi: Worse. Some snitch is already selling plans for their new enclaves.

Bowie: Enclaves?

Nairobi: Gated compounds surrounded by high walls and patrolled by armed guards. The IRS has quietly offered to buy the home of any employee that wants more protection and move him and his family inside one. They're negotiating right now for dozens of isolatable neighborhoods across the country and will harden them as soon as the deals are done.

Fawn finished her fourth glass. The AC shutdown was still on, but it didn't matter so much any more. Thank goodness she was already home.

Nairobi: Anyone hear anything about this passport control thing?

Angelo: They're changing that, too. Now you have to go through Passport Control if you want to leave the country.

Fawn: That's new, isn't it?

Angelo: Maybe technically, but they've always checked you before you left.

Bowie: No, I don't think so.

Angelo: When you leave, do you have to show someone your passport?

Bowie: Just the ticket counter.

Angelo: And what do they do with it?

Bowie: Make sure I'm the one on the ticket.

Angelo: And?

Bowie: I don't know, what?

Angelo: Make sure you're not on the no-fly list.

Bowie: But that doesn't mean much, does it? I mean, I'm not a terrorist.

Angelo: Do you owe money to the IRS? Are you a political malcontent? Wanted for anything? Been to any protests lately? Or are you simply someone they want to keep track of? Then you're on the no-fly list for international flights.

Nairobi: So if it's already in place, why bother with a new Passport Control?

Angelo: Thieves Emporium sells perfect passports with any name you want. Works because ticket agents can't check government passport files. Too many badlanders were getting out with false passports.

Fawn: So?

Angelo: Now, if you want to leave, a trained enforcer asks pointed questions and checks the database. Fake passports are tickets to jail because they're not in it.

Fawn: Can't someone hack the passport records?

Bowie: Good luck at that, luv.

Angelo: As far as I know, no cracker has ever created a false entry in the U.S. Passport Database. They guard it too closely.

Nairobi: And without a record in the database, you better not try to slip a bogus passport past a blackjack who has access to those records.

Fawn: There goes my European vacation.

* * *

Early one weekday morning, long before sunup, a Chicago beer delivery truck broke down over a manhole cover in the left lane of La Salle just north of Hubbard. After several attempts to start the engine, the driver gave up and opened the hood.

A passing police cruiser stopped and asked if the driver needed help, but was told a tow truck had already been called. Since there was almost no traffic at 3:32 am, the officer didn't offer to push the van to the shoulder. It wouldn't have helped if he had, though, as the problem was in the transmission. It was locked in park. Nothing would move that truck until the tow got there.

When he passed the intersection an hour later, the officer saw that the delivery truck had gone. Either the driver managed to unlock his transmission or the tow truck got there quicker than usual. Whichever it was, it wasn't his problem any more. He didn't bother to file a report on the encounter.

Three days later, a large General Services limousine pulled out of the Federal Reserve Bank Of Chicago secure underground parking garage and turned onto Quincy. It went east, then north at the next intersection onto La Salle.

In the front sat a driver and a bodyguard. Both carried pistols and wore bullet-proof vests under their clothing. A submachine gun sat in a rack under the bodyguard's seat. Surrounding the passenger compartment, a cocoon of safety protected everyone with bullet-proof Kevlar and armored glass. The windows were tinted, not just to prevent anyone from seeing in, but also to block radio signals from coming out because they might be used to locate or track the vehicle. No cell phones or WiFi for the limo passengers, but that was a small price to pay for safety.

Maxwell Stein, Governor of the Federal Reserve Bank Of Chicago, sat alone in the back, staring out at a city made dark by the rainy night and the rationing of electricity. Although he felt guilty about wasting the time he spent in the limo, he was too exhausted to do anything productive.

The vehicle proceeded up La Salle towards his residence on Walton. They did not usually take this route, any more than they regularly took any other, but there are only four bridges across the Chicago River. His driver chose a different one each time. This one happened to be the pick for tonight.

Not that it mattered much. At this time of night, there would be no traffic. And La Salle and Michigan offered the added security of being four-lane roads. The driver would take advantage of that by staying in the left lane to avoid any curb-side threats. On average, they drove the La Salle route twice a week, always in the left lane.

Tonight was no different, with one exception. As they entered the Hubbard Street intersection, the I-PASS transponder (which was mounted on the front bumper because of the radio-proof windshield) received and responded to an interrogation request. Had the driver known this, he might have questioned it, as the nearest toll road was over five miles away.

As the limo exited the intersection, the transponder received a second request, to which it also responded. Two seconds later, as its left front wheel passed over a fiberglass manhole cover just north of Hubbard, a magnetic switch in a package fastened to the underside of that cover sensed the vehicle overhead. Already armed by its I-PASS interrogator circuit, a small computer in the package closed a relay. Fifteen pounds of plastic explosive detonated under the cover.

The confined space of the manhole directed the force of the blast upwards, striking the left center of the vehicle, almost tearing it in two. Flying into the air and flipping over, it landed upside down across the gutter, half covering the sidewalk. None of the three occupants noticed the impact, though, as the initial shock killed them all before the vehicle's wheels even left the pavement.

* * *

> Chang: You are right. Your policeman would be a catch if we could turn him. I see nothing in his background to use for a hook,

though. He has never been married, no girl friends, doesn't seem to use any professional services. No drugs, alcohol, gambling or other vices. No debts, either. His only outside interest seems to be coin collecting with particular emphasis on the old Roman Empire. Unless we can bribe him with thirty pieces of silver, he seems bulletproof.

Fawn: He could have gone through a stoolie, used that guy's identity. Instead, he came to us openly. There must be something else there or he would never have gone to the trouble to ask me to do it this way.

Chang: He asked you? Child, how did you meet this man?

Just the thought of it hurt. Now, to actually do it, to lie to this woman who had helped her so much, was like a searing pain. But she had no other option. She didn't dare let anyone know she had been captured. She had to save her girls.

Fawn: The zoo.

Chang: He has interests besides coins?

Fawn: Of course.

Chang: How did he know you were a badlander?

Lies upon lies. Stray away from the truth, and where does the end wait?

Fawn: We've been spending some time together.

Chang: Oh, child, have you been sleeping with him?

Fawn: No.

Not convincing thought Fawn. *Well, in for a penny, in for a pound.*

Fawn: OK. Yes.

Chang: Are you willing to vouch for him?

Damn. What were her girls worth to her? The answer to that was easy.

Fawn: Yes

Chang: OK, we'll take him. But we won't vouch for him. We'll flag him as a known snitch in big letters. Does he understand what that means?

Fawn: Yes. I'll be sure he does. He isn't trying to trick anyone.

> Chang. And one more thing. We are going to send him a message, just to keep him off balance. He needs to know that we know all about him and will be watching him. OK?
>
> Fawn: OK.
>
> Chang: Use your wheels to make him a boot stick and get him a clean laptop, one you buy yourself with cash. Don't use one of your doorbells to send him across, use 34.200.3.96. That will get him the Container Corporation Of Shanghai. Have him ask for Zhu Jiao Lian.
>
> Fawn: OK.
>
> Chang: Good luck, child. I hope you're not digging yourself in too deep.
>
> Fawn: Thank you, I hope not either.

* * *

Fawn's standoff with Weidemeyer put her in a moral quandary. Anything she told him could be used to help civs catch other badlanders. On the other hand, if she didn't prepare him as well as possible, he was more likely to get caught. In the end, she decided her girls were more important. She would provide him with the best set of wheels she could.

"I'm always subject to search at any time," Weidemeyer said as he shook hot sauce over his scrambled eggs. "It's one of the security burdens imposed by the Secret Service. That means not just my person, but my apartment, my car, my communications, my finances, everything I own or have access to. Any of it can be searched at any time without reason or explanation."

They were again sitting over breakfast. She had wanted to hold these discussions at her apartment, but he was worried that someone who knew of her status as a badlander might notice his visit. It might be spy craft that was unnecessary in the age of double-blind communications, but he still worried about it, so they met at this anonymous location.

This latest revelation about his security burden meant that he didn't dare have a dedicated wheels laptop, even a small netbook, anywhere. Or at least, anywhere that it could be traced back to him if it were found.

"Will you ever have to cross from any computer other than your personal one?"

He nodded as he chewed, then swallowed.

"We're not allowed to bring personal computers along when we go to the field. Instead, they let us use our government-issued one for personal business. If I need to access the badlands when I'm traveling on business, it'll have to be with my government computer."

"And they sweep that one regularly, I assume?"

"No. Randomly, average once a month or so. When I'm back in the office."

"Never when you're in the field?"

He shook his head as he swallowed.

No personal computer on the road, no wheels on his government laptop when it was back in the office. And any wheels he had outside of his work computer would have to be hidden well enough to not implicate him if they were found.

They chewed in silence, savoring the subtle bouquet of flavors inherent in greasy scrambled eggs, while she cogitated on the problem.

"OK, I think I can do it, but you'll have to change the BIOS settings on your work laptop. Think they'd catch that?"

"What are BIOS settings?"

"Parameters that your computer checks when you first turn it on, before it loads your system. They're stored in memory chips on the motherboard."

"I think they only sweep the hard drive."

"Good."

"What are you going to have me change?"

"The boot order."

"Which is what?"

"Like I said, computers first execute instructions in the BIOS. When they finish that, they load the operating system which, because it's so big, is stored in an external memory."

"Meaning?"

"The internal hard drive, an optical drive, a USB flash drive, or a USB hard drive."

"So what's a 'boot order'?"

"The sequence the BIOS follows when it's looking for that operating system. For security reasons, I suspect your government laptop only looks at its own hard drive. If it can't find an OS there, it probably just shuts down. I want to change that so it first looks at its USB drives, then the hard drive, then shuts down."

As he struggled to take it all in, a thought struck him. According to her records, she had never had any computer training. Yet she seemed to have this technology pretty well in hand.

"How do you know all this?"

"Every badlander has to know how to camouflage her wheels. You better learn, too, if you don't want to get caught. So pay attention."

Also, it helped that she had spent much of the past two days chatting with HOTWHEELS about this problem. But she chose not to mention that. No one wants to seem dependent on expert advice. And right now, it felt good to have any edge over him, no matter how minor.

"Do you have your work computer with you?" she asked.

"I'm on a business trip, aren't I?"

* * *

The lot was almost empty, with grass growing up between cracks where customers used to park. Around its edges, empty stores showed vacant fronts like gaping mouths of large dead fish. In their center, like a giant decaying tooth, sat a moribund Lowe's, open only through the grace of one of the government's Anchor Store loans.

Weidemeyer's sedan sat in the middle of this gray desert. Officially, he was supervising Fawn's badlands activities, something he was expected to do. Lowe's guest Wi-Fi provided an untraceable Internet access point and the empty lot let them see unexpected visitors in time to log off if necessary. His cell phone sat outside on the hood so it couldn't pick up their conversation. Hers was at home.

On Weidemeyer's lap sat his government-issued computer, a Panasonic Toughbook sculpted out of a single solid block of magnesium metal. It was on and plugged in to the car's cigarette lighter.

Carefully, Fawn talked him through the use of the BIOS access hot-key. He would have to hit it at just the right moment during start-up. Somehow, on the first attempt, he missed. Windows came up.

Restarting his system, he tried again, this time successfully. For his efforts, he was told that BIOS access was password protected. Fortunately, her adviser at HOTWHEELS had anticipated this problem.

For reliability reasons, every Secret Service laptop has to be maintainable at any support location, meaning every tech has to have a full set of passwords for every Secret Service laptop. Someone had apparently needed a little extra money, because the passwords were for sale in the Emporium.

Money changed hands. She had three for him to try. One worked.

"Remember it," she said. "To be safe, you should switch your boot order back after each crossing. You'll need it for that."

"Why should I change it back?"

"They might check when they do a scan. If they do and see that it has been changed, they might become suspicious. Even if they don't, they might reset it."

She showed him how to change the boot order, then she rebooted. After a long wait, the screen finally showed his normal desktop. She pulled a mini-flash drive from her purse and plugged it in.

"Can you see the USB drive I just plugged in?"

He checked and nodded.

"Open it. In the folder TrueCrypt is a setup program. Run it."

He tried, but was told that permission had been denied.

"Well, it seems they don't trust you enough to give you administrator privileges for your own computer. Sorry, I guess I should have expected that."

"What do we do now?"

"Get them to let you install this encryption program or install it for you. It's available on line. If they don't trust it, they can download the source code, then check and compile it themselves. If you want plausible deniability on this laptop, you have to get this software installed."

"What's 'plausible deniability'?"

"It means you want a reasonable and legal excuse for everything you do. This," she said, taking an external hard drive from her purse, "is encrypted. It contains two sections, one of which is hidden. We've placed various files in the overt section, personal files that you might use. Roman history. Coin collecting. Articles about money. And some porno to explain-."

"Stop right there-"

"If your superiors look at what's on this drive, you have to have something a little naughty or they will ask why you bothered to encrypt it. The alternative was to put personal financial information there, but this seemed safer. We can't think of a better way to do it. If you can, then speak up. Otherwise, please shut up and let me finish "

"Why do I need this at all?" he asked, pointing to the thin hard drive.

"You have to store your badlands data files somewhere. If you want to cross while you're on the road, you'll have to have those files with you. The mini-flash drive just holds generic system files, but nothing that can be traced to your real identity. This," she said as she pointed to the USB hard drive, "holds your personal files."

He said nothing, so she continued.

"As I said, there are two sections to the drive. You'll be able to access the overt section with either password, but the covert one will show up only if you use the password that is specific to that section. Right now, we have chosen 'Roman Money' and 'CoVert' for the two. If you use the password 'Roman Money', you'll see only what your bosses will be happy with, assuming they're straight males with normal testosterone levels."

"What about the section that's hidden? Won't they see it, even if they can't read it?

"No. It's encrypted to look like random noise."

"So how do I see the hidden data? Do I type 'CoVert' as my password instead of 'Roman Money'?"

"Only if you booted up using the thumb drive. Boot in Windows and that password means nothing." Then she handed him the external hard drive. "Plug this in and reboot."

He did as he was told. His laptop began the restart process.

"If your BIOS is set to boot from a USB drive first, it will find the bootloader on the mini-flash and run it."

"What's a bootloader?"

"It's the first program your computer looks for after it's finished running the BIOS start-up tasks. Then it loads the operating system on your computer, sets it up, and starts it."

"Why haven't I heard of it before?"

"You been running Windows, right?"

"Yes."

"Then your computer doesn't have one. At least, it's not a separate program. All the start-up functions for Windows are hidden, including the bootloader code."

"And if I use the password 'CoVert'?"

"The bootloader will load a bare-bones Linux OS into your computer memory, convert the password 'CoVert' to the one that will decrypt the hidden section of your external hard drive, run TrueCrypt with that password to decode the hidden section, finish loading the rest of your wheels files that are stored in that hidden section, and then start your Linux OS."

His laptop came up, showing the Windows login screen.

"Don't worry, it's fake. Type in anything but 'CoVert' and it will use whatever you type as a password to start the real Windows."

She saw the look on his face when she finished.

"Yeah, I know it's a lot, but, after you do it a time or two, it'll seem easy. Ready for a try?"

"Why don't I have to have TrueCrypt installed?"

"There's a copy on the mini-flash drive. You only need an installation on your work computer to give you an excuse for why your external hard drive is encrypted. In fact, as long as you have the mini-flash, the external hard drive, and a BIOS set to boot from your USB ports, you can turn almost any Intel computer into a set of wheels."

He nodded to show he was keeping up.

"In case you hadn't guessed, let me stress one point. This," she said, touching the mini-flash that was plugged into his laptop, "contains the only data in the entire system that can link you to the badlands. As long as it isn't examined closely, you'll have plausible deniability. Everything else is explainable, but this chip isn't. If you get into trouble, ditch it", tapping the mini-flash for emphasis, "and they can't get you. It can't be linked to your real-world identity, so as long as you get far enough away from it before it's found, you can claim you never saw it and they can't prove otherwise."*

"Fingerprints?" he asked. He was, after all, a cop.

“Right. If your prints are on it, they can get you. Better always hold it by the edges.”

He didn't reply. She gave him time to ask a question. None came.

"Don't lose that mini-flash. It's your ticket across the border. I've made a spare for you," she said as she pulled another one out of her purse. "Hide them well, but don't lose them," she said as she dropped the spare into his shirt pocket. "They're your only safe way across."

"Questions?" she asked, to give him one more chance.

"Are all badlander's computers set up like this?"

What did she dare say? He was the enemy, anything she told him about other badland systems would spread to the other side. But they had technical experts and none of this was rocket science. They must already know it. Not telling him would only lessen his ability to stay free.

"Yes and no. Most are single-computer systems. They don't use an external hard drive, it's just something else to lose. Instead they encrypt their badland's data on a separate partition on their laptop's internal drive. About half start from a mini-flash like yours, the others just put the bootloader and decryption program on their internal drive. That way they don't have to carry a separate flash drive around."

"Why don't we do that for me?"

"Because they'd find your bootloader the first time they did a security scan

* Drives like this exist today. You can find out about it at https://tails.boum.org

of your computer. That's a dead give-away that you're running Linux because Windows doesn't use one. This way, the bootloader is on your USB drive, not your government-issued laptop."

"So they can't find it when they scan my computer?"

"Right."

She gave that a minute to sink in. When he didn't raise any more questions, she asked "OK. Ready to cross?"

The Rubicon. He nodded.

She talked him through logging on to the Lowes Guest Wi-Fi connection using his new system. When the connection screen came up, she said "Type in 'CoVert'.

He did. The screen changed, informing him that he had not registered any doorbell addresses and to please enter one in the space below.

"Congratulations, this is where you're supposed to be."

"Where do I get an address?"

She handed him a piece of paper.

"Be sure to type the name exactly as it's written, capitalization and all, because it's also a password."

He typed 34.200.3.96 and hit Enter. The display changed to the error screen for a VPN server operated by the Container Corporation Of Shanghai. Who was he trying to reach?

"Type in the name, exactly as written."

He typed in 'Zhu Jiao Lian' without appreciating the joke, as he spoke no Chinese. In Mandarin the phrase means 'Trainer Of Pigs'.

After he hit the Enter key, the screen changed to a chat format.

After a short wait, Zhu Jiao Lian opened the chat with:

> Lian: Welcome to the badlands, Butterfly Killer.

* * *

The use of Weidemeyer's old, almost-forgotten nick-name hit him hard. He got the message, the one the Trainer Of Pigs wanted him to get: They knew his deepest secrets. They had proven to him that their ability to gather information was incredible by using that ability to probe every corner of his past. This was a demonstration of their power. He had just been warned: Watch your step, pig, you're in our neighborhood now.

It also told him something else, something they may not have intended to say: Dancing Fawn had betrayed him. They had to have his real-world name to get this nick-name and could only have gotten it from her. She had turned him in to his enemies, sold him out for some special favor that he could not yet understand.

Joshua Weidemeyer was not a man prone to anger. All his life, he had cultivated a detached demeanor, one that best reflected his professional outlook and his private interests. So this knowledge caused him only a brief flash of rage. Then, it made him cold.

"You turned me in," he accused without looking up from the laptop.

"What?"

"You gave them my name. You turned me in. How much did they pay you?"

She sensed his mood change, heard the coldness in his voice. He turned to stare at her, his eyes burning into her face.

"I only did what I had to do to get you a set of wheels. I didn't sell you out."

"You gave them my name."

"Yes. GOBI DESERT wouldn't indenture you unless they checked you out first. They had to have your name to do that."

"Don't you understand that I could go to jail for this? My bosses can't find out I'm making unsupervised crossings."

"They won't."

"Why not?"

"GOBI DESERT didn't tell anyone you were crossing, only that they were investigating you."

"They said that? And you believe them?"

"More than I believe you." To her surprise, she regretted the statement as soon as she said it. But she made no effort to take it back. Instead, after a pause, she said "I'm well aware that you are all that stands between my girls and adoption. You may rest assured that I will do nothing to risk your professional position."

"You have no idea," he answered. Then, looking up, he asked "Have you plugged into the Internet since you gave them my name?"

"Yes."

"With a cable? Did you use an Ethernet cable, not your WiFi?"

And suddenly, for the first time since her arrest, she knew she held the upper hand. Tipped of by the specifics of his question, she struggled to suppress a smile.

"Why?"

"Just answer the question."

"If you want an answer, tell me why you ask."

"That's confidential."

"Not if you want an answer."

With a sigh, he gave up the battle. "There's a logger in your laptop," he said. "It records everything you type. Including your request for my wheels. And my name. It can't use your WiFi since that would require a change in one of your software drivers, but it can use your Ethernet. If you've plugged in using a cable, that data's been uploaded to DHS."

She had guessed right. Anger and elation surged through her, one because he had tried to catch her friends and the other because she now had something to fight back with. His career, maybe even his freedom, were in her hands. Making a show of her anger, she said "You promised I wouldn't have to turn in my friends."

"You don't."

"I type their names, you arrest them. What do you call that?"

"It wasn't like that."

"What was it like?"

"I had no choice. It's standard procedure. They always bug captured laptops."

"And you didn't warn me."

"Did you plug into the Internet?"

"And if I did?"

"Then we're both dead."

And she knew he was right. One slip by either of them and they would both lose. They were in this together. She may have the upper hand at the moment, but it was still a Mexican standoff. She needed him as much as he needed her, he to further his career and she to protect her girls. Like it or not, they were tied together by the same rope. She dare not push this game too far.

'You think you're playing with children?" she demanded. "Just because we don't work for a big government agency, you think we don't know what we're doing?"

He looked back in silence, assuming it was a rhetorical question.

"Any badlander who's laptop gets taken by you people knows it'll be bugged when she gets it back. So she throws it away and buys a new one. That's our 'standard procedure'."

"You didn't cross with it?"

"No. Your logger's at the bottom of a sinkhole."

Relief tempered his anger. He hadn't been caught. But he wasn't safe, either. His attempt to spy on her had put both of them at risk, but so had her release of his real name. What he did was unavoidable, but what she did was inexcusable. He glared back at her, unmollified. "None of this would have happened if you hadn't betrayed me."

"It was the only way I could get you across."

"You should have asked me."

"And have you get cold feet?"

"You may as well have put it on Facebook."

"GOBI DESERT stays in business because they're discreet. They make a living by doing what they promise. If they say they didn't tell anyone you were getting crossing privileges, then they didn't."

"They have to change my badlands name."

"Why?"

"People know it's mine. Using it puts me at risk."

"I'll see what I can do, but I doubt they'll change it. They didn't pick it by accident."

A moment passed between them, hostile in its silence. Then she unlatched her door.

"I'll take the bus home," she said as she got out of the car. "Change your passwords as soon as I leave, I don't want the responsibility of knowing them." The door slammed and she walked away without turning back.

What could he do? Arrest her? And then have to explain why he was here with an illegal border-crossing computer system?

He went back to setting up his crossing.

Chapter 16

Life As A Double Agent

Arnold Wilson Parker had a problem. For three months, he had been hunting for a replacement for Maxwell Stein, but with no luck. There were a number of qualified candidates to choose from, even several who would follow his instructions, but none that were willing to take the risk that now came with the job. Stein's assassination, along with the subsequent killings of two other Governors, had made that job a dangerous one. In a world of men motivated by personal gain, the risk of losing it all loomed too large to accept. Only men of principle are willing to die for what they believe in. Men of avarice are not.

So he would have to settle for a promotion from far down in the ranks. He would have to take someone who was still young enough to believe in his or her own invulnerability, one who had enough to gain from the size of the promotion to be willing to accept the risk. It meant he would have a weakness at the highest level of his organization, but he had no other choice. Appearance demanded the positions be filled.

The goal now was damage control. He had to find a way to stop the assassinations, to make their threat recede in the minds of potential candidates. If he succeeded, he would be able to recruit strong people to replace the three pups he now had to promote.

That was why he had flown Matthew Hood out to Colorado. The large paneled study in which the two of them sat was warmed, if not heated, by the flickering remains of an earlier fire. Winter sun streamed in through the closed french doors while the mountains across the valley were covered in a layer of silent white. As usual, they sat alone.

"This is not your normal assassination," Hood said in an attempt to excuse his failure to find leads.

"How so?"

"This sort of thing unravels because it's too big for one person to pull off alone. To work together, people have to talk to each other. You know, plan. Coordinate."

"This attack wasn't planned?"

"No, no. It was, of course. But we catch these guys through their communications. Wiretap somebody, catch them passing notes, that sort of thing."

"So do that here."

"Well, that's the problem, you see?"

"Explain it to me."

"These people set this thing up through the badlands. Their communications used Internet links we can't read or trace. We can't monitor their activities any more than they can ours."

"What do you have so far?"

"A stolen beer truck with a hole in the floor.

"Anything else?"

"We know they got an I-PASS interrogator and the limo transponder code. So far, no leads on how they did it."

"Someone sold it to them?"

"Probably."

"Can't you do financial checks. I mean, see who got paid?"

"No -"

"Hood, I don't think you understand how serious this is. These people have damaged our entire monetary system. They have got to be caught. Don't tell me you don't have enough people. Or authority. Or whatever. Get the financial records. Now."

"We can't."

"Can't?" asked Parker, the frustration clear in his voice.

“Payments were made in the badlands. That's where the records are. We can't touch them."

"Then what're they good for? All those NSA toys?"

"Give me a name and I can tell you the guy's shower history. But-"

"His what?"

"Shower history. When he takes his showers. And make a good guess when he'll take his next one."

"Really?"

"If there's a smart meter on his water and power, yes. I can even tell you how hot he likes it and if he showers with a girlfriend. But-"

"How?"

"Showers take longer when you're not alone. But-"

"How do you know it's not the dishwasher? Using the hot water, I mean?"

"A dishwasher cycles on and off. A shower stays on," said Hood, then waited in case there were any more questions.

"Sorry. Go on," said Parker, apparently getting the point.

"Just give me a name," began Hood again, "and I have data going back, what, maybe ten years? And-"

"Can you do that to me?"

"What?"

"Tell when I take a shower?"

"No," answered Hood without, amazingly, any annoyance in is voice. "Your security detail is way too good. May I continue?"

"Sorry," answered Parker, while thinking *Thank God for money.*

"With enough data, my lawyers can always find a crime. They'll prosecute. Bury anyone under legal motions, make his life miserable. Maybe even send him up for some felony."

"Even if he didn't do anything?"

"Of course he did something. We got 100,000 laws on the books, twice that in regs. Somewhere, sometime, by accident or intentionally, he broke one. We get a moving x-ray of his life, all we have to do is find it."

"So why can't you get these badlanders the same way?"

"They don't use their real names. So their data's not in the system."

"Can't you find them some other way?"

"Nothing they use is in the system. They fly totally under the radar. That's the problem. If even one little finger stuck up above the surface, we'd grab it and yank them up. But we can't because nothing shows."

Arnold Wilson Parker was not used to getting 'no' for an answer. He took it well enough, walking to the edge of the balcony to gaze at 'his' valley through the closed French doors. After a minute of silent reflection, he came back to his chair and sat down.

"OK, what are you going to do?"

"If we can't beat them with razzle-dazzle, we'll just have to do it with good old police work."

"Go on."

"Tighten the National Security Firewall, increase NSA listening and decoding efforts, put up more roadblocks, more package inspections, better border searches."

"What do you need?"

"Funding. I can't hire more people without money."

"OK. I'll take care of that. Anything else?"

"More eyeballs. Right now, the army is reluctant to put troops to use in domestic duties."

"I'll try to change some minds. Anything else?"

Hood thought for a long ten seconds.

"No."

"Good. You'll get what you need. But I expect you to perform. Perform. Expect it. Fair?"

"Yes sir."

And with that, the meeting came to a frosty close.

* * *

Getting a badlands name was easy. Getting one that was untraceable was not. After all, you can't just walk up to a known badlander and ask him to recruit you. If you did, and he did, he would still know something about your real world identity. Everyone has to cross for the first time. And everyone has to be recruited in the real world. Your recruiter always knows something about your real-world identity.

Still, Malyy Mishka had done the best he could to hide his tracks. He got recruited by a snitch who thought he was a petty criminal. Then he arranged for his recruiter to die. Next, he changed crossing houses, not just once, but several times, getting a new name with each move. Finally, he bought a house, along with its reputation, and used it to rename himself again.

If enough people asked enough questions and paid enough money, someone might be able to get real-world information on him, but it wouldn't be easy and it wouldn't be much. He didn't have what the CIA called a perfect legend, but it was close.

Now he was proudly indentured to the STALINGRAD Crossing House. Proud because that association carried a certain cachet. If your rep said you were indentured there, people took notice. They took care of their own.

STALINGRAD was an affinity crossing house, meaning its owner enforced a common character on its members. All crossing houses tend to be that way, by accident if not by design, because people recruit those they know. STALINGRAD was different. It overtly restricted membership to certain classes of individuals. You had to prove yourself to be invited to join and, if you failed to keep up with its standards, you were booted out.

He had originally been introduced to the organization through its invitation-only chat room. Presenting himself as a second generation Russian immigrant, he claimed he was a petty thief and part-time mugger in New York City. They probably didn't believe him but, eventually, they recognized in him the necessary philosophical and moral outlook. In particular, he, like their other members, believed the only way to solve political problems was by placing unrestricted authority in the hands of the right individual.

So, to use the slang of the Stalinists that were its indentureds, he had been allowed to 'swim the Volga'. To the best of his knowledge, he was the only one there that did not speak at least some Russian. At first, he had tried to hide the fact, but his inability to write the language quickly gave him away.

When they found out that he spoke no Russian, he expected to be thrown out, as they were all rabid nationalists, but they had grown too used to him.

Or, perhaps, too used to his money. He had become known as a regular purchaser of violent services, something that endeared him to his Slavic associates. The fact that he paid well helped, too.

So, rather than excommunicate him, they gave him an honorary membership, made him a Stalinist by decree. In celebration, they renamed him (again) Malyy Mishka, Russian for Little Bear. At first, it had been done to degrade him, but, as time passed, it became an endearment. He was accepted for what he was.

Now he sat in chat with one of his crossing house brothers, Sasha Filippov, someone he suspected of being a primary contact for the Russian mafia.

> Mishka: What I mean is success. You see that, don't you? The operation has been a success. Big success.
>
> Sasha: Spasibo.
>
> Mishka: But it's done. Over. Wrap it up.
>
> Sasha: Da. Understood.
>
> Mishka: How many still out there? Cars, I mean.
>
> Sasha: Maybe two hundred.
>
> Mishka: That many? Well, get them off the streets. Clean up the evidence. Don't need them any more.
>
> Sasha: Pochemu? Why not keep for future?
>
> Mishka: No. Never needed again. Never. All roadblocks are now protected with GPS jammers. Bombs are just risks to us now. Evidence.
>
> Sasha: OK. We erase. You want kill anyone as part of clean up?
>
> Mishka: Well, if you know of anyone who isn't reliable. I mean, anyone that knows something. Yes, then, of course. Silence them.
>
> Sasha: I check, let you know.
>
> Mishka: Thank you. Good job.
>
> Sasha: Thank also you.

And with that, the chat came to an end. Arnold Wilson Parker leaned back in his chair, alone in his dark study, and looked at the now-still display on his wheels.

Yes, it had been a successful effort. Before he used the badlands against itself, everyone regarded them as just a bunch of criminals. Petty smugglers and minor thugs, to be dealt with by the police. The bombings had energized people, brought the country together in a united front, committed to whatever it took to win the fight. Now his people had the authority to do whatever was necessary to strike back.

But more to the point, he had shown that the anonymity the badlanders loved cut both ways. Now he, too, had the ability to strike from the shadows, to influence events from behind the impenetrable veil of double-blind communications.

Assassination has always been an acceptable weapon for those who were few in numbers. But it worked only if its source couldn't be found. Usually, that was impossible because the communications used to coordinate the attack could always be traced.

Murder as policy is really nothing more than an extension of other lesser forms of corruption such as database sabotage, information theft, and false document production (including scrip, passports, financial instruments, records). If you can provide a safe environment to perform those illegal acts, you can provide it for assassinations as well.

With badlands access, conspiracies to kill high officials could be formed, executed, and covered up without any risk of the communications being detected, much less traced. In addition, resources to perform the acts, such as poisons or explosives, could be easily obtained without leaving any leads back to their source. Like Hood said, fighting a badlands assassination cult is almost impossible.

The problems caused by the recent Fed governor deaths came to his mind. He had always assumed their deaths were ordered by badlanders, but maybe not. Had Van de Groot gained access to the badlands, too? Had she hired killers through the Emporium?

Perhaps yes, perhaps no. There was no way to tell, which was the beauty of the thing. Anonymity worked both ways.

Next week, he would bring up the subject of Van de Groot in the STALINGRAD chat. Someone might be willing to pop him. Or, if not her, then at least some of her people.

Maybe the badlands wasn't such a bad place after all.

* * *

Fawn and Weidemeyer sat in the front seats of her van. Both had laptops open and running. On the dash was a directional antenna which connected Weidemeyer's laptop to the WiFi from the Starbuck's across the square. Mounted on top of the vehicle was another directional antenna which pointed to the WiFi transmitter that the City of Ocala provided for their public square. It was connected to Fawn's wheels. They used separate WiFi sources to make it hard for Internal Affairs to detect that they were both online. Three back-up cameras mounted outside the van gave Fawn an uninterrupted view of the space around them. As usual when she made a crossing, she had left her cell phone at home. His was locked in his car.

Their doors were locked and windows up. The manual deadbolts that Fawn had mounted on the inside of each door after the Bastard's attack were also latched. The engine was running and the air conditioning was going flat out to keep the oppressive Florida heat under control. It was, unfortunately, only partially successful, as shown by the occasional drop of sweat that ran down Fawn's clean-scrubbed face. Outside, in the early-afternoon summer sun, the central square was deserted. Only a few establishments were open, subsidized by the city in an attempt to provide an air of normalcy. The others displayed For-Rent signs in dirty windows. Other than Weidemeyer's sedan, which was in the next space, all the parking in the square was empty.

A loop of string from the USB flash drive in Weidemeyer's laptop lay over his right thumb. Should an Internal Affairs investigator attempt to approach the vehicle or, worse yet, try to open a door, a flick of his hand would jerk the chip out and send it flying into the back. That would instantly reboot his laptop, thus destroying all evidence that he had made a crossing.

She had taken no such precautions as they weren't necessary. After all, she was a snitch and so was supposed to be crossing under his supervision.

Both screens showed chat windows. His had no entries. Hers showed:

Angelo: Where did you meet a cop?

Fawn: Open chat.

Nairobi: How do you know he's a cop?

Fawn: He says he is. He's quite honest about it.

Nairobi: Couldn't he be a blow-hard?

Fawn: Maybe. But better safe than sorry, right? So, please, watch your mouth. Don't trust him.

Nairobi: OK, you've covered yourself. Send him in.

Fawn: Angelo?

Angelo: Yeah. Ready.

She turned to Weidemeyer and said "You're on" as his chat box went active, then turned back to her own screen:

System: Butterfly Killer, male, GOBI DESERT, has entered the room.

Fawn: Welcome, Butterfly.

Butterfly: Thank you.

Fawn: Allow me to introduce Angelo Pisa, a sometimes-protester, and Nairobi Bombay, a sometimes-journalist.

Butterfly: Thank you for meeting with me.

Nairobi: A favor to Fawn.

Angelo: Likewise.

Butterfly: I'm not here to hassle anyone. Really. You two are safe.

Angelo: OK. Ask your questions.

Butterfly: Who finances the badlands?

Nairobi: You do.

Butterfly: I don't understand.

Nairobi: You civs. Your laws, regulations, and restrictions break anyone who isn't rich enough to get around them. Then you hit us with taxes, fees, fines, and inflation. People have to survive, so they go to the only place left and bring what little they still have with them.

Butterfly: To become outlaws?

Nairobi: Your government made us outlaws so they could control us. But the badlands gave us an out, a place to run to instead. Outlaws first, then badlanders, not the other way around.

Angelo: No one came here because he wanted to. You assholes forced us into it.

Fawn: Hey, Clown Face. Turn it down a little, OK?

Angelo: Did cops kill any of your friends? He deserves it.

Fawn: He doesn't run the civs any more than we run the badlands. He's just trying to understand what's going on. So, please, you two. Drop the attitude. Please?

Butterfly: Who owns your reputation reporting system?

Nairobi: Systems. Plural. There's dozens of them.

Butterfly: Who owns them?

Nairobi: Independent competitors.

Fawn: A hundred different people.

Angelo: Tell your bosses they can't control us. That's what they want, isn't it? Well they're out of luck. They can't control what they can't touch. They can't just pay some cop-shit like you to hurt us if they don't like what we're doing.

Fawn: Please, Angelo. Please. He's my guest.

Butterfly: Spoken like a true criminal.

Angelo: Meaning?

Butterfly: Cops keep people honest.

Angelo: Is that what you think you're doing?

Fawn: Stop it. Stop it. Both of you.

Butterfly: We protect people.

Angelo: Not people, just laws. They're not the same.

Butterfly: We're a democracy

Angelo: And that makes your laws moral?

Butterfly: Yes.

Angelo: Your government is a tyranny of the many against a tyranny of the few. How does that make its laws moral?

Butterfly: Don't play holy with me. You're just a criminal, like any other.

Fawn: Butterfly! STOP IT!

Angelo: Like Gandhi? Or Mandela? Or Jefferson? Weren't they criminals, too?

Butterfly: Listen, punk, yo

The sting of the blow jerked him back to the front seat. She had slapped him, hit his shoulder as hard as she could with the flat of her hand. The surprise, more than the pain, got his attention. Turning, he saw the mouse was gone. He faced the eyes of a tiger. She was fighting to keep what little control she had over her life, fighting to keep him tied to her by his need for information. She was not going to let it slip away in some schoolboy fight. For her girl's sake, she couldn't.

"Apologize," she demanded, a single word spit out as if she had yelled it.

He opened his mouth to say something, but she cut him off.

"Now."

And he realized she was right. The cool hardness came back over him. This fight would serve neither of them. Turning back to his laptop, he typed.

Butterfly: Sorry. I got off track.

Fawn: You too, Angelo.

Angelo: What?

Fawn: Apologize.

Angelo: To him?

Fawn: Yes. Now, Angelo.

Angelo: Fuck you, cop.

Fawn: Then leave. Apologize or leave.

System: Angelo Pisa, male, RENAISSANCE, has left the room.

In the car, Fawn gave Weidemeyer an angry look, then went back to her wheels and typed:

Fawn: I apologize for him. He's been under a lot of stress.

Butterfly: I understand.

Fawn: Where were we?

Butterfly: Do you really think the badlands just sprang up on its own? Like spontaneous combustion?

Nairobi: No. It was the work of many dedicated individuals operating in their own self-interest. It didn't just happen, it was made. But not to any plan. Do ants have a plan for their ant hill? Do bees have a plan for their hive?

Fawn: Who runs bee hives? Or schools of fish?

Butterfly: I'm not a fish.

Fawn: Most of the world just runs itself.

Nairobi: We're speaking English, right?

Butterfly: Your point?

Nairobi: English is a complicated communications system. Who designed it? Who controls it? The Badlands is no different. It's just a network that sprang up on its own thanks to the efforts of those who use it.

* * *

Weidemeyer felt like a dog on a leash. His might not be as tight as on an officially authorized crossing, but it still chafed. As long as Fawn guided him around, he would see nothing but her little Potemkin village. Time to take it off, meet his own contacts on his own terms. That's why he got his own wheels, wasn't it?

So he started taking 'unescorted' excursions across the border. Frequently. The one today had to be at least his tenth this month alone. As often in the past, he was lurking in a chat room, just listening, trying to understand the undercurrents of what drove these people. If he could find their true motivations, he might get a lead on who ran things.

Today, an unusually interesting individual participated in the discussions. After introducing himself, Weidemeyer convinced Lucius Magnus to join him in a private chat.

Lucius: You have an unusual rep.

Butterfly: So do you.

Lucius: Mine doesn't say I'm a civ snitch. Are you going to report me?

Butterfly: Hey, give me credit! I'm not just a snitch, I'm a real honest-to-goodness Civ Honcho. Speak to me as you would to God.

Lucius: At least you're an honest one.

Butterfly: And you? You said you picked your own badlands name? I thought no one could do that.

Because I sure would like to change mine.

Lucius: True. People who pick their own names tend to hide a bit of their real-world identity in their picks. But I was lucky. Got around the system.

Butterfly: Could I change mine?

Lucius: Sure. But your rep starts from scratch.

Butterfly: I could live with that.

Lucius: Considering yours says you're a stoolie, I guess you could.

Butterfly: How would I do it?

Lucius: Indenture to my crossing house.

Butterfly: You can change someone's name?

Lucius: I own BARABBAS. Cross with me, I could give you a new name.

Butterfly: That's how you picked your own?

Lucius: Yep.

Butterfly: Great. Where do I apply?

Lucius: You don't. I got standards. No snitches.

Butterfly: How'd you start a crossing house?

Lucius: Had a business in the real world. The government killed it, so I came here. Started BARABBAS with my former employees as indentures.

Butterfly: How'd you get a rep big enough?

Lucius: Money. People trust rich folks more than poor.

Butterfly: That's it? Just money?

Lucius: No. Time, too. Kept my real-world company afloat for three years using badlands contacts before I gave up. It gave me a good rep.

Butterfly: What did your old company do?

Lucius: You're not just a snitch. You're a nosy snitch.

Butterfly: Sorry. I'm new here.

Lucius: OK. Don't pry again.

Butterfly: Can you tell me how the government killed your old company? Or is that too specific?

Lucius: No. That's OK. They did it the same way they kill most businesses: Regulate, tax, inflate, and diddle the interest rates.

Butterfly: Rates are that important?

Lucius: What should I do with my assets? Save? Invest? Speculate? That depends on how some Fed bozo feels when he wakes up in the morning. Market savvy, economic education, or street-smarts can't predict it. Eventually, everyone loses.

Butterfly: You an economist?

There was a pause in the text string.

Butterfly: Sorry. If that's prying, please, forget I asked.

Lucius: It's OK. Yes, I have a background in it.

Butterfly: Doesn't the Fed have to manipulate the money supply to stabilize the economy?

Lucius: Damn. You're not just a civ, you're a damned Keynesian, too!

Butterfly: What'd I say?

Lucius: Just joking. John Maynard Keynes. Principal proponent for debt as money. Some good ideas, but a predatory power structure abused them.

Butterfly: Whoa. That's pretty strong, don't you think?

Lucius: No. The Fed exists solely to support the people who run this country.

Butterfly: Not what I heard.

Lucius: Which was?

Butterfly: It stabilizes the economy.

Lucius: Its primary goal is its own survival. That means keeping its supporters in power. After that, if it can stabilize the economy, fine. But survival comes first, the economy be damned if necessary.

Butterfly: But you agree it stabilizes the economy?

Lucius: I will agree that it has sometimes tried. But it can't succeed.

Butterfly: Can't?

Lucius: No. Can't.

Butterfly: That's pretty hard to accept.

Lucius: Ever heard of anti-fragility?

Butterfly: Robustness?

Lucius: No. That's different. Robust means it doesn't break when I hit it. Anti-fragile means it gets stronger because I hit it.

Butterfly: I don't understand.

Lucius: Suppose I ship a wine glass around the world and it comes back stronger than when I sent it. What would you call that?

Butterfly: Very unlikely.

Lucius: In wine glasses, yes. In other things, no. That property is anti-fragility.

Butterfly: So what? I can't think of a single thing that has it.

Lucius: How about you?

Butterfly: Me?

Lucius: Your body. If you run a mile every day, wouldn't you get better at it? Most living things are anti-fragile.

Butterfly: That's a pretty unusual case.

Lucius: No. It's common. And not just in individuals. Consider groups of living things. Like forests.

Butterfly: Go on.

Lucius: How do you prevent big forest fires?

Butterfly: Hire lots of smoke jumpers?

Lucius: No. Just the opposite. Start lots of small fires.

Butterfly: That makes no sense. None at all.

Lucius: If a forest doesn't have much underbrush, starting lots of small fires becomes a maintenance operation. Ground litter burns away without hurting the big trees because the fire never gets very hot. The small stuff gets cleared away so the big trees get the light and room they need to stay healthy. Shifting, smoldering undergrowth fires are essential for healthy forest.

Butterfly: So why do we have smoke jumpers?

Lucius: At first, because we didn't know any better. Now we do. But we've painted ourselves into a corner. We've kept the forests fire-free for too long. So there's too much dried underbrush. If a fire gets started now, it'll be a hot one. Kill everything in its path.

Butterfly: Yellowstone?

Lucius: Yes. Those fires made us see the problem.

Butterfly: And the solution?

Lucius: Burn the excess fuel a little at a time. Start fires when everything is wet and hope they clear the debris without spreading.

Butterfly: Sounds dangerous.

Lucius: Very.

Butterfly: So what's the point?

Lucius: Economies are like forests. Debt is the underbrush. Bankruptcies are the fires.

Butterfly: You're saying the Fed is Smokey The Bear?

Lucius: Right.

Butterfly: And we have an excess of debt?

Lucius: Right. Thanks to the Fed, that's true.

Butterfly: An excess that will cause a firestorm of bankruptcies if it ever starts to go?

Lucius: Another Great Depression.

Butterfly: And the economic solution?

Lucius: For now or the long-term?

Butterfly: Long term.

Lucius: Lots of small fires. Just like a forest.

Butterfly: Let people go bankrupt?

Lucius: Let everything go bankrupt. Don't help with subsidized lending. Because of politics, the only way to do that is to eliminate central banks.

Butterfly: Who will issue our money?

Lucius: No one. Use gold. Like we did in the US for its first 150 years.

Butterfly: But that caused bankruptcies.

Lucius: That's the idea. Many. Small. And often. So big debt can't ever build up.

Butterfly: But we can't do that now.

Lucius: No. We're in debt too deep.

Butterfly: What can we do now?

Lucius: Pray.

* * *

Of all the contacts Weidemeyer had made so far in the Badlands, Angelo seemed the most promising. The young man's anger and hostility made it likely that he was hiding something. The fact that he was an admitted conspirator would have moved him to the top of the action list even without those emotions.

But how to pursue the matter? In the real world, that would have been an easy decision. A data search would produce an amazing amount of historical information. Video bugs and GPS trackers would add to it. Follow up with a subpoena, maybe an arrest. Fact-based interrogations coupled with isolation usually took no more than a few days to get results.

But this was the badlands. No subpoenas, no power to arrest. He couldn't even do a data search without a real name. He would have to ask for a meeting, depend on this perp's willingness to talk to find out anything. So, as unusual as it was for him, that's what he did. Several text requests, phrased in the most conciliatory language he could think of, finally got him a chat.

After some preliminaries, including a few compliments and an unsuccessful attempt at establishing a rapport, Weidemeyer finally gave up and came straight to the point:

Butterfly: Have your people been killing Fed Governors?

Angelo: You started the war. We're just fighting back.

Butterfly: War? You really think you can win this?

Angelo: Maybe not. But you can't, either.

Butterfly: You bomb the roadblocks, too?

Angelo: We strike where we can.

Butterfly: With terror?

Angelo: Terror? Like you civs carpet-bombing Dresden or Tokyo? That kind of terror?

Butterfly: We were at war.

Angelo: They were civilians.

Butterfly: They were legitimate targets.

Angelo: Ditto for road blocks.

Butterfly: This is not war.

Angelo: Tell that to my dead friends.

Butterfly: Why pick on the Fed?

Angelo: Tyrants use carrots as well as sticks to survive. The Fed's their carrot.

Butterfly: They're not even part of the government. Isn't that what you want? Money controlled by the free market?

Angelo: The Fed's hardly a free market.

Butterfly: Someone has to control our money.

Angelo: Why? No one did before the Fed. Two hundred years and we did just fine.

Butterfly: Fine? You like depressions?

Angelo: Not depressions. Downturns. We never had a 'Great Depression' until we had the Fed.

Butterfly: OK. So why can't we win?

Angelo: Complexity will kill you.

Butterfly: What does complexity have to do with anything?

Angelo: Look at your new National Firewall. You force everyone to update their software and install your certs. You put in new hardware to check and track them. Then you reroute all Internet traffic. You have to do all that to get this thing to work, right?

Butterfly: Yes.

Angelo: We pay a little bribe, spoof a few VPN ports, and we're around it. You spend yourselves to death and you still lose.

Butterfly: That's just one case.

Angelo: No. It's true everywhere. The more you clamp down on a complex system, the more it fights back. So now you're between a rock and a hard place. Either you get total control, the ultimate in a totalitarian state, or you lose it all.

Butterfly: You've got the same problem.

Angelo: Only if we had the same objective. But we don't. Not only don't we care about centralizing control, we abhor it. We consider it the antithesis of freedom. Our world is inherently simple because it's decentralized. There is no King Of The Badlands.

Butterfly: I don't believe that.

Angelo: Wake up, civ. The history of civilization is the story of centralization running into too much complexity. You've hit the law of diminishing returns.

Butterfly: If that were true, how did civilization evolve at all? We're not subsistence farmers any more. You think we're going to go back to grubbing with sticks for our food?

Angelo: Complicated and complex are different. Complicated just means there are many working parts. Yes, our society is far more complicated than it ever has been. Complexity refers to the control of those parts. Civ society has reached a maximum in complexity, meaning a maximum of intercommunicating independent entities if control is to be maintained. There are now too many for any central authority. To survive, your bosses must either reduce independence in the parts or give up on centralized control. And they ain't going to give up.

Butterfly: So how will they reduce the number of parts?

Angelo: Not the number of parts. The number of independent parts.

Butterfly: OK. How?

Angelo: Either stop their globalization drive, stop trying to control international trade and commerce, or reduce local independence. Eliminate the ability of individuals to act on their own. Given their mindset, that's the only option they see available to them.

Butterfly: Even if what you say is true, why does it matter? Can't governments just keep making things more complex?

Angelo: How many cops does it take to catch one badlander?

Butterfly: That's classified.

Angelo: 'Classified'? Never mind. I'll tell you. Over a hundred. Right?

How did he know?

Butterfly: Maybe.

Angelo: And you got equipment, cars, communications. All it takes for us is one laptop.

Butterfly: So?

Angelo: So complexity costs money. Can you afford to keep outspending us 100:1 while your economy collapses? You damned civs are all going down.

There was a pause in the text stream. Angelo seemed finally to have run down.

Butterfly: One more question.

Angelo: OK.

Butterfly: Why do you hate me?

Angelo: Because you want to enslave my children.

Butterfly: I don't even know your children.

Angelo: You're training to do it anyway.

Butterfly: Meaning?

Angelo: You've spent your entire life getting programmed to kill. Civ schools taught you that only the greater good mattered. In the military, civs brutalized you until all you could do was follow orders. Finally, they made you a cop by training you to enforce orders for the greater good. They own your conscience. You're so brainwashed that you think what you do is actually right.

Suddenly, unexpected anger overwhelmed Weidemeyer. With it came the demons, rushing up from the dark corners of his mind where he had managed to chain them. *I'm not Pug*, he thought as he drove them back into hiding.

Then he typed:

Butterfly: You know nothing about me, punk.

Angelo: I know you're a pig.

Butterfly: And you're a criminal thug.

Angelo: Hey, pig. Know the nicest part about the badlands?

Butterfly: What?

Angelo: I don't have to talk to pigs. Including you. Don't text me again.

System: Angelo Pisa, male, RENAISSANCE, has left the room.

* * *

Lucius: In 1421, China sent a fleet around the Indian Ocean. Maybe around the world. 300 ships, some as long a football field.

Butterfly: Never heard of it.

Lucius: Heard of Prince Henry?

Butterfly: Who?

Lucius: Europe's answer to China. Portuguese. Third son of the king. Missed the big spot by two, so he decided to do something else. Built ships and sent them out to explore the world, just like in China.

Butterfly: Where'd he go?

Lucius: He didn't. Afraid of the water, I guess. He just paid for the ships and crews. Like the emperor of China.

Butterfly: Did Henry's ships go to China?

Lucius: No. In 1420, his three ships discovered the Madeira Islands.

Butterfly: Never heard of them, either.

Lucius: They're about 600 miles off the coast of Portugal.

Butterfly: So?

Lucius: China sends 300 ships half-way around the world and the best Europe can do is get three over-sized boats to an island 600 miles away. Who were the bumpkins? Get the point?

Butterfly: OK, I got it. We were idiots. So?

Lucius: So, fast forward 400 years. Britain declares war on the Chinese Empire. Half of Asia at war with some little island on the other side of the world. Funny, really. Except the Brits whip their ass. Take Hong Kong. Now who're the bumpkins?

Butterfly: Big change.

Lucius: Right. The question is why. Do you know why?

Butterfly: I give.

Lucius: In China, the emperor that sent out the fleet died. The new one thought exploration was a bad idea, so no more fleets.

Butterfly: And the west didn't ever stop?

Lucius: They couldn't. Too many competing governments. Prince Henry eventually got his little ships to India, then Indonesia. Bypassed the Arab spice monopoly. Made the Portuguese very rich. Everyone else had to compete or die. First Spain, then Holland, England, and France. It ran away because there was no central control. No central government like there was in China to shut it down.

Butterfly: Your point being?

Lucius: A one-world government will stagnate like the Chinese Empire. Yes, humanity has serious problems. But no global government will ever solve them any more than the Chinese Emperor solved his. It took the competing governments of Europe to banish the horsemen of famine, disease, and pestilence.

Butterfly: But not war.

Lucius: True. But China's peace was the peace of the grave. It wasn't worth four hundred years of stagnation.

The conversation paused as Weidemeyer took another sip of his Virgin Mary. Then he asked:

Butterfly: Why did they stop?

Lucius: Who?

Butterfly: The Chinese. Why did the new emperor stop the fleets?

Lucius: Self preservation.

Butterfly: Who was he worried about?

Lucius: Not who. What. He was worried about change.

Butterfly: I don't understand.

Lucius: Those in power want to preserve the status quo. They like it because it's what got them where they are. Sending fleets around the world would cause change in Chinese society that would upset that status quo. So, he stopped it.

Butterfly: And that wasn't true in the west?

Lucius: Oh, it was. Every western monarch would have loved to stop the clock.

Butterfly: So why didn't they?

Lucius: Foreign competition. China didn't have any, every country in Europe did. Western countries had to change or die. China didn't have that pressure. It's a good thing for them they lost to the Brits.

Butterfly: You think they were lucky to lose the war?

Lucius: Look at the alternative. Suppose China was the only country in the world.

Butterfly: OK. Suppose.

Lucius: Then there wouldn't have been any war. Humanity would still be locked in a 15th century China today, wouldn't it? We'd all be coolies, ruled by soldiers, governed by Mandarins. With no chance of ever getting out. That didn't change in the 400 years before the British. If they hadn’t come, why would it in the next two hundred? Or two thousand?

Chapter 17

The King And The Cop

When the blackmail payments stopped, Caper Oleander decided a bird in the hand was worth more than nothing. He could have contacted Cassandra Carter and asked what was going on, but he had always found her difficult. Now he had a viable alternative. He decided to use it.

When Nobu Bara of Tokugawa Crossing, owner of the KISS'N TELL Snitch House, heard that the database was back on the market, he moved quickly. After all, not only did he have a moral duty to his client, but also a considerable commission at stake. How fortunate that, for once, virtue and avarice led in the same direction.

Within days, gold changed hands. Angelo, Nairobi, and Fawn each became proud owners of a copy of both the encrypted Detention database and the passwords necessary to open it. Those files contained the full and true histories of everyone who was ever held in Heart Mountain Detention: names, dates, status reports, and eventual disposition. All the information that had never before been released to the public was there.

Angelo sent his copy to the people who had paid for its purchase. They, in turn, used it for whatever private political battles they were fighting.

Nairobi promptly published her copy on BadlandsSources.net where it was picked up by several meatspace news services. The next day, headlines all over the world announced that FEMA had been running a death camp. They had admitted through their own records to the killing of over 1,000 detainees.

Fawn looked through her copy to find her husband. Like the rest of the Prometheus inmates, his file showed that he had gone directly into Detention upon his arrival at the camp and so, by FEMA policy, had not had his name released to the public. Eventually, he had been quietly killed and his body had, using a falsified death certificate, been cremated. Only then, to balance the camp head count, had FEMA admitted that he had ever been in one of their camps. The official records were falsified to show that he had been released directly from Detention to the custody of his wife. Only these files told the truth.

When Fawn first heard FEMA's slanderous claim about another woman, she knew it wasn't true. It wasn't that her marriage was perfect. Like any wife, she could not rule out the possibility that he may have moved in with someone else. But she knew that, whatever his defects as a husband, he was the most devoted father she could ever imagine. If he were alive and able to communicate, something deep in his soul would drive him to contact his daughters. They were truly the light of his life. The fact that he hadn't called them, hadn't provided for them, hadn't even asked about them was all she had needed to know to put the lie to FEMA's claim that he was alive, free, and living with someone else.

* * *

Fawn: I've asked Angelo to set up an interview for you.

Butterfly: Who with?

Fawn: King Eddy.

Butterfly: Who is King Eddy?

Fawn: You wanted to meet the man in charge.

Butterfly: I thought you said no one was in charge.

Fawn: That's right. No one is.

Butterfly: Than who is King Eddy?

Fawn: A badlander with influence.

Butterfly: What does that mean?

Fawn: Just that. People pay attention to what he says.

Butterfly: You know him?

Fawn: No. That's why I asked Angelo to set it up.

Butterfly: Angelo knows him?

Fawn: Yes.

Butterfly: How?

Fawn: Ask Angelo. You better thank him, too. He's doing you a favor.

Fat chance, thought Weidemeyer. But he knew better than to type it. Instead, he asked:

Butterfly: Why did you call him 'Clown Face'?

Fawn: Who?

Butterfly: Angelo.

Fawn: He wore a clown mask when we first met.

Butterfly: You've met in person?

Fawn: Yes.

Butterfly: Isn't that pretty rare in the badlands?

Fawn: Uncommon, but not unknown. Recruiters usually meet their prospects. Providers of some services always have to meet their customers. If you went to a badlands doctor because you wanted to keep your medical condition confidential, he would know what you looked like.

Butterfly: Did you meet Angelo professionally?

Fawn: You mean did he pay me to have sex?

Butterfly: Sorry, I didn't mean it that way.

Fawn: We met in a riot. That's another way badlanders meet in person. When they get together to fight you civs, they often see each other's faces.

Butterfly: So you could identify him if you met him again?

Fawn: Planning a line-up? You are a damned cop, aren't you? Sorry, I'd almost forgotten.

There was a long pause in the text stream as both sides tried to decide what to say.

Butterfly: I'm sorry. I didn't mean it that way. I'm just trying to understand how the pieces fit.

Fawn: We've all got a sore spot, here in the badlands. You rub everyone the wrong way because you don't understand it. You need to be more careful.

Butterfly: How?

Fawn: You ask questions for a living. You probe for facts. For background. But, here, everyone values their privacy. You ask too many questions and that puts everyone on edge.

Butterfly: How else can I understand this place?

Fawn: It's not the asking, it's the asking without permission. Don't just go slamming in. That may be the norm in the real world, but here it's not. Here it's trespassing. Go hat in hand, head bowed. Here you are a supplicant, not an enforcer.

Butterfly: Sorry.

Fawn: Don't just say it. Mean it.

Butterfly: I do. I'm sorry for my pushiness. And I'm sorry about the things I said to you about my badlands name.

Fawn: Tried to get it changed?

Butterfly: Yes.

Fawn: But you're still using it.

Butterfly: You were right.

Fawn: That name was the price of your admission. I had no choice.

Butterfly: I understand. That's why I'm genuinely sorry for what I said to you. Please forgive me?

Fawn: You won't prosecute my friends?

Butterfly: I promised, didn't I?

Fawn: Even Angelo?

Butterfly: Even Angelo.

Fawn: Thank you.

Butterfly: Forgive me?

Fawn: OK.

Butterfly: Friends?

Fawn: Don't push it.

* * *

Butterfly: Does BARABBAS have access everywhere in the badlands?

Lucius: I'm not sure what you mean.

Butterfly: Can your people go anywhere? Can your house get you into any market?

Lucius: I understand now. Yes, I don't know of anyplace that won't give us their address.

Butterfly: How long did it take BARABBAS to get that rep?

There was a pause before Lucius answered.

Lucius: COCHISE. Damn you, this is about COCHISE, isn't it?

That took Weidemeyer back quite a bit. It wasn't just the sudden analysis, wrong though it was, but also the anger implied by the words that startled him.

Butterfly: What?

Lucius: This is about COCHISE crossing, isn't it? You're trying to fix their rep, aren't you?

Butterfly: No!

Lucius: Why not? You're a cop, right? Isn't that one of the things they asked you to find out? Why no one will talk with COCHISE?

Butterfly: You know it's a government crossing?

Lucius: Everyone knows. That's why no one deals with it.

Butterfly: I'm not on anyone's errand. COCHISE or any one else's.

Lucius: If you're not snitching for them, why the interest?

Butterfly: Curiosity. Nothing more, just curiosity. I heard COCHISE wasn't doing well and wondered why your crossing works. That's all. I'm not reporting any of this to anyone.

There was a pause in the text while Lucius considered the answer. Then:

Butterfly: That's the truth.

Lucius: OK. Fair enough.

Butterfly: Why does everyone think COCHISE is a front?

Lucius: The way their indentureds act. Like cops. All questions, always pushing.

Butterfly: Like me.

Lucius: You're trying to change.

Butterfly: But I'm still a cop. Why put up with me? Why talk with me but not with them?

Lucius: Good question. You come through GOBI DESERT. They've got a good rep. I guess some of it rubs off. That's part of it, anyway.

Butterfly: But there's more?

Lucius: I don't know. Maybe. Maybe it's like the difference between a gold digger and a hooker.

Butterfly: I don't understand.

Lucius: You know what a hooker wants. She's honest. But a gold digger isn't. They're both whores, but the digger is waiting to stick it to you down the road. Maybe that's it. Maybe it's just that you're honest. Up front.

Butterfly: You speak from experience?

Lucius: Not with hookers, no. But I got stung good by a digger once.

She was going to take my son away, he thought. And, unaccountably, in spite of the risk, he felt the urge to talk about it with this cop. Fortunately, prudence imposed restraint. *Better change the subject.*

Lucius: Where'd you get your badlands name?

Butterfly: GOBI DESERT picked it for me.

And, unfortunately, that's not a lie, thought Weidemeyer.

Lucius: It's not the kind of name they usually pick.

This is getting uncomfortable, thought Weidemeyer.

Butterfly: So I understand.

Lucius: I mean, it's not Oriental or anything, is it?

Butterfly: No, I don't think so.

Lucius: Why'd they pick it?

Is he needling me? Does he know who I really am?

Butterfly: No idea. We can't all be lucky enough to own a crossing house.

Lucius: No. I guess not.

And, as quickly as he could, Weidemeyer changed the subject.

Butterfly: Do you really think all this will last?

Lucius: The badlands? Why not?

Butterfly: It's so new. So different.

Lucius: Not really.

Butterfly: How?

Lucius: What does the badlands offer? I mean fundamentally, underneath it all? The chance to lead our own lives without someone looking over our shoulders. That's not new.

Butterfly: Its not?

Lucius: A lifetime ago anyone could pay cash for a train ticket without an ID. Or make a phone call or write a letter without having it monitored. Or even walk into a store, any store, and pay cash without telling anyone who he was. Not very long ago, the anonymity that now exists only in the badlands was standard for everyone. You always got it. Without even having to try.

Butterfly: That's changed.

Lucius: Yes. Computers did it. On both sides. Suddenly the government could track everyone, spy on everyone, control what we got to hear. And that's the great irony.

Butterfly: What is?

Lucius: We didn't need a place to hide until the Internet came. And when it came, it gave us the badlands. It enabled what may become the most totalitarian police state humanity has ever seen and, at the same time, gave us a place to hide while we fight it for our freedom.

After one brief pause, Lucius typed:

Lucius: The world changes. And still it stays the same.

* * *

Butterfly: I didn't expect to hear from you again.

Angelo: The King asked me to talk to you.

Butterfly: King Eddy?

Angelo: Yes. Why do you want to see him?

Butterfly: He runs the badlands.

Angelo: Fawn tell you that?

Butterfly: I read between the lines.

Angelo: Why should he talk to a spy?

Butterfly: Investigator.

Angelo: Spy.

Butterfly: I'm honest about my intentions. That makes me an investigator, not a spy.

Angelo: OK. Same question. Why should he talk to you? Who do you work for?

Butterfly: Getting a bit personal, aren't you?

Angelo: How does it feel?

Butterfly: I'm entitled to my secrets.

Angelo: And the rest of us aren't? Is that the kind of world you want, civ? Where only government employees have secrets?

Butterfly: What if it is? Just don't do anything wrong. Then you won't have to hide.

Angelo: According to who? You? Or the government?

Butterfly: Meaning?

Angelo: You will when they make something you did retroactively illegal. Doesn't matter what it is, just so they know you did it. Then they got you. They can sweat you whenever they want.

Butterfly: That never happens.

Angelo: Take off the blinders, you damned pig.

This is going nowhere, thought Weidemeyer. *How do I get it moving again?* He had to get that interview. But nothing subtle came to mind, so he just jumped in.

Butterfly: Why do you hate me?

Angelo: I know what kind of world you're trying to build.

Butterfly: Enlighten me.

Angelo: Small. For Ubermenschen, Enforcers, and the rest of us.

Serfs. I won't let my children be Debt Serfs.

Butterfly: Then teach them to stay out of debt.

Angelo: How do they do that? When the only money they're allowed to use is debt? Your masters print more every day. They line their own pockets with it and turn what I've saved into shit.

Butterfly: I don't do that.

Angelo: You hold the gun that lets them do it.

Butterfly: OK. I'm dog crap. Now can I talk to King Eddy?

* * *

Weidemeyer waited quietly, alone in his dark car outside an empty Lowes. His laptop sat balanced on the steering wheel, open, running, and connected. In the badlands, he also waited in a private chat for King Eddy to arrive.

System: King Eddy, male, RENAISSANCE, has entered the room

King: OK, civ, what do you want?

Butterfly: Tell me who runs the badlands.

King: You think it's me? I'm flattered.

Butterfly: I'm told you own most of it.

King: Ah, boyo. Wish it were so. No. Maybe a quarter, that's it.

Butterfly: How do I know you're telling the truth?

King: You want an audited statement?

Butterfly: That would be good.

King: Stuff it, pig.

Butterfly: But you do know who runs it?

King: Yeah. No one runs it. No one can run it. The very term 'running it' implies coercion, which don't exist here.

Butterfly: How do you know that?

King: OK, let's pretend that I control all the badlands. Then someone decides that he don't want to pay me my cut. So, what can I do? Well, I can put a nasty note in his rep file. Right. Big threat.

Butterfly: You could pay a persuasion house to hurt him.

King: If I could fix that sort of problem with muscle, I would fix you. But you still breathe. Know why? Because I don't know where you live. No one knows where you live. We know you're a cop, but there's lots of cops in the world. Which one are you? Give me your meat-space name, then I could fix your problem. Will you do that for me? Give me your name?

Butterfly: Now you can stuff yourself.

King: Right. That's the same problem I got with any situation that I would solve with muscle in the real world. Here it don't work. So, even if I own everything, I got nada unless I got the goodwill of the people I work with. The badlands is a carrot-only kind of place. No stick. So, no control. Influence, yes. Control, no.

Butterfly did not respond. After a long pause, King Eddy typed

King: Look, boyo, you're asking the wrong questions. You want to know who runs us so your bosses can lean on them. You should be asking how your bosses can just stay alive.

Butterfly: Meaning?

King: Do you really think governments go to this much trouble just to catch a few counterfeiters? Hells bells, boyo, they inflate their money supply more in a day than all the counterfeiters in the world do in a lifetime. Don't you see that?

Butterfly: So why do they care?

King: Governments are protection rackets. One of my uncles taught me that business. You use muscle to control violence and live off of the skim. Oh, sorry, I mean 'taxes'. But my uncle couldn't keep it going. You know how governments can?

Butterfly: OK, I'll bite.

King: They take the high ground. The communications. Nations came into existence because the printing press allowed governments to channel communications through a few pieces of machinery. Control those presses, you control what everyone sees and hears. You can run a skim racket without any opposition. When my uncle tried it, he couldn't stop his marks from talking to each other, so they ganged up against him. National governments don't have that problem as long as they hold the high ground.

Butterfly: What about radio, TV, the telegraph, the telephone? They destroy your argument.

King: Hey, you sure you're really a cop? You're thinking too much for a cop.

Butterfly: But it does change things, doesn't it?

King: Look, that stuff just makes the picture bigger, not different. Now, instead of just printing presses, governments have to control telephone exchanges and broadcast stations. So what? Just hire more cops.

Butterfly: What's different now?

King: There's no central control over the Internet. The civs wanted it to stand up to a war, so they designed it without a head. Nothing to cut off. When encryption went public, they couldn't snoop it, either. Double-blind communications came and now they can't even tell who's talking to who. So, there ain't any more high ground. Gone. Bye bye. Adios amigos. No matter how many of you thugs the civs hire, the marks of the world can band together without a pig looking over their shoulders. The badlands makes everyone's communications equal.

Butterfly: Governments still have the guns.

King: Guns don't mean squat without pigs to hold them. But pigs are, I hate to admit it, people too, with wives and kids they want to protect. Once it becomes clear to them that governments can't protect their kin, the pigs stop backing the civs. Yeah, the governments have guns, but without pigs, they got bumpkis. The badlands shows you pigs you're being taken for a ride. Then, guess what? You all quit. No more pigs. Hey, that sounds pretty good, don't it?

Butterfly: Without a government, who controls violence? Who'll protect anyone's kids?

King: Damn good question, boyo. You got my number. If you figure it out, you give me a call, OK?

There was lull in the exchange, then:

King: Hey, pig. My turn.

Butterfly: OK

King: You guys take some oath or something when you become pigs?

Butterfly: Yes.

King: Like what?

Butterfly: We swear to protect the Constitution.

King: Good. Good, I'm impressed. That means, like, the Amendments, too?

Butterfly: All of it.

King: Including the Sixth?

Butterfly: Yes.

King: So you think your masters give everyone a 'speedy and public trial'?

Sven Olson's face sprang unbidden into Weidemeyer's mind. The Wisconsin Dairy Farmer still sat alone in a cell, a staked goat for DHS, held in secret as a terrorist without a trial or even a court date.

Butterfly: According to the Supreme Court, yes.

King: Hey, pig, you a Catholic?

Butterfly: No.

King: What are you?

Butterfly: Mormon.

King: I thought maybe Catholic. Me, I'm Catholic. Your answer was a good Catholic one. But then maybe good Mormon, too, I don't know. I like it. Hey, do you know there's nothing in the Bible about the Pope?

Butterfly: So?

King: Is there anything in your Book Of Mormon about the Pope?

Butterfly: No

King: No, I guess I didn't think there was, either. Well, to be a Catholic, you gotta believe in two things, not just one, because one don't mean the other. Since there's nothing in the Bible about the Pope, you got to believe that God wrote the Bible and that he chose the Pope to interpret it. See? Two things. Independent of each other.

Butterfly: So?

King: Does the Constitution give the Supreme Court the right to over-rule Congress? Or the President?

Butterfly: Of course.

King: Guess again, cop.

Butterfly: The court does it all the time.

King: Only because they say they can.

Butterfly: It's not in the Constitution?

King: Bright boy.

Butterfly: That's not true.

King: Look it up, pig. Article III, Section 2.

Butterfly: OK. Assume you're right. So what?

King: If it's not in the Constitution, then to accept their rulings, you have to independently agree to support them. Just like me and the Pope. Right?

The text stream paused, then:

King: So, what I want to ask is, do you pigs take an oath to support the Supreme Court? Besides the one for the Constitution?

Butterfly: No.

King: Well, hells bells, boyo, that makes you more like some damned Protestant, then, don't it? Looks to me like you have to decide on your own what the Constitution says, right? That's tough, boyo. You got it under control?

Chapter 18

Currency Manipulation

Arnold Wilson Parker sat in the almost-dark of his study, the magnificent view hidden by both night and drawn drapes. Under the light of a single lamp, he looked at Matthew Hood seated across from him.

"This has gone too far, Hood. Too far. We have to sacrifice someone. Someone has to take the blame. Has to. No choice. You see that, don't you?"

"Who did you have in mind?" came the cautious answer, wariness obvious in its tone.

"Carter. What I mean is, we really don't have a choice. Do we?"

"No," came Hood's reply, tinged with a sigh of relief. "But the damned dyke has insurance."

"Insurance?"

"Files. Recordings. She bugged our meetings."

"How do you know?"

"She sent me copies."

Parker smiled, almost a laugh, and shook his head. "It's funny. In the old days, that would have been a problem. Not now." To emphasize his point, he leaned over and handed Hood an envelope.

Hood took it, not sure what to do next.

"Go ahead. Open it."

Reaching inside, Hood pulled out an American passport, a brick of hundred dollar bills, a USB drive, and an envelope. He opened the passport and saw Cassandra Carter's picture over someone else's name.

"It's a badlands crossing kit. The passport's good, but it's not in our system, so Carter can't let anyone who has access to the State Department database see it."

"What are you offering her?"

"A new life. You have to get her around Passport Control. But otherwise, everything she needs is there. All she has to do is keep her insurance to herself. Just disappear."

"What do you need from me?"

"Convince her. To cooperate, I mean. Then get her around passport control. BUNKIE'S will have a private jet at BWI to pick her up."

"BUNKIE'S?"

"Never mind."

"OK. I'll have someone get her out."

"No. Not 'someone'. Do it yourself. Personally."

"Me?" asked Hood with a little surprise.

"If the press finds out we've helped her, we're dead. So you get her quietly on that plane personally. And do it alone. We don't need any more witnesses. Got it?"

Hood nodded, accepting another dirty job as the price for being on top. Then he examined the passport in his hand. It was good. Perfect, in fact.

"How'd you get this?" he asked, holding it up. "You got badlands access?"

Parker nodded. *And I'm changing my mind about the place*, he thought. *Having an out, an escape if I need to run, that's reason enough to keep it alive. If it works for Carter, it'll work for me*.

Changing the subject, he asked "Who's this 'Nairobi Bombay'? Can we get her?"

Hood shook his head, then explained "Don't know her real name."

"Any leads?"

"We got her partner. Badlands name Dancing Fawn. She must know something."

"Sweat her. Hurt her. Bad, if you have to." said Parker.

"She's got kids."

"They matter to her?"

Hood nodded.

"OK, start with that. But if it's not enough, take her out of the country and do whatever you have to."

"She need to come back?"

Parker shook his head.

"Right."

"Any other ideas?" asked Parker.

"I could offer Bombay an interview. In person only, then snatch her when she shows up."

"Not likely. She's too smart. Still, it's worth a try. I'll have someone ask her. Let you know if she agrees. Anything else?"

Hood shook his head.

Well, thought Parker, *I do. Maybe I can rattle her a bit. Scare her. Spook her into doing something dumb, give herself away next time she hits a roadblock.*

* * *

Nairobi received an anonymous text message asking for a chat. Some of her best leads, like the one from Oak, came to her this way so she was more than willing to oblige. Now she sat alone with her new contact:

> Nairobi: What can I do for you?
>
> Sasha: Interview.
>
> Nairobi: With who?
>
> Sasha: Matthew Hood.
>
> Nairobi: Deputy Secretary of DHS?
>
> Sasha: Da. Same.
>
> Nairobi: He asked you to set up an interview?
>
> Sasha: Da.

She glanced again at her new contact's crossing house. STALINGRAD. Not the best choice for this kind of message.

Nairobi: How does he know you?

Sasha: Not me. Associate. DHS badlands agent. Agent asked me ask you.

Nairobi: I'm flattered. Why me?

Sasha: He read articles of you. Want set straight record.

Nairobi: Why didn't he just contact me himself? Through COCHISE?

Sasha: Not want anyone else to know. COCHISE monitored.

Nairobi: Well, I will be pleased to chat with him.

Sasha: Nyet. No. He must have visit. In person.

Nairobi: In person? Why in person?

Sasha: He show you files.

Nairobi: Why not just send me the files?

Sasha: Will not send online. Not want files public.

Nairobi: What information?

Sasha: Confidential FEMA files.

Nairobi: I already have them.

Sasha: Nyet. This more. Show why he act.

Nairobi: I'll have to pass on the personal interview. Will he give an online one without the files?

Sasha: Nyet. Off record only. Not risk recording. In person only way to be sure no recording.

Nairobi: I'm sorry, but there is a safety issue.

Sasha: Da. Understand. Not to worry. Matthew Hood very important man, give you personal guarantee. You be safe. His word.

Nairobi: No. Sorry.

Sasha: You give phone interview?

That took Nairobi back a bit. The question made no sense. If Hood wanted to be sure the interview was unrecorded, why accept a phone interview? She could be recording audio just as easily as text. In fact, because the audio could be tied to him with a voice print, it was actually more dangerous for him than a text-only interview.

> Nairobi: I thought you said Hood refused any interview where a record could be kept.
>
> Sasha: Da. But maybe he change mind. If I ask. You want me ask?

This entire meeting was beginning to smell. True, she had gone verbal with Oak, but that had an entirely different feel to it. Besides, Oak wasn't with STALINGRAD. Big story or not, her gut said the risk wasn't worth it. She would not give DHS a chance to get a copy of her voice print.

> Nairobi: No. No verbal. Text only.
>
> Sasha: Final?
>
> Nairobi: Yes.
>
> Sasha: Please. Nothing to change your mind?
>
> Nairobi: No.
>
> Sasha: Ochen′ zhal′. Hood ask me give you second message.
>
> Nairobi: What is it?
>
> Sasha: He say DHS catch you. After they finish, he give you to me. To STALINGRAD. We kill you whore cunt. Slow and bad.

There was a pause in the text stream, then:

> Nairobi: Isn't Sasha a girl's name?
>
> Sasha: Nyet.
>
> Nairobi: Yes it is. It's a girl's name. Why do you have a girls name?
>
> Sasha: Nyet! Sasha Filippov was boy. Hero. Hero Of Soviet Union.
>
> Nairobi: Well, little boy. Stay away from me or I'll burn your pee-pee off with a soldering iron.
>
> System: Nairobi Bombay, female, DARK CITIES, has left the room

* * *

The young man who used to be called Junior (and still was behind his back) rode tall in the saddle as befitted a man who had grown up in the west. Around him sparkled the summer, sun high and glinting off the last of the mountain snows. Under foot was an alpine meadow, full in the joy of the season. Small flowers shot up everywhere, while the thick tight grass muffled the sound of his horse's hooves.

For the past two hours, he and his father had ridden through their estate. Now they came to a stop on the summit of a small hill near its edge. Looking down towards the valley floor, they saw the perimeter, a ribbon of newly-turned dirt against the lush green grass. A hundred workmen were finishing a fence, installing the last of the wire and sensors along its far side, beyond the tall posts that marked the middle of the scar.

"I remember when this was all open," said the younger Parker (who preferred to be called Will). He was now in his early twenties.

"Hard times require hard solutions," answered his father.

They sat on their horses in silence, taking in the magnificent view. For as far as Will could see, across to the narrow valley and up the towering peaks beyond, only the workmen stirred. The land beyond the fence was quiet and empty. A new preserve, nationalized under eminent domain for a future wildlife sanctuary. And for the enjoyment of the few land owners who, like his father, had the funds and political pull to own property next to it. The masses had their National Parks, his father had this.

A fair trade thought Will.

"Is it going to hurt us?" he asked.

"What?" asked his father in return.

"Dropping the gold standard."

His father smiled. "What do you think?" he answered, again with another question.

"I think you were ready for it," said Will.

His father nodded slightly. Then, after a pause to appreciate the view, he asked "Do you know how?"

"We got out of the dollar before it started," answered his son.

"Good man."

Again, both men fell silent. The view was magnificent, well worth the time for silent contemplation.

"What caused it?" asked Will.

Without a pause, the older man answered "Not enough metal. Can't keep the game going without selling some. We just ran out. No gold left. None."

A breeze slipped by, rustling the grass and making the aspens dance.

"Who caused it?"

"Which snow flake causes an avalanche? Some little man in some little office exchanged one-too-many dollars for gold. Doesn't matter who. Not now."

Again, silence. Overhead, Will saw an eagle soar. Silently he pointed it out to his father. They both watched until it slid behind a peak.

"So what do we do now?" Will asked, breaking the silence.

"Wait. It'll stop. The slide, that is."

"Can we afford to wait?"

"Of course. Knew it was coming. Everything is inflation-proofed. Everything. Just sit tight. Don't sell until the time comes. The right moment."

"And when will that be?"

"After the avalanche stops. Sliding, that is. Downhill."

"How long?"

"No idea. Used to rely on Stein for that. Can't now. Have some young flunky instead. He'll let me know before the Fed tightens up."

Again silence fell over on the pair. Only the sound of their horses eating the new grass disturbed the crisp air. And the wind. And the armored car.

It drove slowly along the near-side dirt road that ran next to the security fence. About a hundred yards ahead of it, a black Humvee bounced slowly along the same path. When the first vehicle reached the work site, both stopped. Three SWAT troops got out of the Humvee and, under the watchful guns of the armored car, checked ID's.

The elder Parker smiled. "Those men," he said, gesturing towards the workers now lined up for inspection. "They worry about their next beer, or a football team, or where to steal a porno movie. Think for today. Maybe tomorrow. No farther. Do they worry that we're running out of everything we need? To survive? As a species. Everything."

Will didn't answer. The question hung in his mind even as the wind blew the sound away. The two watched in silence as blackjacks finished checking ID's and moved on to search the work site.

"Can humanity solve anything if men like those are in charge?"

"No, father," answered Will.

"These problems can't be solved in a few years. Can't. They're long-term. Long term and global."

The younger man just looked and listened.

"Will, I want to leave you more than this land. I want to give you a stable world. Sustainable. With a single government. The kind humanity needs if it is to survive. One that can deal with the big issues. Overpopulation. Resource depletion. Nuclear war. Where real solutions that take decades can be implemented. No. Longer. Generations. Sustainable, over generations. We must have order if humanity is to survive. Must. Stability and unity. Not chaos. You see that, don't you?"

"Yes sir."

"Before I'm gone, I'll give you that dream. The thousand-year solution. You can see what I'm working for, can't you? What I'm going to leave your generation?"

"Yes sir," answered Will.

And the amazing thing was that he could. Because right there, in front of him, was a little piece of it, a microcosm of what was to come. Nature preserved. Safety and security for all. Those with the education, experience, and vision to guide humanity sat on the high ground directing it, guiding it into a bright, sustainable future. Below them, under the watchful eyes of their trusted protectors, labored the rest of humanity, not for some selfish gain, but for the betterment of all.

The future for Will and his father did indeed look bright.

Just as it had for the first Chinese Emperors.

* * *

It started with a knock on the door. One of Weidemeyer's agents, wearing a set of paint-spattered coveralls, looked through the peephole. Should it be needed, she was ready with the cover story. They were renovating the place for a new tenant.

On the other side stood a slim man, also dressed in painters overalls. He held a Secret Service ID up to the peephole for her inspection. Because it is difficult to see much through a peephole, she couldn't tell that it wasn't genuine. So, even though they were not expecting a courier, she opened the door to ask what he wanted.

But she never got the question out. As soon as she unlatched it, the man on the other side slammed it into her face. Her visitor shoved past it, using his shoulder to pin her against the wall. Behind him, six armored blackjacks rushed by, a dark river surging down the hall.

His PS-90 carbine at the ready, Colonel Pug Ringgold led the troopers into the living room. Facing him were folding tables cluttered with laptops attended by surprised Secret Service Agents. While his men speed-walked around the room's perimeter, Ringgold bellowed that this was a DHS security inspection. Disabled by the sudden display of overwhelming force, the five agents in the room did nothing more than stand up.

Except Joshua Weidemeyer. He was livid, then he turned to ice. Striding up to Ringgold, moving closer than polite manners allowed, the planner of Coro confronted its executioner. A stiletto facing down a bowie knife.

Without flinching, the black-clad SWAT colonel reached into a vest pocket, extracted an envelope, and offered it as his only explanation. The stiletto ignored it. Instead, without breaking eye contact, he pulled out his cell and speed-dialed Hood's private number. As he lifted the speaker to his ear, he saw the bowie knife smile.

A beep told Weidemeyer he had no signal. "Anyone got cell service?" he yelled, while keeping his stare on Ringgold's silent eyes.

Seconds later, several 'No's straggled in from his staff.

"Internet's down too, sir."

"Sorry," Ringgold said with a smile that now turned distinctly smarmy.

"Security, you know." Then, dropping the envelope to the floor, he pulled out a cell and held it out to Weidemeyer.

"Please. Use mine."

When Weidemeyer hesitated, Ringgold added "Go ahead. It's not jammed." The smirk never left his face. "Speed-dial four."

Having no other option, Weidemeyer took it and, breaking eye contact, stepped back and dialed. Fifteen seconds later, Matthew Hood came on the line. Their conversation was brief and to the point. Colonel Ringgold had full responsibility for all DHS internal security. And unrestricted authority.

"Someone has to watch the watchers," Ringgold said as Weidemeyer handed him back the phone. "It just happens to be me."

Weidemeyer's only response was a yell to the room: "Everyone back to work."

"What about the Internet?" came a reply.

"Well, Ringgold? What about it?" Weidemeyer echoed.

"The sooner we get this inspection over with, the sooner your people can get back online. Tell them to sit by their laptops and wait."

There was a long silence as Weidemeyer tried to think of any way he could resist this intrusion. But nothing came to mind, so he issued the instructions.

"You too," said Ringgold. That's when Weidemeyer realized that he could be in serious trouble. Until now, he had been too shocked by the speed of the assault to think very far ahead, but now it hit him. Had Fawn told him the truth? Was his Toughbook really clean? If they searched it, this would be its first inspection since she made changes to it. Would it pass? Giving up the last vestiges of his defiant stance, he moved back to his station to wait.

Ten minutes later, a SWAT tech approached him. "Sorry, sir, but I need to check your laptop."

Weidemeyer waved towards it, sitting on the table in front of him. It was open, running Windows. A blank browser covered most of the screen.

Turning the computer so he could get to the keyboard, the tech rebooted it. Seconds later, he had the BIOS screen up. Clicking quickly through the menus, he stopped in mid-keystroke. Then, straightening up, he gestured for Ringgold.

Fawn, you better not have made a mistake, Weidemeyer thought.

"Sir, this computer is already set for USB boot," the tech told his boss when Ringgold arrived.

Turning to Weidemeyer, Ringgold asked "Did you change the boot order on this laptop?"

He had. The last time he had traveled to the badlands, he had made the change so he could boot from the mini-flash drive. Apparently he forgot to change it back when he finished.

Better try something, he thought. *These guys expect an answer.*

"What's the 'boot order'?" he asked.

"Are you denying that you made any changes to the BIOS of this computer?" demanded Ringgold.

"What's a 'BIOS'?"

"Did you ever use a function key on this computer during start-up?" asked Ringgold.

No more evasion. It's time to cross another Rubicon.

"No," Weidemeyer answered without equivocation. The lie came with surprising ease to his lips.

A man's willingness to believe a lie hinges on many factors. In this case, Colonel Ringgold was very familiar with Joshua Weidemeyer's personal history, as he was with all his potential rivals. Nothing in Weidemeyer's resume indicated any particular expertise in computers. That made his claim of ignorance plausible. Backing that up was the fact that the BIOS on these laptops was locked with a password. Weidemeyer was unlikely to know it.

If he hadn't made the changes, who had? Every secure government computer had to go through random IT checks. To perform them, a tech would have had to change the BIOS settings. It was entirely possible that whoever did the last inspection had forgotten to change them back.

If there was still uncertainty in Pug's mind, it was decided by the political pull of the participants. One day he would own Weidemeyer, but, for now, the man had too many friends. Pug would get away with today's show of force because Hood backed him, but calling Weidemeyer a liar would be a step too far. He would have to accept the denial.

"OK," he said to his tech, "Go ahead with the rest of the checks."

The man pulled a small tablet from his pack, placed it on the table next to Weidemeyer's machine, and turned it on. The tablet booted quickly. Using a USB patch cable, he connected it to Weidemeyer's laptop and rebooted the Secret Service machine.

With a USB port now at the head of the boot order, the laptop looked first to the tablet for an operating system. Finding one, it used it. The screen of Weidemeyer's laptop remained blank while it ran the inspection program the tablet loaded into its memory.

Time passed in silence, slowly for the tech because he was bored, but slower still for Weidemeyer because his life hung in the balance. Finally, more to calm his nerves than because he really cared, he asked "What's it doing?"

"Looking for contraband," said the tech, surprisingly willing to talk now that his boss had moved out of earshot.

"What's that?"

"Login records, IP addresses. That sort of thing,"

Weidemeyer had assumed his laptop was being searched for any open-source code as well as any sign that anything other than standard Windows software had ever been loaded onto it. But he hadn't been sure what other checks were being done. Now he knew.

"Login records?"

"Yes. We check to be sure you haven't logged on to any badlands sites or visited any of their addresses. If you have, for your sake, better fess up now. This thing is good."

Weidemeyer sat in silence, waiting to see if Fawn had betrayed him. When the tension got the better of him, he had to have another distraction.

"You do this sort of thing often?"

"No," answered the tech. "This is actually our first time-"

Before he could continue, his tablet beeped and the screen changed. "Good news, sir. You're clean," he announced.

Thank you, Fawn.

"Now I need to look through your brief case. Do I have your permission?"

Crap.

"Go ahead."

The man did a thorough search, coming up with three USB flash cards and the encrypted remote hard drive.

"Are these the only USB devices you have?" he asked Weidemeyer.

"Yes."

"Please empty your pockets, sir."

This is getting way too intrusive, thought Weidemeyer, but he knew he had no choice, so he complied. When he finished, sitting on the table in front of him was a set of keys, a cell phone, and his wallet. There had been no USB drives in his pockets.

"You going to frisk me next?" he asked with more than a little annoyance in his voice. Fortunately, he had the stroke to get away with the question.

"Yes, sir," answered the tech.

Double crap. He hadn't expected that answer.

"Please raise your hands, sir," instructed the tech as he pulled a wand from his pack. Several quick swipes identified Weidemeyer's gun, handcuffs, and belt buckle, but no other metal. And no hidden USB drives. A quick pat-down followed. Still nothing.

Satisfied, the tech gestured for him to put his arms down. Then he began plugging the drives, one by one, into his tablet. His machine ran whatever checks it thought best, flashing a message on its display after it was finished with each device. The hard drive took the longest, but it, like the flash cards, passed with flying colors.

"Thank you, sir," said the tech as he placed the tested articles back in Weidemeyer's briefcase.

"We done now?"

"Yes sir."

"Can I have my Internet back?"

"That's up to Colonel Ringgold, sir. I'll tell him I've finished the inspection."

Two minutes later, with a new password installed on his laptop, he got back online.

The inspection lasted over an hour. Pug's people found nothing. When they finished, they said little and left as abruptly as they had arrived.

Their visit left Weidemeyer with three points to ponder. First, it was no accident that the first SWAT inspection occurred on his team while he was on duty. Colonel Pug Ringgold, like GOBI DESERT, had just sent him a message.

Second, Fawn told the truth. She had not betrayed him. His Toughbook and USB hard drive had passed the inspection with flying colors.

And, finally, he needed a better place to hide his wheels mini-flash. The heel of his shoe was no longer good enough.

Chapter 19

Back In Prison

"Hood is adamant and, frankly, I have to say I agree with him."

What could Weidemeyer say to answer his old boss? Could he say that Fawn had taught him more about the badlands than all his other agents combined? They would ask how, and he dared not answer. If they ever learned that he had made unauthorized, unmonitored trips across the border, his career and perhaps his freedom would be over.

"I review her work every week when she comes back to see her girls. You're both wrong. She's one of our best contributors."

"Joshua" said his boss, "How many terrorists has she named? She's had free rein for over six months now, right?"

"Yes."

"Has she gotten us a single badlander during that time?"

"Her value's greater than just a few agents."

"OK. Just convince me. What has she contributed?"

There again, the unanswerable question.

"Josh, next time she comes back, tell her that it's over. Execute the court order and transfer her to Danbury." FCI Danbury was the nearest Federal Prison with a women's unit.

Perhaps there was still a chance, thought Weidemeyer. *Perhaps if she were finally confronted with all she feared, she would turn in someone.*

"Let me take her and her children to Danbury. Talk to her in the van. If I can't get her to come over with some names, then I'll leave her there and turn her girls over to Family Services. But, please, give her this last chance."

"Why do you need to take the girls?"

"I want to rub her face in it, make her really feel what she is about to lose."

His boss considered it a moment, then asked "Do you think she can deliver

Nairobi Bombay? Hood really wants that one. If she can produce Bombay, I know I can sell it to Hood."

"Maybe. Please. Let me try."

* * *

Weidemeyer stood behind the one-way glass, hands in his pockets watching her in her cell. She was having breakfast with her two girls. Shoving, chattering, and giggling. He almost expected someone to throw a piece of toast. Did people really act this way at the table? His family never did. Breakfast was the time to discuss the day's plans, to put on the grim armor you would need to get through the coming fight. He didn't remember ever even smiling, much less laughing.

In his right hand he fingered a Roman silver coin. Without any conscious intent, he had started carrying it to work. It had become as common on his dresser as his keys, phone, and wallet. Somehow, it gave him comfort. Perhaps it was a reassurance that all the hard things that he might have to do were worth it. The world was an old place and would grow older still after this was over, after he and everyone now in it was gone.

As he watched her girls, his mind ambushed him.

Would the children of Coro have laughed like that? it asked.

Shaken, he struggled to drive the image from his mind. Finally, his iron self-control reasserted itself. His composure back in place, he looked again at Fawn.

Would she denounce him? If she did, could he plausibly deny it? What proof did she have?

They finished breakfast. The matron came in to take the children. Still, even in parting, there seemed to be some magic joy passing between them.

She was due to go back to Orlando later on today. He had given her as much time with her girls as possible so she would appreciate what she was about to lose.

The matron was gone now. Like it or not, now was the time to tell her. Walking around to the other side of the glass, he entered the visitors side of her isolation cell. She heard him walk in, looked up, and actually smiled when she saw him. He couldn't bring himself to smile back.

She saw his face. "What's wrong?"

"I have to execute the court order."

Her face didn't change, just froze, as if her control of it had stopped while she tried to decide if he was serious. Then, when she realized he was, she slumped to the floor.

"I'm sorry. I did everything I could, but Hood forced it. I can't fight that." He dared not say more because he knew the recorders, as always, were running.

She didn't start to cry, she just sat there looking at him.

"Listen, there's still one chance. If you give me Bombay, I can stop this. He really wants her. Please, help yourself and the kids." He had almost said help us, but had caught himself in time. That would not have looked at all good on the recording.

"You said I wouldn't have to turn in my own."

"It's out of my hands. Hood's involved. I'm sorry."

Her gaze dropped to the floor and stayed there, wrapped in silence.

"Well?" he prompted.

"No."

They argued for the rest of the morning, but she wouldn't change her mind. Whatever twisted moral code she had, it was firm. She wouldn't snitch. Not on Bombay. Or Angelo. Or, for some strange reason, not even on him.

* * *

Saturday morning traffic was steady but not heavy on this section of three-lane expressway. Nairobi Bombay drove alone in the middle lane, her mind lost in the sort of wandering thoughts that we all fall into during moments of active boredom.

Several thousand yards ahead, beyond her vision, three police cars drove abreast, one in each lane. Turning on their flashing lights, they begin to slow. The freeway traffic behind them, having nowhere else to go, reduced speed as well.

About a quarter of a mile from the next exit, the parade came to a stop. As soon as the traffic ahead of the stopped cruisers cleared that exit, a small convoy drove back up the ramp and headed towards the stopped police vehicles. When they got to the blockage, they spread out and stopped, one camouflaged army truck facing each cruiser in the right two lanes. The truck in the middle lane was towing a steel bump-barrier which was quickly unhitched and wheeled into place in the fast lane abreast of the truck that had towed it. A black armored car drove onto the left shoulder, facing traffic, and pulled up next to the bump barrier, stopping between it and the center-line concrete wall.

The bump-barrier was designed to slow or stop traffic. It consisted of a low platform made of eight-foot long steel plates as wide as a single lane. At the far end, away from approaching traffic, was a spiked gate that is normally recessed, but could be slammed up instantly to stop all traffic. If it is retracted, the assembly is nothing more than a mild speed bump less than an inch thick. But with the barrier up, it is transformed into a sloping spiked wall angled into any oncoming traffic. In the up position, it was solid enough to stop even the most determined charge that a large truck might make.

When these preparations were completed, the three police cruisers drove over the bump-barrier, circled behind the two trucks, and then pulled onto the right shoulder facing the traffic. Driving slowly to avoid the debris and cracked concrete that always covered the shoulder, they reached the end of the stopped cars in about a mile. Circling behind it, the officers got out and placed a line of barriers across the right two lanes, then got ready to direct traffic.

Nairobi sat stopped in the middle lane, watching the oncoming traffic fly by unimpeded in the adjacent three lanes, unaware of the cause of the stoppage. She saw the two cruisers pass her going the other way on her right. Overhead, she heard the sound of a helicopter. Thinking it a traffic spotter, she looked out her window to see two of them, unmanned, circling the area. Both sported military livery.

Ambling behind the two cruisers, rolling down the right shoulder at a slow speed, came a black Humvee with bullhorns mounted on the roof. She heard it, faintly at first, but then louder as the vehicle approached. Then she saw it, followed by a small convoy of SWAT and army trucks. Rolling down her window, she heard:

"This is a DHS Terrorist Safety Check. If you are stopped in one of the right two lanes, please turn off your ignition and stay in your vehicle. You will be arrested if you move your vehicle or exit from it without instructions from an officer. If you have a computer with you, do not remove it from its storage location or touch it in any way. A DHS inspector will be with you shortly."

They didn't bother to apologize for the inconvenience.

A line of about a dozen trucks followed the Humvee. The last one stopped as it passed her and she watched as a few blackjacks and a dozen soldiers in full combat gear got out and moved towards the cars behind her.

Then the traffic to her left moved. A police cruiser drove by her on the left shoulder, moving against the traffic, the officer in it gesturing for traffic in the left lane to move ahead. Manning the bump-barrier, two blackjacks also gestured for the cars in that lane to proceed over the barrier. Within minutes, the traffic in the fast lane, the one next to her, was moving at a slow but steady twenty mph, easing some of the congestion caused by the blockage of the two right lanes.

This wasn't the first time she had been caught in a flying road block. On at least three occasions in the past, she had been stopped and had her vehicle searched. Each time they asked to see her computer and, each time, as requested, she had turned it on. When her Linux bootloader came up, looking exactly like a Windows log-on page, they lost interest. Terrorists don't use Windows.

She decided to fill the dead time by returning phone calls, but couldn't get cell service, something that was very unusual considering they were in the middle of a major city. Although she didn't notice it, the GPS locator in her phone wasn't working either. Both were being jammed.

So, with nothing else to do, she turned around to watch the show. That included, on several occasions, people being led in handcuffs to the right shoulder where a black Humvee, presumably called by radio, drove up and took them away.

Meanwhile, the civs that got out of the truck had formed into two inspection teams. They start on the two cars directly behind her, one in each lane. She took the opportunity to watch them in action from a close distance.

First, a helmeted blackjack would move to the driver's window and talk with the driver, presumably checking documentation and giving instructions. The hood and trunk were both opened and the contents inspected. Unlike previous inspections she had had to endure, this lot seemed to be well equipped. One army soldier in each team wore an explosive sniffer pack. He would move around the car, sticking a wand that was connected to his pack into every conceivable location. He even checked the air in the tires, letting a little out of each one into the sniffer tip.

The driver (and passengers, if there were any) was asked to get out and stand in front of the vehicle. All were frisked by a second soldier, both with a magnetic wand and a pat-down. The blackjack, the sniffer operator, and another soldier would search the vehicle interior while this was going on. Meanwhile, a fourth army trooper, using a mirror on the end of an extension, would move slowly along the sides of the car, inspecting the undercarriage.

Eventually, the hood was closed. All luggage and packages were then removed from the vehicle and placed on it to receive a thorough manual search, including the use of the explosive sniffer. If everything passed, the driver would be handed back his documents, leaving him and any passengers to repack their luggage and reload it into their vehicle. If anything was found wanting, however, all were handcuffed and led to the shoulder for pick-up.

Assuming there were no arrests, the driver and passengers eventually got back into their vehicle. When the driver signaled that he was ready, one of the soldiers would stop traffic in the left lane long enough for them to leave. No one hesitated, pulling out to leave empty spaces in the matrix of parked cars. Meanwhile, the inspection team would move on to the next vehicle.

At best, this procedure took five minutes. More often, it took ten. So, with the waves of inspectors at least ten cars apart, Nairobi estimated she would be there at least two hours. Well aware of the prohibition against opening any of her luggage, she couldn't even get out a book to read. So she just leaned back to rest her eyes.

A tapping on her window woke her. Rolling it down, she was confronted by an unsmiling blackjack.

"License and registration, please. And unlock your hood and trunk."

She handed him her documentation. "I can't unlock the trunk from inside the car."

"OK, ma'am, please get out and unlock the trunk. Then go to the front of the vehicle and wait there."

She did as she was told, standing in the warm sun while they searched her car. As she waited, she looked across the lane of slow traffic moving next to her. Across the low concrete barrier beyond, three lanes of vehicles passed her at full speed from the other direction. The only thing that separated them from low-income housing on the far side of the freeway was another low crash barrier. She noticed that the helicopters had left, as had several of the cruisers.

One of the soldiers, a woman, came to the front of her car and asked her to lift her arms. She did so and received a quick frisk and wand check.

Meanwhile, satisfied with the cleanliness of her engine, one of the troopers closed her hood. Then they emptied the contents of her car onto it. In her case, that consisted of her laptop, the contents of her glove compartment, some maps, and two boxes of trash from the trunk.

While a soldier pawed through her possessions, his rifle lying on the ground by his feet, the blackjack picked up her laptop case.

"Is this yours, ma'am?" he asked.

"Yes."

"Please take out the computer."

She did as she was asked. He took it from her, plugged a small tablet of his own into one of its USB ports, and turned it on. Only when the screen of his tablet told him to do so did he turn on her laptop. She waited for Windows to boot up, but instead, the screen remained blank. He concentrated on his tablet. Then, without looking up, he asked "You have a bootloader installed on this computer."

Those few words stunned her, no less than if she had been struck. If he knew she had a bootloader, then he knew her system was not running standard Windows. Possession of a computer using anything other than a Windows or Apple package had become grounds for summary arrest. In her case, given her conversation with Sasha, that would be a serious matter. She could deny that this was a set of wheels as long as she wanted, but the result would be the same. Any sane person knew there was only so much isolation, water-boarding, and shock treatment you could stand before you did anything you were asked. She knew she had her limits, too. To avoid the pain, she would eventually give them her password. Even if she used the red one, the crossing would still show them her badlands name, would still tell her captors she was Nairobi Bombay. After that, she could count on a rough time. And, eventually the STALINGRAD House.

Yet what alternative did she have? Like most badlanders, she had a crash bag hidden in a secure place. Even if they got her name and picture from her car registration, they would have a hard time catching her as long as she could get to it. In it were a driver's license, passport, and some credit cards (all in a false name), as well as considerable cash, clothes, and materials to disguise her appearance. If she could get to that bag, she could be on a domestic flight to some distant city in less than an hour. With luck, and the help of a good extraction service, she could be out of the country within a week.

The blackjack next to her had set down her laptop and was turning to call for assistance. With his right hand, he was reaching for the handcuffs in his belt. All that stood between her and that crash bag were four lanes of traffic, cars and trucks that would shield her from pursuit. Only the blackjack had ready access to a weapon, the pistol he carried on his belt. The soldiers were armed with rifles, but had all set them down to concentrate on their inspections. In a rush, most would take several seconds just trying to remember where they left them.

So she bolted.

Crossing the near lane of slow vehicles was easy. Vaulting the barrier, she began dodging through the next lane of traffic before the officer she left behind realized what had happened.

Her years of Pilates and racquetball kicked in. She was no longer a raw-boned awkward strapping with a plain face. She was a world-class basketball player, an Olympic gymnast, or the dancer she always secretly longed to be. Her vision narrowed, her mind concentrated. She jinked, she swerved, she feinted, she floated through the air with the speed and grace of a cat.

The first shots sounded before she reached the middle lane. A total of fourteen were fired, aimed to kill, but none struck her. She was supple grace personified, dodging between the moving vehicles like a champion bullfighter, sidestepping death. Because of the difficulty of firing at a jinking target hidden by at least two lanes of fast counter-flowing traffic, she was able to dance across the road unscathed. The last lane slipped under her feet like a rushing whisper. Ahead lay only the final concrete barrier.

There are no funerals in the badlands. No wakes. It is, after all, not a corporeal place. No one dies there. Only in the flesh-and-blood world does death visit. One of the ironies of the virtual world is that, with a few exceptions, no one knows the real-world identities of even their closest friends. So it was with Nairobi Bombay.

If she stopped crossing, none of her badlander friends would ever know why, nor ever find out. Her emails would just go unanswered, her blog would not be updated. She would just drop out of sight, probably just out of touch for a while. Even had they wanted to, the police couldn't have told anyone in the badlands about her status because her wheels didn't have her unencrypted badlands name recorded anywhere on the hard disk. They had no way of getting her badlands identity unless she gave them one of her passwords.

Only in the real world would anyone know that a suspected terrorist was struck by a swerving semi while trying to escape across an interstate. Even confirming her real-world identity was difficult because her body was pinned against the far concrete barrier by the skidding cab and smeared like strawberry jam on a crust of dried bread.

Chapter 20

Escape Attempt

For the past hour, ever since they left the holding facility in DC, Weidemeyer had sat in the back of the prison van, trying to talk the only adult prisoner into being more cooperative. She protested that she had done all she could, then gradually, fell silent. Now Fawn wouldn't even look at him. She just huddled with her twins, hugging and rocking, not to the sway of the van, but to some atavistic rhythm in an attempt to quell her sorrow.

So now he had to make a decision, probably the hardest of his life. After a minute of thought, he leaned against the cage that separated him from the driver's compartment. "I give up. Pull into that rest area ahead and I'll drive," he yelled to the young matron who sat behind the wheel. She nodded in response.

They were headed north on I95, running late because of morning DC rush-hour traffic. As they turned off the expressway, Weidemeyer at least had the comfort of knowing he had done everything possible to help Fawn and her girls.

They pulled into a space far away from other vehicles.

"I'll pit first," he said. "You four go after I get back. It's still five hours to Danbury and I don't want to have to stop again."

Ten minutes later, the prison matron followed Fawn and her two girls out of the ladies room. Distracted by the stink of overflowing toilets, she didn't pay as much attention to her surroundings as she should have. Suddenly, her world exploded in pain. As she spasmed towards the ground, strong hands grabbed her and helped her sit, half slumping, against a tire.

"Are you OK?" asked a male voice as gloved hands frisk her, taking her gun, radio, and cell phone. Looking up, she saw Groucho Marx kneeling next to her.

"Listen, I'm really sorry about this, but we didn't have any choice, you know?" Groucho said. "Anything else and you might have panicked. Started yelling or shooting or something, you know? So, look, just sit here with me a minute until you feel better, then I'll walk you over to your van. And don't worry, I won't zap you again unless you start acting crazy. I promise. OK?"

All she could do was look back and concentrate on breathing.

"Is she OK?" Came a feminine voice from above her left shoulder. The prison matron looked up to see a middle-aged woman in a long-sleeved frumpy flower dress, sun hat, and white dress gloves. Her face was covered by sunglasses and a large flesh-colored bandage.

"Just a fainting spell, she's recovering now," said Groucho.

"Thank goodness. You understand, don't you, sweetie, that you can get out of this without any more fainting spells if you just work with us?"

Realizing she had little choice, the young matron nodded.

"Good" said the woman in the frumpy dress. "Let's get you up and back to your van." And, with that, they helped her to her feet and supported her, one on either side, as she walked towards the far end of the lot.

Then she remembered her charges. But when she tried to turn to look for them, her assistants stopped her.

"Now, now, sweetie, if you strain yourself you'll have another attack," soothed Mrs. Frumpy Dress.

"But..."

"Don't worry about them. They left right after you got your attack. Let's just worry about your health, OK? Just keep walking quietly with us or you may have another seizure."

As they approached the prison van, the back door opened from the inside. A man in a Federal Prison Service uniform, a very heavy beard, and dark glasses moved aside to make room for her. Inside, she saw Special Agent Weidemeyer chained to one of the prisoner seats. Before she could protest, she was helped through the door and it closed. Someone snapped manacles on her wrists and ankles, then chained her across from Weidemeyer. Mrs. Frumpy Dress sat next to her and the van took off.

Across from her, Groucho Marx pulled out a clasp knife and opened it. Moving quickly, he slipped the point of a long serrated blade under Weidemeyer's chin and slashed hard. The agent's tie fell from his neck. A few more slashes and his shoe laces and belt were gone. Finally, Groucho opened Weidemeyer's collar and took his ID.

"You're next, sweetie." said Mrs. Frumpy Dress. She took the knife from

Groucho and with slow, bird-like movements, cut off the matron's uniform jacket.

Moving to a duffel in the back of the van, she pulled out a set of women's prison overalls. At least, that's what they looked like at first glance. On more careful examination, though, the matron saw that zippers ran down the arms, legs, and back. Fumbling, trying to sort out which end of the complex garment went where, Mrs. Frumpy Dress lay a split pants leg on top of each of her thighs, covering her legs down to just above her shackles.

"Lift your feet up, sweetie," directed Mrs. Frumpy Dress.

The matron did as she was told. Reaching around the matron's legs, Mrs. Frumpy Dress connected the zippers behind the younger woman's calves.

"OK, you can put your feet down, now, sweetie. Give me your arms."

The matron did as she was told and got the same treatment there.

"Stand up for me now, OK, sweetie?"

She did while Groucho steadied her. In seconds, she was encased in what looked from the front like a standard prison uniform.

"Thank you, sweetie. You can sit down now."

While Groucho helped her, Mrs. Frumpy Dress pulled some documents from the duffel bag.

"Sweetie, are you feeling well enough to read?"

The matron nodded.

"Good. Here, look at this," Mrs. Frumpy Dress said and handed her the papers. They were prisoner transport orders, one for her and one for Weidemeyer, correct in every detail, including pictures. Only the names were wrong.

"Do you understand, sweetie? If you make a ruckus, we'll show these papers to anyone that stops us. All you'll get is another fainting spell. Do you see that?

Another nod.

"Good. And, to be sure you keep working with us, I'm going to attach these little wires to the back of your neck. No, don't worry, it's just tape, like for an EKG. We'll take them off before we leave, I promise. But you understand, don't you, that its like a dog's shock collar? I can send you a little warning, like this..."

She felt a tingling in her neck. Not painful, but insistent. Then it stopped.

"Feel that?"

She nodded.

"Good. Now remember, if you make a ruckus, you will have another attack. Got it?"

Another nod.

"OK, now let me tell you what's going to happen. This van has to be moving on the road to the Danbury facility or its GPS tracker will trip an alarm somewhere. We don't want that, so you're going to FCI Danbury exactly as you planned. Well, almost. We'll have to drop you two and the van off a few blocks from the prison, we can't actually drive in there with you, you know. Anyway, the GPS will tell them you're stopped. When you take too long to get moving again, they'll send someone out to find you. You'll be back before sunset with nothing more than a good story to tell your boyfriend. This little health episode will all be just a memory. OK? Will you help us get you back safely into a warm bed tonight?"

Again, just the nod.

"Good, good. Now, we can't make this trip with our masks, so we need you to put on this hood."

The matron tensed. Mrs. Frumpy Dress must have noticed it.

"You're still going to work with us, right?"

She couldn't answer, except to show her fear with wide eyes.

"Don't worry, sweetie, the last thing we want is for you or Special Agent Weidemeyer to get hurt. Honest. Look, this is just a prisoner hood. You put them on other people all the time, right?

The matron said nothing.

"I'll be sitting right here next to you the whole way. If anything goes wrong, I'll take it off. I promise. "

Still no response.

"Please. Work with me on this, OK?"

She got a little nod.

"Let me put on the hood?"

Finally, faint speech: "OK".

Mrs. Frumpy Dress slipped black hoods over Weidemeyer and the young matron. The trip to Danbury continued with two prisoners, a guard, and two administrators.

* * *

Darkness filled Fawn's mind as she walked back toward the van. Preoccupied with her own thoughts, she almost didn't hear the scuffle behind her. Turning, more out of curiosity than for any other reason, she saw her escort slump to the ground in the arms of a muscular man with unusual facial features. Before she could understand what she saw, a strong hand grasped her arm and pulled. A familiar voice said "Fawn. Come on. Now, Fawn." She resisted, turning instead to see who was grabbing her.

And there stood Angelo Pisa.

"What are you doing here?"

"Later. We have to go now. Please," he pleaded and tugged again at her arm. Trusting him, she gripped a girl's hand in each of hers and let herself be led. Five steps and they reached the open cargo door of a white delivery van. Two more and they were all inside. The door slammed and they moved. Seconds later, the van accelerated up the I-95 on-ramp to become just another vehicle in the crowd.

Her eyes adjusted to the darkness faster than her mind did to her new situation. She found herself and her daughters sitting with Angelo and two fit young women. Both strangers wore costume masks. One went to work on her shackles.

"You OK?" asked Angelo.

"Honeys, are you OK?" She got two nods. Then, yes, she was OK, too.

"Good. We don't have much time, so hurry. Change into these clothes while we talk," he said as the other woman handed her a pile of clothes.

"I hope they fit. We had to guess a little about your sizes. Also, we need to deal with your hair. They'll be looking for a brunet with a prison cut. Given the time problem, the best way is to make you into a cancer patient. So Sandy will cut off your hair and eyebrows.

That got her attention. "No. Wait, what?" she stuttered.

"Please, Fawn. There is no time. Just do this, OK?"

She nodded and the first woman, having removed her restraints, got to work with the clippers.

"OK. Honeys, please take off your clothes and put these new ones on. And hurry, OK?"

"What about the man, momma?"

"It's OK, he won't look, I promise."

And, with a smile, Angelo turned his back, but kept talking.

"With luck, they won't know you're missing until about five tonight. When you take into account flight time, that gives us four hours, not long. So, please, less talk and more action, OK?"

"OK" she said and the transformation began. It went well until the makeup case came out. Suddenly, she balked.

"What's wrong?" asked Angelo.

How could she tell him? How could she explain the degradation and servitude that case represented?

"Fawn, please."

The tiger fought with the mouse for her mind, for just a second, then it took over. With a small head movement, she told them to proceed.

Fifteen minutes later, Fawn and her girls were new creatures. She had a buzz cut from her collarbones up. On her head was a blond wig. All three sported conservative, tasteful, and expensive traveling clothes that fit quite well. For the first time in years, she wore makeup. And, for the first time in her life, she wore gold jewelry.

"Your luggage is behind you. Here are passports for you and your girls. We kept the same first names, but you will have to memorize new last ones quickly, as we will be at BWI in less than ten minutes.

"The passports are from South Africa with stamps showing you recently visited London and then the US. You are here on a medical visa to get more cancer tests. Fortunately, those tests showed you are in remission after your recent chemo course. You have a business visa for Cuba, which is your next stop. You also have documents showing that you are an employee of the Meds For Cuba foundation, which is your excuse for being on this flight. You are there to present two cases of fresh vaccine to the Cuban medical authorities as a goodwill gesture. They're in the aircraft baggage compartment. If you need to see them, you can get to that space through the lavatory in the rear."

He did not mention that the baggage compartment was also accessible from outside the aircraft. Nor did he mention, because he did not know, that there were also four empty duffel bags in that compartment. Two were big enough to hold adult bodies. The other two were smaller, child-sized.

"You will depart on a private jet from the general aviation gate of the International Terminal at BWI. We'll drop you off as close as we can to the entrance. Get through security and Passport Control and on to the jet as quickly as you can. The aircraft crew knows nothing about any of this, just that they have four guests and are to take off as soon as all are on board. The only other passenger is already there, so they're just waiting on you."

Only six months ago, Passport Control, Security, and Baggage Inspection didn't exist for charter aircraft flights. For those rich enough to travel by private aircraft, all you had to do was drive up and get aboard. Those times were gone now. Flying out of the country was a lot tougher, even for the rich.

"I can't stress this enough," continued Angelo. "You have to be through immigration in Havana before the Feds realize you're gone. As soon as they know about your escape, they'll alert all border control stations. Then they'll find your picture in the departing visa files, get the name you're traveling under, and ask the authorities in Havana to arrest you. You must be through customs at the other end before that happens or the Cubans will be forced to detain you and we'll be right back to square one.

"You'll be covered until about five tonight, seven hours from now, but, after that, things get dicey. Given the two-and-a-half hour flight time to Cuba and the delays in getting from the gate to the runway, you only have about an hour to get on the plane once we drop you off. Do you understand?"

This was all a bit much and well over a bit too fast, but she did get the gist.

"Yes" she said. Then, turning to her daughters, she said "Girls, we're going to play the Shy Game for a while, OK? If anyone tries to talk with you, don't answer, just hide your faces, like you used to do when the Bastard was around. Do you remember him?"

Two small heads nodded.

"OK, show me."

They both ducked, hid their faces, grabbed their mother's skirt, and tried to hide behind her back. Then, for the first time since breakfast, the giggles came back.

They were very good girls.

"Good, good. Now, if that doesn't work, just start crying. But, whatever happens, don't say a word to anyone, even me, unless I tell you it's OK to answer. Can you do that? This is really important."

Games were fun and they had practiced this one often in the past. Two smiles, two nods.

"OK, we're ready."

"I see that." said Angelo.

"Now, we can't come in there with you, too many cameras and the masks would be noticed, so you'll have to do this by yourself. There's a cell phone in your purse, speed-dial 2 if you get into trouble. Never mind who answers, just ask for me. You shouldn't have any trouble, though, so relax. You'll have an hour to get through security and Passport Control, that's lots of time."

They rode in silence for a minute or so, then she said "I didn't know you did anything besides clown marches."

"I do, but this isn't one of them. BUNKIE'S asked me to come along to make you feel more comfortable. The last thing an extraction service wants is for the target to resist her rescue."

"BUNKIE'S?"

"The extraction service. They're running this show."

"I owe you again, it seems."

As the van pulled up to the curb, he said "Tell me about it next chat, OK? Good luck."

The door slid open and she stepped out, a child in each hand. Almost without her noticing it, two bags appeared beside her. No one else got out. The door slammed shut. Without any fanfare, the van slipped away from the curb and into the departing traffic.

Suddenly, she felt very alone.

* * *

"Excuse me."

She was halfway across the lobby of the international terminal, heading towards the general aviation counter, when the voice ambushed her from behind. She decided to ignore it, walking on, a suit case rolling under each hand, her two children following behind like little ducklings.

Then, a tap on her shoulder. "Excuse me, I think I know you," said a squeaky voice.

This could no longer be ignored. She stopped and turned to confront her new problem. What she saw was a middle-aged man of medium height and heavy build, well dressed in a suit and tie, with a full face that managed to be both red from chronic acne and yellow from some underlying metabolic condition. Clipped to his tailored suit jacket was an ID of some sort. He seemed to be squinting as he looked at her, then smiled.

"Dancing Fawn, isn't it?"

Her heart stopped.

"Where is Agent Weidemeyer? How did you get here?"

To her credit, she didn't bolt. It wouldn't have done any good anyway. She was, after all, in one of the most secure airport terminals in the world. But she wanted to run. Drop everything, grab her girls, and run like the wind.

"Forgive me, we haven't actually met, have we? I'm Matthew Hood, Deputy Secretary of Homeland Security. I know you, though. After all, I signed the papers that sent you to Danbury, remember? Oh, here. Want to check my ID?"

He reached for his badge, obviously enjoying himself, and held it up to her without unclipping it. She was too sick to look at it.

"Now, please, tell me where Agent Weidemeyer is."

Why hadn't he called security? Why hadn't he had her arrested? Why were they just talking here like two old friends who just happened to meet?

"Come, now, I know you can speak. Why aren't you in a prison van with Agent Weidemeyer?"

"What do you want from me?"

Again, the smile, this time with crooked yellow teeth showing.

"For starters, I want to know how you came to be here."

Still, no call for help, no alarm raised.

"Why haven't you called security?"

The smile lost just a little of its smugness. Yes, there was something there. She couldn't have known that he had come here to sneak Cassandra Carter around Passport Control, couldn't have known that he had to get out of the airport undetected, just like she did, or risk exposing his relationship with Carter. He was frantically trying to think of how he could quietly get her into a car so he could take her someplace safe, someplace that wouldn't raise questions, and turn her in there.

"Oh, there's plenty of time for that. But first, I thought we might just talk."

Since before mankind first walked upright, women have been doing whatever it takes to protect their children. She had been doing it all her adult life, more so since her husband had disappeared, and had gotten good at it. Now, all that experience came to the surface.

Unattractive men rarely get attention from beautiful women. Perhaps there was a way.

"This is a pretty public place to have a discussion. Doesn't DHS have suites or something here at the airport?"

There was a pause while he considered the matter. She helped him along by throwing him one of her most fetching smiles.

"We could talk about Nairobi Bombay," she offered.

That got his interest.

"Alone. In private," she added as she arched her back slightly towards him.

Either because of his hatred for Nairobi or for some other baser reason, he must have come to a decision, because he pulled out his cell phone. Without taking his eyes off her smile, he speed-dialed.

"Hey, Margie, I need someplace quiet to work for a while. Are any of the BWI rooms free for tonight?"

A pause. She slipped the tip of her tongue through her lips to wet them while he watched.

"Good, could you put me down for two?"

She sped up her breathing slightly, making each one a little deeper.

"OK, those will do. Thanks," and hung up.

"OK, let's go," he said as he took one of her bags and used his other hand to guide her with a firm grip on her upper arm.

Her mind raced as they walked through the airport. This diversion bought her a little time, but it wouldn't get her family on the plane. And it certainly didn't get her the five or six hours she needed to get to Cuba.

Her mind churned over the possibilities and problems. Were cameras hidden in the room? What if they were monitored? Then any escape she made would be seen instantly. She'd be caught before she left the airport.

She dismissed the worry. If there were cameras, Hood planned to turn them off. He couldn't allow himself to be an actor in an impromptu porno film, especially not with an escaped prisoner that he should have turned in.

How to delay him for at least five hours? Better yet, eight, to give her a safety cushion? Knock him out? Tie him up? This was her last chance to keep her girls. Whatever it took, she would do it.

Five minutes later, Hood used a key to open one of the many anonymous doors that seem to exist in every airport in the world. Behind it was a short bare hall with six more doors, all numbered and closed. He unlocked one and guided her through it. Her children followed, along with her luggage. He closed and locked it from the inside, then did a quick inspection of the closet and bathroom. Satisfied, he took her purse and dumped the contents onto the bed. Seeing nothing of interest, he frisked her quickly but thoroughly while her girls watched.

"Sorry," he explained, "But we do have to follow procedures."

She gave him back a wry professional smile and asked "You have procedures for this?"

The joke seemed to put him at ease, as she had hoped it would.

"What about my girls? Are you going to interrogate me in front of them?"

"Tell them to come with me," he said "and I'll put them in the next room."

This worried her, being separated from her charges, but the alternate worried her even more.

"Honeys, please go with this nice man. He'll put you in another room for a while. Please just sit there quietly and wait for Mommie to come for you, OK?"

Two nods.

Picking up her luggage and opening the door, he gestured for the twins to follow. They did. When they were all out in the hall, he took the precaution of closing and locking her door from the outside. She took advantage of the privacy to get ready for his return.

* * *

The phone rang and Mrs. Frumpy Dress answered it.

"No, sorry. You must have the wrong number," she said. Then, after a brief pause, "This is the Sturm residence." Another pause, then "No need to apologize, these things happen all the time." A last pause, then "Goodbye" and she hung up.

Leaning against the screen that separated the prisoner compartment from the driver, she yelled "We have Mississippi." He nodded and looked in the rear view mirrors. A car in the next lane three vehicles back flashed its lights twice. The driver tapped his brakes once, then twice in quick succession.

Condition Mississippi. The customer was late for the plane. No check-in, no one had heard from her, she did not answer her phone. Perhaps captured, maybe just delayed. Whatever the reason, the charter no longer had enough time get to Cuba before the Feds started their search. Under the current plan, that is. So the plan had to change.

There was a McDonald's at the next exit. The driver signaled a turn, looking back to confirm an answering turn signal from the following sedan. Together, they pulled onto the exit. At the McDonald's, the sedan pulled into a space near the back of the lot, using overgrown weeds in one of the dividers as concealment. The van circled the building once and pulled next to it on the far side to gain further cover.

As soon as the van came to a stop, the tech who was driving the sedan got into its front passenger seat and closed the door, making sure it was locked.

"Ignition on?" he asked as he pulled a small white box from his tool kit. The driver nodded. "Doors?" he asked as he wiggled under the passenger dash. Another nod. The indicator on the driver's dash showed they were all closed.

Rolling onto his back, the tech reached up and pulled a small black cube down from behind the dash. It connected to the vehicle by several colored wires.

This was a commercial GPS tracker, a common variety used by fleet operators to keep track of their vehicles. The prison system had glued the cube to its cable socket so it couldn't be removed from the van, but, otherwise, the installation was standard.

These units locate their position using a GPS signal and transmit it to a central monitoring facility. Included with each transmission is a status word showing the ignition state, door closure condition, and power loss alert.

This last presented the greatest problem. If the unit ever lost voltage, it would use this bit to alert the watchers when the power came back on. Since that would trigger an immediate search, they dare not cut power to the transmitter.

The small white box he brought with him had a cable and connector attached. Carefully spreading apart the wires from the GPS tracker, the tech slipped one into each of four notches in the connector. Closing a cover over the top of these wires, he slipped the assembly into the jaws of a crimping tool.

"Watch the lights, OK?" he asked the driver. The latter picked up the GPS cube and, looking at its LED indicator lights, nodded that he was ready. After a pause, the tech squeezed the tool handle hard with both hands. This drove the four wires down into the four notches. Four sharpened conductors cut through insulation on four wires. Each made electrical contact without severing the underlying conductor.

"Well?" asked the tech as he pulled the crimping tool off the connector.

"We're good," answered the driver. None of the LED's on the tracker had blinked. None of the GPS wires had broken during the operation.

The tech pushed a button on the white box. Inside, a microprocessor detected the voltages coming from the connector and matched them using an internal battery. Now, if the cable were cut, the microprocessor would simulate the vehicle door, ignition, and power signals to the tracker. Four green LEDs on the box face showed the task had been completed.

"We still OK?"

The driver nodded again. No blown fuses, the tracker LED's didn't flicker. The microprocessor must have gotten the voltages right.

Pulling a pair of small dikes from his tool kit, the tech cut all the wires connecting the tracker assembly to the vehicle. The white box, crimped connector, and GPS transmitter came free in his hand. He looked at the driver.

"Still good," came the reply. The tracker LED's had not flickered. As far as the civs were concerned, it was still wired to the prison van, one with closed doors and a running engine.

"Phones?" the tech asked as he taped the wires and crimp connector together to keep them from shaking loose. The driver handed him the two taken from the matron and Weidemeyer. Dropping them and the now-free GPS assembly into a gray canvass sack, the tech grabbed his tool kit and bailed out of the van. Seconds later, both vehicles pulled out of the parking lot and onto the feeder. Shortly after that, they were again traveling together north on I95.

The interruption took less than ten minutes. As far as the prison monitors were concerned, the van had stopped for burgers and a potty break, nothing more. A Google map check would show that the stop occurred at a McDonald's, thus confirming their assumption.

Forty five minutes later, the sedan and prison van parted company when the latter exited the expressway. The sedan, with GPS tracker and cell phones, continued towards Danbury along the route originally assigned for the trip.

At least, it did as far as Union City, NJ where there were two large truck stops.

At one of those stops, another conspirator watched the parked trucks, selecting one that seemed about ready to go. When the sedan arrived, he slipped the canvas sack and its contents under that truck's tarp. Of course, an alarm would go off as soon as the truck moved in the wrong direction, maybe even sooner if it sat there long enough. With luck, the civs would assume the prisoners had hijacked the van and chase it rather than contacting the airports.

Meanwhile, the prison van, now without tracker or cell phones, pulled up to an empty house somewhere outside of Trenton. There it, and its four passengers, would stay hidden until two of them heard their customer was safe.

* * *

After he finished locking the twins in the next room, Hood took advantage of the privacy in the empty hall to make two phone calls.

Several days ago, in anticipation of his efforts to slip Carter around Passport Control, he made arrangements for all the airport security videos to be digitally altered to obscure his identity. The first call he made arranged for images of Fawn to also be altered.

The second was to an agent he could trust. The man agreed to pick them both up out front, take them away from the airport, and, after dropping Hood off, hold Fawn in a quiet place until an APB was issued for her capture. At that point, he would turn her in, claiming that he found her walking along the side of the road. Hood's presence at BWI would be a matter of her word against his, backed with the altered security recordings.

Now all that remained was to get her to go quietly with him into the car. If she decided to make a scene, someone would recognize him, so he had to prevent that. Well, he had four hours to work on it since his ride couldn't get there any sooner. Maybe he could make some sort of trade to convince her that the ride was her release.

Fortunately, the lay-over room was safe, especially since he had turned off all the cameras and mics. Margie would cover the room use records, at least as far as his name was concerned.

When he returned to her room, he found it dim, lit only by light from under the closed bathroom door. She sat on the only bed, her back against the headboard, with her skirt and jacket off and her knees pulled to her chest. Her panties showed between her ankles. The presentation was more forward than she would have liked at this stage, but time was critically short.

She need not have worried. Like many unattractive men, he had a weakness for beautiful women. And, like most in high places, his arrogance had long ago convinced him that he could get away with almost any act as long as he took care to cover his tracks.

They began their discussion with him sitting in a chair across the room, but that separation quickly evaporated. Now he lay naked on his back while she, wearing only her wig, straddled his hips and worked to save her girls.

Of course, he had promised to release her if she pleased him. Her plan required it and she agreed quickly. But she was no fool. The important thing was not that she believed him, which she didn't, but that he thought she did. He had to feel comfortable and in control. She needed the confidence that feeling would bring.

He was getting close. Leaning over, she kissed his neck, his ear, whispering vulgar endearments to speed him along. And it worked. He was very close.

He hadn't rechecked the bathroom when he came back, too distracted by her offer from the bed. If he had, he might have seen the remains of a broken drinking glass in the trash. Now, as he arched his back, distracted by his own wave of pleasure, it was too late. The glass shard she held in her hand slipped through his skin just under his left ear. Before he realized the puncture had occurred, the shard slashed across his neck, below the line of his jaw, towards his Adam's apple. He tried to scream, but she smothered his lips with her own, digging in her teeth to keep her mouth against his. And she slashed, clutching his head tightly against hers with the crook of her left elbow to increase her leverage.

While he was in the other room, she had checked her own neck, found her own carotid artery. So she knew exactly where to strike. And she did. Again and again. His artery, jugular, and windpipe. Hard and deep. She slashed at them all. He struggled, trying to push her away, as blood first spattered then spurted across her breasts and down her side. Hard and fast, again and again, she pulled the sliver of glass through soft flesh.

Finally, he pushed her loose. She rolled off him to her left, anticipating correctly that he would try to escape through the opening she gave him. When he rolled towards the edge of the bed, she grabbed him again, this time from behind. Left arm over his chin, legs over his hips, she slashed the right side of his neck.

Perhaps she found one of her new targets, perhaps the first attack was enough. It didn't matter. Enough damage had already been done. He slid off the bed onto the floor with her hanging onto him, falling over him, red splashing like modern art over the bedding, the walls, and the carpet. The human body holds a lot of blood.

After he stopped moving, rage still gripped her, overwhelming anger at him because he made her do this. He made her cut him. It was so wrong, but it was his fault. Rolling off his body, she grabbed the bedside lamp and slammed it down against his skull, again and again, like a lumberjack chopping wood. Damn him. Damn him for what he made her do.

She swung until her arms could no longer lift the lamp. Only then did her anger fade. Finally, she came out of her killing frenzy. The act done, she stood in silence, suppressing her surging breath, and listened. She heard no sound, no alarm. If there were camera watchers, they had seen nothing.

Quickly, her wig on the floor and her naked body covered with slowly-clotting bits of blood and brain, she pulled her cell from under the mattress. Two missed calls.

Hitting the callback, she grabbed her wig and moved into the bathroom as she listened. Someone answered as she threw the filthy tresses into the sink.

"Hello," came the noncommittal answer.

"Has the plane left yet?" she demanded as she turned on the cold water.

"Who is this?"

Damn, you don't know? You gave me the phone.

"Fawn. Has the plane left?"

"Have we met before?"

SHIT! It sounded like Angelo on the other end, so she took a chance.

"Yes. Has the plane left?"

"What was the name of the bar where we first met?"

"What??"

"What was the name of the bar where we first met?"

"Bar, hell. We met in a riot. Now, dammit, has the plane left yet?"

"No. But it's a mess. How soon can you check in?"

"Ten minutes, maybe fifteen. Will that do?"

"Hurry." And the line went dead.

And she did hurry. Pulling the wet but clean wig from the sink and wrapping it in two towels, she wrung it between them to get it as dry as possible, then spread it out to air. Jumping in the shower, she attacked the clotting blood.

That's when she noticed her hand. She had wrapped the shard in toilet paper to give her a gripping surface, but it must have slipped, because several deep cuts ran along her thumb and palm. They bled profusely, pink streaks mixed with clear shower water even after she was clean everywhere else. She found a Kleenex box and wrapped her hand as tightly as possible, pressing until the flow stopped. But as soon as she took the pressure off, the bleeding started again. In desperation, she rolled up a washcloth and gripped it as hard as she could with her cut hand. That worked. As long as she held tight, the pressure stopped the bleeding. But if she relaxed her grip, blood would be everywhere, and someone would notice. She had to keep her fist clenched until she got on the plane.

She had been careful to place her clothes far from the bed so they weren't spattered. After dressing quickly with one hand, she searched his clothes for keys. She found them, along with a small hammerless revolver.

Not long ago, that gun would have been like a snake, not to be touched at any cost. Now it was magic, a talisman, a steel proof that she still had control over her life. She picked it up, turned it over slowly, then gripped the handle and slid her finger though the trigger guard. Never mind that she wasn't sure how to shoot it, much less if she could hit anything. The comfort it gave her was what mattered. The tighter she held it, the better she felt. Here was a physical manifestation of her decision to never again be a mouse.

Taking the keys in her injured hand with the pistol in the other, she unlocked the door and peeked out into the hall. It was empty.

Stepping out, she crept silently down the row of rooms, pistol at the ready, not even sure it would fire if she pulled the trigger*. Pausing at each door, she called softly for her girls. At the second, she got the answer she desperately needed to hear.

Finding the key that opened that door, she whispered to her girls to please be quiet as she used it. They were good girls, quiet as church mice, but still overwhelmed her with their hugs, not of joy, but of fear when she opened the door.

Pulling her luggage from their room, she dropped the pistol into her purse and locked the door. Stepping back quickly to her old room, she made one last check to be sure she hadn't left anything, then closed the door. After a quick push and a twist of the knob to be sure it was latched, she broke off the key in the lock. That might not be as good as bolting it from the inside, but it should give her a little more time before the cleaning staff found the body.

"OK, honeys, let's go for a plane ride!"

---

* It would. Like most small hammerless revolvers, this one had no manual safety.

Chapter 21

Freedom Flight

"I'd like to check in, please." she said as she handed three passports to the counter agent. "I'm sorry, but I'm rather late," she added, hoping to speed things up.

"That's an understatement," came a quick reply. "They've been looking for you everywhere. Luggage on the scale please." Then, as she reached for Fawn's documents, she noticed the bloody washcloth. "Did you just do that?" she asked in a voice that carried more than the normal concern expected from a good ticket agent.

"Caught it on the edge of the taxi door."

Fawn saw skepticism flash across the woman's face, just for a second, before a veneer of professionalism suppressed it. Turning, she gestured to the other agent who was trying to look busy. When he came over, she asked him something Fawn couldn't quite catch. Then, while she went back to her computer, he slipped behind the wall that separated the back area from the counter.

As Fawn watched her agent work, she grew very cold. Did the woman somehow know the real cause of Fawn's bloody hand? Had the body already been discovered? Had this woman sent the other agent for the police? Or had Fawn imagined the emotions she saw?

"Good. You're all set," the agent said, handing Fawn back her passports just as her co-worker returned. "This was all I could find," he said as he handed an Ace bandage to Fawn's agent. She took it, concern obvious on her face. Then, with a sigh, she turned to Fawn. "Give me your hand," she commanded in a tone that was out of place for her station.

Fawn hesitated.

"Please," the agent asked, with a hint of strain breaking her voice.

Reluctantly, Fawn reached across the counter. Within seconds, she received a quick but competent-looking bandage job, one that encased her entire hand, along with the bloody wash cloth, in a cocoon of snug, buff-colored cloth. Unstained cloth. With pressure from the bandage, she could even relax her grip on the towel.

"That should get you on the plane. We can't have you bleeding all over the airport, now can we?" she asked. Then, her professional demeanor once again in place, she pointed towards the waiting customs entrance and urged Fawn along by saying "Please go straight to security. The aircraft is waiting on you."

Shortly after she got back into the public area, Fawn had realized Hood's gun was more of a liability than an asset. It and his keys had gone into the first trash can she passed. She and her girls easily passed the security scan.

Minutes later, hair still damp and freckles standing out like pebbles on a sandy beach, she stood in front of a muscular but smiling customs agent. He took her passport and those of her girls, confirmed the pictures, then scanned them into the system.

Fawn knew enough about fake ID's to know that this was the critical step. She had no doubt that the quality of the passports and visa stamps would pass any inspection, but she wasn't so sure about the database his scanner was connected to. BUNKIE'S wouldn't have brought her this far if they didn't think it would support her story. Still, mistakes happen, and so she worried.

She need not have, for several reasons. First, BUNKIE'S had an agent planted in the Visa Section of the State Department. That agent had created a false visa approval record, complete with bogus entry dates. The check showed a good record.

But, since the badlands is a belt-and-suspenders kind of place, and since BUNKIE'S hadn't gotten their reputation by taking chances, they also planted trojans in the State Department's visa computer system. These little programs corrupted critical data on a few visa records when they were first created, before any backup was done. This way, when the backup was made, it also contained the same mistake, making it impossible to find using error checks.

The result was that a significant number of searches returned a false fail. Either the visa could not be found (because the passport number or last name had been altered in the database) or the entry dates would have been changed or the country of origin would be different or any one of a number of other mismatches would occur.

At first, DHS had been diligent about this issue, holding innocent passengers well beyond the departure of their flights, sometimes even for days, while the matter was resolved, always in the passengers favor.

So, now, no one at DHS became all that concerned if a visa record didn't match or was missing. As long as everything else looked good, as long as the documents seemed genuine under close scrutiny, they would blame it on State. The passenger would not be delayed.

If that weren't enough, several Passport Control supervisors at this airport had, because of arrangements made through the Thieves Emporium, a personal interest in seeing that the occasional special passenger was not delayed. If there were a mismatch in records, when one of those supervisors was on duty, the passenger in question would get the benefit of the doubt and be waived through to the departure lounge.

Finally, Fawn's documents said she was a wealthy citizen of South Africa traveling on a private aircraft of Venezuelan registry on a good-will mission to Cuba. No supervisor in his right mind, no matter how strict, would delay her any further than necessary. Too many foreign governments would get angry, something that would not help one's career.

So, within minutes of handing her documents to Passport Control, she was boarding her aircraft. No one even seemed to notice her bandaged hand.

Entering the cabin, she saw only one row of passenger seats on each side of the aisle*. Those seats, six in total, faced each other in pairs across small tables. One pair was on her right on the port side of the aircraft, while the other two were across the aisle on the starboard side.

Behind her was the cockpit, occupied by the pilot and co-pilot. The door to it was latched open. This wasn't a commercial passenger flight, so there was no flight attendant on board. The door would be open the entire fight so the co-pilot could act as cabin staff.

In front of her in the first forward-facing seat on her left sat one passenger, a tall handsome-looking woman. The other five seats were empty. So, not wanting to separate her girls, she took the forward-facing seat across the aisle from the woman and gave her girls the two rear ones.

And there she waited. The aircraft didn't move, the engines didn't even start.

She could see into the cockpit. Both pilots seemed relaxed, ready, but not doing anything to get the aircraft into the air. Visions of sirens filled her mind. Would they come with whoops and lights to block the aircraft from leaving the gate? Or would there be a knock on the aircraft door, followed by a civil request for her to come quietly.

---

* See the appendix for a layout of the aircraft.

She could stand it no more. On the pretext of asking for pain killer for her hand, she got up and stuck her head into the cockpit.

"When do we get out of here?"

"Soon as they fit us in," replied the captain with a noticeable Spanish accent.

"I don't understand. Aren't we ready?"

"Si, senora. We have been ready for hours. But we missed our departure slot with Air Traffic Control, so they gave it away. We have to wait our turn for another one." He was too tactful to mention that they lost their place in line because of her tardiness.

"How long will that be?"

"Who knows? Maybe days. No, just kidding, senora. We should get it any second. Here's some Advil, water's in the galley. Just go back and sit down and we'll tell you when we are ready to go."

So, that's what she did, but not in her old seat. If these were the last minutes she would have with her girls, she wanted to really be with them.

There was a settee running lengthwise down the port side of the aircraft across the aisle from where the girls sat. She sat on it now and gestured for them to join her. They didn't need to be asked twice, moving fast as mice, without a noise.

"OK, honeys, the shyness game is over."

"Did we do well?" came the question, repeated in various ways from two little mouths again and again.

"Very. Mona Lisa couldn't have done it better."

"Where are we going?"

"Cuba. You've never been on an airplane flight before, have you?

Two heads shook with enthusiasm.

"You'll like this."

She was about to prepare her little charges for the thrill of takeoff when one of them asked "Momma, why is that woman staring at us?"

Looking up, Fawn saw that the only other adult passenger had changed seats, having moved into the most forward seat which faced backwards. And she was looking at Fawn and her girls with unusual concentration.

Then it hit her. She had seen that woman's picture before. Often. Sitting on the other side of the cabin, staring back at her, the woman who would be with her on this aircraft for the rest of the flight, was Cassandra Carter, the FEMA official who had ordered the murder of her husband.

* * *

"Hawthorne," the Transportation Superintendent for the Federal Bureau of Prisons answered as he picked up the phone.

"Wells, duty, sir. We have a stopped van."

"Where?"

"Grover Cleveland Service Area. Woodbridge, New Jersey."

"How long?"

"Thirty five minutes."

"They didn't check in before they stopped?"

"No sir."

"Did you call them?"

"Yes, both of them, but no answer.

"Who are the prisoners?"

"One woman, sir, a counterfeiter, and her two children."

"Are they still on route?"

"Yes sir. I was told they might take a little longer because they're trying to sweat the prisoner."

"Well, then we need to cut them a little slack. If they don't move in the next half hour, though, have a state trooper stop by, OK?"

"Yes sir."

And, with that, Hawthorne hung up the phone.

* * *

"Get down, honey, I have to talk to the captain," she said to the girl in her lap. The other woman must have been listening, because she stood up and moved to block the aisle as Fawn rose.

"Get out of my way," Fawn demanded when she reached the entrance to the galley.

"Why?"

"Because I know who you are, Cassandra Carter."

The tall woman smiled back, a self-satisfied smirk that Fawn would shortly wipe off her face.

"Are you going to ask the captain to call the police, Dancing Fawn?"

That stopped Fawn.

"Yes, I know who you are, too," continued Carter. "How badly do you want to keep your daughters? That's your choice. All or nothing. Turn me in, you turn us both in."

Fawn looked past Carter into the cockpit. Both crew were killing time in casual conversation. Neither looked back towards the passengers.

"Make up your mind. After we leave US airspace, this Venezuelan crew won't turn back. You'll have to make your case to the Cuban authorities and they'll have better things to do than listen. So, it's now or never. Go ahead. Tell the captain."

Fawn's mind seethed, incensed that she should be trapped here with this filth, incredulous that she found herself hesitating, yet terrified of losing God's two most precious gifts.

"We still have a bit of time for you to decide. Why don't you go back to your seat and relax while you think about it?" And, with that, Carter backed into her seat and sat down. Looking at Fawn in silence, she waited to see what her decision would be.

And, in truth, Fawn knew there was no choice. She should honor her husband by putting his killer behind bars, but he would want her to protect his girls more. She had lied, sold her body, and killed to keep them next to her. But this, she thought as she moved back towards the settee, would always be the most difficult, the most obscene act she would ever commit.

* * *

"Hawthorne," the FBP Transportation Superintendent answered as he picked up the phone.

"Wells, sir. The van still hasn't moved. Should I call the patrol?"

No one wanted to raise a red flag, to cause a ruckus if there was no reason to do so. That's why Hawthorne had been so reluctant to act when the van first stopped. That was also why Wells didn't make the call after the allotted time cushion expired.

"How long has it been sitting there?" asked Hawthorne.

"Almost an hour, sir."

That was too much, even for a trouble-averse bureaucrat.

"Send someone out."

* * *

"Hey, muchachas, good news," yelled the captain. "We just got clearance. Be in the air in half an hour. Please be sure your seat belts are fastened, OK? Gracias."

Even as he said it, the first aircraft engine spooled up. Within minutes, like a ruptured duck waddling to the sea, the jet started rolling slowly towards the taxiway. Twenty minutes later, as promised, the captain shoved the throttles against the firewall. The ungainly aircraft rolled, faster and faster, until it became a graceful bird, screaming upwards towards the sky.

The climb-out was uneventful. As the aircraft leveled off, the captain yelled back "Hey, good news, mis amigas. We are not going to die on take-off. So, if you want to celebrate, this would be a good time to visit the galley. It's help-yourself."

Had Fawn not been so relieved at being out of the clutches of the local police, she might have done just that. Unfortunately, her relief was unjustified. The aircraft she rode in was still within Unites States airspace and, more to the point, within radar and VHF radio range. If DHS wanted her back, all they had to do was pick up a microphone and ask.*

* * *

* See the appendix for a map of the flight route.

One thing the Thieves Emporium does well is distribute unauthorized copies of passwords. Imagine, for a moment, that everyone in your office was given the same pass-code to get into the building. Suppose that you also needed money. What would be the downside risk if you sold a copy of that pass-code? Nothing, as long as you could be assured that the transaction was anonymous. After all, if your bosses ever found out that someone had sold a copy, what could they do? Every occupant of the building had the same code, so they would have no way of tracking down the culprit.

The same is true of the Internet. Many devices that are critical to the operation of that system are not sophisticated enough to have password tables, so each uses a single password for access control. Since any technician might have to maintain any of these devices, they must all have copies of every password. And the full set was for sale in the Thieves Emporium.

Routers are simple but critical pieces of Internet equipment. They direct traffic. When you send a web page request, a network of them passes it along from one to the next until it finally reaches the correct destination, like railway workers controlling track switches in a freight yard, directing cars to the right tracks as they move through the yard.

Messages going to the DHS offices in BWI go through one of three routers. Each has been programmed to forward DHS messages to their network, which is, other than via these three routers, cut off from the rest of the world.

The routers that connect the BWI airport networks to the rest of the world are examples of this simple device. Each has a single password. Anyone responsible for maintaining them must have the password for every one he/she has to work on. And, as was to be expected, someone in that august group of service technicians sold a copy of those passwords in the Thieves Emporium.

As Fawn's aircraft reached the takeoff end of the runway, each of these servers received a message, along with the correct password, to change how DHS emails were to be handled. Until told to do otherwise, each server was to ignore messages directed to the DHS network. All other types of messages would go through, just not emails. For the next four hours, until another message reset the router configurations, emails for Passport Control at BWI airport would pile up in transmitting servers, not erased because the BWI mail server had not acknowledged their receipt, but trapped, waiting in limbo for the router blockage to the DHS network to clear.

Needless to say, no one notified BWI Passport Control that their incoming emails were not getting through.

* * *

"Hawthorne," the FBP Transportation Superintendent answered as he picked up the phone.

"They're moving, sir."

"Who's moving?"

"Transfer van from DC with the woman prisoner. Sir."

"Good."

"No, sir, not good. They started north again on I95, so I canceled the trooper call. But when they got to I80, they turned west. That isn't the scheduled route."

"You're saying they're going away from Danbury?"

"Yes sir"

"Then we have a hijacking. Have you told the state patrol?"

"Yes sir, I called them as soon as the van left I95. They've got three cars on it."

"Good, we should have it cornered in a few minutes. Did you put out an APB?

"No sir. We know where they are."

Maybe, thought Hawthorne. *But, then again, maybe not.*

"APB all east coast border crossings. Just in case."

"Yes sir."

And within minutes, alert notices, including pictures of the prisoner and her daughters, were emailed to every Passport Control office on the east coast, including those at BWI.

* * *

"Transponder's gone," said the co-pilot in Spanish.

The captain looked over at the interrogation light on the face of the instrument and watched it for several seconds. It stayed dark. Normally, it flashed red about once a second, each time the aircraft was stuck with a radar pulse. The fact that it remained dark meant they had flown far enough out to sea to be below the shore-based ATC radar. From now on, until they got within range of Bermuda ATC radar, the only way anyone would know where they were was by their own manually-transmitted position reports. They were too far out in the Atlantic to be detected by any land-based radar. The curve of the earth had put them below the horizon for both Bermuda and the U.S. east coast, a condition that would persist for the next 300 miles. This event had occurred at a little over 200 miles from the U. S. east coast, about right for their altitude of 30,000 feet.

Their official destination was Bermuda because, according to their dispatch service, they could not get clearance from Cuban ATC to fly to Havana. Not willing to lose their take-off slot again because of another delayed departure, and needing a clearance to somewhere before they could take off, their dispatch service had gotten them approval to fly to Bermuda. So they were officially in route to that island, even though they hoped to change course shortly, as soon as they got permission to land at Havana.

This sort of dogleg flight path would use more fuel, but delays were common when flying to Cuba from the United States, so their aircraft had departed with almost-full tanks. If necessary, they actually had enough on board to fly non-stop all the way to Caracas in Venezuela. In fact, they could fly nonstop to any of the Atlantic islands or much of South America, though not to Europe or Africa.

After giving up on the transponder light, the captain touched the transmit switch on his yoke and said "New York Center, YV328CP". New York Center was the air traffic authority currently responsible for directing this aircraft through the sky. This cryptic message was just a request for them to answer the radio.

Several seconds passed in silence.

Again, "New York Center, YV328CP"

Again, silence.

"Out of VHF range, too."

Aircraft voice communications use many frequencies, but all of them fall into one of two ranges, either VHF or HF. The signals behave quite differently in the two bands.

Higher-frequency VHF signals, like those emitted by ATC radars, are line-of-sight, meaning they can't follow the curve of the earth. Like ATC radar pulses, when an aircraft drops below the horizon, it can no longer receive VHF transmissions because the horizon is now in the way. In spite of this problem, they are the main method of short-range aircraft radio communications because their higher frequency makes them easier to understand.

HF radio, on the other hand, is often distorted, sometimes unintelligible. However, their lower frequency has one big advantage, which is the only reason HF radios are ever used: Their signals reflect down from ionized layers high in the earth's atmosphere. Often, they also bounce back up from the ocean's surface. So, if conditions are right, they ricochet around the world like a rifle shot down a curving mine shaft.

Reaching over, the captain changed his radio frequency to the HF band. With luck, signal bounce would keep him in touch with ATC.

But that didn't work out. They could hear a reply when they transmitted, but it was garbled, impossible to understand. Perhaps a solar flare disturbed the ionosphere, or giant thunderheads somewhere made its surface ripple. Maybe their radio needed servicing, though it had worked when they tested it just before take off. Whatever the reason, the captain logged that HF communications was not possible, a situation that was common on long over-water flights.

Fortunately, this second radio failure didn't completely cut them off from the rest of the world. They also had a satellite up-link on board, one that functioned reliably regardless of how far out to sea they flew. However, no ATC organization had the equipment to use this link. It was monitored only by their private dispatch service in Caracas who had to relay communications by telephone to NYC ATC. With the HF down, that was the only way they could receive permission to enter Cuban airspace.

Theirs was an older system, limited to text only, but it functioned reliably enough. To confirm this, the captain sent a message informing his dispatch service of the aircraft's location, stating that they were no longer in radio contact with ATC, and formally asking them to act as a relay. Their service received this request and, as was standard procedure, agreed to perform the duty.

Five minutes later, YV328CP received a new clearance via their dispatch service and the satellite link telling him to depart their current course and fly direct to Caracas. Apparently the people who were paying for this charter had given up on the Cuban clearance.

Making a wide sweeping turn so as to not disturb his passengers, the captain brought his aircraft to its new course, one that would take it across the eastern tip of the Dominican Republic before continuing on to Caracas.

* * *

"Hawthorne."

"Wells, again, sir. She's in the air. On a charter. We had to fax her picture to BWI Passport Control because there was something wrong with their email, but, when they finally got it, one of the agents recognized her. She was wearing a blond wig, but the visa photo of the woman who left the country on the charter matches the picture of our escapee. She also had two girls with her."

"Good, good. Where's the flight now?"

"ATC says they're over the Atlantic about 600 miles east of Georgia. They couldn't get clearance for Cuba, so they started for Bermuda, then changed it to go directly back to Caracas.

"Good. Alert the Bermuda police in case they are still headed there and have ATC order them to land in San Juan."

"We can try that, sir, but it would probably just warn them. After all, the aircraft is flying under a Venezuelan flag in international waters on a Cuban goodwill mission. They would probably just refuse, as would the Venezuelan government if we tried to go through them."

"Then have the Caracas authorities meet them when they land."

"That might be difficult, sir, given the relationship we have with their national government. May I suggest an alternative?"

"Go."

"Their present flight plan takes them over the Dominican Republic. Our relations with that government are quite good. Why not just have their traffic control order them to land in Santo Domingo when they're in local airspace?

"What if they refuse?"

"We declare a hijacking. Then the DR government is required by treaty to allow us to intercept. Should I put an aircraft on standby?"

"Good idea. Do it."

"Thank you, sir. I will."

* * *

"We just got a new clearance," said the copilot of YV328CP when they were dead east of Key West, Florida.

"When will these people make up their mind?" asked the captain, confirming the message that had just come over the satellite link from their dispatch service.

Then, with a deft hand, he brought his aircraft to its new course. Should his actions ever be questioned, the memory in his satellite communications system would confirm that he was following ATC instructions relayed to him via his dispatch service.

* * *

"Hawthorne."

"Wells, again, sir. We got them."

"Go on."

"We got them. ATC says they lost cabin pressure, had to drop to 8,000 feet and head for San Juan. They can't go anywhere else now.

"Why not Caracas or Santo Domingo?"

"Not Caracas. Jets suck too much fuel at low altitude, they don't have the range. They could head for the Dominican Republic, though."

"Better set up for an arrest at either airport. Can the FBI get there in time?"

"Yes sir. The charter had to slow down because of the lower altitude. It'll take them over two hours either way. The FBI will have had plenty of time."

"Good. The woman on board killed Matthew Hood."

"The guy that runs DHS?"

"The same. And she took his gun. Warn our people."

"What do you want me to say?"

"Same as what the FBI guys have been told."

"Which is?"

"She's armed. No heroics. Kill shots are authorized."

* * *

"I'm sorry for your loss," said Cassandra Carter.

The remark took Fawn without warning. Turning in anger, she glared at the other woman's face, but could not bring herself to answer.

Again, Carter spoke. "I truly am."

Facing aft with her back against the galley bulkhead, Fawn sat across the aisle from Carter who faced forward in the next row of seats.

"Go to hell," she spat back.

The aircraft flew on in a silence covered by the muted whine of engines. In the cockpit, both pilots wore headsets, doing whatever amused aircrews during long open-water flights. Behind her, one of her girls lay on the settee and the other curled up in the aft-most seat. Both seemed asleep.

"You seem to think I had a choice in the matter. I didn't."

Fawn just stared back at her.

"Do you know why your husband was in that camp?"

"How could I?" Fawn answered. "You wouldn't let him call me."

"If he told what he knew to the press, Prometheus would have been shut down."

"Shall I tell my daughters that's why they'll grow up without a father?"

"That reactor was this country's last hope. If he had shut it down, your daughters would freeze to death in the dark or die in some radioactive waste hell. We had to prove the plant would work."

"It's running now. Be happy."

"Twenty three more are going up. If your husband shut down the first one, they'd all have been canceled."

She made no reply. None would matter. Her girls would grow up without a father regardless of anything she could say.

"His death was an unavoidable necessity."

Fawn just looked back, too weary to answer.

"There are seven billion people on this planet. Without a replacement for oil, most of them will die. Prometheus is our only chance."

"Did God tell you that?"

"Someone has to take charge."

"Why?"

"If we didn't make the decisions, nothing would get done."

"Meaning my husband would still be alive?"

"Humanity no longer has any choice. We've crawled out too far on the overpopulation limb to just let things go. It's up to us, the best and the brightest, to take control and bring things back to a safe state. That's what we're doing."

No, Fawn thought, *what you are doing is destroying humanity one person at a time to build your ego, your wealth, and your power. You just won't admit it, not even to yourself, because you believe God has made you better than the rest of us. We have to make some other choice, something besides starving to death in our own filth or living as your slaves.*

She turned back the window, feeling like such a fool, not because she was wrong, but because she had tried to reason with a civ. Better to spend her time teaching a snake to dance.

Fifty minutes later, at 31,000 feet because no cabin pressure problem had occurred, the copilot said "We've got transponder contact."

The captain looked over and saw the interrogation light flash regularly. They were back in range of an ATC radar. He changed the VHF radio to the contact frequency for their new ATC center and hit the transmit button.

"Havana Center, YV328CP"

YV328CP's flight path had brought them out of the Atlantic to cross the Bahamas over Mayaguana Island, too far south to be picked up by the ATC radar in Nassau, the only one in the Bahamas. They were close enough to Provo, the capital of the Turks and Caicos, to be in range, but that airport didn't have radar. So, now, after flying most of the way across the Bahamas, they were making their first ATC contact.

He got no answer on the first or second contact attempt, but on the third he got a go-ahead.

"We have radar contact and wish to complete our flight plan." the captain said in Spanish.

There was an acknowledgment and a long pause.

"What did you say your call sign was?" asked the controller, also in Spanish.

"YV328CP"

"I don't have a flight plan for you, amigo."

Mierda, the captain thought. He hadn't had to break cover so far, which was the way he liked it. But this could become a bureaucratic goat-grope if he didn't straighten it out quickly. Oh well, that's what BUNKIE'S paid him for.

"Sorry, Havana, our dispatcher told us that everything was in order," he said in Spanish using his best 'We're all buddies here' tone. "May we land and discuss it then?"

"What is the purpose of your flight, senior?"

"We are delivering a donation of vaccines," answered the captain, again in Spanish. English may be the official language of international pilot communications, but he knew this was not the time to use it.

There was a pause while the controller considered the matter, taking into account the cargo and the fact that the aircraft was Venezuelan, not Yankee.

"I can file for you to divert to Provo or Nassau," the controller offered, obviously trying to avoid bending any rules.

"Gracias, but both are gringo. They have already delayed this shipment for months just to make a point." There hadn't been any delay, but the captain was betting that the controller wouldn't know that.

After a moment of silence, the captain added "Please, senor, the Cuban people need these vaccines."

Finally, the controller came back and asked "Where do you want to go?"

"Santiago is closest, that would be fine with us," answered the captain, interpreting the ambiguity in the question as approval to enter Cuban airspace.

There was a pause before the reply came back. Finally, the controller answered. "Bueno, YV328CP. You are cleared direct to Santiago. Descend to 5,000 meters when you cross the coast and contact Santiago tower at that time."

With considerable relief, the captain read back the clearance. He had earned BUNKIE'S pay this flight, as had the ticket agent who bandaged Fawn's bloody hand to get her through customs.

* * *

"Hawthorne," he said into the phone.

"She's in Cuba."

"Who is this?"

"Wells, sir. Sorry."

"Go on."

"The charter landed in Santiago de Cuba over an hour ago."

"What? I thought it was going to fly through Dominican Republic airspace."

"That's what ATC told us, yes, sir. But now they say they have updated information that the aircraft has already landed."

"Shit. Is the FBI there?"

"In Cuba?"

"Can the Cubans arrest her?"

"FBI says they'll have to go through State. It'll take days."

While they spoke, Cassandra Carter, Dancing Fawn, and two charming little twin girls passed through Cuban immigration.

Freedom is not a moral thing. It is not right or wrong, good or bad. It is a status, like health or wealth. Used for the wrong purpose, it is bad, but for the right, it is good. How it is used is up to the recipient of the condition, not an inherent characteristic of it.

More to the point, it is not something you can pick and choose from like some political buffet. Give government the tools to take someone else's freedom and you give it the power to take yours in the future. Maybe not today, but soon. And when that day comes, it will be your turn to feel the chains. In most cases, it is far better to tolerate behavior you do not like than to risk losing your freedom by giving another the power to prevent it.

Good or bad, right or wrong, just or unjust, Cassandra Carter and Dancing Fawn would benefit from that status. They were now both free.

Fawn and her girls got into an airport taxi by the curb outside the Santiago, Cuba international airport. After a brief pause to negotiate the fare, the cab pulled out and faded into the crowded street. Shortly after that, Dancing Fawn and her girls disappeared into the badlands for the last time.

* * *

Two burly baggage handlers waiting overtime at the Santo Domingo airport in the Dominican Republic were told they could go home. The private aircraft they had been waiting for had landed somewhere else as planned. They were prepared to smuggle four people past willing customs officials by hiding them in duffel bags. Now that would not be necessary.

BUNKIE'S was, after all, a belt-and-suspenders kind of organization.

* * *

The phone rang. Through the darkness of the hood, the matron heard Mrs. Frumpy Dress speak.

"Hello, Sturm residence."

A pause.

"No. You have the wrong number. This is the Sturm residence. There is no one here named Clyde. Yes, I am quite sure. Thank you. Goodbye."

With a click, she closed the phone and said "Customer's safe. We're good to go."

The matron sat on the bathroom floor in the back of a vacant house, still chained hand and foot. A large rope tied her shackles to something solid, though she couldn't tell what because of her hood.

"Good news," Mrs. Frumpy said. "We're done here, so we're leaving. After we're gone, you'll be free to go. For your own safety, though, please wait five minutes before you start on your knots. I'll leave the handcuff keys on the kitchen counter."

Then the matron felt Mrs. Frumpy Dress lean close, close enough to smell her perfume.

"Listen, sweetie," whispered the woman. "We're really sorry about all this. It turned out worse than we wanted, I hope you'll forgive us. To show you we mean that, I'm going to slip this little card in your pocket."

A hand reach inside her prison overalls. She felt motion across her shirt.

"It's for a discount. If you ever need to get out of a tight spot, let us know. As far as we're concerned, you've been a good sport and we owe you. Just give us the number on the card and we'll give you a good deal. I promise."

"Ah, and, one more thing. I'd keep this card thing quiet, if I were you. All bosses are rats, at least everyone I ever had was. If yours know you have this, they'll take it away. That's not why we're giving it to you, so, please, just keep mum about it, OK?"

And, without waiting for a reply, she moved away. Which was just as well, since the matron was too scared to answer. Especially since, in spite of earlier promises, the Taser wire was still taped to the back of her neck.

"Thanks for your patience, folks," the older woman announced from near the door. Then it opened.

"Your five minutes starts now. Good luck."

The door closed. The sound of walking feet faded into the distance. Then there was silence.

Ten minutes later, as they worked on the knots, the matron smelled smoke. Not wood smoke, but burning plastic or rubber. She mentioned it to

Weidemeyer, and he agreed.

Three minutes later, as Weidemeyer got his knot free, they heard fire engines. He pulled off their hoods, then hopped into the kitchen and got the keys. Two minutes later, free of both shackles and her prison uniform, they left the house to look for the fire.

It wasn't hard to find. Across the street, half a block down from where they stood, the remains of their prison van still smoldered, so charred that even the tires were gone. No fingerprints or DNA would ever be recovered from that vehicle. Their captors had all worn gloves and long sleeves, but mistakes still happen. BUNKIE'S was a belt-and-suspenders kind of organization.

As they watched the firemen roll up their hoses, the matron pulled the card from her shirt pocket. It was a double business card, folded down the middle to make it small enough to fit in a wallet. One side and half of the other was covered with what looked like printed instructions. On the remaining white space, written carefully so it could be easily read, was a coupon code and the words:

177.12.212.7:1723

Beau Jangles

Quietly, after checking to be sure no one was watching, she slipped the card down the front of her panties.

Chapter 22

A New World

"So, what the fucking hell happened?" asked Daniel Shelton, Special Agent for the FBI and currently acting chairman of the BS committee.

"I heard a tap on the car window," answered Joshua Weidemeyer who was still, even after the inquiry, a Special Agent for the Secret Service. "When I looked up, I saw a mask and a gun muzzle. One thing led to another, and I wound up sitting in the back of the van cuffed to the prisoner bar."

"You came off better than Hood," said Shelton.

Time passed in quiet contemplation of the female form as seen, at least in Shelton's case, through the pleasant haze of a few drinks. Then Weidemeyer asked "Are you sure she killed him?"

"Fucking hell. Can a guy ever be sure about anything? But, yeah, her prints and DNA were all over the place. If she didn't do the job, she was fucking-well holding the shard and lamp that did it."

"God, I can't believe she slipped away. What did the FAA have to say about the screw-up?"

"No direct contact with the aircraft, so they had to believe the dispatcher."

"You're going after him?"

Shelton shook his head.

"The pilot?"

Shelton shook his head again.

"Why not?"

"They're both telling the truth."

"How?"

"Their satellite system was infected with a trojan. It changed the messages."

"You sure?"

"It runs on Windows. NSA went through a back door.

"Broke in?"

"We don't call it that," said Shelton before he took another sip of Scotch. "Anyway, we know what was sent."

"Who planted the trojan?"

"We'll never know. It erased itself when the flight landed."

"You sure it was really there?"

"Logs," Shelton said with a nod. "It was there."

The two lapsed back into contemplative silence. A waitress with a really nice set showed up and they ordered another round.

"You know," Weidemeyer said after his third orange juice arrived, "This place of yours is starting to grow on me."

* * *

Arnold Wilson Parker sat alone in his relocated study, buried in the basement three floors below his old one. The ambiance here failed by any comparison, but the open, airy spaces that he loved were no longer safe. Perhaps, sometime in the near future, Pug would guarantee that no sniper or drone could crawl close enough for a shot. But not yet. For now, Parker would have to live like a mole, hidden away for his own protection, cut off from the glories of Colorado daylight.

The greatest irony was that none of it had to happen. If he had just known about the badlands, understood their potential, he wouldn't have had to set up the Heart Mountain operation. Like so much else the government did, he could have contracted out the work. Even now, several members of the STALINGRAD Crossing were stalking and eliminating the problems that had been released because of Bombay's meddling. Rather than risk so much again, in the future he would just ask them to handle that kind of work from the start.

And the worst part was that Bombay had apparently gotten away. The bitch just dropped out of sight after she had caused him as much trouble as she could. Unless he was lucky enough to have her surface again somewhere, he would just have to give up on her. Eat his losses, do without the revenge he so longed for.

Fortunately, his financial resources were still intact. Van de Groot had done considerable damage to him politically, but that could be mended. He still owned the Fed. And he had gotten Pug promoted to head the DHS, his one political victory. Pug was a good man. Loyal. He knew how to do what had to be done. And he still had the unwavering support of the SWAT organization.

Pug and the Fed, those were the keys. As long as the Fed printed the money he needed to pay the DHS, Pug would back him. Van de Groot and Congress could all go to hell, he'd be covered.*

No, all was far from lost. Not by a long shot.

Time to plan his next move. Somehow he had to tame the chaos that was the badlands, bring it into line to serve the human race. Otherwise all of the crusades he had embarked on could be at risk, just like Prometheus. Without his guiding hand, mankind would begin the long slide into a new dark age. Only he had the knowledge, the vision, and the power to prevent that. He had to re-impose order. Had to. At any cost. The future, even the survival, of humanity depended on it.

* * *

Joshua Weidemeyer sat in silent darkness watching the suburbs of northern Virginia morph through another sunset. On the other side of his apartment window, spread out below him like a museum diorama, the city changed from gray-green to orange-gold to black-silver.

In the past, nothing pleased him more than to watch the world put itself to bed. The display always gave him a sense of comfort. It promised a tomorrow washed clean by the night, bringing with it a fresh start and, with luck, a chance to make up for past sins.

Which was something he desperately wanted. Because tonight, sitting alone with a glass of cider, faces from the past weighed heavily on his soul.

Faces like Sven's. Locked away because Weidemeyer had done his duty. A

* In 2008, the FED increased spendable money (cash and checking account deposits) by $225 billion. Someone spent that money when it was first created. When they did, they could have paid the operating budget for every U.S. intelligence organization (including the CIA, NSA, and NRA), the U. S. Army, Department Of Homeland Security, and the Department Of Justice, with money left over to buy half of all U. S. TV advertising and pay every political contribution made to or in the name of every Federal candidate in that year. As long as he kept control of how the FED spent the money it printed, he would have it all.

slave forever in servitude to a free and democratic government because of his hand.

Or the children of Coro.

Small faces frozen forever by death and after-action pictures.

Please, Lord. Somehow. Please. Let me wash that away.

He hadn't expected them there, wasn't even in the country when it went down. But the plan had been his. He had organized it, had agreed to leave no witnesses, and had set it in motion. There may not be blood on his hands, but there was splatter on his soul.

It had been necessary, he used to tell himself, t*o protect the life blood of the country. Not just of America, but of the world.*

And maybe it had been. The logic seemed sound enough when he was young. But it had gotten thin with time, like his hair, and now it no longer covered the stain on his soul.

If they'd grown up, he often wondered, *what would they have looked like?*

Where was the happy certainty of his youth? The comfortable stability of Leave It To Beaver, where everyone had a warm place to live and a bright future to look forward to? Where good guys wore white hats and moral ambiguities didn't exist?

Gone. Forever gone. No longer was the distinction between good and evil easy to see. Now moral poles mixed together and the authority which once held them apart was, at best, indifferent to their admixture. Now virtue came in fifty shades of grey while law and justice no longer stood for the same thing.

The middle class, that bulwark of economic virtue, had been driven into poverty, maybe intentionally, by those at the top. Their savings gone, they were worse than de facto renters, tied to their own soon-to-be foreclosed houses, because renters could still move where the jobs were. They, on the other hand, were trapped, dependent on government-subsidized jobs or checks for their daily bread. Eventually, they would all have to choose: Either get good at saying 'Thankee, Massa' for every government handout, or regain independence by going underground.

Serfdom or the Badlands. There was nothing in-between.

When the Fed dropped the gold standard, his life turned into a lie. If the dollar was going to be destroyed by its own guardians, why had he killed those children? He always thought he was fighting for civilization, but now he saw the trick. Money, that magic slight-of-hand that enabled humanity to go from subsistence farming to civilization, was no longer the bedrock our commerce. Instead, it was being devoured from within like the Earth by a massive sinkhole.

Like Rome, we slide back into mud huts because we gave someone the power to print our money.

How could he have been a party to that? How could he have let them turn his act of patriotism into murder?

How could he not? He had taken an oath before his God. Such things are not easily ignored. Life is not always as simple as we would like.

Sometimes, you have to dance with the devil.

Then King Eddy gave him an out. The man had been right, Weidemeyer's pledge of loyalty to the Constitution did not bind him to the Supreme Court's decisions. But, if not to them, then to who? The Constitution was just paper. Someone had to interpret it. If not nine wise men, then who? Not liking the only answer he could come up with, not willing to bear the burden of trusting his own judgment on such a weighty matter, he had locked the question away in the dungeon of his mind, to rest in chains with the demons of Coro and Sven.

But Pug wouldn't let them stay there. Every time Weidemeyer saw the man make another power-grab, they came stormed up from the darkness. And he didn't even know why.

It wasn't because he feared the man. On the contrary, he was confident he could come out on top in any fight, had even begun to plan how. In his spare moments, he found himself adding up his resources, his contacts, his friends. Who could he count on to slip a knife in when asked? Or change sides at a critical moment, or strike from behind when Pug least expected it? The list was long. He had no doubt he would win, especially if, as he planned, he struck first and without warning or mercy.

Then early one morning, he awoke screaming at the dark, covered with sweat and terror. In his dream, he had seen himself standing in front of a full-length mirror admiring his new SS uniform. And he knew why the battle terrified him so.

If he won it, new friends would seek his advice and old enemies would step out of his way. Budgets would swell, staff would increase, and he would quickly climb the ladder. Pug's defeat would bring him power while the struggle would make him tougher, harder, and less willing to worry about those below him.

If he continued to win, each new fight would be easier. Eventually, his word would become law. Supporters and sycophants would move into his camp by the dozens. All would become his men and women, willing to lie, cheat, steal, and even (with the right political cover) kill to curry his favor. And with each new recruit, his conscience would weaken, poisoned by his new power.

Eventually, if he kept on winning, he would become an ego monster.

He would become another Pug.

The fear that tore at the belly of his soul was not of his defeat, but of his victory.

But what choice did he have? This was not a game of marbles. He couldn't just pick up his favorite cats-eye and go home. If he tried, Pug would strike from behind. He would be crushed, perhaps even killed, by an opponent who would give no quarter. Pug would never let a beaten enemy live to strike again. In that respect, he was no different from his piers. At this level, they were all brutal people. In their world, 'suicides' by the vanquished were common, and 'accidents' not unheard of. Only 'assassinations' were rare.

Searching for any way out, Weidemeyer began to look more closely at those around him. Everywhere he saw bulls charging each other, heads slamming together, horns locking in brutal combat. Hooves flailed dirt, trampling on anyone who wasn't quick enough to get out of the way. Below him, the fights were less dramatic, but otherwise the same. And, at his level or above, they were often fatal to both the losers and the trampled. The more at stake, the less likely quarter was to be given. All hierarchies, be they government, corporate, or criminal, have room for only one leader at the top. The more powerful the organization, the more willing its members are to pay any price to gain ultimate authority.

But there are ways of dealing with charging bulls besides charging back. A matador does it by simply stepping aside, dancing out of the way so the brute expends itself harmlessly. Even when facing whole herds, the concept is the same. Just step out of their way. Let them run off a cliff instead of hurting you.

Fawn had shown him how to forge his contacts into a matador's red cape. Whenever he sensed one of his supporters was ready to become a badlander, he would send in a recruiter, just like he had done with the prison van matron. Slowly, he would build his own underground network. Then, whenever Pug made a move, he would neutralize it. The man's plans would always fail and he would never even know why.

Would building a secret organization within the government violate his oath? He had, after all, promised God he would support the existing power structure. Or, at least, the framework on which it rested. And he was a man who took such promises very seriously. Did Pug count? Was he protected by that oath? Could Weidemeyer use the Badlands against him without violating it?

Struggling with the problem, Weidemeyer had asked a man he had known for many years, and for whom he had great respect, for advice. Much to Weidemeyer's disappointment, the Elder sidestepped the issue.

Instead, the churchman pointed out that God gave us all free will. He was powerful enough to have withheld that gift, but He didn't. He could have chosen to force everyone to behave as He wanted, but He chose not to. He give up that power. We were all free, individually free, to run our own lives as we wished because God chosen not to control our minds. We had the power of choice because He wanted it that way.

Given that, what must He think of the Pug's of the world who tried to take that gift away? Would He be pleased to see any of His children forced to think or behave in a particular manner by other men even if that behavior was the kind He hoped they would decide, on their own, to engage in? He had chosen not to force us to be good, so how could he look favorably on anyone else who did so? If Weidemeyer's oath forced him to support an organization that worked against God's will, would the Almighty want Weidemeyer to keep it?

While he was struggling with that question, one of his sources tipped him off about the plan for Fawn's interrogation. The dead children of Coro came screaming out of their dungeon yelling 'NO'.

And they were right. He would not again be party to murder. Ever. For the past, he could only ask forgiveness, but, for the future, never again. God would never hold him to an oath if it lead to another Coro. He was free to act.

So he went to Madam Chang. With only minor assistance from him, she took care of everything.

Now Fawn was free, his soul was clean, and his loyalties were forever changed.

Oh, he still held his job. He was still a much-respected member of the Law Enforcement Community. The support he had given the escape had all been covert. His actions had been hidden, explainable, and accepted. But they were not just acts performed for the narrow objective of freeing Fawn. No, they had a broader meaning. They were conscious steps aimed at bringing down a system that was eating its own children. He was no longer a civ. He had not just crossed the border, he had moved to the other side. Now, and forever more, he was a badlander.

So he sat, as he did on so many evenings, watching the world slip into comfortable darkness. This time, though, he knew the morning would not be better. This time, he knew too much about the forces facing each other. He knew their commitments, their strengths, their ruthlessness. He knew there could be no compromise, no accommodation between them.

This time, he thought, *a revolution is coming.*

Thank you, Fawn, for for forcing me to join the right side.

Appendix 1

Glossary

Badlands*: A community made up of a network of double-blind communications links.

BIOS: The first program a computer executes when it starts up. It is usually quite small and is semi-permanently stored in chips on the computer motherboard. It sets up the computer so it can load and run a bootloader as well as information on where to look for that program.

Bootloader: A program that loads the operating system into a computer. It is usually the first program that a BIOS looks for after it has configured the computer on which it resides.

Boot Order: The sequence of devices that the BIOS looks at when attempting to locate a bootloader. These devices may include an internal hard drive, an optical drive, USB ports, and an external network location. It loads the first bootloader it finds, so, if there is more than one operating system available to it, the Boot Order determines which one will be used.

Bot House*: A business that rents out zombied computers, either individually or, more often, in groups. They also organize these machines to perform different functions, the most common being to link in chains for untraceable communications.

Botnet: A group of zombies linked together to perform a function. The most common purpose these are used for is to establish untraceable communications chains.

Civ*: Supporters of the governments of the Civilized Nations Of The World. In other words, those that would be most opposed to the existence of the Badlands.

Compile: Convert a source code program into an executable. For all practical purposes, this is a one-way operation because information necessary for human understanding of the source code is lost in the process. In other words, source code can easily be converted to an executable but an executable can't practically be converted back to source code.

Cracker: Someone skilled at the arts of breaking into computer software

* Terms not commonly used by the public.

systems.

Crossing House*: A business that makes a living by bringing individuals into the badlands from the real world and supporting them while they are there.

Doorbell*: Another word for the Badlands hailing channel. The first step in anonymous communications is to send an Internet packet out in such a way that a Doorbell server or trojan will hear it and initiate the connection process.

Dual-key Encryption: Encryption which uses two passwords. The first password, known as the "public" key, is used for one-way encryption, meaning that, once encrypted, it may not be decrypted even by the key that encrypted it, except by the second key of the pair, usually called a "private" key.

Encrypted Chat: A special type of private chat room in which all communications between the participants are encrypted directly. This means that, if the operator of the chat room attempts to monitor the conversation, he will be locked out by the encryption.

Executable: A program that may be read and executed by a computer. Because computers and people are different, it is extremely difficult, if not impossible, for a human to understand the code in an executable program.

Firewall: A software structure that controls communications. They are typically placed between a network or individual computer and the rest of the world. A firewall that protects only your home computer may, for instance, be set up to prevent your children from accessing pornography. One that protects a nation may be designed to block politically unacceptable thoughts from entering the country. The software may be running on the computer it protects in which case it is the first software that acts on incoming messages and the last that operates on outgoing ones.

FOMC: Federal Open Market Committee. Federal Reserve committee that sets interest rates.

IP Address: A number in the format of NNN.NNN.NNN.NNN (where NNN is a digit from 0 to 255) that can is used by Internet routers to forward messages through the network. For a badlander, all addresses fall into three classes. An anonymous address is one that can't be used to locate him. The addresses used by zombies while communicating in a botnet fall

* Terms not commonly used by the public.

into this classification. Registered addresses are those that are directly linked to his identity. The address you get when you sign up for Internet service probably falls into this classification. Traceable addresses are those which, though not revealing his real-world identity directly, may be used to work back to locate a Registered address.

Keystroke Logger: A piece of software or hardware that records all actions taken by the operator of a computer including all keystrokes and mouse movements. Usually, they are in the form of trojans that are placed on the target computer without the knowledge of the user. Some send copies of the recordings they make via the Internet to some outside party for analysis.

Kit ID*: An identification card such as a drivers license that is made using a mail-order kit rather than from a centralized factory. The use of such a kit allows the creation of an ID without sending an identifying picture to anyone else, so the security is better. However, because the production facilities are on a kitchen table, the fidelity is not as good.

Linux: An Open-Source software operating system which operates on the same computer platforms as Windows.

Logs: All commercial computer systems record all communications and events that occur to allow traces and troubleshooting. Retention periods run from minutes to forever depending on the laws in effect in the country where the server is located.

M0, M1, M2, M3, or M4: Fed terms to designate various types of money according to their velocity.

MeatSpace: The opposite of cyberspace. A slang term for the real world.

Open-Source: Programs that are distributed in source code format. This allows the user of this form of software to check the function of the software before he compiles it into executable format for his computer.

Operating System: The software program/s that a computer uses to run itself. Common operating systems are Unix, Windows 7, XP, or Apple OS X. These programs are usually quite large and so must be loaded from location with large storage capacity such as a hard drive.

OS: An abbreviation for Operating System.

Port: A doorway through a firewall. All are numbered, some are designated for particular usage. This classification allows software designers to know

* Terms not commonly used by the public.

what type of information to expect from a firewall. A communications concerning a web page, for instance, would usually travel through port 80. There are about 64,000 ports in a firewall. Most are always closed and have no function assigned to them.

Private Key: See Dual-key Encryption.

Proxy: See the servers entry.

Public Access Point: A location where the public can log on to an Internet, either using wireless or by plugging in a cable.

Public Key: See Dual-key Encryption.

QE: An abbreviation for Quantitative Easing, a term used to describe one way central bankers create more money

Registered IP Address: See IP address

RFID Tag: A small radio transceiver that responds to short-range radio communications requests by transmitting back an ID code number. These devices are usually self-powered, cost fractions of a cent to make, and can be smaller than a grain of rice. Because they are also usually waterproof, they can be embedded in tissue, paper, or almost any medium as long as they are close enough to the surface to be able to receive and transmit radio signals.

Router: The 'traffic director' of the Internet. It looks at incoming messages from servers or other routers and sends them out according to the address they are being sent to.

Server: A computer that operates without any human assistance. Some specific types of servers are:

> **Botnet**: A computer that can be programmed to do a variety of communications functions as part of a temporary network. There are usually two classes of this device: Relay botnet servers, which pass messages on, and Master botnet servers, which control the linking and operation of the relay servers.
>
> **Decoy***: Provides cover for a Doorbell server. It ignores badlands communications sent to it. The service it provides for badlands communications is only that it provides an address for a Doorbell server to monitor, thus allowing the latter to remain anonymous.

* Terms not commonly used by the public.

Doorbell*: Captures messages not addressed to it and forwards them to an server other than the one the original message was addressed to.

Email: Transmits, receives, and holds email until the user downloads it,

Proxy: A server that relays Internet communications by changing the return address of the message. The use of such a server insures that the recipient of the message will not be able to find the Internet address of the computer that sent it, only of the relay server.

Print: Forwards documents to a printer and controls the activities of that printer

VPN: Establishes encrypted connections with other VPN servers so that data sent between the two servers can't be read by any third party while it is in transit.

Web: Delivers web pages when asked

Source Code: A type of computer code that can be read by human beings. Programs using this code format can be understood and altered by people, but they can't be used by computers. To be usable by computers, these programs must be converted from Source Code format to Executable format.

Spoofing: The act of making an electronic message seem to be something it isn't. If you send an email with your friend's return address in an attempt to make someone else think it came from him, you are spoofing.

Trace: To follow the path an Internet message takes. Doing so records the IP addresses of all the routers that the message passed through to get to you. It requires routers willing to pass back trace information when asked. Since most private networks don't do this, it usually stops where the path enters a private network. For instance, a trace of a communication to a public library will usually stop at the gateway to the library's internal network.

Traceable IP Address: See IP address

Trojan: A small stealth executable file that runs all the time on an infected computer without the user's knowledge.

Tunnel: To run a VPN through an Internet structure, such as a firewall, in such a way that the communications through that connection are not visible to operators of the structure.

Velocity: In economics, a number that represents how often money is spent rather than saved.

VPN: Virtual Private Network. An Internet protocol that allows encrypted communications between two computers over any Internet connection without any third party that observes the communications being able to understand it.

Wheels*: A slang term given to computers that are used for travel into the badlands.

Zombie: A computer that has been taken over by a trojan.

* Terms not commonly used by the public.

Appendix 2

Characters

The following characters appear or are referred to more than once in this novel.

Abbas, Luke: Divorced father who kidnaps his son and escapes to the badlands.

Angelo: Angelo Pisa, RENAISSANCE Crossing House. Activist, protester against the Federal Reserve. He meets Fawn during a riot.

Bara: Nobu Bara, TOKOGAWA Crossing House. Owner of the KISS'N TELL Snitch House. Fawn goes to him to try to buy the FEMA data base.

Bastard: Fawn's pimp when she is first recruited to go to the badlands.

Bowie: David Bowie, ROCKY ROAD Crossing House. A flirt and social acquaintance of Dancing Fawn and Nairobi Bombay.

Butterfly: Butterfly Killer, GOBI DESERT Crossing House. Joshua Weidemeyer's badlands name.

Carter, Cassandra: Head of FEMA, reports to Matthew Hood.

Chang: Mai Lee Chang, GOBI DESERT Crossing House. Fawn's principle contact in the badlands.

Eddy: A small-time hood with a computer science degree. He tries to go straight but has a hard time of it. Eventually, he acquires the Badlands name of King Eddy.

Fawn: Dancing Fawn, GOBI DESERT Crossing House. A prostitute who is trying to support two young daughters.

Hawthorne: Transportation Superintendent for the Federal Bureau of Prisons.

Hood, Mathew: Deputy Secretary of (and the true power behind) the Department of Homeland Security.

Junior: Arnold Wilson Parker II. Also known as Will. The son of the current de facto King Of The Civs.

King Eddy: One of the founders of the badlands, now one of the most influential men in it. Known in the real world as Eddy. Owns the RENAISSANCE Crossing House.

Kohrob, Edgar: Chairman Of The Board for ENGCO, one of the largest engineering and construction companies in the world. His company is the prime contractor for the Prometheus Project to build the first thorium power plant.

Lucius: Lucius Magnus, BARABBAS Crossing House. The badlands name for Luke Abbas.

Mishka: Malyy Mishka, STALINGRAD Crossing House. The badlands name for Arnold Wilson Parker Sr.

Nairobi: Nairobi Bombay, DARK CITIES Crossing House. Reporter. One of the first friends Fawn makes after she crosses over into the badlands.

Oak: Unknown crossing house. A Cajun oil field worker who obtains information that he wishes to give to Nairobi.

Oleander: Caper Oleander, FRAGRANT PATH Crossing House. A cracker who breaks into a FEMA computer and obtains confidential files.

Olsen, Sven: A Wisconsin dairy farmer who is caught by Joshua Weidemeyer when he attempts to pass counterfeit currency.

Parker, Arnold Wilson: The current de facto King Of The Civs. He owns a large estate in Colorado.

Ringgold, Pug: Former Ranger, Special Forces, fluent in Spanish. Later transferred to CIA, ran covert ops in Central America.

Sasha: Sasha Filippov, STALINGRAD Crossing House. A Russian nationalist thug who specializes in violence.

Shelton, Daniel: Special Agent for the FBI, associate of Joshua Weidemeyer.

Stein, Maxwell: Governor of the Federal Reserve Bank of Chicago and a long-time associate of Arnold Wilson Parker Sr.

Van de Groot: The leader of Arnold Parker's political/financial opposition.

Weed: Milk Weed, WILDERNESS Crossing House. Owner of the LET'S DO IT MY WAY Persuasion House and a long-time friend of the man known to Fawn as Mai Lee Chang.

Weidemeyer, Joshua: Special Agent for the Secret Service. He specializes in the detection of counterfeit currency and the capture of those that produce it.

Wells: A Corrections Officer with the Federal Bureau of Prisons

Appendix 3

Crossing Houses

A Crossing House is a business that provides interface services between the real world and the badlands. Every badlander is indentured to a crossing house which provides him with contacts and support in exchange for some form of compensation. To make identification easier, names of these business are always written in capitals in this book.

The following is a list of the crossing houses mentioned in this book along with any comments that may be relevant.

BARABBAS: Started by Luke Abbas to keep his real-world company afloat, this crossing house specializes in supporting real-world manufacturing operations.

COCHISE: Widely recognized as a front for civ cops.

DARK CITIES: One of the oldest crossing houses. They advertise by naming their indentures after famous cities.

FRAGRANT PATH: A newer house without much of a reputation.

GOBI DESERT: One of the original crossing houses who's indentured are usually former sex workers.

RENAISSANCE: Founded and owned by King Eddy. Reputed to be run by the U. S. mafia.

ROCKY ROAD: An older crossing house with no particular reputation.

STALINGRAD: The place to go if you want something very bad done. Probably owned and run by Russian organized crime. Indentureship is severely restricted to those having Russian hyper-nationalist views and a proven track record of violence.

TOKOGAWA: Probably run by the Yakuza crime syndicate. Indentureds are mostly Japanese or of Japanese origin.

WILDERNESS: An older house of no particular repute.

Appendix 4

Bibliography

This book is first and foremost a work of ideas. Beginning with the conflict between totalitarianism and anarchy, it touches on so many themes that each receives, at best, only minor discussion. Anyone with interest in any of them should guard against the sin of oversimplification by further reading. I suggest you begin with the following sources.

The subject of the economy, money, and central banking is well covered by the following sources:

Creature From Jekyll Island by G. Edward Griffin. History of money, central banking, and how the Fed got started. If you only have time to read the chapter summaries, at least do that.

www.econtalk.org Great podcasts on specific areas of economy hosted by Russ Roberts. If you can't read Hayek and don't have time for Griffin, at least listen to these interviews during your next commute.

The Road to Serfdom by F. A. Hayek. Read it for a common-sense understanding of how our economy works.

Inherent in the concept of double-blind communications is the assumption that all messages are unreadable by anyone who intercepts them. That means encryption is critical to the existence of the badlands. If you wish to know more about that subject, I recommend:

Applied Cryptography by Bruce Schneier. Full details of how computers changed the field of codes and ciphers. You don't have to be a programmer to like the book.

www.schneier.com/crypto-gram.html by Bruce Schneier. An excellent newsletter if you want to keep up with the nuts and bolts of digital privacy and how to keep it.

The Code Book by Simon Singh. Basics of how codes and ciphers operate

Crypto: How the Code Rebels Beat the Government Saving Privacy in the Digital Age by Steven Levy.

Digital Anti-Repression Workshop by Jacob Appelbaum:

www.youtube.com/watch?v=HHoJ9pQ0cn8 and www.youtube.com/watch?v=s9fByRmAHgU.

There is a large body of open-source software available online right now. To find out some of the details of existing packages, I recommend you start with:

www.bitcoin.org A good site describing digital money. Bitcoins are an example of what the badlands might use for money if civs manage to gain control of gold.

Firefox OS Details on an Open-Source OS being written for smart phones at developer.mozilla.org/en-S/docs/Mozilla/Firefox_OS/Introduction

www.openvpn.net Complicated and difficult to use for the beginner, this VPN is by far the most secure on the market.

www.sourceforge.net A library of open-source programs.

www.torproject.org A 'botnet' type of system that anyone can use now.

www.ubuntu.com The Linux distribution used to write this book. Easy to install, easy to learn to use.

www.prism-break.org An excellent list of open-source software replacements.

www.privacytools.io More good privacy analysis tools.

Self-organizing systems are one of the subthemes of this book. Chaos, emergence, and instability in interconnected systems is a complex and interesting subject. The following might help the reader begin to understand them:

Antifragile: Things That Gain from Disorder by Nassim Nicholas Taleb.

Hidden Order: How Adaption Builds Complexity by John H. Holland.

Mobs, Messiahs, and Markets by Bill Bonner and Lila Rajiva.

Ubiquity: Why Catastrophes Happen by Mark Buchanan.

www.peakprosperity.com/crashcourse by Chris Martenson. A good analysis of the use of debt as money and how it drives our economic paradigms.

Rebellion and asymmetric warfare in the modern age. Both illustrate how complexity works against the more powerful party:

Blackhawk Down (The movie) An excellent depiction of the failure of complexity in action.

Little Brother by Cory Doctorow.

Problems that the rulers of any society must struggle with to maintain their control are discussed:

1984 by George Orwell. Excellent description of what happens when those in control manage to impose permanent stasis on a society. If you haven't read it, do so. If you have, read it again.

Animal Farm by George Orwell. Simple. Short. And powerful.

Atlas Shrugged by Ayn Rand.

www.threefeloniesaday.com/Youtoo/tabid/86/Default.aspx Or get the book Three Felonies A Day by Harvey Silverglate. There really is a good reason to keep your personal data out of government data bases.

Production Versus Plunder by Paul Rosenberg. An excellent examination of why authoritarian organizations exist and why they are so destructive to the wellbeing of the human race.

Finally, here are a number of sources that talk further about other issues discussed in this book:

Who Controls The World by James Glatfelder. Want to know what companies Arnold Parker controls? Then check out this excellent TED talk at www.ted.com/talks/james b glattfelder who controls the world and the supporting paper (which does give names) at www.plosone.org/article/info%3Adoi %2F10.1371%2Fjournal.pone.0025995

Cypherpunks: Freedom and the Future of the Internet by Julian Assange et al.

www.energyfromthorium.com by Kirk Sorensen. Find out what thorium reactors can really do.

www.LewRockwell.com by Lew Rockwell. Podcasts and articles on a wide variety of freedom issues.

www.OathKeepers.org What do you do if you have taken an oath and feel you have now been betrayed? This was the problem facing Joshua Weidemeyer. If it is confronting you, this site might help.

Nullification: How to Resist Federal Tyranny in the 21st Century by Thomas E. Woods. If there is no New Badlands, what do those who want to fight the growth of government do? Begin by reading this book.

blacklistednews.com Get all the stories that don't make national news.

www.zerohedge.com Another good news site.

Appendix 5

Do The Badlands Really Exist?

Do the badlands really exist?

That is a very good question.

First, I know of no technical reason why they don't. Everything outlined in this book is technically correct, though sometimes greatly simplified. But that simplification does not change the basic facts. It should be possible for a society based on double-blind Internet communications to exist right now.

But does one exist? There is some evidence that it does or, at least, is beginning to form. For instance, why has it been so difficult for the United States to eliminate international terrorism? Why has the Treasury Department revamped the currency several times in the past twenty-five years? Why is the government trying so hard to pass legislation that will restrict access to the Internet? Why have they been unable to stamp out intellectual property theft? Why does Pirate Bay still exist? What about the Silk Road (not the ancient one, but the one on the Internet). And WikiLeaks? Or the protest group Anonymous? And what are Bitcoins? Why are there over six million botnet zombies in existence right now according to Symantec? Why do others think that number is closer to 24 million?

There may not be a fire yet, but there's smoke coming from some very flammable locations. Spontaneous combustion has already started. The badlands exists right now. Perhaps not at the level of development outlined in this book, but that will come.

Do you have your doorbell address yet?

Appendix 6

Double-Blind Communications

Communications between badlands entities is always done via a double-blind system. This insures that neither party in the communications can obtain the public IP address of the other. The ability of the Internet to support such anonymous communications is essential for the existence of the badlands.

To understand the concepts behind this protocol, imagine that two parties wish to engage in a double-blind conversation: Sally wants to establish a link with George anonymously without him knowing who she is. She doesn't actually know who he is, only that they have a mutual interest that she wishes to discuss. He is willing to help establish this link as long as he can be assured that it will not reveal his identity to her.

Sally first protects her own public IP address (which, on the Internet, is directly tied to her identity) by establishing a botnet connection to an anonymous proxy server. This server acts as an interface, substituting its own IP address for hers in all communications. This server is a zombie, with no connection to her other than by the trojan working inside it. Her connection to this machine is via a chain of zombies called a botnet whose connection sequence is constantly being changed. Any party receiving a connection request from her through this system will not be able to trace the source of her call back to her because such an effort would dead-end at her proxy server.

A botnet is set up and controlled by a botnet master server. That server selects at random a subset of the hundreds or thousands of zombies under its control and directs them to form a chain between Sally's public IP address and her zombie proxy server. To guarantee that no links in this chain can be used to trace communications back to Sally, the server devolves this chain frequently and then rebuilds it with another zombie subset quickly enough to avoid any drop in communications between Sally and George. Any outside party attempting to follow the chain would find that it had disappeared before more than one link was traced.

The botnet master server will know Sally's public IP address as that server must direct the first zombie in the botnet chain to connect to her. This knowledge held by botnet master servers regarding their client's true public IP address is the only weakness in this communications system. As long as this server is run by a reputable person, it will not log Sally's address and so can reveal little if it is examined by the authorities.

Even in the event that the operator of this server chooses to intentionally reveal Sally's public IP address, little damage will be done because this server will have no way of determining who Sally is attempting to talk to. The addresses on the messages she will send through this chain will only lead to the George's decoy (see below) or anonymous proxy server. The latter, being set up by a botnet master server of George's choosing, will not allow its connections to be traced back to George. Therefore, even the operator of one of the botnet master servers will not be able to trace Sally's communications.

Sally initiates her connection to George by sending a request down her botnet chain and anonymous proxy server to a prearranged large commercial VPN server (called a decoy server). This VPN server is one whose IP address George publishes as his contact address. Since Sally's proxy will not be on the allowed customer list for the decoy server, her call attempt will be ignored by that computer.

However, George has set up a server on the traffic path used by his decoy server. This server, called a doorbell server, will see all traffic sent to the decoy server because it is on the same communications path as that server. So it will also see Sally's doorbell request when it goes to the decoy server.

By logging all requests sent to the decoy server and all replies that come back, the doorbell server can tell which communications are ignored by the decoy server. Those communications requests are re-encrypted and then forwarded on by the doorbell server to George's computer. Because of the risk of detection by either Sally or anyone monitoring traffic at the decoy server link, no communications are sent directly to Sally's anonymous proxy server.

George's computer decrypts the message from the doorbell server and informs George that someone wants to establish a connection with him. If he agrees, he instructs his computer to send a request to his master botnet server. That computer coordinates the establishment of a botnet chain between George and Sally's proxy server. The latter forwards George's communications, along with the IP address of George's anonymous proxy server, back to Sally. They can then establish communications with each other's proxy servers without either participant, or anyone else who might monitor the conversation, knowing the real IP address of either of them.

To cover the fact that the decoy server may have received a legitimate VPN request and simply dropped it by accident, George's computer replies to Sally with what appears to be an error web page from the decoy server. That page will give Sally the option to send back identifying information to confirm to George that she really is who she claims and so is entitled to make the connection.

The point of this analysis is not to prove that double-blind communications are occurring in any particular way, but only to show that they could be occurring. Given the demand for such communications that exists today, this demonstration alone is enough to prove that some technique, probably more efficient that the one outlined above, is almost certainly in use right now.

Appendix 7

Hacking And Trojans

A trojan is a program that is designed to perform a clandestine function, one that is hidden from the operator of the computer it runs on. Operating in the background, it starts and runs whenever its host computer starts. Its code, as well as the actions it performs, are designed to be undetectable by normal user inspection. Usually, it is programmed to do something when directed by an external command.

The first problem any program of this type faces is that the commands and its response must come through the Internet. Access to that communication highway is usually blocked by a program called a firewall. This program, supplied either by the maker of the operating system which is running on the computer, or by an outside vendor such as ZoneAlarm or McAffe, is there specifically to block this sort of unauthorized communication from either direction.

Windows provides a generic web penetration of the firewall to allow programs that don't have web access to get to the web. If it is blocked by the firewall, many legal programs don't work. So, this makes an ideal vehicle for a trojan to access the network.

Needless to say, all anti-virus programs sweep for trojans. They know which ones to look for because they build up a signature database from past trojans that have been located and reported to the vendor of the software. The likelihood that a trojan will not be in that database increases with the rarity of the software and how long it has been used. If it is a recent program and is used on only a few computers, it is unlikely to be swept by anti-virus programs. Thus, trojan houses have a need for new virus designs to keep them in business.

Trojans are inserted in various ways, mainly through cracking exploits. A cracking exploit is a successful effort to get across a computer firewall. Like trojans, the more common cracking techniques are known widely and so are unusable against a new firewall because the vendors of firewalls update their products constantly to prevent exploits of known weaknesses. That means that cracker houses, like trojan houses, have a constant business looking for and selling new weaknesses.

The likelihood that a cracker will be able to break through a firewall increases as the number of computers increase and as the sophistication of the user goes down. If a cracker wants to get the U. S. Government's nuclear launch codes, he will have a virtually impossible task as there are very few computers that hold those codes and some very sophisticated professionals working full-time to block his access to them. On the other hand, if he just wants to plant a relay trojan, any computer out of the hundreds of thousands operated by technical-ignorant users will satisfy his requirement. Accomplishing that objective will be quite easy.

Appendix 8

Thorium Reactor Safety

Would a thorium nuclear power reactor require a 'containment vessel'?

This book uses thorium reactors as a point of conflict. Any number of subjects could have been used for that purpose, as nuclear power is not directly related to the issues discussed in this book. However, I choose thorium reactor construction because of the importance I believe it should have in our national energy policy.

Nuclear power as it now exists is the direct result of the Manhattan project of World War II. At that time, three substances were known to be suitable for nuclear bomb manufacture: U235, P239, and U233. In each case, if a sufficient amount of the pure material is concentrated in a small volume, a fission chain reaction occurs which will produce a nuclear explosion.

U235 is a type of uranium which exists in trace quantities in all naturally-occurring uranium ore. When the Manhattan project was started, separation of it from other types of uranium was known to be difficult but was thought to be easier to do than the manufacturing of a new element. The design and operation of machines to do that separation was undertaken at Oak Ridge, Tennessee.

P239, a type of plutonium, does not exist naturally. It must be manufactured. That is done by bombarding the most common component of uranium metal, U238, with neutrons. When one is absorbed by an atom of U238, that atom is transformed into P239. Because P239 is a different chemical from U238, the two can be easily separated after the change takes place. Early in World War II, this process seemed less practical than U235 separation, but it was undertaken at the Hanford, Washington facility as a back-up for the work being done at Oak Ridge.

U233 also does not exist in nature but, like P239, can be manufactured. In this case, it is produced when an atom of Th232 absorbs a neutron. For technical reasons, this seemed to be harder to accomplish than the manufacture of P239, so only the manufacture of the latter was undertaken by the Manhattan Project.

Th232, a type of thorium, is as common as dirt. Well, almost, anyway. It is far more available than uranium ore and also less radioactive.

Eventually, nuclear bombs were successfully made from both P239 and U235. None has ever been made from U233.

Now fast forward to today. Because the technology was well understood through our nuclear bomb programs, all nuclear power reactors now in existence run on either P239 or U235. Unfortunately, the very thing that is desirable for bomb manufacture, the characteristic that makes these materials so good for nuclear weapons, also makes them problematical for power plants: Their reactions are unstable. It is easy to make them go boom but much harder to make them sit still and produce steady power.

This stability issue was well known at the time the current plants were designed. So, to cope with the risk of things going wrong, large airtight steel-reinforced concrete bunkers were placed around the reactors. They had to be strong enough to contain anything that a reactor failure might produce, up to and including a weak nuclear explosion.

For technical reasons, those reactors had to be cooled with pressurized water. As it cooled the reactor, this water would become radioactive. So any containment vessel also had to be large enough to contain the huge volume of radioactive steam that a reactor failure might create. The result is the tremendous domed vessel that has become the identifying icon of nuclear power. Every nuclear power plant in the United States, almost every one in the world, has one. They are large, expensive, and symbolic of all the inherent risks associated with trying to misuse a bomb technology to generate power. When I refer to 'containment vessels' in this book, I am talking specifically about these large structures.

So, back to the subject of discussion: Would a thorium (meaning Th232/U233) power reactor need a containment vessel? There are very good reasons why the answer is probably no. Some type of safety enclosure would still be necessary, but it would be more like a bank vault than a containment vessel.

There are many reasons for this, but two are worth mentioning here. First, unlike current power reactors, a Th323/U233 reactor could be cooled without pumping water through the core. This means no radioactive water, so no radioactive steam during a meltdown. The volume requiring containment can be small, not much larger than the size of the actual reactor.

The second reason concerns the nature of a 'meltdown'. Unlike the power reactors now in use, thorium reactors could use a molten core. In other words, they would have to be in a 'meltdown' condition before they could even be started. 'Meltdown' would be their normal operating condition, not a disaster like in current nuclear reactors which all use a solid core. Rather than using a containment vessel to trap the radioactive products if something goes wrong, in an emergency the core would be drained into an underground vault with a wide, flat bottom. That dump would not only move the radioactive core material to a safer location underground, it would also spread it out, thus forcing the nuclear reaction stop and the salt to quickly cool back to a solid. In fact, this is such a safe and easy procedure that it was actually done every Friday for the thorium research reactors that were run after World War II. The engineers who ran those reactors wanted to go home for the weekends, so each Friday they just dumped the core and let it cool. When they came back on Monday, they reheated the thorium/uranium salt, pumped it back into the reactor, and they were back in business.

Uranium, plutonium, and thorium nuclear technologies are fundamentally different, like the difference between nitromethane, nitroglycerin, and diesel fuel. When it came to nuclear power, our drive to make nuclear bombs forced us to dance with the devil, a dance that can now be ended. For reasons of safety, economics, and waste disposal (Th232/U233 reactors produce very little nuclear waste), it is time we took a serious look at thorium power plants.

Google LFTR, thorium power, or look at the bibliography of this book for more details.

Appendix 9

More On Money

One of the major themes of this book is that we are controlled by those who create our money. The discussions in several places highlight this theme, but leave many questions unanswered because of lack of space. Hopefully, many of those are answered here.

Please return to the scene in Chapter 3 where Arnold Parker and his son, Will, are relaxing by a trout stream. Their discussion continues:

"Is that all money really is?" asked young Will.

"Yes," answered his father.

"Just something used in a three-party exchange?"

His father nodded.

"But what about all that other stuff?"

"What stuff?"

"Didn't Aristotle have a list?"

"Durable, portable, divisible, and have value?" replied Arnold Parker.

The teenager nodded.

"Yes," his father answered with a laugh. "He did. But it wasn't a definition, just a list. Of qualities. Not essential. Only nice to have."

"Money doesn't have to be durable?"

"Wheat isn't very durable."

"And the rest?"

"Indians used sea shells. They weren't fungible or divisible and didn't have any 'intrinsic' value. Yap islanders used giant stone wheels, not exactly portable. Many features are important for money, but their lack doesn't stop something from being used if that's all there is."

"As long as there's a three-party transaction?"

"Right. Money is so essential that something has to serve. Has to. Even if it has nothing on the list."

"Why?"

"Specialization. Of labor, I mean. Without money, people never spend enough time on one thing to get good at it. Have to spend most of it growing their own food, too bad at it to do anything else. Got nothing left for artisans or smiths. Certainly not for something as complicated as a mill.

"What if they can't find anything?"

"Drive them back to the stone age." Which was the horror that external control of money threatened. Control what a man can use for money and you can destroy his society. As a threat, it was only slightly less effective than violence.

"Who decides which thing on the list counts?"

"The marketplace."

"How?"

"By deciding which kind of money to accept."

Of all the desirable qualities that the marketplace might demand of money, the two most important are fungibility and stability. The former means the ability of any bit of money to be substituted for any other bit, while the latter refers to the total quantity in existence at any given time. Without the former, money is almost barter. It can't be used as a unit of account if each measure isn't the same as every other one. Without that, long term financial accumulation and planning becomes meaningless.

Stability of supply means only that the amount in existence, available to act as money, is predictable. It need not be constant as long as those who use it for money know how it will change so they can factor that into their monetary calculations.

Ideally, of course, it should grow at 2-3% a year to match the rate of growth of the real economy, but that isn't an essential requirement. What is a major strike against its acceptance by any marketplace is instability of supply, not knowing how much will be available at any given time due to variations in production or consumption. This is one of the major reasons that fiat currencies are not ideally suited for use as money.

Conspicuous because it is often talked about but is not on the list is 'having intrinsic value'. Money is a token, nothing more. Its 'value' in the marketplace exists only because the marketplace says it does. There may be some secondary value to the commodity not associated with its function as money, but, when evaluated as money, its 'intrinsic' value is irrelevant. What would a Federal Reserve Note be worth if the market didn't use it for money? It would be scratch paper that someone had already written on.

In fact, from a macroeconomic point of view, having an intrinsic value is actually a disadvantage because consumption is required to establish that value and that consumption changes the total amount in existence. It reduces the money supply. Having an inherent value conflicts directly with having a stability of supply. Silver, for instance, had no inherent value until the invention of chemical photography. So, before that event, it made good money. Afterwards, the supply varied so much that it could no longer provide stability and so became much less desirable for use as money. To put it another way, durability is an important characteristic of money because it makes the money supply more stable. If a commodity is irrecoverably consumed in normal commerce, such as silver is by many industrial applications today, it is not, practically speaking, durable.

One of the critical points made in this story is that the marketplace, a collective group made up of the users of money, is the sole arbitrator of what will be used as money. It selects which characteristics are the most important. It, and it alone, will indicate this preference by selecting which commodities are to be used for money.

Does this mean the government plays no part in the choice? Obviously not. But its role is limited to putting forward a candidate. If, as in the past in our country, that candidate has enough of the qualities that the market values in money, it will be accepted. But, as has happened often in other countries, if it loses those characteristics, it will be rejected. Legal tender laws and the requirement that all taxes be paid with the government-backed candidate are strong incentives for the market to use it as money, but there is no guarantee that they will be sufficient.

One final point regarding the definition of money. Many argue that one must measure the economic world in terms of the candidate before that candidate can be considered money. In other words, it must become what is known as a 'unit of account'.

That concept is actually very simple. If your power company asks you to pay your monthly bill once with silver dimes, you will think it odd. If you have to do it every time, you will begin to evaluate your bill in dimes rather than dollars. That act of gaging cost, of deciding what something is 'worth', creates what is called a 'unit of account'. Many claim this is the defining event for money, but I argue that it is just a result of the method of use which, because of it's earlier occurrence, is actually a better definition.

In either case, the point is the same. Money is not what the government decides it is, but rather what the marketplace dictates. We have in our own hands the power to control our commerce if we will just use it.

Appendix 10

Flight Path And Aircraft

The private aircraft that Fawn used to escape was the Bombardier Challenger 300 jet. The layout and a photo of the interior are:

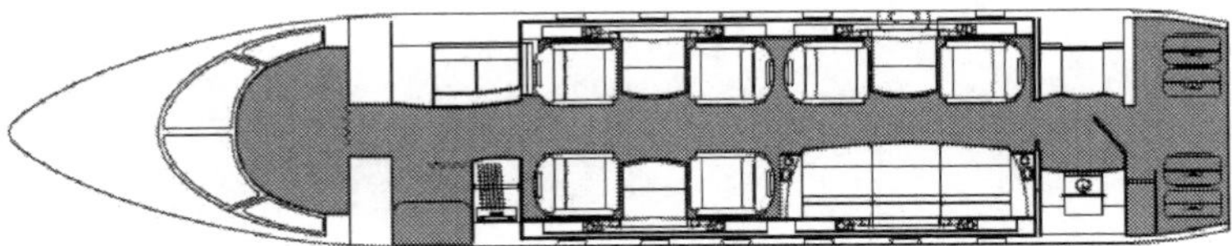

The baggage compartment is accessible from both the outside and the inside of the aircraft.

Everything written in this book about Air Traffic Control's ability to locate and communicate with aircraft outside of the range of ground-based radar is correct. Aircraft location is known by ATC only through crew statements. HF-band communications are unreliable. Satellite communications are never direct to ATC, but only occur if relayed by a private dispatcher.

The following is the path taken by Fawn's escaping aircraft:

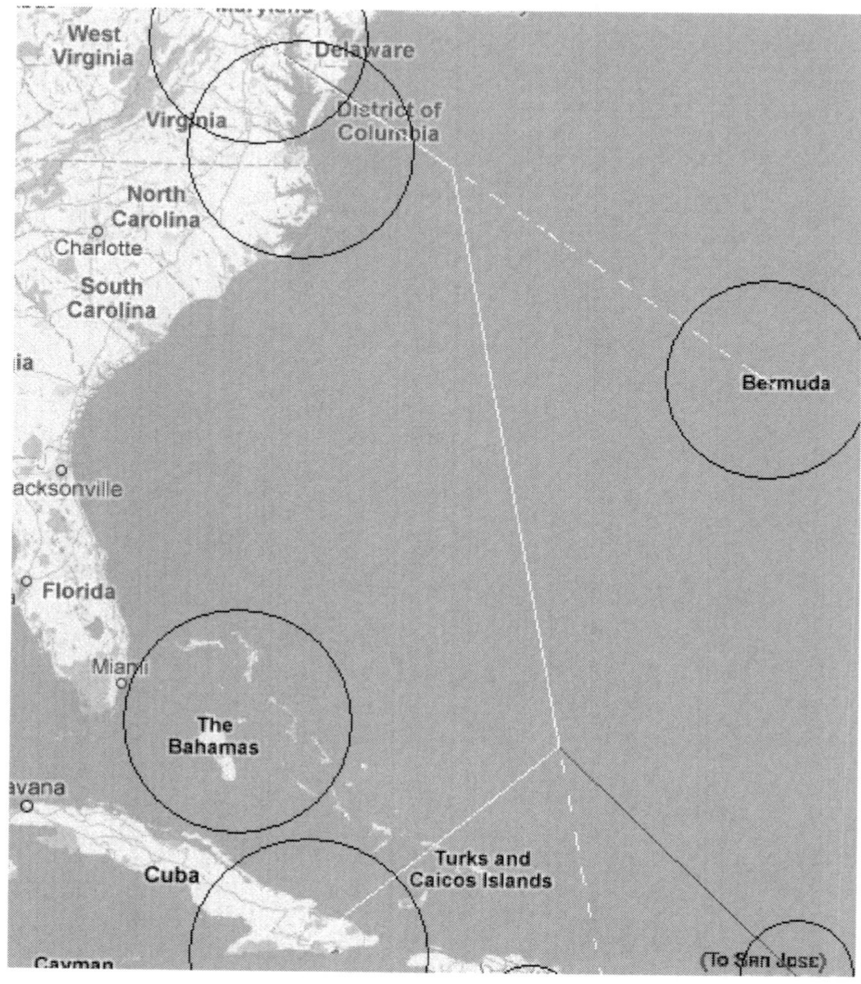

The solid white is the flight path actually taken. The dashed white is that filed for but never taken. Thin dark line is the path ATC was given when it differed from the one actually flown.

The black circles are the limits of ATC radar and VHF communications. The diameter is determined by the height of the aircraft and ground radar antenna. For flights at 30,000 ft, the radius of detection is about 220 nm. For 15,000 ft, it drops to about half that.

Made in the USA
San Bernardino, CA
03 August 2015